MESSINA

Book 1,

The Casa Bella Chronicles

Liz Galvano

Messina
Book 1, The Casa Bella Chronicles
by Liz Galvano

Printed in the United States of America.

ISBN 9781498453073

www.xulonpress.com

CASTELLO
MTT X:XXVIII
AL SUO
SERVIZIO
IN VITA
E MORTE

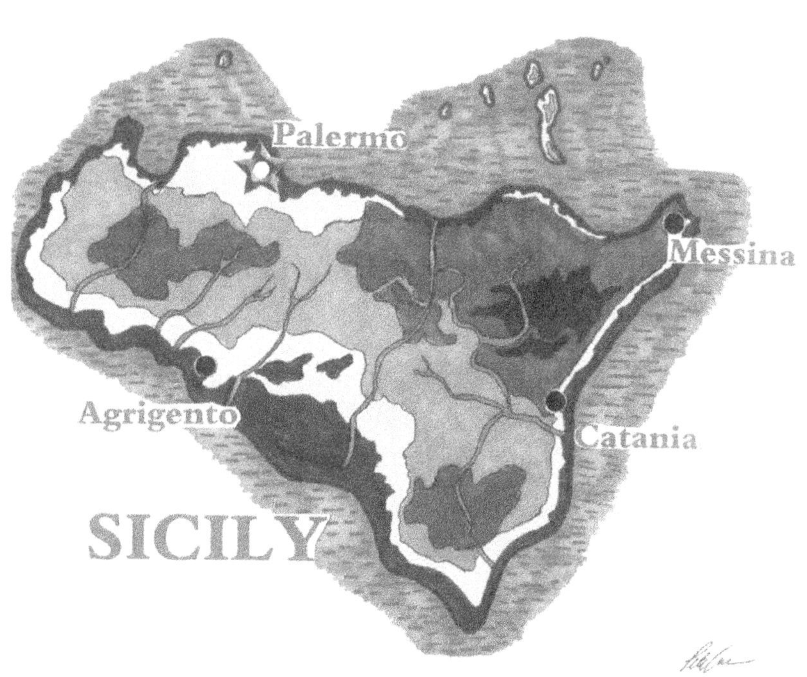
Palermo
Messina
Agrigento
Catania
SICILY

Messina, Sicily December 28th, 1908.
Seventy thousand people never woke up.
Of the first sixty days after the catastrophe it rained forty-five, making rescue extremely hazardous for the doctors, nurses and rescue crews. When all was said and done, the death toll estimate stood at two-hundred thousand people. Some details in regard to the earthquake have been changed to help the flow of this story.
The overall account of this tragedy, however, remains intact.
This is a fictional tale based on historical events,
yet by no means represents all that happened in Messina.
This book is dedicated to the men and women who sacrificed themselves willingly to help during this great tragedy, and to those who were lost that fateful night.

CHAPTER ONE

And we know that God causes everything to work together for the good of those who love God and are called according to his purpose for them. (Romans 8:28)

Rome, Italy December 27, 1908

The last rays of the setting sun danced on the dome of St. Peters Basilica in the heart of Vatican City. Giovanni Castello squinted, then turned his eyes from the brilliance. This time of day always seemed bitter sweet. Like a human life, once beautiful, giving way to old age and death, so daylight succumbed to night. Only a sunset promised a sunrise on the other side. Did the depth of human suffering promise a sunrise too? Who could be sure?

Through shadows of deep purple, Giovanni made his way across *la Piazza San Pietro*. Cold breath rose from darkened stone and mirrored Giovanni's lonely existence. Except for the gaze of the on-looking saints who watched from their rest atop the colonnade at St. Peter's, Giovanni walked in solitude.

Something about this place always bothered him, particularly when he was alone. It felt so eerie; as though the marble statues above would come to life at any moment. The dark-haired Sicilian avoided looking at them as he had avoided their God for many years.

He passed the obelisk in the center of the oval-shaped piazza; a gust of wind blew from behind and debris rose into the air. Giovanni struggled briefly with his hat, and then tightened his coat. He scanned the darkness behind him, certain someone followed. Or perhaps this time he'd see the unseen presence he'd avoided for so long. A cold shiver rose from inside and he turned his back to the familiar specter that called to his heart. Without another look, Giovanni hurried on his way.

The Eternal City. Lucy had always wanted to see it. She clung to the window of the motor coach. No way could she take it all in. Music filled the air, the aroma of superb Italian creations made her stomach absolutely growl. Cathedrals, built who knows when, reached for the stars and the statues; so beautiful, so life-like, so... nude. Why did they have so many nude statues? Lucy averted her eyes. Some things just didn't seem right. She glanced at her father. Henry James seemed unfazed by the things they passed. He'd once told her that they'd be living in the most sophisticated city in the world and here they were, right in the middle of it.

The air, slightly warmer than usual on this December night, made the evening's festivities even more enjoyable. Lucy hated to wear an evening gown at all and a heavy wrap would have just been a bother. But the light pink satin dress she wore made her father happy. And this evening, for his sake, she would put her opinions aside and behave like a lady. Thank goodness tonight felt like spring and Olivia Drake, in whose home they stayed, insisted that a light gossamer covering would be all she needed to accentuate the pearls sewn into the bodice. The car pulled to the curb and the door opened. A holiday gala at the American Embassy, well, no avoiding it now.

Hansom cabs, expensive carriages and motorcars crowded the street, pausing long enough to allow occupants to escape. Lucy and her father made their way up the steps toward the sound of the orchestra.

Inside, the grand ballroom presented a visual feast of gold and greenery. What a Christmas tree! It rose magnificently to the ceiling, lit with brilliant white lights. A hand blown glass ornament hung from every branch. A fireplace roared next to the tree, an enormous hand-carved eagle flew over the mantle. To the right, Old Glory stood proudly.

Couples waltzed in the middle of the room. "Daddy, let's join them." Lucy pulled at her father's arm. "I'm so full of energy I could dance a jig."

"Please don't." Henry James's eyebrows went up, then a smile softened his face. "Your mother loved to dance too. You look so much like her, with your beautiful auburn hair swept up like that." He held out his hand.

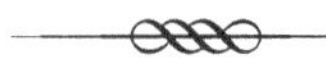

The music stopped with a flourish. Everyone bowed and curtsied, applauding the orchestra with enthusiasm.

"You're every bit as beautiful as your mother. I wish she were here to see how well you dance." Henry James kissed his daughter's hand. "Shall we get some punch, my dear?"

"Yes, please," Lucy smiled at her father's southern drawl. Arm-in–arm, they made their way to the punch bowl full of shimmering liquid the color of cherries. She lifted two cups full of juice and handed one to her father.

"Not just yet, my love. I think I see a collogue heading toward the smoking lounge. If you'd wait I promise to be back by the next dance."

"I'll be right here." Lucy watched her father's bald crown disappear in the crowd. What a dear man. Her heart grew warm. She set a punch cup back on the table and sipped from the one in her hand. Sweet, cool and fizzy; just what she needed.

"Have you met the ambassador from Spain, Delores?" A lady with hair that must have been the result of a bleach bottle stood with a friend at the other end of the table. She slid her mouth around a long, ivory cigarette holder and exhaled lazily. The smoke seeped through her lips to create luxurious billows around her shoulders.

It would be rude to laugh. Lucy bit her lip and tried to find a distraction but the other lady was funnier that the first.

With a face a shade too white and extra rouge on her puffy cheeks, Deloris raised a penciled eyebrow and sipped champagne. "Yes, Gladys, I met his wife as well. She *is* rather fat, don't you think?"

Lucy turned away. If she stuck her fingers in her ears they'd know for sure she'd heard them. She peeked from the corner of her eye.

"Oh yes, but we mustn't judge. You and I are also wider than we once were."Gladys must like to roll her r's.

"You, maybe. At least *I* still have a waistline." Deloris snorted, scanned the room and shoved an *hors d'oeuvre* in her mouth.

"Try one of these." Gladys smiled, at her friend's bulging figure? She handed Deloris a small cake.

"*That* is the author, Maude Howe." Deloris pointed her fan discretely. "Isn't her mother the one who wrote *The Battle Hymn of the Republic*?"

Really? Lucy looked too. A woman who traveled the world and wrote books would be worth knowing. *Maude Howe, wow.* Lucy inched closer. These two seemed to know everyone.

"I believe you're right." Gladys touched the end of her cigarette to a crystal bowl on the table. The ashes fell to the bottom, glowed for a second and then turned black. "The man next to her is her fiancé. I don't remember his name but I do know that he's working on a painting that will be a gift to the American government. We must make sure to meet them both before the night's over.

"Who's the Italian over there; the one that just walked in the door?" Gladys set her glasses back on her nose and squinted. "My, he's handsome."

"Yes he is, but look at his face. He's not at all pleased to be here. In any event, nothing could ever compel me to get involved with an Italian. They're so temperamental, so hard to read, I can never tell what they're thinking. I might be wrong, but now that I look again, I think his uncle is the illustrious Vincenzo Castello. A much better looking man in my opinion." Deloris looked about the room.

Lucy watched the elegant Italian. He moved comfortably in his tuxedo as though he wore one often. He must be used to the finer things in life. Thank goodness she wouldn't have to talk to him tonight.

"*Who* is that woman dancing so beautifully with the older gentleman?" Gladys's exclamation grabbed Lucy's attention. She followed the gaze of the blond with her own.

"Doctor Henry James and his daughter, Lucille, from Boston." Deloris dabbed her mouth. "They're guests of Colonel Matthew Drake. Dr. James will be working for the next year at the University of Rome doing some kind of research."

Lucy's eyes grew big and a smile crept across her face. Deloris had no idea who she watched on the dance floor nor had she a clue who stood three feet away.

"And his daughter, she's oddly attractive, although way too tall." Gladys gave a tiny yawn behind a hand gloved in satin. "Has she no husband? She seems a little old to be unmarried."

"She is by far the more interesting of the two." Deloris leaned in. "I have heard, from a very reliable source, that the young woman is not only *unmarried*, but is in fact a *doctor*. She is an accomplished surgeon just like her father. I learned that piece of news from Mrs. Drake herself."

"Really? I must meet them this very evening," Gladys said. "A woman doctor! Who would have ever thought, in my lifetime, I would meet a woman doctor? No wonder she's a spinster."

"Excuse me," Lucy leaned closer. How could she resist the fun? "Did you say that woman is a doctor?"

Gladys inched her jeweled lorgnette down her nose to peer over the rim. She balanced the long handle of the spectacles and a china plate laden with sweets in one hand, while the other held the accessory that some poor pachyderm gave his life for. She took another drag from the ivory-encased cigarette and turned. "Young woman, I wasn't speaking to you. What is it you want?"

"Did you say Lucille James is a doctor? And she's not married?" Lucy looked across the dance floor at the poor victim of the conversation. *That girl is beautiful. You two should be ashamed of yourselves.*

"What man would have a woman who spends her day in a surgery? Just think of all the blood and other unpleasant things she must see. How unattractive." Gladys swayed to the beat of the music.

"I rather like the idea." Lucy gave a pleasant smile.

Gladys dropped her lorgnette from her nose. "You give your opinion freely for a newcomer to Rome. Who are you?"

Deloris stopped chewing.

"My name is Lucille James. I'm a surgeon."

Applause at the dances end filled the silence.

"She's so skinny!" Deloris looked down her nose.

"Come along Deloris. Eavesdropping is rude. No wonder she's a spinster." Gladys pulled her friend with her.

"I say it's because she needs to eat more." Deloris took one more look over her shoulder.

The icy silence, Lucy had heard before. The crack about her weight, well, it stung but that wasn't anything new either.

"Lucille, what did you say to those women to make them leave?" Henry James had finally returned. He smelled of tobacco. "Nothing, really." She nudged him and spied their host and hostess. Whew, a distraction. "The Drakes are finally here. Don't they look nice?"

The Drakes strolled across the floor, accompanied by the swish of midnight blue taffeta. Even with their matching figures, short and round, Mrs. Drake had managed to outfit her husband in a tuxedo to compliment her dress. They smiled sheepishly when they spotted their guests.

"Henry, Lucille, I hope you didn't mind being sent ahead of us. Olivia likes to make an entrance of sorts." The Colonel fingered the lapel his wife had ordered to match her dress. He rolled his eyes and smiled down at Olivia.

Mrs. Drake swatted her husband with her black lace fan. "If you had put your book down in time to dress, we could have arrived with our guests." The black feather in Olivia's hair gave a floating nod. "Please forgive our rudeness."

Lucy fought a laugh. "Of course you're forgiven."

"Are you finding work agreeable, Doctor James?" The English accent came from outside their circle.

"Dr. Randolph Montgomery, it's good to see you." Dr. James's extended hand welcomed the outsider. "Please allow me to present Colonel and Mrs. Matthew Drake. My daughter, Lucille, you've met."

Too pale, too thin and a handshake like a wet fish. Ew. Lucy gave a nod and latched onto her father's arm.

"I'll be working with Dr. Montgomery at the University." Henry James patted the Colonel on the arm.

"Good to meet you." Colonel Drake stuck his hand out. His vigorous handshakes were the stuff of legend back home. He squished those slimy fingers like a sponge. Lucy watched delighted.

Dr. Montgomery rubbed his fingers. "Colonel Drake, Mrs. Drake, if you wouldn't mind." He gave a slight bow. "I'd love to steal your company for a few moments. More of our colleagues have arrived and I would like Doctor James and his daughter to meet them."

"Go right ahead." Colonel Drake offered his arm to Olivia. "I'm going to try to convince my wife to join me for the next dance."

"I was waiting for you to ask." Olivia curtsied. She must have been something when she was young.

"Henry. Lucille." The Colonel bowed to his wife and they took off in a whirl. Olivia's feather bobbed at every step.

"Dr. Montgomery, why don't you go ahead. Lucille and I will join you momentarily." Henry James renewed his grip on Lucy's arm. The Englishman disappeared in the crowd.

Uh, oh. Now what?

"Please promise me that you will show no garish behavior while we're here." Henry James gave Lucy a stern frown.

"But I've already promised to behave myself while we're in Rome."

"I want to hear you say you'll behave yourself tonight."

"I know it bothers you when I speak my mind." Lucy patted her father's hand. "Don't worry, I won't embarrass you."

"I wish I could believe that." Henry James cracked a smile and held out his arm. "Come on, let's go meet the other doctors."

The group of waiting doctors, gaped like men in a side show. Did they not think she'd notice?

Dr. Montgomery straightened his jacket and smiled a greeting. "Allow me to present Dr. Osvaldo De Stanza from Milan and Doctor Sergio Mortellaro from right here in Rome. Dr. Mortellaro is the head physician at the University Hospital. He'll be our host." He turned to the other physicians. "Gentlemen, I would like you to meet Dr. Henry James and his daughter, Lucille. As I've told you, Miss James is an accomplished surgeon in her own right."

Dr Mortellaro examined Lucy through his monocle.

What am I, a lab rat? No, he *looked* like a lab rat.

"You're very unusual, Miss James. What university did you attend?"

"I graduated from The Medical University of Boston." *Act like a lady. Act like a lady.* Lucy bit her tongue.

"I had the opportunity to observe her work when I visited Boston last summer," Dr. Montgomery looked over his brandy just before taking a sip. "This young lady has convinced me that women, on occasion, can make marvelous physicians."

Lucy bit harder.

"You must have encountered quite a bit of prejudice." Dr. De Stanza's face kind of looked like a weasel. He stepped closer to her with a yellow smile. The suffocating smell of hair tonic and too much cologne made her want to gag.

There's such a thing as personal space. Lucy backed up a step. "Yes, I've encountered a lot of prejudice, but I've yet to meet a fellow physician who doesn't appreciate hard work and study."

"My daughter graduated in the top of her class. I'm very proud of her." Henry pulled Lucy under his arm.

Thanks Dad.

Dr. De Stanza turned to Henry. "I thought you were from Boston. Your accent says otherwise."

Lucy smiled to herself. If only she had a penny for all the times he'd given this answer.

"I live in Boston. Lucille was born there. But I'm *from* the great state of South Carolina." He stood up a little straighter.

"A Southerner." Dr. De Stanza tilted his head toward Dr. Mortellaro. "We must remember to be on our best behavior, especially around..."

Dr. Montgomery's scowled stopped him cold. "Dr. James, I would like to extend an invitation, for your daughter to work alongside our group at the university. I know we'd all like a chance to watch her."

Weasel, lab-rat, and...fish or...cadaver. Hey, dead guy, I can speak for myself, you know. Could her patience last much longer?

"Ask her." Henry James gave Lucy's arm a subtle squeeze.

She bit her tongue again.

Henry James released his daughter. "Lucille is quite capable of making her own decisions."

Dr. Montgomery raised an eyebrow. "Well, what would you say?"

About working with a dead guy and a couple of rodents? "I'd be honored." Especially if they actually allowed her to do her job.

"I'm excited." Dr Montgomery rocked onto his toes. He looked about the room. "There was someone else I wanted you to meet. He said he had a meeting to attend at the Vatican this evening. I hope he's here."

"At the Vatican?" Dr. De Stanza snickered. "What on earth for?"

"I'm not sure." Dr Montgomery searched the crowd again. "He said something about the chief magistrate of Rome and what else I don't know."

"Oh. He met with his uncle." Dr. De Stanza blew through his nose.

Dr. Montgomery rolled his eyes and shook his head. "Where is that rascal—ah here he comes."

Lucy turned. Just perfect. The unhappy Italian, from the socialites' conversation, wove through the crowd to meet them. He looked to be in his early thirties with light olive skin and soft black hair. His serious dark gray eyes and well-built frame commanded an air of casual elegance. No doubt he had a firm place in Rome's high society, but something about him said he might also possess a depth of character. What exactly did he hide beneath the surface?

"This is Dr. Giovanni Castello." Dr. Montgomery gestured his hand toward the man. "Dr. Castello, I would like you to meet Doctors Henry and Lucille James."

Dr. Castello executed the most graceful bow she had ever seen. Lucy curtsied in return and, when she rose, found a curious expression on his face. Before she could decipher it, though, he turned and extended a hand to her father.

"Dr. Castello is one of the finest young surgeons that the University of Rome has produced in recent years." Dr. Montgomery rubbed his hands together. "I was lucky enough to steal him away from Italy. He worked with me in London for a while. He recently opened a practice in Messina, Sicily. Remind me, how long have you been there?"

"I've been there for almost two years now." He had a beautiful voice and a rolling Italian accent.

"I was hoping to convince Dr. Castello to join our group. He really is quite the expert on infectious diseases, and actually had a chance to work with Sir Joseph Lister for a short period. However, Dr. Castello would rather spend his time working in his small office and surgery among people who can't even pay him. Once he's made up his mind..." Dr. Montgomery shrugged his shoulders.

"Rome has plenty of doctors." Dr. Castello tilted his head toward Lucy. "The need is much greater in the smaller cities."

"But Messina is not exactly a small town," said Dr. Mortellaro.

"You're right. The population is quite large, but it's made up mostly of peasants and laborers who need to be educated on every level. There simply are not enough physicians to keep up with the population."

"So you've chosen to work among the peasants?" A humanitarian? Lucy leaned in a bit.

"Yes. I don't believe that anyone should be denied medical treatment. In addition to the lack of good physicians, the city lags behind in modern conveniences. We might be living in the twentieth century here in Rome, but many Sicilians live as though it's still the fifteen-hundreds. They have no understanding of proper sanitation or of disease prevention. Many people have yet to see their first light bulb."

"It must be difficult." She might just have to admire him.

"Yes it is. We must sometimes do emergency surgeries by candle light. You gentlemen know how difficult that can be."

Lucy raised an eyebrow, but remained pleasant.

Giovanni bowed toward Lucy with a slight smile. "Living in the medical community I'm surrounded by men. It is easy to forget one's manners, Miss James. Forgive me, I did mean to include you in that statement."

Ah, a lab-rat, a weasel, a cadaver and…a patronizing peacock. Lucy sensed her father's gaze so she pressed her lips together.

A swell of music drowned out the conversation. Dr. De Stanza looked at Lucy as if to ask a question. Yikes. No way did she want to dance with that creepy guy.

Dr Montgomery's eyes grew round.

Dr Castello threw a sideways glance at Dr. De Stanza and quickly stepped in front of him. "May I have this dance Miss James?" He offered Lucy his well manicured hand and the scent of soft cologne followed. The darkness of his eyes looked into her soul.

Her father frowned. She shouldn't dance with him? Why not? How could she in good manners refuse?

"You really don't have to dance with me, Dr. Castello." Lucy walked with her escort to the dance floor. Perhaps he, too, wanted a way out.

"Would you have rather danced with De Stanza?" Giovanni stopped and faced her.

"No." Lucy shook her head. She shivered and knew that her partner felt it. "It's not a practice of mine to dance with a man I hardly know."

"Don't consider this a dance then, consider this a rescue. I don't like the way he looks at you."

"You noticed?" *A protective peacock, hmm.*

"How could I not notice? I know the man well. You shouldn't dance with him."

"I would have told him no."

"You could have told me no." Giovanni shrugged. "But you're in a foreign country among new colleagues."

"You're right." Lucy allowed him to lead her to the center of the room. "I wanted to make a good impression. Thank you for the rescue, Dr. Castello."

"Please, call me Giovanni. I'm at your service." He took her in his arms with a warm smile; and the waltz began.

Okay, so you're not a peacock. I might just have to like you. "If I'm to call you by your first name, then I insist that you return the favor. My name is Lucille, my friends call me Lucy."

A wisp of genuine kindness lit her partner's face. *Maybe you're as nice as I first believed. You're a good dancer too*. She circled the floor with her partner, enjoying the music.

"Tell me Lucille; Lucy," Giovanni's light hands guided her easily, "what convinced you to become a doctor? I would imagine that someone in your…" Dr. Castello looked over her shoulder and then back at her. "…position would be much happier married and raising a family."

"What position would that be?" Lucy had heard this question more than once.

"A woman, attractive, eligible, obviously from a good family, why bother? Although I must admit, I can see the reason in becoming a nurse. That would, in itself, be valuable knowledge to bring into a family. But why become a doctor, much less a surgeon?"

"I love this profession. Medicine runs in my family and I seem to be good at it. My father is a doctor and my mother was a brilliant nurse. Father always said that, given the opportunity, Mother would have been just as accomplished a surgeon as he. My older brother graduated with a medical degree three years ago. Why shouldn't I be allowed to do the same?"

"Why should any woman put herself on display?" Dr. Castello's hand on her waist moved slightly. "A degree such as yours will only prove to be useless education or worse. If you marry, I don't know any man who would want his wife doing surgeries. It's too ugly a job for someone like you. As for the medical community, it took years for them to finally admit that Florence Nightingale was right in her discovery of hospital sanitization. I'm not sure how readily they will receive such a wonder as you. If they accept you at all, they'll see you as a novelty and exhibit you like a glorified circus act. I would wager that the physicians here tonight have already invited you to join them just so that they can watch."

"Yes, as a matter of fact they have." *Rats, you're right.*

"Don't think for a moment that it is because they see you as an equal. You'll be nothing more than a trained monkey."

Jehoshaphat, you too? The hairs on the back of her neck started to rise. She faked a smile. "I sincerely believe that God has given me a gift and I must use it. Somehow, He'll find an avenue for what He's given me. As for marriage, I have no intentions of marrying unless I can find someone with whom I can work as a partner. You don't think women make suitable physicians, do you?"

"Since you've asked plainly, I'll not pad my answer. No." Dr. Castello shook his head. He smiled as though he instructed a child. "I certainly believe that women are intelligent enough; I simply have yet to meet a woman who is emotionally stable enough. Unlike you, I don't believe in God so I don't believe that he gives gifts. Unfortunately that puts us at opposite sides of the medical table."

"But you've worked with Dr. Lister. Word has it that he has a strong faith in The Almighty."

"He does indeed, and a more humble individual you will never meet. But he's old and set in his ways. He wouldn't even consider the possibility of Darwin's theory. You do know what Darwin's theory is?"

Could she make him trip? "Something about someone like you being related to an ape? Tonight I could almost believe it. I suppose you embrace Darwin's theory of evolution?"

His mouth twitched. "I do."

"I think it takes just as much faith to believe in your religion as it does mine."

Dr. Castello slowed their step. "Are you always so impertinent?

Lucy glared at him. "*Impertinent?* I'm too delicate to be impertinent. I'm emotionally unstable, or…or… a trained monkey! I don't understand a thing I'm saying." She stopped dancing and stepped back. Who cared if the whole room watched!"*Porco*!" The word came out of her mouth before she could think. The music stopped and so did the dancing crowd. The weight of one hundred-fifty staring people brought heat to her cheeks. She saw her partner's mouth tighten, could he possibly be fighting a smile? Lucy's blood boiled.

"Where did you learn language like that? You're father should wash your mouth out with soap." Dr. Castello was definitely trying not to laugh.

Lucy almost swallowed her tongue. *Some things just don't mean the same thing here. Pig is a bad word?* Then she saw the spark of humor in his eye and her anger returned. "You speak English, you know exactly what I meant and you deserve it!"

"Oh, yes. I should have remembered. I'm sorry to have corrected you for calling me a pig." He raised one eyebrow and smiled like a cat.

"You're *sorry*?" she seethed. "No, I'm sorry; sorry that I danced with you and sorry I thought-" The floor under her feet vibrated. What on earth? "Did you feel that?"

"Feel what?" Dr. Castello cocked his head, his gaze swept her face. "Miss James, have you had too much..." Tinkling from above must have caused him to look overhead, at the crystal chandelier. It moved back and forth and then swayed. The crowded room began to murmur. Lights flickered and a vase filled with lilies crashed to the tile. Someone screamed.

"Quickly, to the alcove!" With a vice like grip he grabbed her wrist.

Lucy fought against him and the vibration grew. "Daddy. I need to find him."

"He'll be fine." The strong Sicilian dragged her through the crowd of confusion.

"What's happening?" Lucy finally gave in. A small foyer, leading to a marbled patio, waited.

"Earthquake! Get down." He pushed her beneath him, wrapped in his protective arms; the scent of warm cologne clung to fine silk.

The room went dark.

CHAPTER TWO

Thank goodness it was only a tremor. But if a tremor could be felt as far north as Rome, how devastating must the earthquake have been? The idea did not bode well. Giovanni settled at the bow of the *HMS Fortitude*. His hand went to the Marconi gram in his breast pocket.

Earthquake.
Messina.
Help.

Three words, most likely sent by Alfredo the station operator. How would the man have known the reach him through *Zio* Vincenzo? Maybe Padre Dominic managed to send this note to his uncle. Whoever sent this must not have had much time. Faces of people he knew flashed through his mind and the knot in his stomach tightened. He would give his life for any one of them and right now he was stuck on this slow moving steamer.

In the fading distance, people milled about the stone harbor at Palermo, some weeping, others poring over the local news. Normally he would have gotten off here. His parents would understand; Castellos always helped. Hopefully, Mamma would get the note before long.

Palermo would wait his return. To the right Mt. Pellegrino, adorned with the shrine to the patron saint of the city, stood as a shining farewell to all who left this place. Giovanni gripped the railing, breathed in the sweet salty air to relax and prepare his mind for what lay ahead.

"Have you any news?" Giovanni stopped the first officer when he passed.

"Just what's come over the wireless. Nothing from the city itself." The man fidgeted with the pages on his clipboard and dropped his pencil. "Ships from Russia are there right now. The word they keep sending is: devastation. That's all we've got."

Giovanni picked up the pencil at his foot and handed it to the man. He grimaced. "A fault line lies underwater, through the Straights of Messina."

The first officer lowered his gaze and nodded. "So I've heard."

"If it produced a tidal wave..." Giovanni's jaw tightened.

A comforting hand rested on Giovanni's shoulder. "Try not to think about it yet. You're a doctor, right?"

"Yes."

"Maybe you should get some rest."

"Messina. One hour." The call came from outside Giovanni's cabin door. He rolled off his cot and rubbed his eyes. Who knew what lay ahead?

He stepped into his trousers and pulled suspenders over his shoulders. What a week. A day and half ago he was dancing with that feisty thing from America. Too bad he had to make a quick exit. It would have been worth hanging around that awful research group just to get to know her. Lucy from America. Maybe this quake really wasn't as bad as everyone thought. Sicily had been through so many. Hopefully it wouldn't take much time to clean up and Giovanni could find a reason to return *Roma*.

Anxiety gripped his stomach. His hunches were usually right. What he hoped for was a minor tragedy. Reality, well, maybe he should just wait and see. Fingers slid through the handle of his leather bag. He tucked a canteen of water over one shoulder, his knapsack over the other and pushed the cabin door open.

Cold moist air stung his face. What a dark gray sky. The British steamer made its way through the fine steady rain. They only had to round Cape *Peloro* and then the sickle shaped harbor came into view.

How could he have prepared himself for this? At first glance, it appeared as though a giant foot had stepped on the middle of the city. Giovanni leaned against the railing and narrowed his eyes. The urge to wretch almost overcame him. Giovanni grabbed his belly and took several deep breaths to force his stomach to still. The harbor swam with debris. A mountain of wrecked fishing ships piled on top of what should have been a home; a lace curtain dangled, limp and torn. The *Palazzata*, a magnificent structure that stretched for almost two miles along the harbor, bid them welcome. Only the outer wall with its sculptured façade of elegant goddesses remained. Along the water and high into the air crept a dark cloud of smoke. After the earthquake and the tidal wave, the city began to burn.

Giovanni sat in one of three large skiffs, suspended above the water by chains. He hugged his knapsack and medical bag to his chest and moved up against the side of the boat to allow what little room was left for the doctors, soldiers and supplies. With a lurch and a squeal of metal on metal, the gears began to turn and the boat descended.

Hundreds of bodies floated in the water, most of them naked, all of them with expressions of horror frozen on their faces. They bumped up against the boat that painfully pushed toward shore. Giovanni held back a sob, wiped the rain from his face and fought, with every ounce of strength, to retain control.

Through his tears, the blurry image of another boat appeared. He rubbed his eyes to get a better look. With so many people aboard how did it float at all? They moaned, reached their hands toward him, begging for water, half-crazed. Not able to help, he turned his face from them and wept.

The launches pulled up to the heavy stone quay. The land looked as though the sea itself froze in one place. Some places were sunk six feet below the waterline while others pushed high into the air.

Giovanni climbed out of the boat and struggled to hold his composure. To his left, a woman's body washed back and forth in the tide. It took all his strength not to stand and gape like a helpless fool. It took even more strength to move on, as he knew he should. He scanned the city, to recognize buildings and streets. The cathedral of Messina, with its bell tower, lay in ruins. Corpses lay here and there, tossed about like rag dolls. Scores of homeless wretches wandered about aimlessly. Some cried, some looked for loved ones, some did nothing at all. A few brave souls actually tried to identify bodies pulled from the water.

Never in the years he studied in the schools of Rome, nor in the days he served in the slums of London had he seen such a horror. Giovanni dove into the recesses of his memory to the time he learned to shield his heart against pain and sorrow. He was a child then, but now, the ability served him well. If he were to be able to help these people at all he must detach his emotions. He slammed shut the door to his heart and steeled his eyes.

A man stood on a pile of rock, barking orders to those around him. Maybe he was in charge. Giovanni made his way to him. "I'm a doctor. Where are you taking victims?"

"Why? Are you hurt?" The man asked.

"No. I said, I'm a doctor." Giovanni showed the man his bag. "Where's the hospital?"

The man scratched his head. "There is no hospital. Can't you see that?"

"I know there's no actual hospital. Where are you taking victims?"

"All over the city. There are stations everywhere. Look for the tarpaulins."

"Is there one near the Chapel of St. Francis?"

"I believe so. It's a long walk from here, I hope you feel better soon."

"Thank you." Giovanni shook his head.

Giovanni stepped over a beheaded statue and moved a broken high-back chair. The road seemed to clear where the train tracks lay. Then, the remains of the chapel of St. Francis lay before him. How long did it take to get here? A dim sun glowed silver behind heavy clouds. It must be late afternoon. At least he'd made it this far.

In the distance, a large tarp had been strung between poles and lashed with rope. It must be the hospital. The rain made it sag sadly in the center and water ran in a steady drip as it overflowed from its middle onto the street. What a nightmare. He shuffled to the corner of the tent.

Victims lay shoulder to shoulder on the ground. The doctors, covered in mud and blood, nodded to Giovanni and continued their labor. He looked down at the person lying at his feet. The man smiled weakly and Giovanni noticed his crushed arm. He dropped his knapsack on the wet ground and stooped to help.

The poor man winced when Giovanni touched him. He must have been there for quite some time.

"*Per favore*, help my wife first." The man turned his head toward the woman next to him and reached with his good arm to stroke her cheek.

"*Mi dispiace, signore*." Giovanni's voice broke when he saw her blue lips. "*Sua moglie è morta*."

CHAPTER THREE

Giovanni rubbed his weary eyes with the back of his blood stained hands. His face felt gritty, his clothes stale. If only he could wash he would feel so much better.

He looked across the tent. Two patients down, a foreign doctor with a bald head could not stop coughing. *He's not going to be able to stay long*.

The man looked back at Giovanni, deep circles under his bloodshot eyes. "This is no hospital, it's a slaughter house and we're the butchers."

"Be careful what you say, some of these people speak English." Giovanni glanced down at the woman he knelt beside. Her face tense, she gripped her rosary, her mouth moved in silent prayer. If her broken hip healed at all she would be lame for life. "I agree, this is the by far the worst thing I've ever seen."

"I wasn't sure *you* spoke English. I'm Emmett Wissig."

"Giovanni Castello." Giovanni stepped over his last patient to get to the next.

Dr. Wissig gave a nod and went back to work.

Giovanni took a deep breath and started to cough as well. The fumes from the smoldering city stung his nose and made his eyes water. The air was better when he stooped to the ground, but he had stooped for so long that his leg muscles screamed for relief. Maybe if he knelt this time.

He moved to his knees, but that hurt too so he sat on the pavement, no longer concerned about what he sat in or on. Giovanni examined the deep gash in the man's side.

"Am I going to die?" His patient grabbed Giovanni's arm with a vice-like grip.

"I don't think so." Giovanni peeled the man's fingers away and sutured his wound. "I'll do everything I can to save you."

He moved on the next person. How many had there been? Was this someone he'd see before or just a look-alike? All these injuries were overcoming his ability to remember faces; which patient belonged to him and which to the other doctors. But his colleagues struggled to remember as well so he took one more look at the sea of injured people, drew a deep breath and kept going.

A fractured shoulder; Giovanni could do nothing to ease the pain.

A dislocated hip; at least this was fixable. With the screaming man's friends holding him down Giovanni pushed the leg back into place.

A severed artery; he could stop the bleeding but with all the rain and no place to dry, would it be better to let this man fall into sleep as he bled to death or to save his life only for him to die in agony with gangrene? *It is not my decision to make*. And so Giovanni saved him.

Compound fracture of the left radius. Didn't I just remove this man's arm? He shook his head and re-focused. "I'm afraid we're going to have to move you." He couldn't look at the fear in the man's eyes.

Giovanni noticed a boy huddled with his mother in the rain. She had a toddler in her arms and another young boy to her left. "*Signora*?"

"I need some help with this poor man."

"What can I do? I have children to hold." She turned to her oldest child. "This is not the first tragedy we've seen. Pietro has been the man of the house for a year and a half now. He'll help you. Then maybe you can help us."

Giovanni nodded. "Whatever I can do for you, I will. How old are you?" He focused his attention to the boy in rags, who shuffled to his side.

"Ten." Pietro stared at the bone protruding from the patient's arm.

"Then you're a man." Giovanni clasped the boy on the arm. He stood his patient and helped him to the piece of wood resting on a pair of saw horses; the closest thing to an operating table they had.

Giovanni managed an encouraging nod first to his patient and then to Pietro. "He needs something to bite down on."

"He can have my hat." Pietro pulled the cap from his head and gave it to the man.

"*Grazie*." The patient shoved the cap in his mouth.

Giovanni touched his head. "I'm afraid I have nothing to give you for the pain. I'm sorry."

The man nodded, closed his eyes and turned his head. His face, already pale, turned even whiter and tears streamed down his face.

"Pietro, I want you to stand right here and you must be brave." Giovanni moved the little boy to the patient's shoulder. "I need you to hold his arm like this with all your strength. Lean on him, see?" Giovanni leaned on the patient. "You try."

"Like this?' With eyes like saucers, Pietro did as he was told.

"That's it. Now turn your head and close your eyes." Giovanni's heart sank. This boy should be out fishing, not helping with a surgery.

"Pietro, you were a big help." Giovanni knelt by his patient, once more on the ground. He wrapped the severed arm with his last clean bandage and then handed Pietro his canteen of water. "Take this to your mother. It's all I have at the moment, but I'll boil more. Will you be here to help if I need it?"

"*Si.*" Pietro grabbed the flask and licked his lips.

"Aren't you thirsty? Take a drink."

"No, my mother drinks first, then my sister. I'm a man, I can wait." Pietro disappeared from sight.

Giovanni felt someone kneel at his side.

"You're Sicilian aren't you? I heard you talking to that boy." The man spoke with a British accent.

"Yes." Giovanni rested a reassuring hand on his patient.

"Dr. Wissig said that your practice was here in Messina."

"Yes," Giovanni said again.

"You're the first local doctor I've met."

Giovanni let out a deep breath. "That is because all the others have died. I was fortunate enough to have been out of town when this happened."

"I'm Doctor Davidson. It seems the authorities have put me in charge of this bloody mess. I need a second in command. It would help to have someone who knows the local dialects."

"I can do that," Giovanni said. "You've been speaking to the authorities? What have they said about supplies? Blankets, clothing? These people are suffering from hunger and exposure as much as anything else. The mainland of Italy is just a stone's throw from the harbor. Has anyone sent anything yet?"

"I keep hearing that help is on the way, but I haven't seen it. You're right, these people *are* cold and hungry." Dr. Davidson wrapped his damp jacket more tightly around his shoulders. "How long has it been since you've had any food?"

Giovanni tried to ignore the claw in his stomach. The doctor in front of him looked as hungry as he felt. "Almost forty-eight hours. Who needs food?" He smiled for the first time in days. "And you?"

"About the same." Dr. Davidson smiled back. "Thank you for keeping things positive."

"Whatever you need." Giovanni turned back to his patient. "Let me finish this man, and then I have an idea."

"What I need are morphine and clean bandages." Dr. Davidson gave a dry laugh and began to help Giovanni.

A gust of wind blew rain into the tent. The doctors covered the patient with their bodies.

"*Santa Maria*!" Giovanni checked the arm he had just bandaged patted it dry with a cloth.

"Does it always rain like this? I thought Sicily was a sunny place."

"Rain is normal here in the winter, so is the cold." Giovanni looked across the tent to the rain that dripped outside. "I've never seen anything like this."

"*Pioggia dal terremoto*." Giovanni's patient whispered.

"You're awake. *Si, amico*." He rubbed the patient's right hand and translated. "Earthquake rain. The locals are all calling it earthquake rain. Try to sleep." Giovanni stood stiffly, grateful to straighten his legs. He gave Dr. Davidson a hand up.

Dr. Davidson straightened his back and stretched his neck. "So, what's your idea?"

"My house is not far from here. I know I have enough food in dry storage to feed us for today, at least." Giovanni looked at all of the people at his feet. "I have some blankets, but not nearly enough." He shrugged. "Some is better that none."

"We have food for today." Dr. Davidson gave an encouraging nod. "Did no one tell you?"

"We do? Where?" Giovanni scanned the tent, and then as if his nose came to life, he smelled garlic and onions.

"Just outside, on the other side of the wall." He pointed to the main support of the tarp."

"*Mamma mia*, why didn't you say so?"

"I don't know. I suppose I thought you knew."

Giovanni stepped over a patient and headed into the misty rain, toward the tantalizing aroma. Never had food smelled so inviting.

He rounded the brick wall and a ray of hope filled his heart. Before him, under a smaller tarp, behind an enormous kettle, stood a balding priest in a tattered brown robe.

"How did I know if there was food, you'd be involved?" Giovanni's voice cracked, but so what? "Isn't that the laundry kettle from my house?"

"Giovanni!" Father Dominic dropped his spoon and grabbed Giovanni in a bear hug. "I knew you wouldn't mind if I borrowed a few things." He raised his eyes to heaven. "*Grazie a Dio*."

"I got your message." Giovanni pulled the crumpled paper from his breast pocket.

"I didn't send this. It must have come from Alfredo." Father Dominic examined the Marconi-gram. "I hope he's ok. I haven't seen him."

Giovanni smeared his tears with his hand. He had to get a grip on his emotions. "What's this?" He peered into the bubbling soup.

"I believe it's everything in your pantry." Father Dominic grinned.

"Is it edible? Who said you could cook?"

"He didn't cook this. The nun did." Dr. Davidson stabbed his thumb toward a surly looking nun. She pushed the priest out of the way.

"*Dio mio*!" Giovanni exclaimed before he could stop himself. "You survived, too?" He grabbed the nun, who struggled, and kissed the top of her head. Then he ducked behind Dr. Davidson, but not before Sister Francesca knocked him on the head with her spoon. She turned around mumbling, angry, and shuffled back to her pot. She wiped the spoon on her dirty apron and continued to stir.

"What was that about?" Dr. Davidson laughed.

Giovanni smirked and rubbed his head.

"He took The Lord's name in vain." Father Dominic spoke to Dr. Davidson, but leveled his eyes at Giovanni. "He's lucky I wasn't holding the spoon."

"So these are your friends?" Dr. Davidson leaned against a brick wall, eating quickly.

"Yes. They're like family." Giovanni, next to him, pulled a handkerchief out of his pocket to wipe his mouth and then saw the filth covering the hanky. He sighed, shoved it back where he found it and used his sleeve.

"I'm glad for you." Dr. Davidson pulled his hanky from his pocket as well, looked at the stains, rolled his eyes and stuffed it back in its place.

"I've known the *Padre* for a very long time. I don't know what I would do without him," Giovanni said.

Father Dominic came around the corner and sat with them, on a pile of mortar.

"And yet you don't believe in God?" Dr. Davidson asked.

Giovanni raised an eyebrow. "Is it that obvious?"

"You never pray for your patients. It's a common practice for many doctors." Dr. Davidson drank the remains of his soup.

"No. I don't believe in God."

"Giovanni has claimed to be an atheist for quite a few years now." Father Dominic folded his arms and looked at Giovanni with a wistful smile. "He doesn't see the hand of God in his life. How he was spared and how he is now able to help the people he loves during their greatest hour of need."

"I don't know how you can still believe after all of this!" Giovanni glared. He regretted the explosion the moment it left his lips. "*Padre*, please. Let's not have this discussion now. I have to get back to the wounded. Thank you for the soup."

He straightened and handed the bowl back to the priest. Normally he had a good grip on his anger. This place made him feel raw. His gaze met his best friend's. Would the priest forgive him, yet again?

Father Dominic patted his cheek. "One day you'll learn that even in the greatest of tragedies, God is good. I'll be here if you need me."

Lucy snapped the clasp on her trunk and stood up to smooth her hair and dress. She turned to the mirror, hung on the back of the door. This berth might be small, but it had everything. She grabbed the extra fabric at her waist, pulled it tight. Would this dress look better if it actually fit? Not really.

"This is at least two sizes too large." Lucy scrunched her nose. "And it's so ugly; I hate this shade of beige. It looks like the inside of a newborn's diaper." She pulled her white smock apron over her head and tied it in the back. "Even this is too big." She moved the apron side-to-side. "I could put two of me in here."

Lucy plopped in a chair and pulled on a pair of black boots, made just like the dress; poor. A good rain would soak them through. She stood in front of the mirror again and pinned her nurse's cap on her head. She frowned. In the sea air, her normally curly hair frizzed like a tumbleweed.

"Nurse's uniform, lady-like bun on my head," Lucy mumbled. She tried again to get her hair to stay in place. She yanked the cap off her head.

"This may be the look that they want, but it's just not practical." Lucy took the pins out of her dark auburn locks and then pulled her hair into a neat simple braid, which fell down her back. She combed her bangs forward and tilted her head to the side. "Now I look like a teenager wearing my mother's dress, but at least my hair won't bother me."

She gathered her cape and stethoscope and made a face at the Lucy in the mirror. "Well, you're here, even if they don't want to admit you're a doctor."

She scooped up her well-worn black leather Bible and stroked it. Mother said to never be without it. *Lord, I believe you're the one who got me accepted on this ship in the first place. I believe you convinced Daddy to not only let me come, but to come with me. And I believe you're the one who convinced the people in charge that I should replace the dear man who has asthma. Please help me do a good job.*

A knock at the cabin door interrupted her prayer. "Lucille, may I come in?" Her father slowly opened the door, peeked in. His mouth turned up in a smile, but his eyes spoke of worry. "You look very professional."

"Good morning, Daddy." Lucy kissed him. Maybe if she joked she could put him at ease. "Nice try. Just look at this dress, it's huge and it's poo brown, and these boots, —I would have been better off with the cowboy boots that Uncle Roy gave me. Lucy shoved her cap in her pocket. The Bible she slid into her shoulder bag. "I'm ready to go, are you?"

Her father's smile became genuine. "I see what you mean about the boots, but since when do you care about what you wear? As for being ready, I think I should be asking you that. This is not an easy thing you've volunteered to do. If I had any indication that you intend to marry I would stop you. But you've chosen this spinster life and I'll let you live it. I pray that you don't one day regret your decisions."

Lucy touched her father's cheek. How this man had shaped her life. Now that the time came to leave she didn't want to. "You know that the only reason they're allowing me to go is that they don't know what to do with me here."

Henry James chuckled. "You're right, of course. Maybe it's best that we just offer ourselves to God, and let Him take care of today. I'm proud of you, Daughter. I know your mother is, too." He opened the cabin door. "After you."

"Morphine," Lucy called out. She read off the clipboard while her father checked the items packed and waiting on deck to be delivered. "Oh, that's wonderful." Around them, crewmen moved wooden boxes to waiting skiffs. Their excited chatter added to her anticipation.

"Check." Her father, three feet away, bent over the supplies.

"Alcohol. Nice."

"Check"

"Ether. Wow, not much of this at all."

"Check. What did you say?" Her father looked up from the crates stuffed with straw and glass bottles.

"I said, there isn't much ether. How about bandages?"

The ship beneath her feet rocked and icy wind burned her cheeks.

"Daddy?" What had silenced the entire crew? Lucy's fingers grew cold. Her father stared at something. She turned to look as well.

"Lord Jesus." The appeal for mercy escaped her lips. From where she stood, she could see the entire port of Messina; and the mist shrouded *Peloritani* Mountains that surrounded the city. Floating objects filled the water like algae on a stagnant pond. Pieces of wood, furniture, a railway car and a ghastly amount of dead people rocked together with the motion of the waves. Buildings smoldered, hidden in smoky shadow. A cold yellow sun fought a losing battle with ugly gray clouds. It brought precious warmth for a moment and then vanished without a trace.

A horrible odor filled her nostrils and her stomach turned. Lucy scanned the marina for the source. Her gaze fell upon the group of soldiers at one end of the harbor burning bodies pulled from the water.

Along the shore near the remains of a stone pier, a small group of people, mules and carts waited.

"I'll bet they're here to meet us." Lucy set her clipboard on top of a crate. For sure her courage would be tested. "This is an impossible mess."

Her father's low voice mumbled. "And you've volunteered to jump in the middle of it."

"Give me your hand."

The voice sounded so familiar. Lucy stood in the rocking boat, tethered to the sailor who tried to hold it close to the dock. The fact that the heavy stone quay had sunk at one end, with the other end three feet in the air made the leap especially tricky.

Her father's hands gripped her waist from behind. She looked to see who had spoken and spied the hand that must be attached to the speaker. The owner of that hand grabbed her arm and hauled her to safety.

"Miss James, if I remember correctly." Those familiar gray eyes, that smooth Italian accent. "Would you move so I can help your father?"

"I've got it." Lucy wheeled about, planted her feet and took her father's hand. Giovanni narrowed his eyes and grabbed the other.

"Thank you, Lucille, Dr. Castello." Henry James regained his balance beside them, then guided the small group toward the wagon. "Let's step over here and give the sailors room to unload the supplies. We've brought as much as we could muster for the time-being. Though I dare say, with all the fundraising around Italy, this won't be your only delivery. Are you Dr. Wissig?" He looked up at the bald man who sat in the cart, mouth covered with a filthy handkerchief.

"I am. I hope you last longer than I did. This place is hell." Wissig climbed down from the wagon. His gaze went to the Venezia anchored beyond the harbor. "Just to be able to breathe again will be so wonderful."

"He's not replacing you, I am." Oops. She spoke before she thought again. *Cat's out of the bag now*. Lucy smiled at Giovanni.

"You?" Dr. Castello straightened. His eyebrows went up. He looked first at Lucy and then to her father. "This is no time to joke."

"We're not joking." Her father handed Lucy her black leather medical kit. She ducked her head and placed the bag in the wagon, under the front seat.

Dr. Castello glared at her. If he kept up, she might just have to tell him off again.

The red tint to her father's face said she wouldn't have to say a word.

"This may be hard for you to swallow," Henry James used his most authoritative tone, "but Lucille is a capable surgeon. She fully understands the risks involved in coming and so do I. If she's volunteered to work here, I'll not stand in her way and neither should you."

Giovanni let out a heavy sigh. "Climb in. I'll take you to our station. You can see for yourselves how bad our situation is."

With the wagons loaded, Henry James climbed into the back, and Lucy took the front seat. Next to her, Giovanni gathered up the reins and gave a sideways glance. He urged the mules forward, the gray sky turned even darker, Lucy felt like her heart turned gray, too.

The mule's pace through the remains of Messina only amplified the urgent need of those they passed. Rescuers crawled like ants over piles of mortar.

"When did you get here?" If only she could have arrived sooner.

"Thirty six hours after it happened." Giovanni shook his head.

"But we had no word in Rome for two days. How did you…?"She had to know.

"I have my sources." He scowled. Then he turned. "What's that smell?" He leaned closer and breathed in. "It's you. Are you wearing rose water?"

Was that an accusation? Lucy raised an eyebrow. "Is that okay with you?

Giovanni turned the mules down a new street. "I'll ask the patients."

Lucy watched the scene roll by. Shivering survivors dug with their bare hands. Some walked around in an insane kind of indifference, while others talked to imaginary voices that spoke to them from under tons of stone. Most of them wore little or nothing at all.

"Where are their clothes?" Lucy undid the throat latch of her cloak. She'd give it away if need be.

"Lucille, no!" Her father touched her shoulder.

"You'll need that cloak." Giovanni closed his eyes and rubbed them. "It's an ancient Italian custom to sleep in the nude. The earthquake happened while they were still in bed. That's why they're naked. Clothing is beginning to arrive from the mainland. You need to take care of yourself or you won't last a week here."

Lucy re-buttoned her cloak and tried not to see the woman ten feet away quiver in the rain.

They rounded a corner of debris. A soldier had a man by the collar of his soiled uniform.

Giovanni stopped the mule. "What goes on here?"

"This worm is a convict who escaped the prison. He was caught cutting off this woman's finger to steal her ring." The soldier pointed to the man's clothing.

Oh. He wore a prison uniform. Then Lucy's gaze went to a corpse on the ground. The bloated victim no longer had a ring finger. Lucy closed her eyes and turned away.

The cart began to move again.

"What will happen to him?" Lucy opened her eyes. She pulled her mother's ring from her finger and handed it to her father. He put it in his breast pocket. The crack of a rifle echoed through the streets. She turned around to see the thief fall to the ground, shot through the head. There were no words to describe this place.

"I'm glad you witnessed that." Giovanni kept his gaze straight ahead. "Now maybe you'll understand. We're under martial law because the local prison was full. A good many of the worst felons in Sicily have escaped to pilfer what's left of Messina. Curfew is at sunset. You must make sure you never walk these streets unattended while you're here. This place isn't safe for anyone. It's even more dangerous at night. Lately, packs of wild dogs have been coming in from the mountains to feast on the dead. They're not as bold in the daylight. The soldiers have shot hundreds of them."

Lucy shuddered. *Lord please protect us*. In the misty mountains above them she could almost see yellow eyes watching.

"There it is." Dr. Castello gave a nod.

"That?" Lucy followed his gaze. Several large tarps had been set on poles. The sides, a collection of different colored tarps, moved in the motion of the wind.

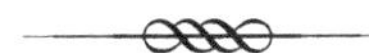

"Thank you for coming." Father Dominic extended his hand. The crack in his spectacles and his warm demeanor relaxed Lucy, right away. "This is Dr. Davidson from London. He's in charge."

"We're so glad you're here." Dr. Davidson shook Lucy's hand and then her father's "I'll make sure your daughter gets safely back to the ship."

"His daughter doesn't need an escort back to the ship. She's the one staying." Giovanni came from behind, hands on his hips; he narrowed his eyes at her.

Dr. Davidson peered down.

"Excuse me for interrupting." Father Dominic leaned toward Lucy. Could he sense the tension? "Someone found coffee and brewed it in your honor." He handed a cup to first to Lucy and then to Henry. "Between you and me, we haven't had much fresh water around here. I wouldn't be surprised if it was made with salt." Father Dominic slurped his coffee and made a face. "Let me take them on the nickel tour."

The head doctor's gaze never left Lucy. "Go on. We'll settle this in a minute."

The priest led the way through a flap on a corner of the tent.

"Did you say the *nickel* tour?" Lucy found herself in an area used both for storage and for eating. Odd shaped tables made from debris from the earthquake had been surrounded by chairs in every form Lucy could imagine.

"I said that right, didn't I?" Father Dominic rubbed his bald head.

"Yes." Lucy smiled despite her surroundings. "Have you been to America?"

"No. I heard Giovanni's Uncle Vincent use the expression. He travels to America quite a bit. I've been waiting to use it." The priest smiled. "I'm glad I got it right. This is where we feed the population and ourselves. We put supplies in that corner." He pointed to a corner with just a few boxes in it.

"Were you here when this happened?" Henry James motioned for Lucy to step in front of him.

"Yes." Father Dominic grew sober. "It was the most frightening thing I've ever experienced. Everything shook so violently I couldn't stand. I had to crawl to the doorjamb of the church. By the time it was over, most buildings were left in rubble and the people buried under them."

"Then the water came. I spoke to one poor woman just yesterday who said that she looked out of her window and saw a large ship on top of the wave as it came toward the town. Although how she saw anything, I don't know; it was completely dark out."

"The odd thing is that every now and then you find a house that's barely damaged at all, standing right next to piles and piles of mortar. Only God knows the difference."

The tent and ground below them began to shake and rumble. Had God heard the priest's remarks? Lanterns swung and glass tingled. Lucy grabbed her father to keep her balance. People everywhere started to scream. Just like that, the tremor stopped.

"Aftershocks make surgery extremely difficult. Fortunately, none of them have been very strong." Father Dominic made the sign of the cross and looked up.

"And this hospital was set up the day it happened?" Lucy tried to peek through the next flap. There must be patients here somewhere.

"Yes. It certainly has changed since then. When Giovanni, excuse me, Dr. Castello found me, we had been working under a plain tarp, strung between posts just to keep the rain off. Now that ships like yours are starting to arrive we at least we have more of a tent with walls and cots. Even so, supplies are painfully low. We fear an outbreak of cholera or worse might occur." Father Dominic's gaze met her own. "You're headstrong. But I see compassion in your eyes. Would you like to meet the patients?"

Should she be insulted or flattered? "I would." Lucy's father put a hand on the small of her back. She shut her mouth.

"Right through here." Father Dominic led them through the next flap.

The smells of blood and body odor almost knocked Lucy over; then she saw the faces of the people and wanted to meet every one. This is why she'd come here. This is why she'd studied so hard. If she gave her life here so be it. At least her life would be given for a reason.

Doctor Davidson came from a room they had yet to see. He wove his way between the cots. "We'll be sending wounded to the Venezia straight away. Are you sure you want to leave your daughter here?"

"She's going to surprise you," Henry James squared his shoulders. How wonderful that he vouched for her.

"I hope so." Dr. Davidson crossed his arms. "Wissig really pulled his own weight around here. She'll be hard-pressed to fill his shoes. If she can't, I'm sending her back."

He shook hands with her father. Henry James grabbed Lucy and planted a kiss on her forehead.

"God be with you, Daughter. I'll be in touch before we ship out. Just because I stood up for you doesn't mean I not afraid for you. Do your job. Do *not* be a hero. Be strong. And don't take guff from anyone, especially him." Henry James nodded toward Dr. Castello who disappeared out the door of the tent.

"I promise to behave. And don't worry, I can handle him." Lucy patted her father's whiskery cheek.

"It's not handling him that worries me." Henry James gave Lucy one final hug and stepped into the rain.

Lucy swallowed the lump in her throat. From behind her, she could feel Dr. Davidson's stare. She turned, taking in the image of the pitiful tent and then gave her attention to the physician in charge.

He shifted his weight and adjusted his glasses. "If we weren't so desperate for help I would have insisted that you leave with your father. You'd better not be a hindrance. For now, I want you to assist Dr.

Castello." He stuck his head out of the tent and shouted, "Dr. Castello, may I have a word with you?"

The Sicilian ducked inside and spied Lucy with her bag at her feet. She gave him a sarcastic smile. He scowled.

"Dr. Castello." Dr. Davidson put an arm around the irritated man. "I'd like you to meet your new assisting physician."

Dr. Castello closed his eyes. "You think this is funny, don't you?"

"Extremely." Dr. Davidson patted the doctor on the back. "Please be sure to make her welcome and, oh yes, have Sister Francesca assign her to a cot." With a soft chuckle he left them.

Lucy stared up at her new boss. Giovanni stared back. Lucy waited

"If you'll come this way, we'll assign you to a cot, and then we can get to work." He turned and she followed him further into the tent.

"We work very quickly under long hours." Giovanni walked briskly. "Our primary job is to mend what we can and send the worst to the arriving ships. Unfortunately, the ships fill up fast, so we end up doing a lot of what should be done in a sterile environment. The people we cannot fix are in that corner." He motioned. "From that end of the tent they can be most easily moved to be burned once they've died."

"After we've done our job, the nurses and volunteers prepare patients and their families to be transported out of Messina. There are groups of people working at every train station in every major city in Italy to receive the *profughi*. However, not all of the *profughi* are willing to leave Messina. You'll meet them as well. They come here for food, clothing, blankets, medical attention or anything else that we can distribute."

Giovanni walked Lucy to the farthest section of the tarps. Two makeshift rooms had been created, up against a brick wall. "This is your suite, *signorina*."

Giovanni pushed the flap aside and Lucy followed him into the space that the doctors and nurses used to sleep when circumstances allowed. A large curtain had been strung to separate the men's area from the women's. To the side of the room stood a surly-looking old nun. Gray hair peeked out from under her habit, which seemed to be on too tight. It made her look a bit surprised as well as cross.

"This is Sister Francesca, the nurse in charge." He picked up a roll of socks that had fallen to the ground and gave them to the nun. "Sister, this is Lucille James. She's my new assistant. Do you have a cot for her in here? Or does she need to sleep with the men? She's a doctor, you know."

The gruff nun turned her dark eyes to Lucy and then pointed to the lumpiest cot in the room, the one up against the curtain, in the corner. "You can take that one." She looked Lucy over from head to toe. "*Dottore?* I wonder how long you'll last." She lifted her tray of bandages and disappeared through the door.

Lucy removed her cloak and retied her apron. She pulled her stethoscope from her pocket, hung it around her neck and made sure that her clinical thermometer was where it should be.

Dr. Castello waited at the door, watching her every move.

Oh, it's going to be hard keeping my mouth shut.

"Unless I tell you, you'll only assist me." Dr. Castello spoke with his back to her. The surgery held two tables for operations and several counters full of instruments and supplies. With walls of tarp and a cobblestone floor, the surprisingly clean room, smelled of antiseptic. Rain hammered the tarp above and dripped down the walls outside.

"You mean I'll be your nurse." Lucy bit her tongue. Too late. This guy had already met her temper once. Why should she hide it?

Her partner stiffened, and turned to face her.

"You will be doing *whatever* I tell you." Dr. Castello steeled his eyes. "Once your skills have been proven, the other table might be yours. Then you might be allowed to work alone; for now, you will help me."

"Why…"

"Silence." He stared at her. Daring her to speak.

Lucy narrowed her eyes but shut her mouth. She'd prove herself.

"If you need to throw up, your bucket is there." He pointed to the pail on the ground. "If you pass out on me more than once, I *will* send you back to the ship. Welcome to hell, Miss James. You've no idea what you've just signed up to do."

CHAPTER FOUR

The flap to the surgery rustled. A dark haired man pushed through escorted by Sister Francesca. Wet from head to toe, he had his hands wrapped in a blood-soaked, floral scarf.

Dr. Castello quickly doused his hands in disinfectant and went to the patient.

Lucy followed his example. The smell of antiseptic always made her want to sneeze. She fought the urge and remembered not to dry her hands on her apron.

Sister Francesca gently unwound the scarf to reveal hands literally worn to the bone.

"Oh no." Lucy focused. Did he speak any English? She did her best to look sympathetic.

The man bobbed his head and smiled.

Is he crazy? Lucy looked more closely at what used to be a thumb.

"You understand that there's nothing I can do to fix this." Dr. Castello's steady gentle voice made Lucy do a double take.

"*Si,* I had a feeling that's what you'd say." The patient nodded. "My cousin told me what a good *dottore* you are. You're clinic is next to the Chapel of Saint Francis."

"Was. It's fallen like everything else. Who's your cousin?"

"Alfredo Barzini. *Sono Luigi*."

"At the wireless station. He must have been the one to send word to me in Rome. How is he? How are his wife and his children?" Dr. Castello put a hand to the man's back. "Are they still here?"

"Yes, they're still here." Luigi's shoulders slumped and his face contorted. "They are *sotto le macerie*."

Lucy scoured her memory to translate. *Sotto means…umm.. under. Macerie…mortar?* She held her breath. Then she saw the doctor's face. Eyes closed, his jaw tightened and his fingers wound into a fist.

Dr. Castello stood with his hand on Luigi's back and for a moment the sound of rain dancing on the canvas above them filled the void. He gave the man a gentle push, his voice tight. "We need to take care of your hands.

I'll trust you to do what's right." Luigi looked at the table with its leather straps and the shiny instruments laid next to it. "I think I'll need help."

Dr. Castello moved a small stool with his foot. "Step up on this." He gave an irritated glance over his shoulder. "*Signorina* James, are you going to help or just stand there?"

"I'm right here." Lucy moved around the patient and narrowed her eyes at Dr. Castello. How awkward to be such an outsider. Maybe a kind smile would communicate to Luigi.

"What a nurse." Luigi winked at Dr. Castello, his cheery disposition, at the surface once more. "It's good to know that there's *some* beauty left in Messina."

He must be mad. Lucy tried to steady him at the elbow.

Luigi stepped up on the stool. He smiled down at her. "You want to know how I did this?" His English was broken but clear as a bell.

"S-sure."Lucy helped him sit.

"My dog woke me in the middle of the night. He wouldn't let me sleep. He insisted we go for a walk, that we should walk to the middle of town. I thought, what a crazy dog! It was then that the earthquake hit. If I hadn't listened, I would have been buried in the rubble, trapped along with my family. That dog helped me survive. When it was over, I ran home. I could hear my wife and my children calling to me from under the stone. I had no shovel so I dug them out with my hands."

What a story. "Didn't you notice what you were *doing* to your hands?"

"No." He turned his hands over. "Not until everyone was standing in front of me. My wife wrapped them in her scarf." The man started laughing. "I would do it again, for we are safe!"

"What happened to the dog?" Lucy eased his shoulders onto the table.

His face grew sober. "The last I saw of him he was swept away in the water. I called him crazy, but he saved our lives. We'll never forget him."

"Miss James." Dr. Castello cleared his throat. "Can we please begin?"

Lucy bit her lips. *So you can take time with them, but I can't.* Her father always took the time to pray and so would she. Lucy placed her hands on the patients arm and said softly, "*Father, please guide our hands and keep our minds clear.*"

From behind her, she felt a wave of anger.

Lucy swatted at a lone winter fly that flew in lazy circles above the patient on the table. *Welcome to hell, Miss James*. Dr. Castello's words kept repeating in her head. *He certainly was right. I knew things here were awful, but I never imagined just how awful.* The drumming rain grew louder and a torrent of water cascaded down the outside wall. A puddle shimmered its way under from the street.

Lucy shivered. Damp and cold the tent held little protection from the elements; still it was worlds better than the scene that played out beyond its walls.

She made the mistake of glancing at her mother's tiny broach-like watch, pinned to her dress at the shoulder. *Two o'clock. Five hours. I should never have looked.*

Lucy laid a gentle hand on the petrified soul stretched out in front of her. "*Father, please guide our hands and keep our minds clear.*"

Dr. Castello glared at her. She smiled in return.

If you think I'll stop praying just because it makes you mad you have another thought coming. Lucy walked to the head of the table with ether in one hand and a cloth in the other. They had come to the end of their supply. If this bottle had enough to put the man out, it would be a genuine miracle. She tipped the brown glass container on its end and emptied its contents. Thankfully, their shivering victim faded into oblivion.

Dr. Castello picked up his knife and began his work to take the man's arm off above the elbow.

Lucy checked the patient again, still out cold. She set the bottle and cloth to the side and moved to aid her partner when he grabbed his saw. The fine doctor hadn't said two words in hours. *If I pay attention I can show him that I know what he's going to do before he does it.*

He gave one strong fast stroke with his blade. Lucy held her breath and caught the severed limb in her hands. *I can't even count how many of these we've done today.* She carried the arm to a basket that sat on the floor by the tent wall. A pool of bloody water leaked from underneath it. *Ugh, it's full.* Lucy turned her head. *Don't look, don't look.*

Lucy caught Dr. Castello watching her. "Yes?"

"I thought you were going to faint."

"Not me."

'Hurry up then."

Lucy trotted back to grab the spray can of carbolic acid, but the sickly sweet odor in the air told her it had already been used. In fact, Dr. Castello had nearly finished the job. *How does he suture so quickly?*

His dark eyes gave no invitation for conversation, so Lucy kept her mouth shut. "Sister Francesca, we're finished here." Dr. Castello faced Lucy. "Move."

"Excuse me." Maybe he would take the hint. Maybe not. Lucy stepped to the side.

Without another word, Dr. Castello walked to the head of the table and checked the patient's breathing. "We're finished here," he called again.

Soldiers came through the flap and carried the patient to the next room.

The flap rustled again and a beautiful young woman limped in with the aid of Sister Francesca. The poor thing had several large bruises on her tear streaked face and a large scrape across her right arm. Her dark curly hair, completely undone, clung in wet ringlets to her muddy blue dress.

Dr. Castello went to the woman's side and patted the table. His Italian so fluent, so quick, there was no keeping up. He took her by the hand and helped her first to the stool and then onto the table. He gently moved her hair out of her eyes and spoke again. "*Testa*..." That meant "head." Something about her head. How frustrating.

"Her arm isn't bad either. Just a really good scrape." Dr. Castello frowned as Lucy stepped in front and examined the woman's arm.

More fluent Italian ensued. He smiled at the young woman and touched her leg.

"*Voglio morire*." The woman sobbed, her face wet with tears. "*Voglio morire*!"

"What? What's she saying?" Lucy took the woman's hand. *She's just a girl. She couldn't be more than eighteen.*

"She wants to die." Dr. Castello spoke softly. He rolled up the woman's skirt to examine her injured leg.

"*Perche'?*" Lucy had to know why.

Still gripping Lucy's hand, the peasant started speaking franticly. Not a word sounded familiar, until she said what the first patient said. "*Sotto le macerie.*" The woman buried her face in her hands and wept.

Lucy wrapped her arms around the woman and let her cry. She looked over to her partner expecting his usual attitude.

He sighed and hung his head. "She was to be married, today. Her fiancé was trapped under the mortar. They could only find his head." He looked up at Lucy, compassion in his eyes. "I know you care, but please don't ask anyone anything else or we'll never get through this."

Lucy shut her mouth and helped the girl from the table. *Huh. I like this side of you.*

"*Basta!*" Someone yelled from outside the surgery.

"What's going on out there?" Dr. Castello helped the young woman out the door and walked into the recovery room.

Lucy followed. She could see another woman, a peasant with wild eyes, struggle among a group of nurses. The woman held her arm close to her side like it might be broken.

Father Dominic stood next to her. "Lea, we need to take care of that arm."

"Dig out my family first," she yelled. At least this woman spoke more clearly and Lucy could understand. "Please, I'm begging you dig out my family."

"Is anyone doing as she asks?" Dr. Castello walked to Father Dominic.

Father Dominic turned his back to the woman, lifted his spectacles and rubbed his face with his hand. "Her family was pulled out two days ago. They're all dead. She says she can hear them calling her from under the rocks."

"But my Agathia, she's gone! I can't find her!" Lea grabbed Father Dominic, her wild eyes pleading.

"Agathia?" Lucy couldn't stop herself. Dr. Castello glared.

"*Mia figlia!*" Lea screamed, hands toward heaven. Lucy stepped back.

"Her daughter." The padre reached for the distraught woman. She pushed him away.

"Take a break *Padre*. Let me try." Dr. Castello softened his countenance. "Lea?" He smiled into the woman's eyes. "We're doing everything we can for your family. You need to be strong for them."

The woman sagged sadly and gave a nod.

For a tyrant, he sure is good with people. Lucy helped the woman into the surgery.

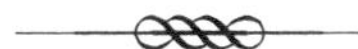

Must you pray for *everyone*, all the time?' Dr. Castello growled. "That last man couldn't even here you."

Would the beast ever stop? Anger pooled in her tummy and she opened her mouth.

Don't contend with him. Apologize. Pray to God silently, He'll hear you. Lucy felt the gentle check in her heart. Had God put her here to learn to control her own temper? It would be so much more satisfying to tell Dr. Jekyll off.

She closed her eyes, counted to ten. "I apologize, Dr. Castello. I can pray silently."

"*Impossibile.*"Dr. Castello's low grumble made her wish she'd yelled instead. Maybe she would.

The surgery door flew open and a soldier came in with a young girl in his arms. Poor little thing! Forget Doctor Jekyll. This little girl came first. Lucy wanted to scoop her up.

"We found her wandering around looking for her mother." The soldier eased her onto the table. The child protected her broken arm and gave a pitiful cry.

"Any luck?" Dr. Castello leaned toward the soldier.

"No." The Russian shook his head and then disappeared through the door.

She's so beautiful. Lucy touched the girl's back. She cried louder.

Dr. Castello put a gentle hand on the child and spoke in soft Italian. "It's all right. We're going to make your arm feel better."

The girl took one look at Dr. Castello's blood spattered apron and started to scream.

The doctor quickly slipped his apron off and tossed it over a chair. Then he stooped to the girl's level with a reassuring smile. He pulled the sobbing child into a gentle hug until her tears subsided.

Lucy removed her apron too. She watched Dr. Castello's gentle face and listened to his soft voice. There had to be more to this man than what he'd shown her so far. *Children can usually tell what a person's really like.* She came to his side to help soothe the girl.

"What's your name?" She kept her voice soft. The girl pulled her head up and wiped her nose with the back of her hand. Lucy took her hanky from her pocket and wiped. "Do you have a name?"

"Agathia."

Agathia? Wait a minute.

"Your *mamma,* is her name Lea?" Dr. Castello must have recognized the name too.

"*Si. Lea Scarpelli. I want Mamma!*" Her soulful eyes overflowed with tears.

"Where'd she go?" Lucy grinned.

"Padre has her in the mess tent." Dr. Castello smiled back. With the girl still in his arms, he stuck his head out the flap in the surgery. "Sister, go get Padre and the woman who just left here. *Pronto!*"

Wait a minute. He smiled? Lucy looked again.

"Let's set this arm." Yep. The smile remained.

"You know my Mamma?" Agathia rubbed her eyes and smeared dirt across her wet face. At least the tears had stopped.

"I think so." Lucy ran a light hand over matted curls.

Dr. Castello looked over Agathia to Lucy. "I can see no other way to set this arm than to strap her down," he said in a low voice. "How I wish we had more ether."

When Dr. Jekyll acted like this he was almost likeable. *Lord, please give me an idea.*

"I have it." She took the child's good hand in hers. "My name is Lucy. I have a little brother. His name is Max. Will you let me hold you for a moment?"

The girl hesitated and then nodded. Lucy took her from Dr. Castello and then slid onto the operating table with Agathia in her lap. She folded her arms around her good one and across her chest leaving the injured arm exposed. She hugged her for a moment and waited for her breathing to relax. Did Dr. Castello understand her intent?

He held up three fingers from under his folded arm. Okay, then.

"I'm going to count to three, Agathia. Can you count with me? *Uno... due...tre.*"

When had the sun set? Instead of seeing gray light through the cracks in the tent Lucy now saw darkness. Inside, several lamps gave much needed light, in limited quantities. The one placed on a stand that bent over the patient helped, but not much.

Dr. Castello had been right; surgery under lamp light was extremely difficult and yet her new partner had not complained once. She wanted to complain though; her legs ached, her back hurt and the steady stream of water that ran under her feet from outside the tent had soaked all the way through her boots. Lucy allowed herself to look at her mother's watch, something she had refused to do for a quite a while because knowing the time made the day drag on. She gave a quick glance and then, just like before, she wished she had not. Eleven-thirty; it had been over twelve hours.

Dr. Castello looked up at Lucy and she re-adjusted the light. He nodded and went back to work.

How was he doing it? She could see circles under his blood-shot eyes and exhaustion written all over his face. He stretched his neck and kept on going. If he could do it, so could she. Lucy prayed for strength.

She turned her attention back to Dr. Castello, completely focused on the abdomen in front of him. He shifted his weight and stretched his fingers before he took the forceps from Lucy. Despite the fatigue, he had such strength and compassion that Lucy caught her breath.

God, you're using him and he doesn't even know it. No way could she feel tired now. Excitement grew, watching the miracle take place in front of her.

Lord, please use me the way you do him.

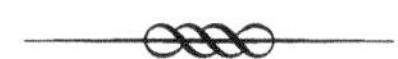

Lucy removed her mask and followed Dr. Castello through the door of the surgery. The doctors relieving them certainly did not look well rested. She re-pinned her watch to her sleeve and dropped her filthy apron in the basket by the door. Part of her hoped that the moody Dr. Castello would recognize her proficiency. Lucy let her eyes track his movements. He must have sensed her gaze, because he turned to look back at her. Lucy's first instinct was to look away, but she forced herself to look the man in the eye.

He stared at her for a second and then looked down at her soaking feet. His mouth tightened, he turned his back and walked away.

Oh well. I guess thank you is too much to ask. Lucy let her thoughts roam as she walked back to her cot. The water in her boots made a squishing sound and her soggy stockings scrunched up under her toes.

"*Buonanotte.*" She nodded to a pair of nurses who stared at her. As soon as she spoke they turned away.

Like I've never seen that before. Lucy thought of all the people who had shunned her at home, if those society belles could see her now, it would only confirm their snooty opinions. Lucy squared her shoulders, glad that she had chosen this life instead of wasting her time on frivolous matters like fashions and table settings. *Thank you God, this is so much more important.*

She pushed aside the flap and walked to her cot past a sleeping nun. The image of Agathia's muddy face flashed into her mind. The joy on that little girl's face when she saw her mother was priceless. *Lord thank you for reuniting her with Lea.* Lucy slipped out of her dress and into a thick flannel nightgown. She sat her aching body onto the lumpy cot, brushed the sand off her damp feet and pulled on a pair of her father's thickest socks. Did they ever feel good.

She remembered how Dr. Castello's countenance had completely changed when Agathia came in the room. What gentleness and concern the man had for his patients, especially when they were children.

Lucy put her feet under the covers. *And at the same time, he can be so rude and condescending.*

The doctors in Rome held him in such high regard. At least now she knew why. The man really was a very gifted surgeon. Then, when his genuine compassion shown through, Lucy simply had to admire him; the way he treated each patient with the utmost respect, the way he could gain confidence and quiet the fear in the most terrified individual. *Maybe,*

I'll be as good as he is one day. Lucy's eyelids refused to stay open any longer. She lay her head on her pillow and let out a sigh. *I'm sorry Lord, I'm too tired to think of how to pray tonight.* She opened her eyes once more and it was morning.

"This is a really good orange. Do you want some?" Lucy peeled apart a wedge and took a bite. Sweet and juicy, it tasted like sunshine on a winter day.

Just outside the surgery wall, Lucy watched Father Dominic tend to his mule. The damp pile of mortar that served as her seat threatened to soak her skirt through to her bloomers, but who cared? After a week and a half of this place things that used to matter just didn't anymore.

"No, thank you. I had one earlier." The priest brushed the mule in short swift strokes. He stopped to step around a sandbag, something Lucy hadn't noticed before.

"No wonder the surgery floor has been so dry lately; someone's anchored the tarp." Lucy stood to get a better look. "They go all around the outside wall of the surgery. This had to be your idea, thank you. My feet were so wet the first two days, I just couldn't get comfortable."

"I appreciated the thanks, but I'm not responsible. Are you telling me you haven't been outside this tent in a week and a half?" Father Dominic pulled a hoof pick from the folds of his robe.

"Not long enough to notice this. It's been raining pretty hard." Lucy looked up at the smoky gray clouds overhead. "This is the first real break I can remember."

Father Dominic began to clean the hoof in his hand. "I have an umbrella. Just let me know and I'll go with you. Fresh air would do you good."

"Thanks for caring." Lucy patted the mule on his shoulder. "What's his name?"

"The mule? Jonah." Father Dominic stretched his back and looked at the sand bags. "I'll bet Dr. Castello had something to do with this. He's always up early. If he saw your feet wet it would be like him to try to fix the situation."

"I don't know." Lucy finished the last of her orange and threw the peel into a pile of mortar." If he fixed this it would be because standing water doesn't belong in a surgery not because he's concerned about my feet."

"If that's what you think, you don't know him very well."

"You're right about that. I hardly know him at all and what I do know I don't like very much."

"I know he can be hard-headed."

"Hard-headed?" Lucy laughed. "Try condescending and mean."

The priest gave her his full attention.

"Look, I know the fact that I'm a woman and a doctor bothers him. As a matter of fact, I know it bothers everyone here. Dr. Castello seems to lead the pack." Her voice trailed off.

Father Dominic leaned against the mule. Jonah flicked an ear in his direction. "I have noticed how cold the staff is toward you. You can tell me, I'll listen."

Lucy winced. "*Padre*, I know he's your friend, but he's just awful, he's so rude. Everyone here has been rude, but Dr. Castello is the worst. He rarely says anything to me at all, unless he has to or if he feels I need to be corrected. Then when he does speak, it's in Italian. I understand some of it and believe me, it's not very nice. Most of the time he ignores me like I'm not standing next to him at all."

"And yet he lets you pray for the patients."

He did didn't he? "Um, he does. How did you....?" Lucy sank onto a large piece of mortar.

Father Dominic chuckled. "Word gets around." He came to her side and sat on a rock. "That he's letting you pray at all tells me a lot. I've never known him to allow anyone he doesn't like into his operating room." Father Dominic put an arm around Lucy's shoulder.

"You think he likes me?" What a novel idea.

"Yes. You and the work you're doing. If he wasn't pleased, he would have sent you back to the ship days ago. He'll come around, give him time. Everyone here will come around. The idea of a woman doctor has never occurred to them, they don't know what to do with you.

"I don't bother you?"

"No. I've lived long enough to know that God will use any vessel that's willing. I'm glad you're here. In the meantime, maybe you could pray for all of us and I'll help you with your Italian."

"Miss James! I don't want you out here by yourself." The subject of the conversation came out through the flap in the tent. He spied Lucy with the priest and his tone softened. "Oh. *Buongiorno, Padre*. Are you finished? I need her help in the surgery."

"Yes." Father Dominic stood and gave Lucy a hand up with a raise of his eyebrow. "Go on. He doesn't want you out here alone because it's dangerous and he *needs you* in the surgery."

Maybe he did. One look at those dark, penetrating eyes changed her mind.

Dr. Castello disappeared into the shadows of the tent and Lucy followed.

Lucy stood in her usual spot. If this man needed her he certainly failed to show it. He'd been completely silent for hours. What other choice had she than to pay strict attention and guess what instrument he would need next?

Dr. Castello glanced at her. Why? Lucy shook it off and focused on the soldier with the gash in his arm. A spray of carbolic acid would do the trick if the bandage on this arm remained dry.

A man with a smashed thumb took Lucy's attention next. Dr Castello glanced at her again; this time a little longer. Did he want something? Lucy frowned at him. He turned back to the peasant and prepared to amputate.

Lucy bandaged the hand, now missing a digit, then sent the man into the next room.

Dr. Castello moved to the washbasin. The disinfectant they used to sterilize their hands also dried their skin. He held his breath and doused his hands. That had to hurt. He had several large cracks in the skin around his fingernails. Lucy had a good one too. It smarted like the dickens to douse her hands but how could she complain when the patients they worked on now had to suffer through with no morphine or ether?

Lucy took the bottle from Dr. Castello and washed. Her hands stung to high heaven. Lucy closed her eyes and released a slow breath.

"Your hands look awful." Dr. Castello had been watching her?

"Yours are worse." Lucy pointed at his swollen thumb.

"Yes, but I've been here longer and I knew what I was getting myself into."

"And I volunteered to come. I choose to be here."

The flap rustled and a man came in supported between two others.

"Let's get him to the table." Dr. Castello moved the stool. The patient's friends helped him up and then left.

Lucy moved to her usual spot. Why was Dr. Castello staring again? She stared back."Do you need something?"

"You *have* chosen to be here. Let's see what you can do." He walked to Lucy's place and pushed her into his spot. "Go ahead. Take over."

CHAPTER FIVE

This felt wrong. Dr. Castello now stood where she usually did. He had all his attention directed at her. *Is he sick?*

His lips pressed together. "*Signorina* James, this will be your only chance. Are you going to faint?"

"No."

"All right then." He pointed to the patient on the table.

One look at the man's mangled foot told Lucy all she needed to know. *Pull it together, Lucille. Concentrate. Lord help me keep a clear mind.*

She gently removed what was left of his shoe, cut away the bottom of his trousers and tied a tourniquet below his knee. Lucy cleaned the entire area then looked for Dr. Castello.

"I've got him strapped in. Go ahead." He walked to the other side of the table and leaned across the patient. He gave a compassionate look to the poor man. "Bite on this." He wedged the man's handkerchief in his mouth. "Here's my hand. Hold on to me." Dr. Castello put his other hand over the patient's eyes.

Lucy acted as soon as she knew the man could not see her. *I've done this before. Fast. He's awake. I've got to be fast.* Lucy grabbed the sharpest knife. *Cut through the skin and muscle first.*

The patient jerked and a frightened cry escaped his lips.

"No, don't look. I've got you. You'll be all right." Dr. Castello's voice soothed.

Tie off the major vein and artery. Reserve some muscle. Lucy pushed flesh away from the bone and grabbed the saw.

The patient wailed again. He trembled violently.

"Hold on to me. You have to be brave. We're almost through." Dr. Castello looked over his shoulder to Lucy and gave a nod.

No! No! The table's too high! I'm too short to get good leverage! Something bumped her foot. *The stool!* Dr. Castello must have slid the footstool from under the table with his toe. *Thank goodness.*

Quicker than she could think, Lucy hopped up and with one lightning stroke, had the poor man's foot off just above the ankle.

"No!" The man screamed and thrashed, but Dr. Castello had his full body weight across the patient's chest.

To do this with no anesthesia! How horrible! Lucy held back her tears. "I'm so sorry. I know it hurts. We're almost finished." She made a reach for the spray pump of carbolic acid and found Dr. Castello holding it for her.

"He's passed out."

"I'm so glad." Lucy sprayed the leg and sutured everything into place. She could feel her partner's stare. "Did I do all right?"

"You need to grow six inches."

"That's not what I asked." Lucy took a roll of bandage from the doctor and wrapped the leg.

"Humph."

Lucy looked up from the bandage. "Well?"

Dr. Castello raised an eyebrow. "Hurry up, you've got another patient waiting."

"Finish." Dr. Castello gave a nod to Lucy. He washed his hands in the basin, removed his apron and walked out of the surgery.

This was the fourth night straight he had done such a thing. *It's as though I'm back in med school.*

Lucy made sure that each stitch was perfect and arranged a bed in recovery for the patient. *I'm so tired, if I don't sit down for a moment, I might just start crying and that would only prove to doctor wonderful that I shouldn't be here.* She stretched her neck and pulled off her blood-stained apron.

Lucy washed and then headed to the mess tent. She grabbed an orange, a crust of bread and some milk, found an empty table and collapsed onto a chair. Her throbbing feet and aching legs made a wonderful souvenir from the grueling day.

Lord Jesus, he's always trying to tell me to do something I would do on my own anyway. He's so cross. So demanding. So bossy. I don't care what Dr. Castello thinks of me, I only want to serve you.

Dr. Castello walked into the room. He grabbed some food and looked for a place to eat.

Lucy ducked behind her hand. Maybe he'd sit with the nuns.

He spied her. The irritating smile he wore on the dance floor in Rome floated on his lips.

"No," Lucy moaned. She slid down in her chair an inch and put her face in her hand. *Anywhere but here.*

The Sicilian walked to her table and, without invitation, sat.

Lucy picked at her bread. If the man sought conversation he would not get it. She scooted her chair farther away and sort of turned her back.

Now he stared at her as he often did in the operating room. *How annoying*. "Yes?"

"I want to know why you wear a nurse's uniform." He rested an arm on the table with a fork in his hand.

"Does it matter what I wear?" Lucy pulled at the sleeve of her ugly frock. Why should he care?

"It does if I have to look at you," he snorted. "That has to be the most unattractive dress I've ever seen. It doesn't even fit you. You should eat more; maybe you'll fill it out one day. Besides, I don't want you fainting while we work tomorrow."

"In case you haven't noticed, I don't faint." Lucy scowled. "And, if you think you're the first person to point out that I'm skinny, you're dumber than you look. Get in line!" She turned away, but her temper wasn't finished. "And *don't* tell me what to do." She tossed her bread on the plate. "I'll be your trained monkey in the surgery, but nowhere else."

"*Scimmia piccola*, you're the most frustrating creature I've ever met." Giovanni was clearly trying not to laugh. "I've been wondering if you remembered our first conversation. You've been well trained."

Well-trained? Like a dog? Lucy gritted her teeth. "And you are still arrogant, conceited and condescending. I couldn't get away from you fast enough! "

"And after I saved you."

"From what? A tremor? Big deal! It doesn't change who you are."

"Who I am? You demand the job of a man and expect to be treated like a lady. I've treated you no differently than any male I've worked with."

Lucy smacked her hands on the table and stood. "Exactly how many males have you called little monkey? Do you monitor what they eat? I'd like to see you do it."

"No, men in general know they must eat when it is time to do so. Really *Signorina* James, you have proven your point: you *don't* faint during surgery. I must admit, I'm impressed with that. You should go back to Rome now."

"I honestly don't care if I impress you or not. If I was on my death bed, I wouldn't go back to Rome. These people are much more important than your opinion and if it irritates you that I'm here, good!" She spun about and walked quickly through the tent flap, past the quiet laughter of everyone in the mess tent.

Giovanni caught Lucy's uneaten orange before it rolled off the table. He put it back on her plate and watched her pigtail bounce as she ducked through the door.

"Why are you choosing to irritate Dr. James?" Father Dominic pulled out the chair that Lucy had occupied and sat. "She's just trying to do her job, Giovanni."

"She's fun to irritate. I love her temper."

"Giovanni; the truth." Father Dominic leaned forward with a frown.

Padre." Giovanni let out a sigh. "She just shouldn't be here. Look at her. She's soft and feminine; this place is bloody and full of death. I want her to return to Rome because it's safe. I don't understand why her father let her come."

"Giovanni, I know that her presence here goes directly against your deeply ingrained code of chivalry, but Lucy is skilled. She's strong on the inside. Has she been unable to perform during surgery?"

"No, as a matter of fact *Signorina* James is surprisingly efficient. The harder I work her, the better she gets. I expected her to collapse on the first day, but as you see she's still here." Giovanni shoved his empty plate away.

"So you *like* working with her."

"I can't hide anything from you can I?" He picked up her orange and held onto it.

"No."

"With a face like hers and all that red hair? What man wouldn't like to stand next to her all day? That doesn't change the fact that Messina is too dangerous a place and that she should not be doing a man's job."

"Think about what you're saying for a moment." The priest leaned forward again. "Think about Dr. James and what her life would be like if she were married. Just how many men would be willing to acknowledge her intelligence? Is she good?"

"More than good."

"Gifted?"

"Okay, I will say to you that she is gifted, but to no one else." Giovanni scowled.

"Wouldn't it be a shame for her to be locked away? You know how hard it is to find a good surgeon. And, Dr. James likes to work with the poor, just like you. But I suppose you think she'd be better off pregnant and rubbing some man's feet at night."

Giovanni pursed his lips and ran a hand through his hair. He did not like the picture in his mind. "But she's a woman."

"Yes, a very talented woman. You know, history is full of women, who, given the opportunity, have served God and country as well as a man. If I remember your family history correctly, you have several in your family tree."

"Yes, but they are exceptions."

"Can't Dr. James be an exception?"

Giovanni looked at the uneaten bread on Lucy's plate. Outside the tent somewhere, a dog barked. Did the priest always have to be right?

"You've been doing this to me for a long time." Giovanni turned the orange in his hand.

"Doing what? Trying to teach you? You're as stubborn as a mule."

"Yes, I am." Giovanni had to smile. "I still don't like the idea of a woman doing surgery."

"Even though you're allowing her to lead now and then?"

"Did Sister Francesca tell you about that?"

"Yes."

Giovanni thought for a moment before he answered. Lucille James certainly did not behave the way he expected. "I was curious. She's much more efficient than the nurses. I never have to ask her for anything, she anticipates what I need and has it ready. So, I wanted to see just how much she knew. *Signorina* James knows quite a lot. Still, I don't understand why she's not married by now. She should be raising a family.

"Maybe she would rather be a doctor."

"I cannot imagine why."

"Maybe men irritate her."

Giovanni looked up from the orange. That thought had never occurred to him.

"If she were a man would you send her away?"Father Dominic raised an eyebrow.

"If that woman was a man she would lead her own surgical staff. She is a strange creature."

"You're leaving God out of the equation again, Giovanni." *Padre* took the roll off Lucy's plate and bit into it. "Dr. James gets her strength and her skill from the Lord."

"You know I don't believe in God," Giovanni said to his friend with a smirk.

"Yes, you do." The priest chuckled. "I wouldn't be surprised at all if Dr. James has been sent here to remind you of just that."

Giovanni stood and grabbed the orange. She'd eaten nothing because of him.

"What are you going to do with that?" Father Dominic grabbed the plates.

"I'll think of something." Giovanni put it in his pocket.

Mamma mia. Lucy pulled her nightgown over her head and climbed onto the lumpy mattress. *This is what I should have done in the first place*. Her stomach growled. *Except that I didn't eat and I'm still hungry.* Lucy stuck her feet under the blanket and scooted up against the curtain that hung behind. She crossed her legs like a tailor and took out her prayer journal and Bible, but it was too dark to read. Her thoughts turned to Psalm 46:1-3.

God is our refuge and strength, a very present help in trouble. Therefore we will not fear, though the earth be removed, and though the mountains be carried into the midst of the sea; thought its waters roar and be troubled though the mountains shake with its swelling...."

A low rumbling sound filled the room.

What on earth was that? Lucy felt a cold chill.

Then Sister Francesca exhaled. The sleeping nun's lips made a funny flapping sound before she began another loud snore.

Lucy stifled a laugh. *This psalm is about an earthquake and that old lady snores like one*. Lucy slipped from her bed and gently rolled Sister Francesca to sleep on her side.

Ah, peace and quiet. Lucy crawled back in bed. *I have to finish the psalm; the end is my favorite part.*

Be still; and know that I am God; I will be exalted among the nations, I will be exalted in the earth The Lord of hosts is with us; The God of Jacob is our refuge.

I blew up at dinner, just in case you didn't notice. Lucy rolled her eyes to heaven as she prayed. *I lost my temper...again.*

That man just makes me so angry. God, I'm sorry. Please help me to show Dr. Impossible Your love. We need you here. I need you here.

Please be with us. Please give me strength. Please give strength to the other doctors who are working here with me. They've been at this for so much longer. If I'm this tired how much more exhausted are they? Help us to sleep peacefully so that we'll be fresh tomorrow. Please help me to write in a straight line, because it's too dark to see. Her gaze drifted around the dark tent from person to person. Why did that man have to say what he did?

"I know I'm skinny." She wrote the words and whispered to God at the same time. "I just wish people would stop reminding me." She put her Bible and prayer journal under the covers.

Lucy rolled on her side against a big lump in the bed by her pillow. *What on earth is that?* She reached above her head.

An orange?

Lucy sat up, smelled it and her stomach growled. *I don't remember bringing this to bed with me. Maybe I did.* She peeled the orange and ate each section slowly, letting the juice burst on her tongue at just the right moment. It was the best meal she'd had in days. But where did it come from?

"God be with you." Father Dominic handed a fresh blanket and a small gunnysack of oranges to a barefoot woman in a ragged dress. "Come back tomorrow, another ship is coming in." He stroked the woman's cheek with his thumb and she gave a toothless grin. *Thank the Lord for these supplies, these people need so much.* He watched the peasant leave the mess tent and turned his attention to the next person in line.

"What's this?" The priest heard Lucy's angry question through the wall of the tent. The surgery stood just on the other side of the tarp.

"I thought the stool helped you see better," Giovanni retorted.

Silence followed. Father Dominic breathed a sigh of relief. Maybe that would be it. He gave a warm hand to the peasant in front of him.

"Go ahead, leave." Giovanni's voice reached Father Dominic's ear.

"I'm *not* leaving. I wouldn't give you the pleasure!" Everyone in the mess tent burst into laughter, except Father Dominic.

Seconds later, Sister Francesca came out of the surgery carrying Lucy's stool.

"They're at it again." Father Dominic stood in her way. "This is the third day in a row. It's a wonder they get any work done at all. What's it about this time?"

Sister Francesca gave a wry smile and held up the small stool in her hand. Across the top *M is for monkey* had been written in boot black.

"You know that's not funny." The priest crossed his arms.

"I'm not laughing at the stool." Sister Francesca put it on the table. "I've never seen a woman put him in his place before. Dr. Castello has finally met his match."

"I think so, too." Father Dominic handed a sack of oranges to another peasant. "In any event, Sister, I think Dr. James just might need a woman to help her understand our wayward Giovanni. I, for one, don't want her to go."

"Then stop acting like a man!" Giovanni's muffled voice floated through the tarp again.

"Don't worry, I'll take care of Dr. James." Sister Francesca turned her head toward the surgery. "I've judged her too harshly, I know that now. Dr. James has a heart for God and His people." She tilted her head toward the priest. "Just like that stinker."

"Just like our Giovanni." Father Dominic nodded. "We'll have to plan."

CHAPTER SIX

Lucy plodded into the mess tent. Her heart felt as heavy as the dreadful boots on her feet. She'd almost lost her composure today, in front of Dr. Castello too. Maybe a little food would keep at bay the swarm of emotions threatening to surface. But she kept seeing the face of a handsome young soldier brought to them on a stretcher.

He couldn't have been more than nineteen. His body, bruised and broken by a fall, had internal injuries beyond repair. To make matters even more heart wrenching the young Russian remained awake through the entire examination. He even thanked them for trying. Dr. Castello sent him to the *Venezia* as a final hope.

To hold it together around all these dying people was hard enough without having to deal with a tyrant too. Maybe she should call him Captain Bligh; then she could mutiny. She took a bowl full of lentil soup from the cook. "*Grazie*."

"You're welcome." He gave her an extra piece of bread. At least she had one ally besides the priest. Lucy gave him a grateful smile. Now to find a place to eat.

There, by himself, Dr. Castello sat at a table in the far corner. His dark eyes big and round, focused on nothing at all, his bowl of soup yet untouched. Could he be sad too?

Go sit with him. The idea nudged her heart.

Lucy sighed. *But I don't like him; he doesn't like me. I won't know what to say to him, we'll just end up fighting.*

She found refuge at another table. Then the words she read that morning came back to her. *"Blessed are the peacemakers, for they shall be called the sons of God." It would be the right thing to do. I don't have to say a word. He looks so lonely. He needs to know that God loves him.*

Lucy rolled her eyes and gave up. She walked to Dr. Castello's table, pulled out a chair and sat next to him.

The pain on his face slowly disappeared. "Do you need something?" His voice flat and low.

"No, I was hoping that you wouldn't mind some company." Lucy bowed her head and thanked the Lord for her meal.

Dr. Castello watched her, she could feel it.

Lucy kept her eyes on her plate. She could be a peacemaker if only she could control her tongue. Lucy shoved a spoon full of food in her mouth, hoping it would do the trick.

"He died, you know." Dr. Castello's flat voice gave away his feelings.

Her heart hurt. "The Russian soldier?"

"Yes."

"I know." Lucy's eyes filled with tears, but she fought them back again. She found Dr. Castello watching her. His eyes filled with tears too.

Dr. Castello sat with her the entire time she ate, even though he finished well before she did. He said nothing more. Before she stood to go to bed for the evening, her heart nudged her again.

Take his plate.

Lucy stood and so did Dr. Castello. With her plate in one hand, she scooped up his.

His face lifted, then he gave a wicked smile. "You might take my glass as well." He put his glass on top of the plates that Lucy held.

She should hit him with these plates!

Blessed are the peacemakers…. The thought interrupted her anger. Lucy bit her lip, counted three and then turned to leave.

"*Grazie, Signorina* James."

She turned and searched Dr. Castello's face once more; his eyes soft and kind. How could she stay mad at him?

"*Prego.*" Lucy looked away. *It's warm in here.* Maybe tomorrow would be better.

Lucy sat on her bed lacing her boots. She did her best to ignore the small hole in the tent wall next to her bed. Through it, a cold gray dawn announced another day of rain. Next to her, on the cot, an orange balanced on the corner.

"That took forever." She stood, grabbed her brush off her bed and yanked it through her tangled hair. The orange rolled to the middle.

"I have a note from your father." Sister Francesca came in from the door and handed a folded paper to Lucy. "Let me help you with your hair."

"You want to what?"

"You read the letter, I'll brush your hair. You know how important punctuality is to Dr. Castello."

Could she be dreaming? Lucy handed her brush to the nun.

"Have a seat." Sister Francesca gave Lucy a gentle push toward her bed.

Lucy sat. The orange jumped.

"You know you're not supposed to have food in the dormitory." Sister Francesca picked up the orange and handed it to Lucy.

"I know, Sister. I keep finding oranges under my pillow. I don't know who's putting them there." Hopefully, the nun would believe her.

Sister Francesca looked from the orange to the curtain. "Maybe you should read your letter." She began to work the brush through Lucy's curls.

My darling Lucille,

The Venezia is full to capacity and we are preparing to ship out. You have the choice to return to Rome with me now, or to continue with the temporary hospital until I can come for you in two months. The choice is yours, but believe me, no one would blame you for leaving. It has been a grueling two weeks.

Love,

Daddy.

Lucy let the letter fall to her lap. She really wanted to stay, but she could read between the lines; her father wanted her to return.

"Is something wrong?" Sister Francesca tied a blue ribbon at the bottom of Lucy's braid.

"Yes. Daddy is shipping out and he wants me to return to Rome with him."

"Is that what he wrote?"

"No, he always gives me the choice and then expects me to choose what he wants. I know him. He wants me to return to Rome." Lucy kicked a small stone by her foot.

"What about your work with Dr. Castello?" Sister Francesca sat to face her.

"What about it? It's been rewarding, but Dr. Castello's made it clear that he would rather me leave than stay. He won't miss me."

"I wouldn't be so sure about that." The nun handed Lucy her brush.

"Sister, I'm not blind. No one wants me here. Except for Father Dominic and the cook, no one even likes me here. Why would I stay?"

"Because we've been wrong." Sister Francesca took Lucy's hand. "I've been wrong and I hope you can forgive me. Can you?"

Really? "Yes, of course." She gave the nun an awkward hug and patted her bony back. *What a miracle.*

"You must understand, Dr. James, Italy is a very old country and people are very set in their ways. Women have well defined roles here, as do men. Our ways might not be perfect, but they are so deeply ingrained that most of us cannot see any other way to live." The nun pulled Lucy's hand to her lap.

"Has Dr. Castello ever said that he *doesn't* like you?"

"No." Lucy fingered the letter in her hand. "He hasn't."

"Then you can trust that he does. Sicilians are very private people, especially the Castello family. If you pay attention, you will see who he is; good with children, good with his patients. Did you know he requires no payment at all when he runs his clinic?"

"No. No, I didn't" Lucy looked up. "I'm just so tired of fighting with him."

"Then don't fight."

"But he always starts it."

"The only concern you should have is the condition of your heart before the Lord. *I* will talk to Dr. Castello."

"You? Will he listen to you? You're a woman."

"Not to Giovanni, I'm not. I'm a nun *and* I'm his aunt. If he doesn't listen to me, I'll tell his mother." Sister Francesca stood and pulled Lucy to her feet. "You'd better hurry."

"*Signorina* James?" Giovanni stood at the flap in the door. "Are you ready?"

"*Un minuto, signore*!" Sister Francesca pointed a crooked finger at the door. She turned to Lucy and whispered, "If he didn't like you, he wouldn't be waiting for you." She handed the orange to Lucy and gave a discrete nod toward Giovanni.

"But he's so bossy," Lucy whispered back. *There's no way it's him.*

"Yes, he's Sicilian." The nun winked and pushed Lucy toward the door.

I'll stay. Daddy's not going to like it, but I'll stay Lucy shoved the orange in her pocket and ran through the door after Dr. Castello, already three feet in front of her.

Had Daddy really left three days ago? Even though she seldom saw him, just knowing her father worked aboard the ship, anchored beyond the harbor, gave a sense of security. Who knew this place would feel so lonely without him.

Thank goodness for her prayer journal. Lucy poured her heart into the dog-eared tablet and it felt like a long lost friend. What a grueling day it had been. Sitting in bed, in the dark tent allowed for some needed quiet and a little time alone with God. Sister Francesca was true to her word; Dr. Castello had stopped picking on her. Instead, he reverted to stoic silence. *Well, at least he's not yelling. Did I hear glass tinkling?* Lucy looked around the dark tent.

My imagination is getting the best of me, Lucy closed the journal and started praying *God is our refuge and strength, a very present help in trouble—*

Her bed began to vibrate, and then it began to shake. She tucked her journal under her pillow. *Oh no. Here we go again. All the patients will wake up.*

The shaking got worse, the crash of glass made her jump.

This is no tremor. Lucy stood, grabbed her robe and shoved her feet into her shoes. The tent around her began to sway. She felt her way toward the wall, through the pitch dark and the deafening noise.

Patients screamed, children cried. *Lord, help me to make it. I can hardly stand*.

The other women in the room were on their feet now. Lucy bumped into Sister Francesca.

"Sister, I am going to calm the patients." Lucy and the nun held onto each other for support.

"Go ahead, I need to calm my nurses." Sister Francesa squeezed Lucy's hand.

Lucy stumbled toward the flap in the tent and the shaking stopped. *Whew*.

A great heave and a crack came from above. Then something heavy knocked her to the ground.

CHAPTER SEVEN

Lucy's heart beat a mile a minute and she struggled to move, but she couldn't. The absolute darkness only added to the confusion.

Oh, my head. She fingered the aching knot at her hairline; her hand came away sticky. *No, this can't happen. I've got to think. I've got to stay conscious. I need to get out of here before someone steps on me.*

Lord, please help me. Lucy tried to push the amazingly heavy object which lay on top of the tarp that held her down. *This is a tent pole. Oh, Lord Jesus, help me keep my wits.*

Maybe I can slide out from under it. Lucy pulled herself forward on her stomach. *Yes, I think I can. Ouch, glass. Rats.* She wiped her skinned palm on her nightgown. Sharp pain said that hand needed some attention. *Jehoshaphat! That's all I needed.*

Sweat trickled down her neck, the air so thick it became a labor to breathe. Lucy moved her hair out of her eyes and pulled herself further along. A foot stepped very close to her face, but she was under the tarp and they on top.

"Help!" Lucy tried to grab at the person, but they moved before she could. She crawled forward, to feel her way in her dark, oppressive prison.

I'm not sure I can go much further. She stopped to rest her aching muscles. Then a cool breath of fresh air reached her face. Lucy gasped and looked to her left. *Light! Oh thank you, God! Oh, help me*.

"Someone's down here." That voice had to belonged to Dr. Castello.

She neared the hole and the tarp swept back. Heavenly, cool air filled her lungs and touched her face.

"Are you all right?" Dr. Castello knelt beside her and pushed her hair out of her eyes. "Can you stand?"

"Yes." Lucy sat up and gave him her hands. "Watch out, I've got glass in my palm."

Dr. Castello's face went soft. He turned her hand over and looked at it and then at Lucy. "Your head is bleeding, too. Let's get you on your feet and I'll take a look."

He took her other hand and his strong arm wrapped around her waist and lifted her to her feet. She found herself standing in the recovery room. A quick glance behind revealed that the roof now sagged to the ground, the surgery and the dormitory lay flat.

"There are more people under there!" Lucy pulled away and tried to lift the tarp.

"Let me look at you first. Then we can help." Dr. Castello grabbed Lucy and pulled her back. He put his hands on either side of her face. "Stay still."

"My head's fine. Just get the glass out of my hand and I'll be good." Lucy shifted, heat rose in her cheeks.

"Would you please stay still?" Dr. Castello held his shirtsleeve to her head for a moment and then examined it gently. "You're right, about your head, at least on the outside." He tapped it.

"Hey!"

"Turn around." Dr. Castello turned Lucy by the shoulders. He ran his fingers through her hair.

"What are you doing?" She grabbed her head and stepped away.

"Stop arguing and stand still." He moved her back in place and braided her hair faster than she could. "I'm just pulling your hair out of your eyes so you can see." He pulled a leather string out of his pocket and tied it in place.

"You're better at this than I am." Lucy could not help but giggle.

"I have nieces." Dr. Castello said over her shoulder. "Let me see your hand."

Before Lucy could think, Dr. Castello turned her around, grabbed her hand and picked the glass out.

"Ouch. Was it in deep?"

"No, *bambina*, but that's the best I can do until we've gotten this tent up. We've got to move before a fire breaks out."

Lucy retied the sash on her robe, watching Dr. Castello. "I'm confused," she muttered.

From outside, a soldier yelled something in Russian. The sound of running feet promised help.

Dr. Castello frowned. "*Signorina* James?" he grabbed her shoulders.

"Yes?"

"Are you going to live?"

Lucy smirked. "I might." She spun on her heels. "Come on, I've done this before." Lucy began to walk her hands on the low hanging roof, toward one of the collapsed poles. "My father loves to camp. We usually go for two weeks every summer. My tent always falls. This tent is much larger, but the idea of standing it will be the same."

Dr. Castello stood behind her with a hand on his hip and a twinkle in his eye. "I know how to raise a tent. What I meant was that we needed to raise it." He came to her side and helped to push the tent back in place.

"I apologize." She giggled again, while she held the tent up. Russian soldiers replaced the first pole. "I just have a hard time thinking of Italians as campers."

"Where exactly did you think this tent came from?" Dr. Castello tied a rope. He stood up panting, but still in a good humor. "Italians have been camping since the days of Rome."

"Okay, so Italians camp. Did you have to make such a heavy tent?" Lucy breathed heavily and her arms began to shake. Dr. Castello came to her side again to support the tent.

"Rest for a moment." He lifted the tent out of her hands. "I can hold this."

"Thanks. There was a lantern in this part of the tent. Have we found it?"

Dr. Castello scanned the ground. In the corner on its side was the missing lantern. "There it is."

"One disaster is enough for anyone." Lucy quickly picked up the fallen lantern and hung it back in its place. She returned to help Giovanni.

Lucy helped their last patient down from the table and out the surgery door. She stood still, bleary eyes and exhausted ears taking in the silence of the morning. The tent was up and everyone accounted for, but they had worked all night. A bird sang outside the tent as though nothing had ever happened. Dr. Castello looked as exhausted as she felt.

Lucy's head throbbed, but in the intensity of the night, she had forgotten all about it. She reached up to feel the dried blood at her hairline.

Dr. Castello followed her hand with his gaze. His brow creased. "We've finished everyone else, now it's your turn. Let me take a better look at you."

She leaned against the table and watched her partner reach for the alcohol. He winced?

"You're hurt, too?" She could not believe she hadn't noticed. "Your rib cage?" Lucy reached her hand to his side, but he squirmed away.

"You first." Dr. Castello pushed Lucy back against the table. "Let me see your hand." He began to gently clean her wound.

"I don't get it." Lucy took a quick breath, with the cold sting of antiseptic.

"I'm sorry, I know it hurts. Don't get what?" He blew on her hand, in the way he had soothed so many children. He wrapped it and tied a tiny knot.

"Why the sudden change?"

"How do you mean?"

"You're being nice to me. Why?"

Dr. Castello paused before he stepped closer. His mouth tightened into a slight smile.

Lucy tried to back up a step, but she was already up against the table. His warm breath kissed her forehead.

He dabbed her cut with cotton. "Has anyone ever told you, you have beautiful skin? I can tell with certainty, you've not spent much time in the sun."

"You're not going to answer me, are you?"

Dr. Castello tilted his head and leaned back a bit. "I'm glad not to lose another physician. Two nurses and Dr. Davidson are enough. If you weren't here, we'd have to close this hospital."

"But you were being nice to me before we knew just *who* was hurt. Are you going to let me look at your side?"

Giovanni straightened up and backed away a bit.

Lucy shrugged and turned to leave. "I'm too tired to argue. I'll get someone else to look at it for you."

"No, wait." Dr. Castello reached for her arm.

Lucy stopped when she felt his touch.

"You don't have to prove yourself to me anymore. I know how professional you are." He tightened his lips and unbuttoned his shirt to reveal a large purple bruise just under his right arm.

"That's huge." Lucy caught her breath and walked to his side. She moved his arm to see better.

"One of the poles hit me as I was making my way toward recovery."

"And you lifted the tent and all those people like nothing was wrong." Lucy looked up into his gray eyes, just inches from her. "How could you? Didn't it hurt?"

"Others were hurting more." Dr. Castello nodded at Lucy's head.

"I have to touch you. Is that okay?"

Dr. Castello rolled his eyes. "Yes, yes. Hurry up. I'm getting cold."

Lucy probed his side and he flinched. "I'm sorry, I know it hurts, *bambino*. Hold still." She touched him again. "Nothing is broken; you're just really bruised and swollen." She straightened up and caught him smiling at her.

He sobered up right away.

Lucy put her hands on her hips. "You're going to be sore for a while. Let me wrap it for you, so we can at least support your rib cage until you're better. What's so funny?"

Sister Francesca walked into the room and placed a basket of clean bandages on the counter. She turned steel eyes on Dr. Castello before she left.

"Nothing." He looked over his shoulder at the nun and then back at Lucy. "Don't waste the supplies. I'll be all right." He slowly buttoned his shirt.

Lucy began to clean and set up for the day.

"You did well tonight," Dr. Castello said.

She turned to find him leaning against the operating table watching her work. His shirttail still hung loose, his soft black curls disheveled. He stood to his feet and, for the first time, began to help.

"You've been working in your nightgown, *scimmia piccola*. Why don't you go and change?" Dr. Castello smiled at her again. "I'll finish here."

Lucy looked down at her filthy robe and sighed. She retied her sash again and tried to brush the dirt off. His words still stung. She turned to leave.

"Dr. James."

Lucy turned back, quickly. "*Doctor* James?" Her eyes went wide.

"I was wrong to call you a monkey. I won't do it again."

Really? "Thank you." Lucy couldn't help but stare.

"Hurry up." Kindness and a tinge of regret looked back at her.

From just outside the surgery door Father Dominic listened to the conversation. Sister Francesca listened too, so at least he could kind of justify this breach in etiquette.

The muffled conversation revealed Giovanni's repentance. "*Grazie a Dio!*" the priest whispered, eyes toward heaven. He wrapped his arm around the old nun and kissed the top of her habit.

"Finally, we have peace." The nun hugged him back. She turned away just as Lucy came out of the door.

"Not so fast." Lucy's Italian had improved so much she could now talk to anyone, even the children. She wiped a little boy's dirty mouth. "Take smaller bites. You might choke." To her right, next to the table where she sat, stood six ragamuffin children—the offspring of Sicilians determined to make a new life in the devastated city. Their presence was always welcome in the dreary mess tent. "Go ahead." She moved the plate of rolls closer. "You may have another."

The children sat at the table and began to stuff bread in their mouths.

To Lucy's left, Sister Francesca sipped a cup of coffee and darned the socks of one of the doctors at the hospital station. Hard to believe such a strong friendship could form in so short a time.

"Have we heard from Dr. Davidson?" Lucy broke off a piece of bread and dipped it in some olive oil.

"Yes. It's only been a week, but he wrote that his concussion is healing nicely. Sisters Maria and Margareta are recovering nicely too. They all send their regards." Sister Francesca dropped a small wooden darning ball into a sock. She let it fall to the toe and held it up to see the severity of the damage.

"Wow." Lucy bit the peppery oil off the roll. *Umm.* "Who's sock is that? There's barely anything left."

"Who do you think would wait so long to ask me to darn this?" Sister turned her head. "David, that roll belongs to Eleanor. Has Dr. Castello assigned you to work with anyone else?"

"No." Lucy shrugged. "I thought he'd be glad to give me away. Especially now that he's in charge. And yes, we're getting along better. I don't know what you said to him, but it worked."

The nun turned toward her; a slow smile crept across her wrinkled face. "I've not said a word."

"But-"

"*Dottoressa* Lucia?"

"Yes, David."

"If I broke my arm could you fix me?"

"Yes. I would fix you right away."

"What about me?"

"You too, Eleanor."

"And me?"

"Yes, you too, Pietro. You children all know to come here if you're ever hurt, don't you? Dr. Castello and I will do our best to make you better."

David slid out of his chair and came to Lucy's side. Even covered in dirt, his light brown curls and olive skin made him stand out from the rest of the children. He held up a dirty piece of lace and proudly handed it to her.

"What's this? Why thank you David." Lucy took him in her arm. The boy reeked, but who cared?

"We all found it." Pietro chimed in.

"Then I'll just have to hug all of you." She hugged them one at a time. The children beamed. "Tell me, where did you find this? It's beautiful."

"In the old house on the corner." Pietro stepped closer.

"The one that's leaning to the side?" Lucy's heart skipped a beat.

"Yes."

Lucy turned her full attention to the ragged group. "The lace is beautiful, but you must please promise me to never go in that house again. It could fall at any moment. Think about your *Mamma*, Pietro. And your *Nonna*, Deloris. If anything were to happen to you who would take care of your families?"

The children grew very quiet.

"Do you promise?" Lucy leaned forward a bit.

"Yes," they answered one-by-one.

"Good." Lucy put her hand on her chest and relaxed.

"There you are." Dr. Castello walked into the mess tent. He took one look at all the children and moved another plate of rolls in front of them. "*Mangia*." He moved the olive oil too.

"This is a former colleague of mine. He's the best assistant I've ever had." He put a hand on Pietro's head. "You're still going to be a doctor when you grow up aren't you?" Dr. Castello smiled down at the boy.

"*Si.*" Pietro patted Dr. Castello's leg and stuffed a piece of bread in his mouth.

"I didn't know you two were friends." Lucy's heart melted at the feasting children.

"Oh, yes. We're old friends. Are you ready?"

"I'm sorry. I was just finished." She stood and ran a hand across Pietro's head too.

"We have a patient who refuses to let me help him." Dr. Castello took a half turn back toward the door, but he waited for her. "You remember Carlo, don't you?"

"Yes. Is he hurt? I saw him not an hour ago. What happened?"

"You'll see." Dr. Castello held back a laugh.

"And he won't let you touch him?" Lucy took a large step to catch up. "You know, it's really not funny that he's hurt."

"No, I suppose you're right." He looked like a cat who had swallowed a mouse. "He won't let me touch him because he likes you."

CHAPTER EIGHT

Lucy's legs stopped working. "*No.*"

Dr. Castello held the flap aside. "After you, Dr. James."

"Oh my goodness." Lucy put her hand to her head and forced her legs to move.

"*Signorina* Doctor!" A bald man with no teeth sat on the table. He held his tattered hat in his hand. What was left of his hair decorated his scalp in a gray mess only from the ears down.

"Carlo, *come va?*" Lucy did not see anything wrong.

The smelly old man only smiled wider and held up a faded yellow flower.

"*Grazie.*" Lucy took the flower and set it aside. She glared at Giovanni.

"I'll just leave you two alone." Giovanni bowed and left.

"Dr. Castello? No. Don't leave. I need your help. Oh, dear." Lucy turned her attention to Carlo.

"Is there something you need?" Then she noticed his ratted-out shoe on the floor. Lucy looked at his bare foot and he held it up for her.

"Oh, my goodness." Lucy put her hand to her mouth. The biggest splinter she had ever seen in her life jutted out of his heel. "Carlo, why didn't you say so?"

He shrugged.

Lucy washed her hands and then washed his foot. When she finished it was two shades lighter than the rest of his body. She wedged his ankle under her arm and grabbed a pair of pliers. "This is going to hurt. I'm sorry, I can't help it."

Lucy closed her eyes, counted three and pulled. When she looked again, the splinter had come out neat-as-you-please and Dr. Castello stood in the doorway with his arms crossed. Lucy couldn't tell if he was pleased or touched.

She cleaned the wound and turned back to her patient. "Carlo, are you all right?"

"*Si, grazie. Grazie, Signorina* Doctor." Carlo cocked his head to the side and pointed his dirty finger at Lucy. "*Grazie, Santa Lucia!*"

"*Santa Lucia.*" Dr. Castello hadn't moved an inch. "You removed the thorn from the lion's paw and now you have a new name."

Lucy wrapped the old man's foot. "I really hope you're wrong."

"*Grazie, Santa Lucia!*" The peasant woman patted Lucy's hand. The tattered blanket Lucy covered the woman with offered little protection from the damp air but the recipient oozed thankfulness.

"*Prego*. Please don't call me that." Lucy smiled back at the peasant. "You don't understand English do you?" Lucy repeated the phrase in Italian.

The woman blinked and continued to smile.

"The fact that they've named you says that they've accepted you." Dr. Castello stood next to a cot on the other side of the tent. "You might as well get used to it. It wouldn't do for you to hurt anyone's …."

The ground shook followed by a thunderous crash.

"Oh, no." Lucy remembered to breathe and she reached to calm the now frightened peasant.

"We'd better wash up." Dr. Castello's tight face said he expected the worst.

"*Casa Angilino* has fallen!" Carlo ran in his voice cracked with emotion and tears streamed down his face. In his arms, a small boy lay limp. "C*hildren!* Children are inside!"

"Not David!" Lucy ran to the child and felt for a pulse. "*No.*" She moved her hands to his neck and started to cry.

"It's broken, isn't it?" Dr. Castello's voice sounded strained.

"Yes."Lucy stroked the little boy's soft brown curls.

Her partner took David from Carlo and laid him gently on a cot.

"There are more." Carlo wiped his eyes and made a step to leave the tent.

"Stay here." Dr. Castello straightened up and ran behind the ragged man.

Stay here? How can he say that? Lucy spied a black leather bag. G.C. tooled into the leather. *He forgot his bag, now I have a reason*. Lucy ran after them. *I'm helping*.

The remains of *Casa Angilino* could be seen right away through a thick haze of dust that hung in the air even in the fine drizzle of rain. The house had not been but half a block from the hospital station. A crowd of people dug desperately at the fallen pile of mortar amid the pleading prayers of parents.

Lucy almost turned back. She had seen a lot since arriving, but never anything so horrible. Dr. Castello, face tight, eyes dark, bent over several children stretched out on the pavement.

Then she spotted Father Dominic in the crowd of people. Even in the midst of tragedy, Lucy gained courage from him. Covered in dirt and sweat, sleeves rolled to his elbows, the priest moved large rocks with the strength of two men.

"Giovanni, we've found some. I can hear them crying!" He shouted across the chaos.

Dr. Castello climbed over the fallen stone and Father Dominic pointed.

Lucy finally made it to where they stood. "Who's in there?"

"We're not sure. I thought I told you to stay behind." Dr. Castello turned slowly.

"You forgot your bag."

Dr. Castello's face softened and took it from her. "Thank you. Please go set up the surgery. We'll be there soon."

"But."

"Stop arguing." Father Dominic dropped to his hands and knees. He peered into the rubble. "If we move this stone, what's over the children might collapse."

Dr. Castello knelt beside the priest. "We'll just have to go in after them. I think I can fit."

"I *know* I can fit." Lucy stooped down too. She could see a few feet into the pile of rubble. It seemed easy enough.

"I was talking to Padre."

"I'm too big."

"You really think I should take her?"

"That's why she's here."

Dr. Castello squared his jaw and nodded. "Let's go."

"Just a minute." Father Dominic reached in his pocket, pulled out a large handkerchief and tied it around Lucy's nose and mouth.

Dr. Castello pulled out his own handkerchief while the priest said a quick prayer.

Dr. Castello moved aside and Lucy crawled head first through the hole in the mortar. *Lord, please protect us.*

She inched her way through the dirt and rock guided now and then by a faint shaft of light from above. How stale the air had become in such a short time. Even with her protective covering, Lucy found it hard to breathe.

"Can you see where you're going?" Dr. Castello slid on his stomach behind her.

"Yes. We're almost there. *Bambini?*" Lucy called. Dust fell from above.

"No more yelling," Dr. Castello whispered. "All of this could fall."

The rocks made a steep drop so Lucy slid down hands first and found room to sit up, on what had once been beautiful brown tile. A wall to her left still had shreds of whimsical bunny wallpaper. Then Lucy saw a demolished cradle. She turned her eyes quickly and moved over to allow Dr. Castello room.

"This must be a supporting wall." Dr. Castello pulled himself through the rocks. He scooted close to where Lucy sat. "They're nearby, I can hear them."

The whimper of a child reached Lucy's ears. "I hear them too."

"If we follow the wall there's bound to be an archway. Right around... Dr. James, they're here."

Lucy crawled after Dr. Castello who already had Dora sobbing in his arms.

"They're fine." Dr. Castello's eye's filled with tears. He took the cloth from his mouth and held it to Dora's "Just some scrapes and bruises. Breathe through this, *cara mia*."

"Oh Marcello, I'm so glad." Lucy wiped the dirt from the little boy's head and wrapped his nose and mouth as well.

"We're sorry." Marcello ducked his head into Lucy and she held him tight.

"I'm sorry too. I want my *Nonna*." Dora stuck her thumb in her mouth.

"You're forgiven and your *Nonna* is waiting for you." Dr. Castello kissed Dora's matted hair. She snuggled into his neck and closed her eyes.

"Is there anyone else down here?" Dr. Castello spoke with his cheek resting on Dora's head.

"Eleanor…and Pietro they're both hurt." Marcello sat up and tugged at Lucy's hand.

"Where are they?" She held her breath.

"Under the rocks." Marcello pointed to what had once been a bedroom; now a pile of stone where most of the house landed when it fell.

Dr. Castello set Dora down, moved quickly to his knees and peered into the rock. "Pietro, my friend, can you hear me?"

"My arm is stuck. I think we'll have to cut it off." Pietro's whimper sounded like music.

"He's alive." Lucy's heart gave a leap. She took Dora in her lap next to Marcello.

"Don't worry about your arm. I'll make it better. Is Eleanor with you?" Dr. Castello looked from another angle.

"Yes, but she's not moving."

Dr. Castello moved a piece of stone. A shower of small rocks and plaster rolled down from above. He ducked, covered his head.

Lucy pushed the screaming children underneath her body. *Lord, please protect us*. She held them firmly and closed her eyes.

Dr. Castello coughed and gasped for air.

"Are you okay?" Lucy called.

He coughed again. "Yes, we've got to get these children out of here."

"You're right." Lucy moved to let them sit up again. She pulled up her skirt, tore two pieces from her petticoat and tied the smaller one around her nose and mouth. The larger piece, Lucy handed to Dr. Castello. "There should be enough for you and the other two."

Dr. Castello touched Lucy's hand, his hair white with plaster. "You've been very brave to come down here. Do you think you can get these children to the surface by yourself?"

"Yes, but that will leave you alone." She felt a cold chill. "If this falls there will be no one here to help you."

Dr. Castello's eyes turned dark. "If this falls there will be little anyone can do to help me. At least I will know that these children are safe."

"But..."

"Please do as I ask."

Lucy's eyes filled with tears. She gave a nod and took Dora. "Marcello, you go first. It's like climbing a ladder. See, up through there. It's not far at all." Lucy showed the path through the debris to Marcello, surprised at how short a distance it really was. She swung Dora onto her back. "Just hold onto my neck."

Lucy slid on her knees through the arch. She turned back one more time to her partner. He looked so alone.

Dr. Castello gave a nod and a slight smile and Lucy began to climb before her tears made it too hard to see.

"Dr. James?" Dr. Castello's voice made her turn around. He crouched at the place that she had just climbed from.

"Yes?" Lucy re-adjusted Dora on her back.

"If I don't make it would you tell my mother I love her?"

"Of course," she whispered and turned so he would not see her cry.

"Dr. James?"

"Yes?" She looked again.

"You're an excellent doctor. Don't let anyone tell you any different." Dr. Castello turned slowly and disappeared from view.

"Quickly, now." Lucy pulled herself up another three feet and then pushed Marcello on ahead of her.

"Dr. James?" Father Dominic's round face appeared at the top of the hole.

"We're here." Lucy never felt so glad to see anyone.

The priest dropped on his stomach and reached in to pull Marcello up.

Marcello gave his hands to the padre and kicked his feet. A good sized rock rolled down and hit Lucy square on the face before she could duck.

"Oh man, that hurt." Lucy rubbed her cheek on her shoulder.

"Did that rock hit you?" Father Dominic was closer than she realized.

"Yes, right on the face."

He pulled Dora from Lucy's back. A moment later he re-appeared, hooked his hands under her arms and lifted Lucy into the fresh air. She pulled her mask from her face and looked around for Marcello and Dora. She found them safe with Sister Francesca.

"Dr. Castello is down there with Pietro and Eleanor. The children are trapped under a pile of rocks." Lucy grabbed the priest's arm.

"How far down are they?" Father Dominic touched his thumb to Lucy's bruised face.

"Not far. Only about eight feet. But the stone is so unstable, it could fall at any moment." She turned quickly from the priest. "I'm fine, really. We've got to get them out."

"Padre?" Giovanni's voice drifted to them from under the rubble.

Both Lucy and Father Dominic dropped to their knees to listen.

"Giovanni?" Father Dominic called.

"I have them. I need help."

"Say no more." Lucy moved to her tummy and slid back into the hole. It really wasn't as far as it seemed the first time. In a matter of seconds, she landed at the bottom along with a hundred tiny pebbles.

Dr. Castello sat on his knees with Eleanor in his arms; a large knot on her head, her eyes closed, her head rested against the doctor's chest. "She's breathing."

Pietro, his face pale, sat on the ground and leaned against Dr. Castello too. He wore a sling on his left arm made from the doctor's coat.

"It's a clean break. We'll be able to set it." Dr. Castello looked over Eleanor to Pietro. "He's going to need some stitches, but it's nothing life threatening. "

"We'll move fast. Eleanor needs a sling too. We can use my petticoat. Don't look." Lucy narrowed her eyes at Dr. Castello.

He turned his head and then put his free hand over Pietro's eyes.

"Hey, I can't see! What's going on?" Pietro tried to move away.

Dr. Castello leaned over him. "Stay still. A gentleman doesn't watch, especially when a lady is trying to help."

Lucy untied her petticoat and pulled it off from the bottom; a trick she had learned when camping with her brothers.

"I'm good." Lucy crawled to Dr. Castello.

"That was fast." His eyes went round.

"Let's tie her like a papoose. Then you can climb freely." She ripped the garment, bottom to top and spread it on the ground.

"A what?"

"An Indian baby. Put her here." Lucy patted.

Dr. Castello gently placed the little girl onto the petticoat. "A baby from India? Oh, you mean an American Indian." He nodded.

Lucy worked quickly. She wound the fabric around Eleanor's feet and then her body, leaving two straps to tie around Dr. Castello's shoulders.

"I never would have thought of this." The child firmly in place, Dr. Castello moved to his knees. His bruised and bleeding hands really needed attention.

"Your knuckles hardly have any skin left." Would he be able to use them in surgery? "We have to get them clean." Lucy made a reach for Pietro.

"Yes, I know. Let's get out first."

"Come on." She nodded at him. "It's not that far."

Giovanni struggled to untie his apron with swollen fingers, then finally just pulled it off over his head and dropped it in the basket. When had he ever been so tired? On the floor lay a small shoe. What and awful, horrible day. He bent, picked it up and tossed it in the basket as well. *Pietro is all right, Marcello will be fine and so will Dora. If we're lucky, Eleanor will make it too.*

A hot tear fell on his hand and he clinched his fist. *How is it possible that You are real?*

In his mind he saw beautiful little David held to his mother's breast as she wept. Giovanni shook his head to shake away the memory, but the images in his mind would not stop. Those grimy little faces eating all that bread just days ago filled his vision, then each of them carried in one by one.

And Lucy. How determined the young woman was. She went from child to child as unwilling as he to lose even one of them. Could he finally admit he was glad to have her with him? Yes, he could.

"I promised to fix them." Lucy had wept openly. Sister Francesca held his partner and cried too. To see them grieve hurt him even more, so he sent them on ahead and cleaned the room alone.

Everything done here. It would only be right to try to find her. Or… was it that he really just wanted to see her again? Her face lit his mind. At least *she* was still all right.

Once in the mess tent, he finally found her tucked in a corner, curled up in a chair. She held her Bible in her lap. A Bible? Even after today? She wiped her face when she saw him approach, as though her tears might be an embarrassment.

Uncertainty coursed through him. Had he intruded? Maybe. Would she even want his company? The questions that pressed at his heart compelled him.

"Will you go for a walk? I need to talk."

Lucy stood slowly and followed him outside the tent. For once, the rain had stopped and thousands of stars dotted the sky like diamonds. The wet pavement beneath their feet shimmered, tainted by the faint smell of smoke that misted around them.

Giovanni checked behind. No one followed. Good. The young woman waited, her face cast in the dim light of a lone lamp by the door.

"I need to know how you can still believe in God after all of this?" This question he voiced had lived unanswered inside him for years. Not that Padre hadn't answered it many times, but still understanding avoided Giovanni's heart. His voice cracked. "After a day like today. We lost five children today, five beautiful children. Can't you see that you're deceiving yourself? Can't you see that this God you keep talking to is just a fantasy?"

Giovanni breathed deeply. The urge to yell at the woman in front of him overwhelmed him. Why should he yell at her? She had given just as much as he had today. Shouldn't he be yelling at God? He spoke through his clenched jaw. "If God were real, if he was as good as you and *Padre* say, then how can he just let people–innocent children—suffer? How can he let them die?"

Lucy closed her eyes for a moment. Did she pray? Most likely. Why did her hands shake? Did she find his presence so intimidating? Or maybe… his disgraceful behavior in effort to scare her home, worked better than he imagined. And yet she remained. Remorse crept to the corners of his heart.

"You're not seeing the big picture." Lucy studied his face and her voice trembled. "Death is not the end of life. It's more like—-a door to the next life. It's harder on those of us who are left behind in this mess, than it is on those who go on to be with the Lord."

"So death is a door." He'd hear that before. "That doesn't answer my question about suffering. Today was as hard on you as it was on anyone else. You've cried through most of it. Admit it; you don't have all the answers."

"You're right." Lucy's eyes filled with tears again. "I don't have all the answers. I wish I knew why things happen the way that they do. What I do have is faith in God. I know without a doubt that He's real and that He loves us. That He loves *you*. I know that *all things work together for good for those who love him*. I've seen Him take the worst of circumstances and bring something good out of it. Something good will come of this, if nothing more than an opportunity for us to behave as He did and lay our lives down for these people. I'll be praying for an answer, Dr. Castello, when I get one I'll let you know." A tear rolled down her cheek and seemed to pierce his heart.

"More tears." If only he could say something to make them stop. Giovanni softened his tone. "We've all cried enough today. I didn't mean to make you cry more."

"I guess I'm not as tough as I thought I was." Lucy looked down at her hands. She held a piece of lace.

"And I behave like *asino*."

Lucy's brow creased."You mean a donkey?"

"Yes."

The corners of her mouth twitched. Good.

"Your tears are not a weakness; they show compassion." Giovanni inhaled deeply, looked around at the ruins of the city and then at Dr. James. She really was a bright spot in this miserable place. Before he could stop himself, he brushed the tear from her bruised cheek with his thumb.

"Look at your face. Did this happen when all that debris fell on us?"

"No. Marcello got me with a rock as we climbed to safety." Like a ray of sunshine on a cold winter day, Lucy smiled through her tears. Then her bottom lip quivered and she started to sob.

Giovanni's heart broke. He could no longer fight his instinct so he pulled her to his chest.

Lucy locked her arms around his waist, leaned into him and cried. "I'm so glad you didn't die in that hole."

Such a child-like hug. Giovanni blinked back his own tears. "I'm here, bambina. I'm glad you're all right too."

He bent to kiss the top of her head, but then stopped himself. He held her for a moment feeling a little awkward. He stroked her head and patted her back. *How does she always manage to smell of rose water*?

He spoke softly in her ear."Better?"

Lucy pulled back and nodded, her face streaked, but smiling. "Can we be friends now?" She sniffed.

"Yes." Giovanni handed her his hanky, glad that for once it was clean. "Let's be friends now."

Lucy wrapped her arms around him again, tucked her head into his chest and sighed.

Giovanni hugged her back and allowed himself to kiss the top of her head and the heaviness in his heart seemed to ease.

"*Buongiorno*, Dr. James." Dr. Castello always beat Lucy to the door of the surgery. Freshly shaven, he stood just on the outside and held the flap for her. The bruises on his fingers had turned a deep blue. "Are you doing better?"

"Yes, thank you. I think we're all doing a little better." *He seems subdued today, but I suppose we'll all feel the effects of yesterday for a long time.*

"How are your hands?" Lucy grabbed his left wrist and gently touched his knuckles. "They're so swollen. This will be arthritis when you're old you know."

"So I've heard." He pulled his hand from her and took a closer look at the bruise on her face. His eyes, a soft gray today, seemed to invite friendship. "I don't always believe everything I read."

He gave her cheek a stroke with his thumb and then walked to Lucy's spot. "Since you're so concerned for me. Why don't you take the lead today and I'll give my hands a break."

"If you rest I'll be surprised." Lucy slid into his place thrilled at the relaxed atmosphere. "Let's see how long you can restrain yourself."

Lucy glanced at the watch on her shoulder; three o'clock and Dr. Castello hadn't interfered yet. Who would have thought? If today hadn't been on the heels of such an awful one it would have been fun. Dr. Castello assisted her most attentively. He chatted, pleasant and helpful.

"Suture." Lucy checked inside the gash she'd cleaned. Her patient, a short Sicilian man, peeked over her shoulder at his leg.

"Do you mind if I show you something?" Dr. Castello watched Lucy, ready with a needle and cat-gut. He looked up at the peasant. "Do you mind if I teach her?"

"No, go ahead." The motion of the man's hand seemed to say.

Lucy wrinkled her nose. "I knew you couldn't just assist all day. Please." Dr. Castello was so fast with a needle; maybe he would show her how he did it.

He raised an eyebrow and his mouth stretched into a bit of a smile. "I'm not taking over. Step left a little." He moved next to Lucy and fingered the needle. "Your stitches are good and strong. But if you want to go faster, try starting from the bottom, then clip it like this. See?" He drew the needle through a few times. The leg moved and he took the peasant's hand. "Hold on to me and don't look. Watching only makes it worse."

The Sicilian turned his head.

Lucy took the needle in hand. The new motion felt awkward at first but then as she worked it became more natural. "This *is* quicker. I get it." Lucy smiled through her mask.

"*Si*, that's it. *Brava*." He bumped her elbow with his and then smiled at the patient. "You did a good job." He wrapped the patched up leg, helped the man off the table and out the door.

"Thank you. That was fun. " Lucy walked to the basin to wash her hands.

"You're a quick learner." Dr. Castello poured water over Lucy's hands and then did the same for himself. He dried his hands on a towel.

"Dr. Castello?" Father Dominic stuck his head in the surgery door. "We've been given a task."

CHAPTER NINE

"If the authorities needed people to distribute these things, they should have sent soldiers." Giovanni stomped around the wagonload of blankets, clothing, food and other essentials.

Lucy bit her lip. Best to let the man rant and not say a thing.

Father Dominic looked up at her with a quick wink and then narrowed his eyes at her partner.

"I understand the need to monitor the people for disease. I understand that there might be people who are not able to make it to the hospital station to pick up supplies. But to simply drive into this city with a wagonload of goods…" Dr. Castello shook his head. "…no escort, no gun. It's as if they've forgotten that Messina is not a normal town anymore." He came around to the left side of the wagon and scowled up at Lucy. "*I* will drive. Move. Move."

Lucy scooted over to the right and Giovanni hauled himself into the driver's seat. With a flip of the reins, they rolled off into the city and the fine rain misted about them.

The condition of the city sure hadn't improved much. With any hope of finding survivors gone, people raced against time, burning and burying bodies as quickly as possible. Still, the threat of epidemic loomed. It seemed every kind of cart imaginable could be used to move the corpses. Now and then, a gaily-painted Sicilian cart rolled by loaded to the top with coffins or bodies; the large wheels and multicolored sides splattered with mud. What had Messina been like in happier days?

The mule plodded along in a slow steady rhythm, his head bowed to the misery of the cold rain. Lucy said not a word. How could she with a partner so stoic? They rounded a pile of mortar. Only an arched doorway stood. The stone cross above said the building must have been a small church. St. Francis held his marble hands out to a withered garden.

"That was *Padre* Dominic's chapel. It's a wonder that he escaped unharmed." So Dr. Castello would speak after all.

"You're from Messina?" Maybe a little conversation would lighten things up. Lucy held her hood in place to keep the rain from stinging her cheeks.

"No. I live here in Messina. The Castello family, my family, lives just outside of Palermo. We used to come here in the summer when I was a child. Two years ago I returned and started a medical practice in that building there." He pointed to the pile of rocks just a few doors down from the church. "Sister Francesca works with me as my nurse. I've known the *Padre* since I was seven."

The fog of silence settled in again.

"I'm so sorry this happened." What else could she say? Lucy peeked out from her cloak.

"I am, too." His eyes kept straight ahead.

Jonah gave a snort and shook mud from his ears.

"This mission bothers you." Lucy touched his arm. "Are we really in that much danger?"

Dr. Castello frowned. "You've seen the conditions of our patients. You've heard the reports of rape and kidnapping; someone goes missing every day. The best people who lived in this city are either dead or living somewhere else by now, the refugees living in these streets live like animals and we have no idea where the majority of the prison convicts went. Personally, I don't think they've gone very far."

"I wondered about the logic behind this." Lucy looked hard at a peasant hauling a load of scavenged clothing. "If you don't mind I am going pray."

Giovanni shook his head. Finally, a smile hinted.

"What?" Lucy raised her eyebrows.

"You never stop praying." He shrugged and shook his head again. Then he started to laugh. "Go ahead, pray. This would be a good time to do so. Put in a good word for me too while you're at it."

"I've been praying for *you* for quite some time now."

"You and everyone else I know," he mumbled.

"Excuse me?"

"I believe you, Dr. James." He gave a look of mock fear, and then chuckled softly.

Beyond the demolished church and medical office, stood a row of small huts constructed out of junk wood and debris. Someone had used a door for a roof. Naked children huddled in dark doorways and stared at the doctors with hollow eyes.

They drove the wagon closer and stopped.

"It's too quiet." Giovanni sat up straight and looked about them. "This feels wrong."

The hairs on Lucy's arm stood on end and she moved closer to Giovanni. "Where are all the..."

"*Pane! Acqua!*" Someone yelled from inside a hut.

Then people came running; a swarm of them. How many? Who could count? Shouting and flailing their arms they rushed the poor mule and then the wagon. A scream forced its way out and instinctively, Lucy scrambled to the top of the bench seat. The wagon lurched and rocked. Would it be pushed over?

Peasants pulled things off the wagon, fighting over the items they stole. Someone tore at Lucy's cloak; another snatched at her feet and yanked at her boots. Lucy grabbed the side of the wagon to keep from being pulled into the crowd.

"*No*!" Giovanni shouted. His strong arms wrapped around her waist. He wrenched her free of the person who held her cloak, kicked the man at her feet and pulled her to the middle of the cart. He cracked his whip at the mob to back them off and moved between Lucy and the crowd.

"The mule! "Lucy screamed. "They can't take him!" She tried to stand, tried to reach for the mule. Someone grabbed at her arm, but Giovanni held her back and protected her with his body.

"Stay with me!" He yelled above the din.

A series of gunshots rang out. Giovanni pulled Lucy close and ducked. The mob scattered like scared rats. Two men lay dead.

"Filthy Eye-talians."

"Watch what you're sayin.' Someone might understand you."

"Nuts! They don't understand a thing. They're like animals. Did you see them?"

Giovanni heard the faint conversation distinctly. He relaxed his protective hold on his partner and they stood. Had she heard it too? "Are you all right?" He looked down at her head against his chest. Lucy moved slowly and he pushed the hood of her cloak back to see her; face pale, lips trembling. If she *had* heard he would have known right away.

"I've never seen anything like that. Yes, I'm all right. Are you okay?" Her hazel eyes, round like she might not want to admit to fear, searched his face.

"I'm fine."He patted her back. "We're okay. It's over."

Lucy looked at his arms clasped around her and her cheeks turned a lovely shade of pink.

"Sorry, I was trying to protect you." He pushed Lucy away gently, his heart strangely light. How ridiculous. After what just happened he should be outraged not glowing. Maybe he was just relieved that they were both unharmed. Giovanni sat her on the seat.

"Hey! Are you people hurt?" The sound of running feet made them both turn.

A group of soldiers came down the street followed by some officers in a wagon.

"Thank you for coming to our aid." Giovanni jumped from the wagon. He shook the Captain's hand. "I'm Dr. Giovanni Castello. Whoever thought we should come into the heart of this city without an escort must have been out of his mind."

"Captain Curtis Bauer. I'm glad we were in the area. You could have been killed."

The captain kept talking, but who could listen? A young officer a few feet away kept looking at Lucy. That was not the problem; Giovanni liked to look at Lucy. No, it was the *way* he looked at her; from head to toe with his head tilted to the side a little. The man had enough intelligence to try to be subtle but, Giovanni had been around the block enough times to know exactly what went though his mind.

"Are you all right, ma'am? That mob almost had you. You need to be more careful." A young officer tipped his cap.

"Yes. I'm fine." Lucy noticed her shaking hands and shoved them under her cloak. Thank you for saving us. You're Americans. Where are you from?"

"Petty Officer Wendell Jackson at your service, ma'am. We're here aboard the USS Celtic."

Giovanni frowned at them from over his shoulder. Something displeased him, but what?

"I'm from New York." Officer Jackson returned Giovanni's icy stare. "Who's that?'

"Dr. Castello. He's in charge of the temporary hospital on *Via San Francesco*."

"He sure seems unfriendly."

"Aren't you going to introduce us Wendell?" Two more handsome Americans stepped forward, caps in their hands and smiles on their faces. Officer Jackson patted the back of the first. "This is Hershel Collins from Maine and Arthur Bean from Milwaukee."

"Hello." Lucy returned the smile and the nod.

"Ma'am," they said together.

"May I ask where you're from?" Officer Jackson had blue eyes, sandy blond hair.

"I'm Lucille James, from Boston. What part of New York are you from?"

"Manhattan." Officer Jackson gave a wink. "Do you know it?"

"I love New York; such wonderful museums and what an amazing library. And the park; whoever would have thought to put a park that large in the middle of a city? It's ingenious."

"Where're you working?" His blue eyes twinkled.

"At the temporary hospital four blocks from here." Lucy pointed in the general direction.

"The one on *Via San Francesco?*"

"Yes."

"If I can escape for a while, maybe we could have tea sometime. You can tell me about Boston." Mr. Jackson glanced once more at Dr. Castello. "Are you sure you're safe with him? I mean he seemed to be holding you awfully tight."

"You didn't see him protect me from that mob?" Lucy shivered. "I'm glad he was there. In any event, I'd love to chat with you. You'll have to stop by the hospital station if you get the chance." Lucy shook his hand.

'We must be going." Dr. Castello climbed into the wagon and once again turned steel eyes on Lucy's new friend.

Petty Officer Jackson returned the glance, and quickly re-adjusted his jacket. He tipped his cap. "Doctor, Ma'am. It was nice to meet you." He turned to re-join his regiment.

"This was foolish." Giovanni gripped the reins and moved them across the mule with a slap. The cart lurched forward. "The next time a team comes into the city I will insist that soldiers go along." He glanced sideways at Lucy.

Who cared if he ranted, she had a new friend. A smile surfaced.

"And you. You're too nice. You don't even know that man and you're willing to have tea with him."

What?"That is none of your business." Lucy tightened her mouth and glared at him. "Officer Jackson was nothing more than a gentleman, unlike some people." She scooted to the far side of the seat; a cloud of angry silence settled in like fog.

"*Aiuto*! *Aiuto!*" A frantic woman screamed.

The wagon stopped.

"Where's…" Lucy looked in the direction that her partner did.

Dr. Castello held up a hand for silence, his face stern. "I think we need to go this way." He turned the mule cart through a series of fallen buildings.

"*Mamma!*" This scream could have only come from a child.

"They're taking my daughter!"

Lucy spied the source of the struggle. By an abandoned storefront, under its dangling wooden sign, a peasant woman gripped the legs of a young girl. The red-faced girl, screamed while two men pulled the child.

“Not while I’m around!” Lucy grabbed the side rail.

“Stay in your seat.” Dr. Castello pulled her back and jumped from the cart.

“Nothin’ doin’!” Lucy slid to the ground and raced after her partner.

CHAPTER TEN

"Aiuto!" The woman yelled all the louder only to be drowned out by the wails of her child.

Giovanni got there first. He caught the man closest in the chin with the heel of his left fist. The rogue's hat flew from his head and he fell to the street with a string of Italian words Lucy had yet to learn.

She saw her opportunity. With that first guy out of the way she wedged herself between the second kidnapper and the girl. This guy however, was big; really big.

"Let her go!" Lucy growled at his face with all the fierceness she could muster. Had he ever brushed his teeth? She had the child by the waist now and Dr. Castello had hit him twice but the burly man wasn't giving up so easily.

Lucy felt a vice like grip on her arm and then a yank. She landed on her bottom in the mud: oh, yea, the first guy. The smaller man grabbed the girl over his shoulder and started to run with the mother screaming after.

Lucy looked for her partner. His hands were full; the big guy had produced a sword from somewhere. The dangling sign caught her eye; the word *Armi* painted on it. The picture of a sword beneath the word explained it all. *Oh...no.*

The ogre swung with the force of ten at the young physician. With each move Giovanni stepped lightly out of the way.

Should she help Dr. Castello or go after the girl?

The man swung again. Giovanni ducked under, grabbed the ogre's wrist and flipped him onto the ground. That settled it.

The rain came down full force.

"Just perfect!" Lucy looked up at the sky and then glared at the man. She stood to her feet, with her arms out to the side for balance in the slick muck.

"I said, let her go." Lucy ran after the man, grabbed him by the hair and yanked. He spun backward, the girl dropped to the ground. Her mother jumped after her. The man turned to crawl after the girl. Lucy pushed herself between him and his victim and gave him a shove.

"Hey!" he yelled and pushed Lucy back.

Lucy landed on the ground. In that moment, she saw two things: Giovanni now sword to sword with the big man. The other thing she saw brought chills; the other rogue reared back with a large piece of mortar in his hand. The peasant woman screamed and covered her child.

Lucy moved her matted hair out of her eyes and launched herself at the nasty piece of work. She hit him in the stomach like a linebacker. They landed hard and mud splattered. Now to take advantage of his surprise. Lucy pinned him face down in the mud with her knee in his back, and his elbow firmly locked behind him. *Oh. Look.* He had a piece of rope hanging out of his pocket. The guy tried move, but Lucy tightened her half nelson.

"You should have let her go!" Lucy pushed harder and he screamed. She yanked the rope from the man's pocket. Perfect; long and thin. A slip knot went around his feet and then another around his hands.

"There!" She spoke through her teeth at the man face down in the mud. "Just like Uncle Roy taught me with the pigs back on the ranch."

Breathing hard, all Lucy could hear was the rain, beating on everything around her.

Just like that; it stopped.

She swung her wet hair out of her eyes and saw six American soldiers gaping at her; the same guys she'd met earlier. Dr. Castello's opponent lay on his back out cold.

Her partner stood over his victim, but he watched Lucy. Wet hair in his eyes, mud caked all over, he grinned at her. "You took that man down like a pro."

She grinned back and then remembered the Americans. "Were you going to help?"

"We came running when we heard the screams, but you had it under control." Officer Jackson eyed her. "What a tackle!"

The other men laughed.

"Would you mind taking these two to prison?" Giovanni gave his sword to the Captain.

"*Grazie! Grazie!*" The peasant woman ran to Giovanni. She grabbed his muddy face in her hands and planted a smooch on the mouth.

"*Prego.*" He hugged the mother first and then gently patted the girl on her cheek. "You two go climb into the wagon. You're coming to the hospital with us tonight."

Two short curtsies gave answer and the mother and daughter made their way to the where Jonah stood patiently.

Dr. Castello offered a hand. "I thought I told you to stay in the cart."

"Like you could have taken both men at once. Admit it, you're glad I didn't listen." Lucy let him pull her to her feet.

He only shook his head. "Let's get out of these wet clothes."

I hate this rainy weather. Lucy squished her toes inside saturated socks. It had rained so much harder lately that water managed to seep though the sand bags. She balanced the small scissors in her hands and pulled one foot up to let her boot drain.

She handed the scissors to Dr. Castello and, with a sigh, put her foot back into the water. She watched her partner, always attentive to his patients, but often aloof when it rained. *I hate it when he's quiet like this.*

Lucy glanced at the weak light glowing under the tent wall and then at their muddy patient. The relentless rain had continued for three days. It soaked soldiers, laborers and *profughi* without mercy. The blanket of wet filled the streets with slick mud, knee deep in some areas, cruelly bogging down beasts of burden employed in the task of moving wagonloads of bodies. Individuals, like this one, who dug for victims, often became victims themselves. They climbed over and dug through slippery mortar, risking their own lives in an effort to find those who had died almost two months before. *This poor man was only trying to help.*

Dr. Castello lifted the patient's leg. Lucy grabbed a bandage roll. Damp.

"We'd better soak this in carbolic acid until we can dry some bandages." She tossed the roll into the basket and reached across the counter for the spray can of their most valuable disinfectant. Lucy felt Dr. Castello's mood grow darker. "Don't you yell at *me* because you don't like the weather."

"I was not going to yell at you," he snapped. "You're standing in water again. Why don't you use the stool?"

Lucy rolled her eyes at him.

"All right, then let's trade places."

"Then we'll both have wet feet. What's the point?"

"*Mamma mia!* Do you have to be so stubborn?" He scowled at her.

She scowled right back "*Mamma mia!* Do you have to be so bossy?"

Dr. Castello held back a laugh.

Lucy threw her hands up. "What?"

Dr. Castello patted the man on the table. "I have to be careful not to say the wrong thing. She's been known to knock a man to the ground on occasion."

"Will you never let that go?" Lucy tried not to look at their patient, now staring at her, eyes like saucers.

"Sister Francesca?" Dr. Castello peered over his shoulder. "We're finished here. Would you please try to find a dry place for this man? How many more are waiting?"

"Three at the moment, but with all the rain, you know to expect more." Sister Francesca helped the man ease off the table and limp from the room.

Lucy went to the washbasin to scrub. "You've said almost nothing in three days. Is there a reason?"

"It's not you." Dr. Castello came to join her. He held her gaze with his own for a moment. Did pain touch his eyes? "Rainy days bring back some very bad memories."

Oh. "Is there anything I can do?"

"You can use your stool so I don't have to worry about your wet feet."

"You worry about me?"

"No." Dr. Castello rolled his eyes at her.

Maybe she could make him smile. "Did you have to tell that man what you did?"

"Yes." He winked at her.

The sun began its descent across the Sicilian sky, the clouds that it hid behind glowing a brilliant silver. The people of this island must have looked with awe at what they once thought to be Apollo and his chariot. The rain paused long enough for the glowing sphere to find a small window in the sky. A single ray of light poured through, shooting down over the harbor like a golden arrow from heaven to earth. The ray hit the water and illuminated the waves.

Lucy removed her surgical mask and pushed the gap in the tent wall aside a little more. She let the breeze touch her face and breathed in the smell of salt air, instead of the infirmary or the smoking city. *What a day.*

She scanned the horizon one last time, and turned to follow Dr. Castello through the curtained wall of the surgery. *Ahhh, off duty at last.* Now for a bath, but Sister Francesca's hot soapy wash tub and scrub brush did not appeal. Through her mind ran the picture of the very deep tub and very hot water at the Drake's house. And that bed! How heavenly. Well, she shouldn't wish for what she couldn't have.

Lucy untied her apron and slipped it over her head. What had she forgotten? Her brothers? *God please protect them.* She lifted her hand to smooth her hair and realized that she still held her apron. Maybe that was it. Lucy leaned halfway in the surgery and tossed her dirty apron in the basket on the floor. She spun around and ran her face into the chest of Dr. Castello.

CHAPTER ELEVEN

"*Scusi*." Lucy lost her balance and tried to right herself but she stepped on his foot.

Giovanni grasped her firmly by the arms and stood her up. "Actually, *Mi scusi*' is what you say when you're about to speak. If you would like to get by someone then you say *permesso*. You didn't see me standing behind you?" Their earlier exchange must have loosened him up.

"Um. No. Sorry. I've forgotten something and I can't remember what. Thank you, *permesso*?" Lucy stepped left to pass, but Giovanni caught her lightly with his hand.

He squared his shoulders and took the posture of authority that he often did when he instructed; but then his shoulders relaxed and his expression turned gentle.

"Dr. James, I've never thanked you for the work you do. I told you once before that you're an excellent physician. I want you to know, that I'm glad you're here." His lips pressed into a rueful smile. "You certainly are capable of leading your own team, but I'd like to ask that you remain my assisting surgeon until you leave."

"Thank you." Lucy's eyes widened. Then she caught the humor beneath his request. "Believe it or not, I like working with you, too."

She cocked her head to the side. "I might actually be better for the experience." That would make him smart right back. Lucy waited.

He only smiled at her...but something behind his eyes...

"Is that it?" She shifted her weight to her right foot.

He shrugged and nodded in the direction of the mess tent. "Will you have something to eat? Come, join me for some dinner."

Food! That was it! Lucy suddenly felt faint with hunger. He looked as tired as she felt. How could she refuse? "Lead the way."

Lucy followed him through the hospital; cots on either side of them. She'd keep a safe but cordial distance. He peeked at her from the corner of his eye. *I wonder if he's as uncomfortable as I am?*

"*Buonanotte, Santa Lucia. Buonanotte dottore Castello.*" The sleepy voice of Giovanni's favorite assistant drifted to them.

"*Buonanotte, Pietro*. Goodnight." Lucy tucked him into his cot, and arranged his broken arm so he could sleep better. "Your *momma* will be back to see you in the morning."

"*Buonanotte, Santa Lucia.*" Dora opened her eyes.

"*Buonanotte, dottore Castello.*" Marcello sat up.

"*Buonanotte, a tutti. Silenzio*. No more talking." Giovanni touched a gentle hand to the cheek of each child before he turned to wait for Lucy.

"Lay down now." Lucy fluffed Marcello's pillow. The boy snuggled into it.

"*Santa Lucia.*" Giovanni watched her with the softest expression. He gave her his hand and she stood.

Lucy's cheeks warmed. How silly to feel so bashful.

"Children love you." He now stood closer than usual.

She tried to hold his gaze. "They love you, too. You can call me *Lucia,* but please leave off the *Santa.*" She should look at the children instead. Or maybe food would be a better distraction.

"What kind of meat is this?" Lucy peered into her bowl. The soup looked hardy enough, filled with pasta, beans and vegetables; but the meat? It looked a little odd.

"Beef." The cook smiled a little too much. He glanced at Giovanni. Why?

Wait a minute. "I thought we ran out of beef last week." Lucy tried to hand the bowl back.

Giovanni moved her along gently. "*Lucia.*"

Lucy stopped, and turned back to him. "*Lucia?*" He took her request seriously?

Giovanni turned her around again. "If cook says it's beef, then beef it is." He leaned to her ear. "Sometimes, it's best not to ask."

"But…" It looked a little too gray.

"*Andiamo, Lucia*. Have a seat." He found a table and pulled a chair out for her.

Table? This was no table; it was someone's front door. It bore the Roman numeral XXXVI on its front and lacked a doorknob.

"This must be new. I've never seen it." At least it felt more like a table. She sat on the remnant of an embroidered chair. The intricate flowers must have taken someone a good deal of time. "This is new too."

"Yes. Padre found them yesterday." Giovanni sat on an old trunk.

She bowed her head and gave silent thanks for her meal. When she finished her prayer, Lucy found her partner watching her.

"I always want to know what you're thinking when you watch me like that." Lucy put her napkin in her lap.

"Most of the time, I'm thinking what a wonder you are. Right now, I'm thinking how much you would like my mother. She prays a lot too, you know."

Really? Now what should she say? Lucy took a nibble of bread.

"I'm telling you, it's beef." Cook's voice rose above the chatter in the room.

Giovanni cleared his throat. "Are you planning to return to Rome anytime soon? If I remember correctly, you were working at the university with your father."

"Actually, Dr. Castello, I was only volunteering at the university." Lucy fingered her spoon. "You were right, you know. The men at the university never did treat me as an equal. I'm amazed that you have."

"*Lucia*?" Giovanni wiped his mouth and leaned forward.

"Yes?"

"Would you please call me Giovanni?"

"S-sure." Wow. Ok.

He smiled and shrugged. "You're welcome here. Permanently, as far as I'm concerned. Good doctors are hard to find. Good surgeons, even harder. I've known those idiots in Rome for a long time. They're a proud bunch and very set in their ways."

He tilted his head to the side. "Not that I'm much better in the way I initially felt about you. But, as I've said, you're indeed an excellent physician. When are you planning to head back to America?" Giovanni took a tiny bite of soup. His eyebrows went up. Could it be that bad?

"We leave in November." Lucy ate more bread. "Since you've put it so nicely, I'll stay as long as I can. Although, I'm not sure how much longer this station will be standing. Aren't there plans for a new hospital?"

"Two." Giovanni nodded. "I spoke to a Captain Belknap recently. He told me that they've drafted two new hospitals and that portable houses are being sent from your country."

"Portable houses? How do you mean?"

"They're building components in America; all the pieces of a house. When the pieces arrive here, they'll simply be nailed together. The plans are for two villages with a hospital on either side of Messina. Even so, I don't think it will be enough to handle all of the *profugi* living in the city."

"So what about you?" Nice to have a decent conversation for a change. Lucy looked hard at the spoonful of gray meat in tomato broth. Her stomach growled. She took a bite. The meat was chewy. It went down her throat like a rock.

Giovanni smirked.

She'd ignore that. "Your building is destroyed. Are you going to stay?"

"Without question." Giovanni pushed his empty bowl away and took a sip of his coffee. "I've made a commitment to the people in this end of town. My villa isn't far from here; it sits just outside of the city limits. Thankfully, it isn't heavily damaged. I'll turn one of the rooms into an office and work from there until I can move back downtown. I'm hoping you'll join me at my practice, if we move soon enough."

Join him at his practice? Lucy tried not to inhale so she could finish her mystery meal. Excitement rose inside. But…"Where would I live? Certainly not with you."

"No, of course not." Giovanni spoke quickly. "You could live in the American village once it's finished, maybe with Sister Francesca."

That could work. Lucy's mind wandered over the last several weeks.

"Your best friend is a priest, your nurse is a nun, *and* your aunt. You're so good with your patients and you have such a passion for the poor. It's hard not to see you as a believer in God."

"I was raised in the church." Giovanni's face lifted in a half smile. "I find the principles of Christianity to be pure. You already know it's God Himself I question. I simply don't believe in Him the way you do."

Lucy leaned forward, encouraged by his openness, but still tentative. She slid her fingers into his. "I'm still seeking an answer to our conversation the other night. But, Giovanni, I know that if you talk to Him, He'll answer you."

"You didn't answer my question." Giovanni looked thoughtful and he did not let go of her hand.

"Did you ask me a question?"

"Not directly. Would you partner with me until you leave? I think we make a good team."

She'd need to pray.

"You want to pray about it first." Giovanni spoke before she could. He kept his voice kind. "Go ahead. Find out what Jesus wants you to do." He gave her hand a squeeze and then released her.

They stood to leave. How light Lucy felt. To have someone befriend *and* accept her made even the ragged mess tent seem a beautiful place. She gave in to her impulse and hugged Giovanni from the side as she would one of her own brothers. He stiffened so she pulled herself away.

"My aunt says I'm way too forward. I'm impulsive." Lucy put her hands on her warm cheeks and stepped back. "I did that to you the other night too. We hug a lot in my home and I'm so grateful that we've become friends. Please forgive me."

"You chatter when you're nervous. I wonder why." He scanned her face with his gaze. "If I recall, I hugged *you* the other night. It's all right, you just surprised me." He ran his hand lightly across the top of her head. "If you want to fit in around here, friends kiss on both cheeks. Like this." He tilted her chin up and softly kissed first one cheek and then the other.

From the corner of her eye, Lucy saw three natives smile at them and nod. She felt heat in her cheeks again.

Giovanni slipped his gentle arm around her shoulder. "In my family, however, we are very affectionate, even with friends." He pulled her into a real hug and held her a little longer than Lucy thought he would.

"You should get some sleep." Giovanni gave her braid a soft tug, and let her go.

Lucy nearly floated back to her cot. If she had music, she'd want to waltz.

Thank you, Lord! What a great day.

Lucy lifted her dress over her head. Giovanni's scent still clung to the fabric. *How does he smell so good after such a long day?*

She ran a brush through her hair and remembered the light in his eyes when he kissed her. *Why do I feel like crying?* Lucy touched her cheek and stared at her pillow. No, no, no. *Oh, I can't like him. I have to get that out of my head. Men don't like me. I have a career.* A bed spring creaked from the other side of the curtain.

"Good night, *Padre*." Giovanni's muted voice came through to Lucy's side.

He must be going to sleep. Warmth touched her heart. How nice to be so close. Lucy pulled back her blanket and crawled into bed.

How many Saturdays have I seen here? Lucy sat in the mule cart next to Giovanni. *At least the rain's stopped.* But the clouds hung so low, it wouldn't be long before they'd be soaked to the skin again. The cart sludged its way though muddy streets. Poor Jonah did his best to stay steady in the goo. *That mule deserves at least a lump of sugar.* Maybe she could find one at the army camp they were headed to. Lucy put a steady hand on top of the giant pile of blankets balanced precariously, in the wagon, behind her.

From far off, the military base looked like hundreds of tiny pyramids all lined up row by row. "This could be Egypt." Lucy caught the top blanket before it slid. "Or a farm for really large chickens."

Giovanni cracked a smile and turned the wagon down the middle of the camp. "And I let you into my surgery. These aren't chicken houses, they're tents made out of wood to keep soldiers dry."

Oh, he was good. She shook his arm. "You don't think I was serious do you?"

"I don't know…you Americans are a strange bunch." Giovanni pulled Jonah to a stop in front of the largest tent.

Lucy grabbed the rail.

"Stay here." Giovanni pointed to the wagon seat. Then he jumped down.

Of all the…

"Hey, Boston." Petty Officer Jackson strolled towards her with a shovel over his shoulder.

Now she had a reason. Lucy jumped to the ground.

"Last time I saw you, you were covered in mud." He bowed and tipped his hat. "I'm glad to see you've recovered."

Rats. He did see the wrestling match didn't he? "T-there was no one else to help I couldn't just let that man kidnap the little girl…" Maybe she should get back in the wagon. She could feel the young man's gaze. Lucy turned away.

"I thought you wanted to invite me to tea."

Really? Lucy examined his face. His smile seemed honest. "Y-yes. When can you come?"

Officer Jackson put his hand to his chin. "What if I were able to break away this evening? May I join you for supper?"

"Yes. We eat at seven." Lucy clasped her hands. He wanted to spend time with her? "Do you think you'll be able to come?"

"I'll do my very best." He took her hand in his and with a bow, kissed it.

Giovanni never should have left *Lucia* alone. He glowered, with a clear view from the officer's tent. The man was slime. The way he kissed Lucy's hand, the way his eyes roamed her face made Giovanni want to wretch. *She's so naive. She's just a child. How am I supposed to pay attention to the camp doctor when all I want to do is punch the vermin?*

With the blankets unloaded Jonah turned his head toward home.

Giovanni took a deep breath. This would be a good time. "I saw you talking to your friend from America." Eyes on the road, he tried to sound pleasant.

"Yes, he might be joining us for dinner tonight." Lucy must have felt his agitation because she turned to him slowly.

CHAPTER TWELVE

"I am not trying to tell you what to do." What an awful way to start. There must be a better approach. Giovanni tried to think.

"Then please don't." Lucy gave him a razor sharp look and scooted to the far side of the wagon.

Giovanni held his tongue, but with every turn of the wagon wheels his agitation wound tighter.

"How old are you?" Did that question really come out of him? Yes, and he had a point to make.

"*What?*" Lucy's eye grew large.

"How old are you?" Giovanni spoke a little louder.

"If you must know, I'm twenty-six." She turned away.

"In your twenty-six years of life, how many men have you known?" What a dreadful thing to ask. His mother would be appalled. But this girl needed to see truth.

"What do you mean? I have two brothers. I know them. I know my father, the professors at Boston University, I know you." Lucy turned to face him directly.

Of course *Lucia* didn't understand the question. Giovanni stopped the mule. "No. I mean how many men have you courted, dated or whatever you call it?"

Her pale face spoke of humiliation. "That's none of your business. Besides, I haven't had much time to date. I've been in college and then working and now I'm here."

Frustrating. Could she be this naive? He examined her face, void of color, and round eyes. Maybe… "Did your mother never discuss with you the nature of men?"

Lucy turned away and grew very still. Had he made her cry?

"No. She wasn't around." Her voice sounded thick.

He should back off but…was the woman too busy to raise a child? *This is why Lucia is clueless*. "You've never been kissed have you?"

"Of course I have, my father kisses me all the time!" She turned around, fire in her eyes again.

What a temper. Giovanni smiled through his frustration. Maybe she would listen now. "*Lucia*, there are a lot of honorable men in this world, but there are many more who would take advantage of you. Of the honorable ones, even fewer would allow you to work outside the home and use your gift. This young man, I can tell, likes you. But he doesn't respect you. He may even be an honorable man. But he's not the kind of man who honors women."

"How do you know?"

"I've seen how he looks at you. I don't like it."

"That's what you said about Dr. De Stanza. You were right that time, I saw it myself. But Officer Jackson has done nothing wrong. He's only been a gentleman. I think you're way too suspicious."

Why did she have to be so stubborn? "Of course he's acting like a gentleman. He knows it's the only way to win someone like you. If you married, he would be abusive. He would keep you pregnant and in the kitchen. I apologize for being so vulgar, but if I'm to be your friend, you'll find that I'll speak to you truthfully, even if what I say is not pleasant. Do. Not. Get involved with him."

"Who said anything about marriage? I just want to be friends." Lucy looked down at her feet and sighed. "Men don't find me attractive enough to get involved."

"*Lucia*, men don't want to be friends with women; they either use them or marry them." Waite a minute. "What do you mean men don't find you attractive? Wherever did you get an idea like that?"

"I can't believe I'm saying this to you." Lucy's face turned pink. "My aunt, my teachers, my professors, and the people I grew up with. All my life I've been told that God gave me brains instead of beauty." She fidgeted with her fingers. "I am way too skinny, you even said that."

"I did not say you were skinny." Giovanni suddenly regretted his words. "I said your uniform is too big."

"What's the difference?" Lucy looked down at her feet again and then into his eyes. Did he see shame?

"My hair is always a mess, my feet are too big and I would rather dissect a frog than go shopping. I can take out an appendix, but I can't cook at all. What man would find that attractive? Besides, I've never been asked out once. How much more proof do I need?"

Mamma mia! No wonder she's this way. And I've only added to the problem. What kind of people would tell a young girl she's ugly? He looked at her delicate features painted with pain.

Time to say what he'd always thought. "But you're beautiful."

"Giovanni, please don't tease me. I really want us to be friends. We are friends aren't we? Or are you going to try to 'use' me?"

"*Lucia*, I will never tease you in that manner. When I said what I did, I was trying to protect you." He spoke in a quiet voice and leaned forward so she would look at him. "I wanted to make you mad enough that you would go back to Rome because this place is so dangerous."

"You were trying to protect me?"

Giovanni took her hand in his and nodded. "Yes, we are friends. No, I will not use you, but I *am* different."

"How are you so different?"

In so many ways, she still seemed like a little girl. "It's difficult to explain." Giovanni let her go. "It has something to do with how I was raised. I just am." He moved the mule forward.

Lucy stared at her feet, quiet for the rest of the way home.

Giovanni would keep an eye on the soldier from New York if he came.

Lucy walked into the mess tent. Would the young man be there or would she face another humiliation? Would it matter? She'd been rejected so many times, why would this one make a difference? Giovanni's conversation in the wagon came to mind. Why was it so important to prove him wrong? If only Giovanni had left well enough alone. The question about her mother really set Lucy's emotions on edge. If this guy didn't show she might just have to find a place to…

"Hey, Boston."

Lucy's heart lightened.

Officer Jackson strode toward her from across the tent. In his dress uniform, he bowed with his hat in hand and sword at his side. He reached for her fingers and kissed her hand.

The handsome American pulled out a chair. "When were you in New York?"

"Just last summer." Lucy slid into the seat. "Daddy took my brothers and me for two weeks. What does your family do?"

"Shipping. That's why I got into the Navy. Father thought it would be good experience before I help him run the company."

"What kind of things do you ship?"

"Oh, anything at all. New Yorkers have sophisticated tastes; they keep us in business." Officer Jackson pulled a beautiful cigar from his pocket and handed it to Lucy. "Here, give this to that doctor you work with. It's from Havana, he'll enjoy it."

"Thank you. That's very kind." She set it on the table next to her plate. "I'm not sure Dr. Castello smokes but I'll be sure he gets it."

"So, what's it like working with Italians? Most of these hospitals are full of British doctors or Russians or even French. I'm surprised they let you work with so many of them."

"So many doctors?"

"So many Italians."

"I like working with them very much." What a weird question. Lucy raised an eyebrow. "Why?"

Officer Jackson shook his head. "Never in my life did I think I would be here, of all places."

"What do you mean?" Lucy sipped her tea. Where could he possibly take this?

"I've seen so many Guineas back home, I've had my fill. They're taking over entire neighborhoods, living together in squalor, smelling of garlic, not speaking English. They've been caught hunting in Central Park. When they're not poaching the squirrels, they're stealing. The only reason we hire them is that they'll take half the pay of a black or Irish man. Now I find myself here, where they come from."

"So you're saying you don't like Italians." Lucy put her tea cup down.

"Oh no, I like 'em fine as long as they stay in their place. It does make me uncomfortable, though, knowing that someone like you is living in this tent with them. Where's your father? What does he do?"

" Daddy's in Rome, he's a physician. When this earthquake happened we both came to help. He returned with the *Venezia* and I stayed because there's just so much to do."

"I get it." Officer Jackson gave a warm smile. "You're father's a doctor and so you're a nurse. No wonder you feel obligated to help. My mother has a compassionate heart too. Besides, if you hadn't stayed, we never would have met."

"Dr. James, do you mind if we take your dishes? We're almost out and we have more people to feed." Cook leaned over them politely; sleeves rolled to the elbows of his giant arms, his bushy eyebrows pinched together and his eyes followed every movement that her dinner guest made.

"Of course." Lucy gathered their plates and handed them to Cook. "Here you go. *Grazie*." Cook waddled off. He looked across the tent and when he spotted Giovanni he gave a nod.

Lucy hadn't seen her partner come into the mess tent; he sat in the corner slowly sipping espresso. And though his dark eyes focused on his meal, an occasional glance said that he watched; Giovanni was protective like that. She'd never realized how much she preferred Giovanni's company to the man who sat with her.

The man who sat with her? No; the man who now stared at her as though he saw a freak in a carnival.

"Is something the matter?" *Oh, he heard my title. Okay, here we go.* Lucy sat back in her chair.

"Did that man just call you *Doctor?*"

"Yes." Lucy kept her face serene. She'd milk this for all she could. "Dr. Castello says I'm an excellent surgeon."

"Are you serious?" Officer Jackson squinted and leaned forward. "A surgeon, who cuts people up and such?"

"Yes." She squinted back.

"And your father allows it? He left you here with all these...these people so you can play doctor?" A different kind of light filled his eye. "There has to be more to this than you're telling me. I can only think of one reason a father would leave his daughter, here." He grabbed Lucy's arm, dragged her to her feet and pulled her close. "I might let you doctor me for a wh-"

Giovanni shoved his way between them. He wrenched her free and had the man's sword out of its scabbard before the American could reach for it. Giovanni knocked him to the ground and held him at sword point.

"*Andiamo! Andiamo!*" The shout of some peasant somewhere beyond the tent walls broke the sudden silence.

Had every person in the tent stood to defend her too? Apparently. Wow. Even Cook had a brass kettle in his hand.

"I thought you lacked brains the first time I laid eyes on you." Giovanni's icy voice grabbed her attention. He wore a glare that would put fear in the bravest. "I can hardly believe that even you would be so stupid. Did you think you could touch this woman in the presence of all these people and get away with it?"

The red-faced man on the ground only scowled.

"You owe the lady an apology." Giovanni stuck the tip of the sword to the man's throat.

"Giovanni, I'm okay. Let him go." Lucy tugged his arm.

"Apologize." He poked again. Giovanni turned his head away and winked at her.

Oh.

"I apologize." Officer Jackson mumbled.

"Louder," Giovanni poked the man once more.

"I apologize," he said clearly, but anger blazed on his face.

Giovanni let him stand. "Now leave before I slice you and serve you over pasta."

People behind him chuckled.

Officer Jackson picked himself up and eased his way toward the door.

"M-my sword?" He hesitated at the threshold.

"Oh, yes. I almost forgot." Giovanni broke the sword over his knee and handed it back to the soldier. "Get out of here."

Officer Jackson quickly disappeared through the flap.

Lucy slid into a chair and hid her face in her hands. At least she wasn't surrounded by overfed debutants this time. But Jiminy! Again?

"It's all right, everyone," Giovanni said. "Dr. James is unhurt." Conversation filled the tent once more.

He slipped his hand around her wrist.

"*Lucia*?" Giovanni gently tugged and she dropped her hands to her lap. Stooped in front of her, he looked like he might still be angry.

"Did you hear what he said?"

"Most of it."

She tried to hold his gaze but the depth of his eyes made her want to cry. How stupid. "I'm so embarrassed. Not all Americans think the way he does."

"Don't you think I know that? I don't care what he thinks. I knew he'd eventually insult you, but when he grabbed you…" Giovanni's eyes grew dark. "That was enough to make him my enemy." He rose and sat in a chair facing her. "Are you all right? Did he bruise you? Let me see your arm." He reached for her wrist.

"My arm's fine. I guess I should have listened." Lucy tried to push his hand away but he took her fingers in his own. "You knew he was like that?"

"I've seen his kind before."

Wow. "He seemed fine until he found out I'm a doctor." Maybe her father was right. Maybe she should just pursue her career because… "Daddy always says that men don't like women who've been educated."

"He's right." He rubbed her hand. "A lot of men feel threatened to know that a woman might actually be smarter."

"Does my education bother you?"

He gave a soft chuckle. "No."

"But you were so adamant in Rome."

Giovanni rubbed his forehead and grimaced. Then the smile returned. "I guess I'm old fashioned. It wasn't your education that bothered me, it was your confidence. And when you pair that with your temper! *Mamma!*" He looked to the heavens.

"So my confidence makes me unattractive."

Giovanni looked up quickly. "Maybe to the average person. But not to me."

He's trying to make me feel better. "Do I bother you still?"

"Sometimes, but if you weren't so confident you wouldn't be able to do what you do." He gave her fingers a playful tug. "I've come to enjoy arguing with you."

Lucy had to laugh."Really. I'll remind you of that the next time we're fighting."

Giovanni laughed too. "I'll try to listen. I think you should stay here and work with me. Have you gotten your answer yet?"

The softness in his eyes drew her in. How could she say no?

"Yes. I'll work with you through the summer; until September. Oh, here, this cigar was for you."

"Even if I did smoke, I wouldn't touch it now." He tossed it on the table. "You look sleepy."

The urge to yawn almost overtook her. "I am. If you don't mind, I'm going to head to bed. It's been a long day." Giovanni stood when she did.

She leaned into him, her heart still heavy. The weight of his arm about her shoulder stirred her spirits. He'd held a man at sword point for her. Through her mind flashed the image of the mud fight. He'd held a sword then too…"Where did you learn to handle a sword like that? Were you in the army?"

"My uncle taught me. But it's not a story for tonight. Maybe, another time. *Buonanotte, Lucia*." He turned her to face him. "Have you always found me to be truthful?"

"Yes."

He touched her chin. "You truly are beautiful. Anyone who tells you different is lying."

"Thanks." *Nice try. Daddy says the same thing*. Somehow, though, Giovanni made her feel safe. Maybe she could reveal a small piece of her heart.

"Remember your question from earlier today?"

His clear gray eyes grew softer still. He nodded.

"No one has ever kissed me." She shrugged."But then, I have yet to find anyone that I would like to kiss me. Or, better yet, anyone I would like to kiss back." Lucy pulled her hand out of his.

"I'm off to bed. *Buonanotte*, Giovanni. See you in the morning."

"*Sogni d'oro, Lucia.*"

"Finally some sunshine." Lucy breathed deeply and relaxed. The idea of a springtime drive to see Giovanni's villa and plan the clinic could not have come on a more perfect day. The cart rolled along pleasantly; the crunch of gravel under the wheels and the clop of hooves lifted her spirits even more. "Padre was right we needed to get away. Even if it's just for the afternoon."

The warm sun and beautiful blue sky gave her a new perspective on the city where she lived.

"This was my idea too, you know. We thought you might enjoy this." Giovanni turned the mule down a cleared road toward the open countryside, into the sloping sides of the pine-clad mountains.

"Once you're out of the city, you can hardly tell there was an earthquake at all. The trees are still standing, everything's turning green. Giovanni, it's all so beautiful. Are those orange trees?"

"Yes, and lemon, too. They were loaded with fruit just a few weeks ago." He pulled the mule closer and broke off an early white blossom. Giovanni put it to his nose and smiled; then he held it for Lucy.

"I've never smelled anything so wonderful."

"In a few weeks all of these trees, all of the citrus trees in Sicily will be covered with these flowers. The air will smell sweet even in the center of town. It's one of my favorite times of the year." He handed the flower to Lucy and urged the mule forward.

No way could she let herself forget this. Birds sang and bathed in the puddles along the road. The whole place smelled sweet and musty at the same time; a mixture of wet earth, warm sun and salt air. *Even in the midst of all the tragedy, Your creation continues to rejoice. Maybe I'll hear the rocks sing out, too.*

The cart neared a hilltop that overlooked the city. The vast ruins of Messina lay before her. The harbor shone in the distance; beyond the harbor, the straits of Messina. Even further in the distance stood Reggio Calabria, the city on the tip of the boot of Italy. They, too, suffered the effects of the quake.

Surrounded by water sparkling under the brilliant yellow sun, the scene set before her seemed surreal and breathtaking.

"It must have been a magnificent city." Lucy spoke softly not wanting to break the quiet.

"It was. It will be again. This is not the first time Sicily has had to rebuild, you know." Giovanni let the reins sit loose across his lap.

"Our cities have been destroyed often and in many ways, through thousands of years of wars and natural disasters. The next time we're out, I'll show you Mt. Etna. It's not far from here." He waved in the opposite direction. "You can see it, just over these mountains. That volcano has been responsible for a good many tragedies."

"When I was a child, I often read the story of Kronos and his scythe. He threw it and created the harbor of Messina." Lucy squinted in the sun. "I never thought I would get to see it."

"You like mythology?"

"I love it."

"Actually, the harbor is so perfectly rounded that geologists believe it to be the cone of a dead volcano."

"Yes, so I've heard. But the story of Kronos is much more fun."

"*Andiamo a casa*." Giovanni turned the mule, who bobbed his head and gave a snort.

"Tell me about your family." He had such a beautiful accent that sometimes Lucy just liked to listen.

"I'm the youngest of five brothers; Vito, the oldest, Michael, Antonio, and Giuseppe. I don't expect you to remember them all. Two of them work with my father. I'm the odd one, choosing to be a doctor. Two of them have passed away."

Giovanni grew still, staring across the orange grove. Where had his thoughts taken him?

He refocused. "Then, there are the wives. Adella and Celeste. And the children; Michael Jr., Filippo, Elisabetta, Ricardo, Guglielmo, Pietro, Teresa and Maria. And, of course, *Mamma*. Her name is Rosa. And Papa. I am named after him, but we just call him Papa."

"And they all live together?" It must be such fun to live with so many.

"Yes, but you must remember that we have a large estate. It's not unusual for Italian families to live together when they can."

"Has your family always lived in Palermo?"

"No, we're originally from Rome. One of my ancestors liked to grow olives when he was not away at war. He learned that Sicily was a fine place to cultivate them and so he moved here.

The mule stopped before a garden, enclosed by a vine-covered wall and a wrought iron gate. The villa, nestled into the mountainside, overlooked a gently sloping valley. Giovanni jumped down from the wagon. He pulled keys from his pocket, unlocked the gate and swung it open.

CHAPTER THIRTEEN

"This is it." He climbed back up and drove the cart down the tree-lined driveway.

The house sure had a warm and friendly feel. The same lacy green vines that decorated the garden wall, grew up its creamy stucco façade on one side. Even with a few tiles missing, the red terra cotta roof made the perfect complement.

"It's beautiful." Lucy wrinkled her nose and squinted at the green canopy of leaves above.

"*Papà* gave me the keys to it when I graduated from medical school. I call it mine, but in reality it belongs to my entire family. We used to spend summers here when I was a child."

"I can see the sense in a walled garden." Lucy took in the length of the stucco wall that surrounded the garden. It had fallen in some places, but she could easily imagine a young Giovanni playing here with his brothers. "A mother could let her children play in relative safety. With a yard like this where could they go?"

Giovanni gave a slight smile. "Over the wall. It's a wonder my mother has any hair left with sons like us. We would pretend to be prisoners of the Bastille. To escape we would shimmy up that tree over there and drop to the ground on the other side. That's how I met Father Dominic you know. I had escaped jail and he returned me to the warden."

"And he's been guarding you ever since." Lucy hopped to the ground.

"I was going to help you down." Giovanni watched her from his seat.

"Thanks, but I'm good." *Rats. Why do I forget things like that?* Maybe she could distract him. Lucy walked ahead among the palm trees and small statues made of stone. Giovanni followed. Saint Francis lay in the corner, on his back, next to a collapsed bench. *Perfect.*

"Let's stand him up again so that he can watch for the birds." She tried to lift him upright.

"If you grab his head like that it will come off. Let me help you." Giovanni stepped in. He reached around her and lifted the statue.

"You're so good with sutures; You'd be good with mortar too." Lucy ducked away when she found herself trapped in his arms.

"Very funny. Did I bump you?" He brushed the dirt from his hands.

"Almost, but I'm too fast." Lucy moved a stray hair out of her eyes.

"You've just dirtied your face. Hold still." Giovanni reached in his pocket and pulled out a handkerchief. He held her chin and wiped Lucy's face. "My niece, Teresa is as messy as you. I should introduce you."

"I'm sure she's an exceptional child. Her father must be proud."

"Most of the time he is. I wouldn't want to be your father. I feel for the man." He narrowed his eyes and a spark of humor shone. He handed her the handkerchief. "Stick this in your pocket in case you need it again."

"Thanks, I always lose mine."

"I know. This one is yours. I keep finding them."

Lucy stuffed the hankie in her pocket.

"I'm afraid I haven't had much time to spend cleaning this place." Giovanni took a step toward the house. "But, come on, I want to show you the rest."

He led her through the front door, still firmly on its hinges. A pile of plaster mixed with broken glass blocked their way. Giovanni offered his hand.

"Really, Giovanni. I won't fall." She navigated the wreckage without him.

"Fine." He shut the door. "Manage on your own."

Lucy followed him into the great room with its marble fireplace and stone lions to guard it. Shattered plaster covered the floor, fallen from a crack in the ceiling, along with the shards of a vase. The furniture must have vibrated its way to the center of the room. A large coat of arms hung above the fireplace, beneath the crest a single sword and scabbard, mounted on the wall.

"This is *perfect*. Do you mind if I see the rest?" Lucy's voice seemed enormously loud in the silent house.

"The dining room and kitchen are this way." Giovanni smiled; at her enthusiasm?

He led her through French doors to the left. "This is a painting of my mother.

"She looks kind. I'll bet we'd be friends.

"She is, and you're right; you would." Giovanni looked from the portrait to Lucy. He reached up and straightened it.

"We can have that re-hung," Giovanni waved his hand at the fallen chandelier of Murano glass. It draped sadly across a mahogany dining table.

"Just look at the gouges in the wood." Lucy ran her hand across the table

"I'm not worried about it; as long as the legs are still good we'll be able to use it. My idea was to have the patients wait in the great room and use the dining room for examinations."

"The kitchen we could use as a laboratory." He led Lucy through the double doors.

"It's huge." Lucy stopped at the door. "Just look at all these cupboards….and running water." She flew to the sink and lifted the faucet handle, but nothing came out. "Rats."

"The water isn't safe to drink, so I disconnected the pump." Giovanni turned the faucet off. "I'll have a new well dug, but that won't be for a while."

He walked toward the back of the kitchen. "The servant's rooms are down this hall to the right. They have a full bath between them." He led her down the hall to the clean, efficient bedrooms. "We can keep people here during emergency if the hospitals are full."

Giovanni ran his hand through his hair. "I'll have to buy a new microscope. Mine was destroyed downtown. Maybe I could find one in Palermo."

"Mine's in Rome. When Daddy comes, I'll ask him to send it upon his return."

"That would be fine." Giovanni motioned for Lucy to follow. "This last room is my favorite."

Giovanni took a right down the back hallway and led Lucy into a large room with thick red carpet on the floor, two overstuffed chairs in front of a fireplace and a carved mahogany desk in the center. The right side of the desk opened to a large bay window, which overlooked the back garden. Empty bookcases lined three of the walls with most of their occupants piled on the floor.

"What a mess." Lucy picked her way through the books. "Don't worry, we'll have this organized before you know it.

"At least I was wise enough to keep the best of my collection in this room. We'll have plenty of reference material and it will be a good place to escape from the patients when we need a break."

"Hey, *Gray's Anatomy*, I love this book."

"Only you." He gave a low chuckle.

What did that mean? "What? Don't you like it?" Lucy looked up from an essay on the digestive tract.

"It's one of my favorites. It's just that most women read novels."

"I like a good novel." Lucy shut the book.

"That's not the point." He grabbed her hand. "Come on, we're almost finished. This hall leads to the back door and ends at the stairs to the upstairs bedrooms. You don't need to see them."

Giovanni put a hand to his head. "You know, it's not really fair that I live in a house while you're somewhere else. Maybe I should let you live here and I will go to the American Village. Would you let me use the bathtub?"

"But it's your bathtub." *Wait a minute.* "You'd be willing to let me live in your house?" Padre said the man was self sacrificing, but "Couldn't we take turns living here? That way we'll both have a chance to use the bathroom."

"I suppose we could trade off and on. We'll figure it out."

Lucy followed him back into the great room.

"This is very nearly how our home and office are set up in America." Lucy wrinkled her nose and examined the crack in the ceiling. "The difference is that Daddy had an actual medical office built to the side, off the kitchen. I'm amazed this place has so little damage."

"It has a foundation of granite." Giovanni pushed an end table back into its corner. "I think the fact that this house was built on rock is what saved it."

"Just like in the Bible." Excitement rose inside and Lucy paced about the room. "A house built on a rock will stand when storms come, while a house built on the shore where there's sand will fall."

Lucy sensed Giovanni's patient gaze. She turned to face him. Would he understand? "My constant talk of God bothers you."

"I'm surrounded by people who speak of God. At least you try to be nice about it. *Padre* and Sister Francesca, they just say what they think I need to hear. Giovanni smirked then he rubbed her arm. "You don't bother me.'"

"What's this?" Lucy walked to the fireplace, put her hands on the mantle and looked up at the coat of arms.

"The Castello family crest." Giovanni joined Lucy at the mantel.

"I've read about these, but I've never actually seen one before. If I remember right, all of the images have a meaning." Lucy tilted her head and squinted. "A sword with a crown above it, held by a lamb. Hmm." Lucy turned a bit toward her companion. "What does the inscription below the sword say?"

"It reads; *In His service by life or death*."

"In whose service?"

"I'd rather not say."

What exactly are you hiding? Her fingers touched an old military cap on the mantle. She picked it up and blew crumbs of plaster off. "Whose was this?"

"It belonged to my brother, Vito." He eased the cap out of her hands. "That was his sword. Vito died of cholera when I was young. His death affected me terribly. For many years I couldn't say his name." Giovanni touched the hat once more before he spoke again.

"If only we knew then what we know now. His death may have been prevented. So many people were lost in that epidemic. At the time, all they knew to do was to burn his possessions. I saved his hat. I hid it for years. His sword was presented to my mother at his funeral. She gave it to me. Except for a photograph at my parents' house, this is all that's left of my brother."

"You must have been very close."

"I was eight, he was eighteen. Vito was my hero."

What happened to Giuseppe?"

"He died of gangrene from a cut that he got on an olive press."

Lucy closed her eyes. This was the source of his pain.

"There was an epidemic of influenza in our town when I was ten." She stepped closer and took his hand in hers. "My parents worked night and day. They saved a lot of lives. Despite all of their precautions, my mother came down with it, too. Mother died." Lucy paused, allowing him to see that she also understood grief. "Daddy said that if Mother hadn't already been so exhausted from their long battle against the sickness, she might have had a chance. Losing someone you love is something that never quite leaves you."

"Finally, I understand you." Such tender compassion filled his eyes. "I don't think my family would know how to function without my mother. I know you miss her."

"Every day. But knowing God has made her absence easier." She gave his hand a pat and let it go.

"You mentioned your aunt the other day," he said softly. "She's the one who raised you, isn't she?"

"Yes. Aunt Lucinda came to live with us shortly after Mother died. She's a wonderful woman who spent her life teaching school. Aunt Lucinda actually encouraged me to become a doctor just like Daddy did. "

"And she never married?"

"No."

"So your Aunt Lucinda decided that you wouldn't marry, either. Did she tell you that you were ugly or was it inferred?" Giovanni kept his voice gentle. Did he know he walked on tender ground?

"Honestly, Giovanni, she meant no harm. I think that she was only trying to protect me from rejection. To this point, she's been right. I've had no suitors at all. So, I'll serve God as a single woman and a doctor. It's not such a terrible fate."

His eyes grew dark. "And the other people in your life? Your teachers, your neighbors?"

"You have to admit I'm unusual." Lucy shrugged and pulled away. Why was it so hard to look him in the eye? "When all the other little girls in my neighborhood were learning to sew and cook, I was either wrestling with my brothers or hanging around a medical office helping to roll bandages. By the time I was nine, I could name all the bones in the body. Why wouldn't they find me strange?"

"Yes, but having intelligence doesn't make you unattractive." Giovanni tilted his head slightly, forcing Lucy to look at him.

"But acting like a 'tomboy' as my aunt puts it, doesn't help. Face it, Giovanni, I'm loud, Daddy say's I'm garish. I share my affections way too easily. Look at us, I act as if you're one of my brothers." Lucy grabbed his hand and squeezed it.

"But, you fit right in around here. If you're my friend, then I consider you to be family." Giovanni squeezed her hand in return. "If you're family, then I see you as a sister, nothing more. You have my protection and my affection."

Lucy almost laughed. "This might be all right as long as I'm in Messina. Once I return home, I'll face the same dilemma. I'm the kind of woman to run an office not a house. I have no desire to focus all of my attention on needlepoint or on how to set a proper table. Impressing society doesn't interest me."

"But that doesn't mean you're unattractive. "

"It's all right." Lucy sighed. "God's given me peace about it. I'm happy to be able to serve him. As you said, what man would allow me to continue practicing medicine anyway? I have yet to meet him."

His thumb swept across the back of her hand. "What about your father? Is he bitter?"

"No. Mother's death made him want to know God better. The Bible promises that Daddy will be reunited with Mother one day."

"A man of science who embraces the Bible. And he's taught his daughter to do the same. *Lucia*, there have been many times that I've been so frustrated at you that I've wanted to throw you from the surgery."

"But—"

"No, not for lack of skill, let me finish. It was your strength that frustrated me. I've come to understand that your strength comes from your faith. I've seen you completely covered in blood and able to hold your concentration under the very worst of conditions; wet feet for example. I've not exactly been easy on you. You have the surgical skills of a man, yet you have faith in God like a little child. I've seldom met anyone who could combine science and faith the way you do. On you, it seems to fit."

"I'm far from perfect." Lucy grinned. "Would it make it easier if you knew that at times I've bitten my tongue so hard I thought it would come off? I'd think I could control myself, but then I'd tell you off anyway."

Giovanni laughed softly. "How could I not notice? I like your temper. I've a feeling that man you beat up will never be the same." He slipped his arm around her shoulder.

Lucy leaned into him. "What's out back?"

"An orange grove. The fruit's already been picked. Still, there might be one or two left. It's worth looking. Let's go find out."

Giovanni led her out the back door onto the stone patio that overlooked a rolling lemon and orange orchard. Off in the distance, the mountains rose again, making the entire property feel extremely private.

Together, they descended the stone steps and walked among the orange trees. "The *profughi* could have used this citrus." Lucy looked through the branches of the short shaggy trees.

"They did use it. Don't you remember all of the oranges and lemons we gave away in January?"

"They came from you? I had no idea. Giovanni, that was really good of you."

He shrugged and motioned for her to follow him further into the orange grove.

"Oranges!" Lucy took a step closer and grabbed his arm to make him stop. "Tell the truth. Are you the one who put the oranges on my pillow?"

Giovanni gave a sheepish frown.

"You stinker! Here I thought you hated me and all along you really did care." Lucy punched him in the arm, hard.

"Ow!" Giovanni laughed and backed up a step. "Of course I cared. I told you I was trying to protect you." He stepped out of the way when Lucy tried to land another punch and caught her arm. "Would you stop? I'll be in need of medical attention if you keep up."

"Wait a minute." Lucy tried to pull her arm free. "Your family raises olives. All that really good olive oil we've been eating for the last two months; that came from you too, didn't it? Would you let me go?"

"Are you going to stop hitting me?"

"Are you going to answer the question?"

Giovanni threw his head back and laughed, but he let her go. "Actually, the olive oil came from my parents."

Lucy noticed an upside down kettle in the dirt. It matched the ones that Cook used. She put a hand to her forehead. How could she have been so blind? "You've provided more than just fruit and olive oil, haven't you? Have you been feeding our hospital station… and all of those refugees… all this time?" Lucy saw the answer in his eyes though again he did not speak. "You never said a word about it." She felt like scales fell from her eyes. *He is a really good man.*

"A lot of other people donated as well." He scratched his head and shifted a bit. "The tea, the coffee…When people are hurting, you do what you can. My actions haven't been so extraordinary."

"Yes, they have," Lucy said softly. Her mind went back to all the long hours he stood in the operating room. "You've worked circles around all of us. I've never once heard you complain. Come to think of it, I've never even hear you say that you were tired."

"*Mamma mia*! What am I, a saint? That's enough." He rolled his eyes grabbed her hand and pulled her along with him. He wrapped his arm around her shoulder and squeezed. "I am *no* saint as you well know, and many people have given a lot more than food. Besides, we came out here to look for oranges."

He released Lucy and squinted into the branches of a particularly large tree. "I see one. It will probably be sour, but still..." He searched the ground. "There should be a ladder around here somewhere."

"Who needs a ladder?" Lucy grabbed a lower branch and climbed halfway up the tree in three moves.

"*Santa Maria!* This woman is a frustration." Giovanni growled. "*Lucia*, come down from there, you'll get hurt." He moved beneath her. Would he try to catch her if she fell?

Lucy grinned down at the frown on his face. He really didn't like it. "Don't worry; I do this all the time back home. We have apples."

Giovanni blocked the sun from his eyes with his hand and paid attention to the branch that Lucy stood on. "Are all American women as stubborn as you?"

"No." She giggled. "I'm much more stubborn than average…I think I can reach it." Lucy held on to a branch with her left hand and reached for the orange with her right. "Got it!"

Giovanni hadn't moved from his spot. His mouth tightened. That had to be a smile he fought. "Congratulations. Now get down."

"Thanks. Here, catch." She tossed the orange to him and swung down to the ground. Giovanni stepped out of the way.

Lucy's skirt caught a branch, she landed on her bottom with a squeal and they burst into laughter. Then Lucy's knee hurt.

"That's the funniest thing I've seen in a long time. *Scimmia piccola* fits you just fine. Let me help you up." He stooped beside her.

I've done it again. Lucy went quiet. *Will I ever be normal?*

Giovanni touched her chin. "*Lucia*, are you all right?"

"I think I scraped my knee." *Tomboy*. She could hear Aunt Lucinda scold.

"What?" He sat on the ground next to her and let out a sigh. "Let me look at it."

Of all the stupid things to do. Lucy gingerly moved her skirt to reveal her injured knee.

"That's not so bad. We should get you inside so I can clean it." He rubbed the top of her head.

Like a child; that must be how he sees me. "Aren't you going to yell at me? I deserve it."

"Yell at you?" His eyebrows went up. "No, of course not." Then he smiled. "Unless you want me to." He started to laugh again, with the sunlight on his hair and such a beautiful light in his eyes. Couldn't she just find a place to hide?

Giovanni stood and pulled Lucy up with both hands before she could protest. "Let's go inside," he said. "I'm an expert at scraped knees."

They made their way up the steps and went in the back door.

"Your first aid kit is in the kitchen?" Lucy lagged behind.

"Yes, come on, right this way." Giovanni motioned for her to catch up. They entered the kitchen; he went to the cupboard and opened it. "I always keep the medical supply here in the cabinet. You know, just in case I fall out of a tree."

"Still clean." He closed the cabinet door with his elbow.

"Thank you." Lucy pulled the alcohol and cloth out of his hand without looking at him directly. Why suffer further humiliation?

"Go ahead, do it yourself." He sounded disappointed. Now what?

"Excuse me?" With her foot on a chair and the bottle in her hand, Lucy looked over her shoulder.

"You're so independent." He crossed his arms.

"What's wrong with being independent?" Lucy forgot her knee for the moment.

"Nothing as long as you learn to admit when it would be best to let someone help you. You know I can see your wound better than you can. Is it that you don't trust me?"

Oh. "If I didn't trust you, I wouldn't be here alone with you," Lucy said, quietly. "I'm embarrassed that I did this. I don't want you..."

"But you showed me your knee just minutes ago, outside, remember?" He tilted his head. Lucy felt his gaze sweep her face.

"You *are* embarrassed," he said slowly. Then she saw him go soft. "I didn't realize you were this shy. After all we've seen together, been through together." Giovanni came to her side and sat on the kitchen table. "This is a side of you I never noticed. I've never seen you act like a woman." He kissed her forehead and Lucy blushed beet red.

"Oh, I'm so mad at myself," she muttered. "I just want to hide."

"*Bambina*, I only want to clean your cut. I won't even look at your leg. You have my word as a gentleman." Giovanni gave a hopeful smile and then pulled the bottle and cloth out of Lucy's hands.

"I'm sorry." Lucy slid onto the table and put her feet on the chair. "I know I'm not being very professional." With her elbows on her knees and her chin in her hands, she hoped her cool fingers would make the redness go.

"No one is professional all the time." He stuck his hand in his pocket. "Hold out your hand."

Lucy did as he asked and he put a lemon drop in her palm.

"I got them in the mail yesterday, from my mother. I always keep these on hand for serious wounds such as this." He winked at her and began to clean her knee.

"Ouch," Lucy scrunched her face and laughed. Her bashfulness evaporated.

Giovanni leaned toward her with a playful smile. "I know it hurts, *bambina*, but you really shouldn't be climbing trees." He touched her chin. "You haven't eaten your lemon drop. Go ahead, *Mamma* sent a whole bag of them."

"I haven't had one of these in years." She popped the candy in her mouth and rolled it around on her tongue. "Thank you, for the surgery and the medication."

"You're quite welcome." Giovanni stood to put the bottle back in the cupboard and hang the cloth over the sink.

"Giovanni?"

"Yes?"

"Please don't tell Daddy that I fell from an orange tree. I would be in so much trouble."

"I will keep this a secret only if you promise not to tell anyone where the food has been coming from. Do we have a deal?"

"We do." Lucy hopped down from the table. Her knee felt stiff.

I used to dread having to work with him all day. From her seat in the cart, Lucy watched Giovanni lock the gate.

The old lock screeched when he turned the key and the ground began to vibrate.

A shower of leaves fluttered to the ground like a thousand butterflies.

"That's not good." Giovanni pulled the key from the lock and slid it in his pocket.

"Do you always have such frequent earthquakes?"

"No and they're rarely very strong. I've never seen anything like what we've experienced lately. We'd better get back in case someone's been hurt."

"That didn't feel too bad."

'You're forgetting the granite we're standing on. Nothing ever feels as strong up here." Giovanni climbed into his seat and urged the mule into a canter.

"I hope you're wrong." Lucy gripped the side of the cart to keep from bouncing out.

They made the turn and she could see groups of people, some on stretchers, some leaning, supported by friends, all heading in the direction of the hospital.

"It looks like we might be in for a long night." Giovanni focused on the crowd. "You go and prep. I'll find someone to take the mule. Never mind, I see Father Dominic."

The good priest waited for them to pull up. He caught Jonah by the bridle. "Two more buildings collapsed. Of course, there were people inside, soldiers mostly. I've sent word to the regiment's physician."

The tiny watch on her shoulder said 9:25. When had day turned to night? And would that army doctor ever come to help?

Giovanni held his hand out and Lucy placed the pump-spray into it. A sickly sweet smell filled the room. How good it was to have disinfectant at all.

The flap moved. A man entered with a brisk pace. "I'm Dr. Le Beau."

It's about time. Lucy took the spray pump from Giovanni.

"You can go now." He stepped in front of Lucy and examined the man on the table.

"That was rude." Anger flashed in Giovanni's eyes.

"He doesn't know." Lucy walked to Giovanni's left. "I know someone else who used to do the same thing."

Giovanni narrowed his eyes at her.

"*Aiuto! Aiuto!*" Two ragged old men ran into the surgery.

"Padre, get these people out of here," Giovanni yelled.

The priest walked into the surgery and stepped between the peasants and the table.

The oldest man clasped his hands. "Please, we've found a woman at the bottom of a building. She's going to have a baby and we can't move her."

Father Dominic put his arm around a peasant. "Giving birth is one of the most natural things. If you show me where she is, I'll bring her here. She'll be fine."

"But she's hurt." The man gave a pleading look to Giovanni.

Lucy knew what Giovanni would say before he said it. She took off her apron and grabbed her bag.

"I can manage from here." Giovanni nodded to her.

"I shouldn't be long." The army doctor moved away from the table.

"No," Giovanni ordered in the same tone that he had once used to speak to Lucy with. "We waited long enough for you to get here. I know *she* can do it. *You* stay with me."

Lucy stifled a grin and ran to follow.

"*Lucia*!"

Lucy turned abruptly.

Giovanni blazed with intensity. "Do *not* climb any trees."

"I'll be safe." Lucy nodded.

"*Padre*, go with her!" Giovanni yelled as she ran outside.

CHAPTER FOURTEEN

"Where is she?" Lucy searched the dark streets, squinting. She and Father Dominic climbed down from the wagon.

"Down there." One of the men pointed. He climbed on top of a mountain of mortar and looked down.

Lucy started to follow, but the priest grabbed her arm. "Lucy, those rocks will be very unstable. This is not at all safe."

He turned to the men and shouted. "You said she was at the *bottom* of a building, not *under* it."

"What's the difference?" One man threw his hands in the air. "She still needs help and we can't do it."

A moan came from below the pile of rubble.

"Please, *Padre*." Lucy pulled away. "At least let me look."

"*Santa Maria!*" He looked to the heavens and then at her. "All right, all right. But be careful!"

Lucy climbed little by little to the top of the mortar. She peered into the hole and held her lantern over it, to see the bottom.

"It's a basement. It couldn't be more than ten feet to the floor below," she yelled over her shoulder. "There's a ledge I could climb on. After that, it'll be a piece of cake. I'm going down there."

Lucy climbed back down and ran to the cart, trying to ignore the scowl on Father Dominic's face. She grabbed the rope from the back and tied it around her waist.

"Here, hold onto me." She shoved the other end of rope into Father Dominic's hands. "I'll need you to pull us back up. This makes me glad to be so skinny." She smiled at the priest.

"Lucy." He growled. "Giovanni would not approve. Let me send for some soldiers. Surely they could dig her out."

"Do you see soldiers anywhere near?"

"That's my point. It's just me out here. And those two." He jabbed a thumb at the two old peasants.

"But I've done this before, remember?"

"Yes, but before you had Giovanni with you and dozens of people to help."

Another moan floated from below the rocks. "She could be dying. We don't have time to wait for soldiers."

"But you are endangering your life."

"Father Dominic, listen to what you are saying. Jesus said, '*Whoever saves his life will lose it; whoever loses his life will save it.*' Please, if I die tonight I'm ready. I'm here to save lives. I couldn't live with myself if I didn't at least try. I promise if the mortar seems unstable, you can pull me right back up."

"That is not the entire scripture, *Signorina*." Father Dominic peered down at her. "But I understand what you are trying to say." He looked around again for soldiers.

"*Dio mio, l'donna testarda!*" Father Dominic looked to heaven once more. He shook his hands at the sky.

"*What* did you say?" Lucy's eyes went round.

"I was praying; you stubborn thing." The priest scowled at her. "You know exactly what I said." He looked around once more. "Very well!"

Father Dominic exhaled loudly. "But I will hold the rope, not them." He put his hands on her head. "Lord *please* keep her safe."

They climbed to the place where the mortar separated just enough for Lucy to squeeze through.

"Hello. Can you hear me?" Lucy stuck her face through the opening. She could hardly see a thing.

Another moan floated up from below.

Giovanni threw a pair of forceps into the wash bin. *I should have paid better attention to where she was going. She's too impulsive, too independent…too stubborn. If she gets hurt it will be my fault.* He grabbed a pair of scissors off the tray without even asking Sister Francesca for them.

A rogue wind whipped through the tent from the far end. The canvas ceiling lifted and slowly descended back into place.

Had someone touched his shoulder? Giovanni paused his work. "Something's wrong, I can feel it." He looked sideways at the nun. "Bringing a pregnant woman back to the hospital shouldn't take this long."

With everything in him, Giovanni wanted to go after Lucy; to be there with her. But so many poor people still waited for his help. He could not work fast enough. He glanced over at the tedious army doctor and grumbled under his breath. The man only slowed things down. Giovanni became so frustrated; he gave the man his own table just to get him out of the way. Now he out-worked the turtle two to one.

Soldiers carried in another patient. Giovanni gritted his teeth. Then, without knowing that he would, he began to pray in his heart.

It's been a long time since I've talked to you and I know you've no reason to listen to me. I want nothing for myself, but please, if you are there, protect Lucia.

Lucy put the lantern over her arm, along with her bag and slid on her stomach, feet first until she could just feel the ledge under her feet.

"I need more rope, *Padre*." The rope became slack; Lucy dropped to the ledge. The outline of the woman lay in the darkness below her.

"I'm going down to the bottom, hold tight." Lucy looked up at Father Dominic, his face tight. She got down on her stomach again and started to slide. She made it about halfway when one of the rocks from above came loose and she lost her grip. The rope around her waist jerked hard and she smashed into a jagged edge of mortar. Sharp pain seared the spot she had scraped that afternoon. Warm blood trickled down her leg. Then the rope went slack and the ground came at her fast. Lucy landed with a bump. *Lord have mercy.* Her heart raced.

"Lucy!" Father Dominic's panicked voice floated down from above.

"I'm okay!" She yelled back. *Except for my knee. Man, that hurt.*

The shadowy body of the pregnant woman rested just a few feet away. *Never mind my knee.* "I see her."

Lucy crept across the wet cement. Why couldn't she hear that woman breathe? The only sound came from the drip of water in a corner she couldn't see.

Lucy placed the lantern next to her patient. Yellow light bathed the two of them; large black shadows danced across the wall. She knelt and held the light to the woman's face; then she saw her head.

"Oh, no." Lucy almost choked. A halo of blood surrounded the woman's head.

Oh, Lord. She sat back on her heels and felt for a pulse; it was hardly there. *There's nothing I can do for this poor lady, but maybe…Lord, please help me.* Lucy turned to look for the baby. *It looks like her water's broken and she's dilated.* Lucy reached inside of her and felt a foot.

Lord Jesus, I need your help.

"What's wrong?" *Padre*'s voice floated down from above.

"The woman's going to die." She felt her pulse again. "No, she's dead. Father, the baby's breached. I'll do my best, but this is in the Lord's hands," Lucy called back.

Lucy fumbled through her medical bag.

Quickly, Lucille. She pulled out her knife and immersed it in alcohol. She made a quick incision in the woman's abdomen. Blood and water leaked from the cut. Lucy reached in and felt for the baby. It moved.

Thank you, Lord!

"The baby's still alive!" She shouted up at the Priest. "It's a boy!" Lucy pulled the infant from its mother and cut the umbilical cord. She tied it with string, dabbed it with alcohol and then cleaned him with the hanky Giovanni had given her that afternoon.

"Come on, little one, breathe!" She cleaned out his mouth, massaged his little chest and then gave him a smack on the bottom. The tiny boy sucked in his first breath and started to cry.

The ground began to vibrate and then to rumble. A shower of plaster fell on top of them. *Lord save us.* Lucy covered the infant with her body.

"Lucy*?"*

"I'm fine Padre." She grabbed the shawl off the baby's mother and wrapped him in it. Then she noticed a locket around the woman's neck. With a quick yank, the chain gave easily. Lucy stuffed it in her pocket.

She rose to her feet with the baby in her arms, turned off the lamp and left it behind. She grabbed her bag and ran to the place directly under the opening overhead.

"Pull me up!" The rope tightened and then her feet left the ground. Up they went toward the fresh air. Father Dominic took the infant from her hands and the men pulled Lucy to safety.

Laughing with relief, Lucy and Father Dominic loaded onto the cart, baby and all. They turned the mule's head toward home.

A deafening crash from behind them made Lucy jump.

The remains of the building collapsed sealing the infant's mother in a tomb of mortar.

Lucy's tiny watch read 12:47 when the pair returned to the hospital with the baby. The soft yellow light from the hanging lamps gave the place a peaceful and friendly feel.

Lucy let out a sigh, glad to be back. She found Giovanni in the recovery room, sitting on the edge of a cot, just finished with his last patient. When he spotted her, the relief in his weary smile warmed her heart.

"We lost the mother." Lucy touched the baby's little face and then handed him to a nun.

"I was getting concerned. You were gone a long time." He tucked a blanket around his patient and then turned slightly.

"I know. I'm sorry, I didn't mean to worry you. The woman had fallen into a basement. I had to climb down to get to her."

Giovanni stiffened and pulled back. His eyes turned black.

Lucy stiffened too. A cold chill went down her spine. She had to think a moment before she could speak. "I was completely safe. I had a rope around me the whole time."

"*Santa Maria.*" Giovanni rubbed his forehead. "I said no trees." He walked to the door of the operating room. "We need to talk." He held the flap aside so Lucy could walk through it. Once they were alone, he wheeled around to face her.

CHAPTER FIFTEEN

"Let me see if I understand you correctly," he said, in a low steely voice. "Going against a direct order from me, you climbed down into the basement of an unstable building to save a woman who was already dead?" His piercing glare made Lucy want to recoil, but just a minute... She had good reason to go down there.

"I didn't know what condition she was in." Lucy put her hands on her hips. "When we called to her, she was moaning. She *was* pregnant, you know. I had to do a cesarean section to save the baby. Giovanni, you would have done the same thing. As a matter of fact, you've *done* the same thing. What was I supposed to do just let him die?"

"I know I've taken chances too. I'm glad the baby was saved." He took two deep breaths. "The point is that you did something I asked you not to do. You put your life at risk. What if that building had collapsed? Do you really think a rope would have saved you?"

The echo of the falling mortar sounded through her memory, and she shivered.

"I-it did collapse." *Uh oh, that was the wrong thing to say.* "But Giovanni look at me—I'm fine!"

"*What*?" Giovanni grew deathly quiet. His jaw tightened and his fingers wrapped into a fist. "You could have been killed."

"I'm prepared to take that chance," Lucy snapped.

"*No*!" Giovanni roared. He pounded his fist on the counter with such force that a tray of instruments jumped. "That is *not* an acceptable answer! *I* am in charge here; *you* do nothing unless *I* tell you. You do not take chances with your life. Do you understand?"

Lucy backed away and started to tremble. She'd known he had a temper, but this! After what they shared just that afternoon?

Giovanni examined her face. She looked him straight in the eye. She'd never reveal her heart to him again.

His gaze went to blood on her skirt and her shaking hands. Lucy stuffed them in her pockets.

"What happened to your leg?" His voice demanded but his features softened.

"I hit a rock on the way down." Lucy looked at her skirt too. The sudden urge to sob took her by surprise. "I haven't had a chance to look at it yet."

"*I* will look at it. Sit. Down." He pointed at the operating table.

Lucy trembled so. And now that he'd mentioned it, her knee really hurt. She tried to scooch up on the table but somehow her coordination had vanished. Maybe she should find her stool.

Giovanni closed his eyes from either regret or frustration, who could tell? "Let me help you." His voice was rough, but at least he'd stopped yelling.

Lucy let Giovanni lift her by the waist and set her on the table. How could he be so gentle and so angry at the same time? She bit her lower lip.

He pulled up a stool and sat. Giovanni rolled up her skirt and put her hand on the hem. "Hold this."

He looked up at her, his eyes still black. "This is the knee you scraped this afternoon."

Lucy nodded, she'd *not* let herself cry. Tears filled her eyes. *How can I be so emotional? Lucille, this has got to stop*. She waited until Giovanni looked down and then quickly wiped away the evidence.

"Your knee is packed with dirt." Giovanni's jaw tightened again. "*Lucia*, this is going to hurt and there is nothing I can do about it." He put her hand on his shoulder. "Squeeze me if you need to."

Like I'm a sissy. "Do what you have to, I'll be all right." Lucy sat rigid. She kept her hand where he had placed it. He was right. This was gonna hurt.

She grabbed him and sucked in when he began to probe and scrape her cut with a pair of small tweezers.

He flushed it with alcohol and Lucy nearly lost her breath. From the corner of her eye, she saw Giovanni glance at her. She knew that look; he was concerned? He finished with a spray of carbolic acid. "I think we can get by with four stitches." Giovanni double-checked the wound.

This would be the worst part. Lucy closed her eyes and then squeezed his shoulder at the first stab of the needle, her leg moved by reflex.

Giovanni placed her foot on his knee to steady her. "Almost over." He encouraged her with a rub, his voice gentle.

Lucy nodded, but kept her eyes closed. Hopefully he'd finish soon. *Lord please, help me through this. I don't want him to see me cry. I knew better than to trust him.*

"*Finito*." Giovanni had to lighten things up again. In his life, he'd never lost his temper like that and he regretted it. He tied the bandage in place. What could he say to make her laugh?

Lucy jumped off the table and left the room.

Giovanni grew still. If only he hadn't yelled at her. If only…

Father Dominic pushed his way through the flap wearing the kind of expression Giovanni had only seen a few times.

"I could hear you yelling all the way outside. Have you lost your senses?‽" The priest frowned. "That young woman has taken the same Hippocratic Oath as you. She fully understood what could have happened tonight and she made a tough decision. You were way out of line."

"I know." Giovanni looked down at his feet. He fidgeted with the corner of his apron.

"You've been extremely hard on her ever since she came here! I've never seen you act this way. She's only been out of medical school, how long is it?"

"Just under a year."

"I think she's held up beautifully, considering how you've treated her. It's a wonder she hasn't gone back to Rome. You're not a cruel person. What's the problem?"

Giovanni searched his heart for a good answer but found none. He merely hung his head.

"Is she not capable?"

"No." Giovanni looked up at the priest. "She is extremely capable."

"Is it because she's a woman?"

"In the beginning, but now, no..."

"Then why, Giovanni? Why would you yell at her like that?"

"I did worse than yell at her."

"What did you do?" Father Dominic squared his shoulders.

"I frightened her." Giovanni forced himself to look at the priest again. "I have never frightened a woman in my entire life. I don't understand it, *Padre*. I was so relieved to see her walk into the tent. But then she told me what she had done, what happened to the building. The thought that *Lucia* could have been killed tonight….it sent me over the edge. I can't believe I exploded that way. I…"

"Stop beating yourself up." Father Dominic rubbed the back of Giovanni's head. "Go apologize. Lucy will forgive you."

"I hope you're right. I don't see how." Giovanni stood to his feet and took off his apron.

"Give her a few minutes." Father Dominic led Giovanni to the door and pulled back the flap. In the far end of the tent, a dying soldier lay on a cot. Lucy sat with his hand in hers. She washed his dirty forehead with a cloth.

"Is that the man who came for dinner?" Giovanni whispered.

"Yes, Officer Jackson. They just brought him in," Father Dominic said. "He was asking for her. I think he wanted to make things right."

Giovanni closed his eyes. It felt as though a knife had gone through his heart.

Lucy held the young man's hands and prayed for him. She folded them on his chest and pulled the sheet over his face.

"She'll be all right." Father Dominic kept his voice low. "God is with Lucy. She knows where her strength comes from; she'll draw it from Him."

Then the priest turned toward Giovanni with the oddest expression on his face.

Father Dominic looked first at Lucy and then again at Giovanni. He closed the flap and then pointed his finger at Giovanni's chest. "You're in love with her."

Giovanni's heart felt as though it stopped. "No... I'll admit I've grown very fond of her..."

"And if Lucy were to go back to Rome tomorrow?" Father Dominic crossed his arms and looked down his nose.

Giovanni caught his breath. "But she's promised to work with me." Did that come out of his own mouth?

"What if she went all the way back to America and you might never see her again?" The priest smiled slightly.

No, Lucia. Something akin to fear fingered its way through his soul. "I would have to find her," Giovanni whispered.

He peeked at Lucy through the flap, now aware of the pain in his heart. "How can I be in love? I've known her a total of two months."

"You've been together for eighteen hours a day, seven days a week, under extremely grueling circumstances. I'd say that's enough time to fall in love." Father Dominic watched her, too.

Giovanni thought back over every encounter he'd had with her since they had met. He could remember minute detail.

"You are in love with her, aren't you?" Father Dominic put a hand on Giovanni's arm.

Giovanni stared at the ground. His heart thumped loudly in his chest. His breath felt labored and the room too warm. He spotted Lucy's stool in the corner and he wanted to take back every cross word he had ever said to her. He ran a hand through his black hair and then looked back up at the priest. "I think you're right."

"Does Lucy know how you feel?"

Giovanni's heart sank. "After tonight? There's no way."

Lucy left the recovery room and Giovanni followed quietly behind. He paused long enough to look at the little orphan, in his cradle, and touch tiny fingers. How brave *Lucia* had been tonight.

Thank you for keeping them safe. Giovanni prayed. Did he believe? Or didn't he? He couldn't be sure.

He would give her a moment to escape; time to seek her God. He knew where she'd go. The door-table had become their unintentional space.

He walked in silence to the mess tent and melted at what he saw.

Her head lay on the table, cradled in her arms. Her dark red braid, almost completely undone, fell across her shoulders and down her back.

He watched her weep and then she prayed.

"*Lord, I know what I did was right. I'm tired of people telling me what to do. I'm so tired of being yelled at for no good reason. And tonight; I've never seen him so angry. Why do I even try? I give up. I'll go back to Rome. Daddy will be happy, Giovanni will be happy. Who cares how I feel about anything? Okay, I know you care. But that's why I come to you.*" Lucy sniffed, her head still in her arms.

How many times have I made her cry? His hand squeezed into a fist, then he squared his shoulders. *This will never happen again.*

He made his way to where she sat and stroked her beautiful hair. She gave a start under his hand and he wanted to beg for forgiveness. She turned to him and he knew what she felt.

"Don't go back to Rome." Giovanni pleaded, in a near whisper. "Stay here. Work with me."

"Why? Will you yell at me?" Her voice sounded tight from crying.

"I might." That should make her smile.

Lucy would not look at him.

"May I sit with you?" He'd keep trying.

"No." Lucy hugged herself and looked away.

Giovanni pulled a chair next to her and sat. "That army doctor was a turtle." He turned a bit toward Lucy. Would that work? She wouldn't lift her eyes.

"The baby is beautiful." *Please, Lucia, say something.*

Lucy pulled out the locket and put it on the table. "This was his mother's. At least he'll have something to remember her by."

Giovanni picked it up and opened it. Inside, the locket held a tiny picture of a smiling couple. "See, he'll know what they looked like."

Lucy nodded. Eyes full of tears, she looked very much like she needed to cry again.

If only he could hold her. "*Lucia*," he said in his softest voice.

She looked away.

"*Lucia*." Giovanni touched his fingers to her hand.

Lucy turned to him but she pulled her hand away. Stabbing him would have hurt no less. He must make amends.

"I never should have yelled at you." Giovanni paused to let his words sink in. "Not tonight or any other time. The decision you made to save that little boy's life was a good one. I was wrong to blow up the way I did."

Tears began to roll down Lucy's cheeks again, but she continued to look at him. "You hurt me."

"I know." Giovanni hoped she could see his heart. "I know I hurt you. Even worse, I know I frightened you. I cannot begin to express how deeply I regret it."

Giovanni reached his hand slowly to Lucy's face, afraid she would recoil again.

He wiped a tear. How fragile she felt under his fingertips. He had to keep talking before he started to cry, too.

"I didn't fully realize what I had sent you to do until you were running out the door. That's why I sent *Padre* to go with you. I would rather put myself in danger than to risk you. You were gone so much longer than I expected, I had the worst feeling that something was wrong. I was so uptight I yelled at that French doctor who was so rude to you. I even prayed. *Lucia*, it has been almost twenty years since I've prayed anything at all. When you came back, and I found out I might have lost you..." His voice cracked.

Giovanni drew a deep breath to steady himself. "We've seen so many horrible things. The idea of seeing you, broken, on that table in there...I couldn't take it. I exploded. I was angry at myself for letting you go and I took it out on you."

Giovanni released a heavy sigh. *Please.* "Can you ever forgive me?"

Lucy's eyes softened through her tears. What a miracle.

Padre, you're right. His heart gave a leap in his chest. If he could hand it to her right now, he would without hesitation. But first, he must make things right.

He asked again a little more softly. "*Lucia*, please forgive me."

Lucy started to sob. She shook her head, "Yes."

Giovanni put his arm around her and pulled her to his shoulder. She heaved as she wept and his arms tightened.

"I will never frighten you again," he whispered in her hair. "I'm so sorry." He kissed the top of her head. He held her gently, he comforted, he stroked her forehead, he waited for Lucy to calm down. She felt so right in his arms. Every time he held her, she felt the same way; as though she had always been a part of him.

Why did it take me so long to admit the truth? He pressed his cheek to her hair. *How am I ever going to tell you? How are you ever going to believe me after how I've treated you?*

Lucy's tears finally subsided she lifted her head, and looked up at Giovanni.

"You're crying too?" She stroked his face.

He almost kissed her fingers, but he smiled instead and moved a stray hair from her face. "You mean more to me than you realize."

Lucy sniffed.

Giovanni pulled a handkerchief from his pocket.

"Is it mine or yours?"

"Mine. See the initials?" He showed her the corner.

Lucy wiped her tears and blew her nose. She grinned and tried to hand it back.

Giovanni made a face of mock disgust. "Thank you, no. You can keep it. What happened to the one I gave you this afternoon?" Her smile made his heart so light.

"I used it to clean the baby."

"I see."

Lucy stuck the hankie in her pocket and laid her head back on Giovanni's shoulder; she snuggled into him like a child. Giovanni wrapped his arm around her, closed his eyes and savored the moment.

"You smell," she said.

"So do you." He wanted to laugh.

Lucy relaxed and her breathing became steady. Maybe she had fallen asleep.

"Did you really pray for me?"

"Yes."

"Does that mean…?"

"Don't jump to conclusions." He kissed the top of her head again.

Her breathing became steady once more.

"Are you still mad at me?" Lucy looked up from his chest; her puffy eyes sparkled.

"Yes." He smiled down at her.

"Maybe we should get some sleep before the sun comes up."

Giovanni stood and lifted Lucy to her feet. He tucked her under his arm and they walked to the door of the nurse's room.

"*Buonanotte, Lucia*," Giovanni said. *Buonanotte, amore,* his heart whispered. He gave her dirty forehead a tender kiss.

Lucy threw her arms around his waist and hugged him one more time. Giovanni hugged her back. If only he could hold her forever.

He forced himself to pull loose, turned her around by the shoulders and sent her through the door.

"You're still up?" *Padre* Dominic came from the direction of the recovery room. He paused next to Giovanni. "Well?"

"She forgave me." If Giovanni could fly, he would.

"And?" The priest cracked a smile.

"I love her." He wanted to shout it.

"You haven't told her yet, have you?"

"No. A thing like this shouldn't be done here." Giovanni could only think of one place to proclaim his love to *Lucia*.

"Good." Padre nodded. "Let's do some planning."

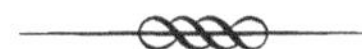

Father Dominic climbed from the cart and gave his faithful mule a good scratch on the shoulder. The animal snorted with pleasure, stretched his neck and stuck out his top lip. "That feels good doesn't it, boy? One day things will be normal again and I'll have a stall for you to rest in." He slipped the bit out of the mule's mouth and tied him to a pipe that stuck out of the mortar.

From the other side of the cart Father Dominic could see a pair of black sensible shoes and the hem of a long brown skirt.

Sister Francesca ducked under the mule's neck and gave him a pat. "Well?"

"The orphanage will take the baby and I left them at the temporary station on the north end of town."

"That's not what I meant." Sister Francesca looked up at him, her gray eyes intense.

"What did you mean then?" Father Dominic gave the mule a flake of hay. He knew exactly what the nun wanted, but took great pleasure out of making her say it.

"You know the saying," Sister Francesca tilted her head and raised an eyebrow. "No one ever goes to *Casa Bella* the first time unless God has brought them. Lucia will not come back the same."

"No, she won't come back the same, I certainly didn't and neither did you." Father Dominic put a hand on the mule's withers and looked down at the wrinkled old saint. "Neither, I think, will our wayward son."

"Even though he's lived there most of his life?"

"Yes, because now, I believe, he's ready to listen."

"I wish I could be a fly on the wall."

"So do I."

CHAPTER SIXTEEN

"Look at all the people." Lucy and Giovanni stepped from the train into the bustling Palermo station. She followed Giovanni through the crowd, toward the street.

"No one's injured, no one's naked. It's so good to see life again. Giovanni, thank you for making me come. I didn't realize how much I needed this."

The street took her breath away. Hansom cabs clip-clopped by, people on horse or mule or bicycle all going different directions without colliding. An occasional automobile drove by and added to the noise.

Cathedrals and towers older than her own country rose toward the strong yellow sun. Street vendors bartered noisily with shoppers whose arms were laden with purchases. Someone nearby was frying fish. *Mmm.* Her stomach grumbled. Lucy readjusted the baby in his basket.

"*Cerino,*" Giovanni yelled but his voice was drowned out by the city din.

He turned to Lucy. "Wait here." Giovanni pointed at the pavement then disappeared into the crowd.

Lucy stood alone with Max in his basket, at her feet, hidden among their bags.

A nice-looking young man approached her. He made eye contact with Lucy when he passed by. "*Che bella*." He smiled.

Oh my goodness. Lucy watched the stranger disappear into a building.

"*Signorinaaa.*" A masculine voice sang. A group of college students approached from the other direction. All five of them laughed and grinned. They elbowed each other and nodded their approval when they passed.

Yikes! Lucy picked up the baby to protect him. *Giovanni, where are you?* She tried to spy him in the sea of people.

"*Bellissima.*" A man peddled a bicycle and tipped his hat.

"*Lucia*," Giovanni shouted from her left. He jumped from a cab and came to her side.

Lucy grabbed his arm. "The men here keep talking to me. Why are they talking to me?" She held Max tight.

"Welcome to Sicily," Giovanni said with a smile. "Even in a dress like that, we know a pretty girl when we see one. If anyone pats you on the *anti-pasto*, let me know." He picked up the luggage. "Just stay close to me."

You betcha. Lucy edged in tight.

Giovanni gave the bags to the cab driver and took the baby from Lucy so she could get in.

"Giovanni, who is this?" the cabbie asked. "Have you been keeping a wife behind our backs?"

"She's a co-worker from Messina." Giovanni turned to Lucy. "*Lucia*, meet my friend Cerino. Cerino, the baby is an orphan. We need to go to the Benedictine orphanage *per favore*.

The cabbie nodded and watched Lucy with the same expression as the college students. "*Che bella*."

Lucy climbed in and sat as far in the corner as she could. Were all the men here so cavalier? Did Giovanni not see it?

Giovanni gave the cabbie a sharp look before he followed. He closed the cab door and sat across from Lucy.

"This is normal?" Lucy arranged her skirt. In all her years, no man had ever given a second glance. How awkward.

"Do you know what he said?" Giovanni smirked.

"Yes." Lucy crossed her arms."Why would he say a thing like that to a perfect stranger?"

"You don't believe him?"

Was he avoiding the question? "Giovanni, please, let's not start this now."

"Well, Max and I agree with him, don't we, Max?" He cooed to the little boy in his arms. "The men in America must be blind as bats."

Lucy's heart grew warm and she fought a smile. Aunt Lucinda would be mortified. Maybe a threat would hide her pleasure. "If you weren't holding that baby I might be tempted to sock you."

"*That* is why I'm holding the baby. But you can still sock me if you like, whatever that means. I won't mind. Oh, we're here."

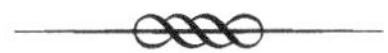

Lucy followed Giovanni to the door while Cerino waited for them. He pulled the rope on the bell and a kind-faced woman dressed in full habit came out.

The nun led them into the nursery of the orphanage; a warm, beautiful room with rich wooden floors.

"We'll keep him safe." The nun turned to Lucy. "Are you the one who saved him?"

Lucy felt heat in her cheeks and she found it hard to speak.

"Yes, sister," Giovanni answered for her. "Dr. James saved Max's life."

Lucy nodded a little too enthusiastically and then handed Max to the nun.

"If you'd like to see the church, the door around the corner is open. Stay as long as you like." The nun showed them to the door. She laid her hand on Lucy and then Giovanni. "The Lord be with you."

"I don't know why I couldn't answer her." Lucy's her eyes filled with tears. "I'm going to miss that little boy."

Giovanni pulled Lucy into a gentle hug with one arm. He leaned his cheek to her head. "Max will have a good life. He couldn't be in better hands. And *you* are not alone, nuns used to do that to me when I was a boy. Eventually you get used to them."

"But I'm not uncomfortable around Sister Francesca."

"Yes, but family is different."

"But she's not my…"

He took her by the hand and nodded in the direction of the church. "Come with me. I know you'd like to see this church from the inside."

Giovanni led Lucy back outside and around the corner. He must have been there before, because he knew exactly where he to go.

He opened the door and led Lucy into an extraordinary church with a high arched ceiling, ornately painted with scenes from the Bible. At the far end, over the altar, hung a life-sized crucifix. The place was so peaceful after the chaos of Messina, she wanted to soak in the profound silence.

"Do you mind if we stay a moment?" Her whisper sounded like a shout.

"That's why I brought you," Giovanni whispered back. He guided her to a pew close to the altar.

Lucy had to put all of her weight on one knee so that she could kneel without tearing her stitches but she managed just fine. She prayed for a little while and then sat back in the pew and closed her eyes. Contented, she sighed and turned to Giovanni. Completely still, he stared off at… what? His eyes were wide and then he gave a quick look at the crucifix.

"Are you all right?"

He nodded, but he still didn't focus on anything in particular.

"Are you ready?" Hmm. He didn't seem to hear. Lucy put her hand on his arm to get his attention.

"Yes," He answered, still staring at something she couldn't see. Then he focused on her. Surely something about him had changed. "Come, on, let's go to Casa Bella."

The drive through the Sicilian countryside seemed an adventure through a flower-filled wonderland. The farther away from the city she went, the more beautiful it became. Everything; every tree, every bush, every blade of grass answered the call of spring and filled the air with fragrance. Then the land became more rolling and in the distance she could see…

"Are those olive trees?" Lucy perched on the edge of her seat. There must be hundreds; all lined up in perfect rows as far as the eye could see. Through the trees, in the distance a grand home stood, framed in the background by a rock hill covered in cypress trees.

"Yes. Our property starts here." Giovanni pointed. "Most farmers choose to live in town and come to work on their farm every day. Just on the other side of that hill is the village of *Castello Nuovo*. Many of our workers come from that town. I'll show it to you sometime."

The cab made a left turn into a long drive lined with willowy almond trees; their blossoms almost gone, taken over by tiny green leaves. At the end, sat the magnificent, sprawling Italian mansion surrounded by a stone courtyard. The entire structure was made of gray stone, topped with green terracotta tile. They drove under a large arch from which hung an ornate, black iron gate.

The gate opened to a wide circular drive with a three-tiered fountain in the middle, topped by a lion that spilled water from its mouth to the fish down below. To the left of the house sat a large coach house and stables, to the right an extensive vineyard and orchard. The cab pulled up to stone steps that led to the massive, wooden front door.

Lucy felt so light-headed. Had the world begun to spin?

Giovanni helped her from the cab. "Welcome to my home, *Lucia*. Welcome to *Casa Bella*."

"When you said your home was large I thought I could imagine it, but I was wrong." Lucy looked down at her faded uniform. "Giovanni, I'm not dressed well enough…"

"Don't be silly, you look just like I do. Besides, *Mamma* will see *you*, not your clothes. They don't know we're coming. Let's have some fun."

"Wait a minute." Lucy grabbed his arm. "They're not expecting us?"

"No." He shrugged. "But I know Mamma would love to meet you. Come."

Lucy followed, her stomach in knots.

Giovanni opened the front door and put his forefinger to his lips. They slipped inside, left their bags in the foyer, and stepped into the great room.

Lucy found it hard to breathe; the place looked like a museum. The great room stood a full two stories high. Arched windows lined the entire back wall, stretching from the floor to the ceiling. They overlooked first a large patio, then the olive groves and made the room feel like it was part of the rolling countryside. A grand staircase of black marble adorned the back wall starting at one of the windows; it climbed to a balcony and archway that must lead to sleeping chambers.

"Come," Giovanni, said again, this time with barely a sound.

He pulled her toward the far end of the cavernous room, to the black grand piano just beneath the balcony. On the wall, next to the piano, a fireplace big enough to stand in met Lucy's eye. Above the mantle hung the crest of the Castello family, exactly like the one in Messina. Only this one, twice as large and obviously the original, looked very old. To the left and right of the crest several jewel-encrusted swords graced the wall.

She followed Giovanni across marble tile of black and white and sat in a red-brocaded chair, just behind the piano.

Giovanni began to play a compelling melody.

Her eyebrows went up."You play beautifully. What song is this?"

He hesitated. "*Santa Lucia*. I've been singing it in my head ever since you came. I hope you're ready."

"For what?" Lucy scanned the empty room. What could possibly happen?

"You'll see."

Uh, oh.

The door burst open and what looked like herd of people came running in.

Jehoshaphat! It's an army! Lucy wanted to duck behind the piano.

All of Giovanni's family; brothers, sisters-in-law, nieces and nephews surrounded him all at once.

"Giovanni's home! *Evviva*! Giovanni!" The children piled on top of him hugging and kissing.

He stood smiling ear to ear and the children slid to the floor around his feet, except for a small girl who had latched her arms around his neck like a spider monkey. Giovanni hugged everyone one at a time.

"Who's that?" A small voice rose above the commotion. The room fell silent and everyone turned to look at Lucy.

Oh dear. Lucy swallowed and managed a shaky smile.

"Everyone," Giovanni gave a sweep of his hand, "this is *Lucia* James. She is a doctor from America and she's my friend."

He pulled her out from her hiding place. "*Lucia*, meet my family; Michael and Adella and their children, Michael, Filippo, Pietro and Teresa. And, *this* is Antonio and Celeste and *their* children Elisabetta, Ricardo, Guglielmo and Maria."

No one made a sound for five full ticks of the grandfather clock.

She had to break the ice somehow. Lucy took a deep breath and gathered her courage. "I think I have it. Michael, Adella, Michael, Filippo, Teresa and Pietro." She pointed to each person. "Antonio and Celeste, Elisabetta, Ricardo, Guglielmo and Maria."

"*Brava*, she did it." The family burst into applause. Children quickly surrounded her, jumping and cheering. Lucy shook their hands at first and finally gave in to their hugs and kisses.

"Where are *Mamma* and *Papà*?" Giovanni set Maria on her feet.

"They should be right behind us," Michael said. "We heard you playing; of course we knew right away who it was."

"Here she comes." Ricardo knelt on a chair and looked out the window.

Giovanni took a step toward the door. Should she follow?

He leaned back and grabbed her hand. "It is all right. They love you. I knew they would." He dragged Lucy with him.

The crowd followed.

The back door opened and Rosa Castello entered the room followed by her husband. She searched the crowd of people and a smile lit her face; her laugh lines disappeared and her soft gray eyes sparkled with tears.

"Giovanni!" Rosa grabbed her son and kissed him. "I've prayed for your safety every day. *Grazie a Dio, sei la casa.*"

"*Ti voglio bene, Mamma.*" He kissed his mother and hugged her gently.

Lucy's heart grew warm.

"*Benvenuto a casa, figlio.*" Giovanni's father patted him on the back and with the grace of a nobleman, pulled him into a strong embrace.

Then Rosa focused on Lucy. She touched her husband's hand and her kind, round face glowed both with hope and curiosity. "Are you not going to introduce your beautiful friend?" His mother looked from Lucy to Papa with an approving nod.

His father looked at Lucy with the same air of confidence as his son. His face softened. No doubt they would make her welcome. But…

Oh, boy. They think we're together. Lucy opened her mouth to explain. Giovanni wrapped his arm around her shoulder and pushed her forward.

"*Mamma*, Papa, meet *Lucia* James from America. *Lucia*, these are my parents." He gave a formal sweep of his hand.

What would be proper, a curtsy? If only Lucy had listened more closely to Aunt Lucinda.

But Rosa Castello grabbed her by the shoulders. "You had to go all the way to America to find a girl?"

"*What?*" Lucy mouthed to him just before his mother pulled her into a strong hug.

"*Benvenuta bambina.*" Rosa kissed Lucy on the lips, then held her at arm's length. "Giovanni, she's so skinny. Haven't you been feeding her?"

Everyone burst into laughter and Lucy couldn't help but relax.

"What a warm home you have." Lucy followed Giovanni up the stairs. "You never told me how wonderful your family is."

"I'm glad you feel welcome." He made a turn down a long hallway with polished floors and crimson carpet. "It wasn't until I spent time in London that I truly grew to appreciate the warmth of an Italian home.

Who knows, maybe one day I'll meet your family." They passed a couple of bedrooms, one done in greens, another in blues.

Lucy put her hands on her hips. "Your mother thinks *we* are together and you let her."

Giovanni paused in front of a door with a glass knob. "What's wrong with that? My family knows I would never bring a woman to my home unless I was serious about her. This is your room," he said, in the same breath.

Lucy felt that he meant to distract her. It worked. He led her inside and set her bags on a chair.

"If you need me I will be right across the hall." He pointed. "The bathroom, I'm afraid we'll need to share."

"Oh my, a bathtub." She sighed "It's been months since we've had a normal bath."

"I should warn you." He chuckled. "We're a very open family and my nieces love a bubble bath. If you don't lock the door you may find that you have visitors."

"I'll lock it." Lucy remembered the fascination that she had with bubbles as a child.

"We have just enough time to freshen up. Supper is at seven. That gives you about forty-five minutes." Giovanni gave Lucy a kiss on the top of her head and then closed the door behind him.

Lucy stood quietly in her room. She didn't want to touch a thing.

The dark hardwood floor had been polished to a high sheen and covered with a honey brown oriental rug that ran almost to the walls. On the rug sat a handsomely carved mahogany sleigh bed with crisp white sheets trimmed in lace and a wonderfully fluffy, ice blue satin down comforter on top. Piles of pillows covered the bed and the two comfy chairs with a lamp and table between them invited her to read. One wall had a beautiful brass fireplace with a marble mantle. Against another stood a hand-carved dresser topped with more marble and an ornate gold leaf mirror. After two months in Messina, this room was a little overwhelming.

Lucy unpacked the one nice skirt and blouse she'd had in Messina. She pulled the periwinkle blue skirt from her bag and gave it a shake, then unwrapped her white lace blouse from its paper and smelled it.

Good, you're still fresh, too.

The events of last night ran through her mind while she dressed. How grueling it had been, but what a wonderful team they had become. She remembered the look of relief on Giovanni's face when she came back to the hospital carrying baby Max.

Lucy stooped to put her shoes back on and felt her knee. She smiled again, this time at the memory of their fight and the sweet apology from Giovanni.

He really was afraid for me. Lucy sat on the bed and looked at her reflection in the mirror. If she closed her eyes, she could still feel his warm lips on her forehead.

Her eyes flew open.

I can't think this way. We're just friends. We're colleagues. The memory of his words at the door drew her hands to her cheeks.

Lord he can't possibly mean that he's serious about me in that way. Please help me control my heart. I've never met anyone like him, but if he doesn't serve you, I can't even consider him, no matter how much I want to.

She stood to straighten her skirt and figure out what to do with her hair. *I think I can remember how make a French braid.* Lucy worked with her unruly mess until it at least appeared to be tangle free and tied her ribbon to hold everything in place. She held up a hand mirror and turned around to review her work. How funny it felt to actually pay attention to her appearance. This was the first time she could remember ever caring, except for the dance at the American Embassy. But Olivia Drake had helped her then. *I wish she were here now. I wish I had someone to teach me how to be pretty. Well, this is the best I can do. If I look funny, I can't help it. He'll just have to accept me for who I am.*

A knock at the door startled Lucy out of her thoughts. She opened it and found Giovanni standing on the other side. He looked like a new man. He had on simple dark trousers, a white linen shirt and a black tie. His black hair fell softly around his freshly shaven face. The stark white of his shirt, against his olive skin and dark features made his appearance even more striking. He smiled at her and Lucy saw something in his eyes that made her heart flutter.

"*Come sei bella*. You should wear your hair like that more often." He offered her his arm.

Why did his compliments make her feel like hiding? "When did you become so sweet?" Lucy slipped her hand into the crook of his strong arm.

"I've always been this way."

"To whom? Your mother?" She laughed.

"Yes."

The formal dining room had a feeling of family. Portraits and photographs detailing the Castello family life hung along the walls. A massive oval table of heavy mahogany was covered by more food than Lucy had seen in months.

"Oh, my. I thought you said supper was a light meal."

"It is," said Giovanni. "Wait until you see the midday table."

He helped Lucy into the chair next to his, then sat.

"Giovanni," his mother said. "Will you say the blessing?"

Lucy tried not to grin as she watched Giovanni out of the corner of her eye.

He gave her a smug look and began without hesitation. "In the name of the Father, the Son and the Holy Ghost, Amen. Bless us, oh Lord and these, Thy gifts, which we are about to receive, from Thy bounty through Christ our Lord, Amen."

"Well done," she whispered.

Out of the corner of his mouth, Giovanni said, "*Never* argue with my mother."

"*Signorina* James." Papa Castello smiled in her direction. He had gray eyes too and salt and pepper hair in soft loose curls. He must have been as handsome as his sons in his youth. "We'd like to know you better. What will you tell us?"

"Please everyone, call me *Lucia*. Let me see. I grew up in a small town just outside of Boston, Massachusetts. I have two brothers, Fredrick and Maxwell. My father is a physician and so is my brother, Fredrick. "

"And you have been working in Messina with Giovanni. Is that how you met?" Giovanni's brother Michael helped Pietro with his napkin.

"No." Lucy smiled at the memory. "Actually we met in Rome, at the American Embassy."

"At the Embassy ball in December?" Giovanni's mother turned abruptly her eyebrow raised.

"Yes, at the ball." Lucy fingered her silver fork and then picked it up.

"This is the woman you danced with?" Rosa looked her son in the eye. "I had a feeling there was more than what you wrote me."

What? Lucy shot a surprised look of disbelief at Giovanni.

"Yes, *Mamma*. Didn't I tell you she was beautiful?"

Rosa gave a warm smile. "Yes, you did and you were right."

Lucy quickly popped a *rigatoni* in her mouth and looked away.

"One day you will believe me," Giovanni whispered in her ear.

"When Giovanni introduced you, he said you're a doctor. What does that mean?" Antonio looked up from his food.

Michael answered before Lucy could speak. "She is not really a doctor. You are a mid-wife or a specialized nurse; am I right?"

Lucy smiled patiently. "I am a full-fledged doctor. I graduated from the Medical University of Boston almost a year ago."

Michael Sr. shifted in his chair. Antonio cleared his throat. The clock on the mantle chimed the half hour.

"You're a doctor?" Little Teresa broke the silence.

"Yes, I'm a doctor." Lucy smiled at the beautiful girl.

"Women don't become doctors." Young Michael frowned.

"Michael," his mother scolded softly. "Your manners."

"Are you really a doctor?" Teresa licked the back of her spoon.

"Yes," Giovanni said. He then addressed his family. "*Lucia* is a doctor, just like me. She is as fine a surgeon as I have ever met."

"How wonderful." Michael's wife Adella sat up in her chair. "Finally, a woman doctor to work with women. I would no longer dread examinations."

Her husband nodded and relaxed.

"I do have a lot of women patients." Lucy kept her tone gracious. "But I have men patients as well."

"She practices medicine on men?" Michael turned to Giovanni.

"Yes, every day."

"And you let her?"

"Yes."

"Giovanni, it's unnatural. She's so young, not even married. For her to be examining male patients goes against the laws of nature, the laws of God even."

Giovanni laughed. "That's ridiculous. Not only do I let her, she's so talented that I've asked *Lucia* to work with me at my practice in

Messina. As for going against the laws of God, she is not fornicating. *Lucia* is saving lives."

"Giovanni, your language." Rosa frowned at him.

"But, *Mamma*, that's what Michael is accusing her of."

"I am not." Michael wiped his mouth quickly. "However, no woman should examine a man, especially one who is single."

"Despite what you believe, I think God approves of what *Lucia* does. In fact, I think He gave her the gift of healing." Giovanni calmly took a sip of water.

No one but Lucy saw the look of wonder on Rosa's face.

"But she's a woman." Michael put both hands on the table this time.

Would the whole family enter the argument? Lucy watched wide-eyed. Yes; except Rosa who seemed to referee. No one really shouted, but when Michael all but came across the table at Giovanni, Lucy lost her appetite. Those poor children. She gave a quick glance across the table; they had to be upset too. But, no; happy as clams amidst the fray, they kept right on eating as though this was the most peaceful, quiet dinner table in Palermo.

How could she stop this? What could she do? Lucy put her fork down.

Rosa grabbed her husband's hand and nodded toward Lucy.

"Enough, everyone. Let it go Michael." Papa gave Lucy a comforting smile. "*Lucia*, please forgive us. We're an open family and often debate around the dinner table. We've not had such a fine topic in a long time. Even so, we should have been more sensitive."

"It's quite all right." Lucy cleared her throat. "I now see where Giovanni gets his love of argument."

"I wouldn't want a woman doctor to examine me," Young Michael said.

"Why not?" Giovanni turned to his nephew. "*Lucia* has taken care of many boys just your age in Messina. I saw her do it."

"I would be too embarrassed." Michael looked down at his fingers.

"He thinks she's pretty." Pietro snickered.

"She *is* pretty." Teresa kicked her feet.

"It's nothing." Giovanni raised an eyebrow toward Lucy, as if he had proven his point. "I hurt my ribs several weeks ago and *Lucia* fixed me. I had to let her examine me to do it. If she can fix me, she can fix you."

"Giovanni, stop." Lucy touched his arm to make him listen.

Giovanni gave her a mischievous smile.

"Don't worry, *Lucia*," Antonio said to her from behind his right hand. "We know he likes to exaggerate."

"Giovanni, you got hurt?" Rosa leaned forward.

"And *Lucia* fixed me. Let me tell you what happened."

Giovanni shared—with great relish—the story of the earthquake and the fallen tent. By the time he finished, the children thought Lucy was some kind of heroine.

She kicked Giovanni under the table. He laughed and spilled his food.

"I like her," Antonio said to Michael while their brother wiped his spill.

"What I want to know," Lucy leaned forward. "is how all of you speak such beautiful English. And your manners, I've never seen children so well-behaved at dinner and so adept at conversation."

The children all sat up a little straighter.

"The Castello family has spoken English for a long time," Giovanni said. "We speak Spanish and French as well. Their schooling will be quite extensive before they're grown. And manners?" He challenged the children. "Who teaches manners?"

"*Nonna*," they said together. Maria pointed at Rosa.

"I hope they didn't offend you." Giovanni escorted Lucy back upstairs. He paused at her bedroom door.

"No. They're very sweet. I love your parents, and the children. What beautiful children. And you." She crossed her arms. "You're a completely different creature around these people. I had no idea that you could be such a rascal. I love seeing this side of you. Thank you for bringing me here."

"Thank you for coming." Giovanni stepped a bit closer. "To Sicilians, home and family are sacred. These are the people I love most in the world. I'll be myself around them before I will anyone else. I am very sorry though, that I have not been myself around you."

Lucy kissed his cheek and his eyes softened.

"It's okay. You're forgiven, remember?" Lucy put her hand on the doorknob. "What time do we need to head into town tomorrow? Is the hospital far?"

"Let's take it easy in the morning. We can be ready around ten if that's all right." He looked, for a moment, toward his bedroom door as though he remembered something. "Actually, I was thinking about giving you the choice of going with Papa and me in the Ford or staying here and relaxing. You don't have to answer now. Let me know in the morning."

Lucy nodded.

"In the meantime, we both need to bathe. You take your bath first. That will give me a chance to visit with my parents. You can have the freedom to do what you do." He waved his hand toward her Bible on the bed. "Do you want me to look at your knee?"

"I think I can manage." Lucy rather regretted her answer.

"There's one more thing." Giovanni smiled suddenly. "I have a gift for you. Wait here." He stepped inside his bedroom, returning with a small book, which he handed to Lucy. "This is to commemorate your first visit to the Castello home."

"I love books." Lucy beamed. She turned it over to see the cover, it said *Demeter and Persephone*. "I love this story."

"I remembered your fondness for mythology. This is one of the books that helped me learn to speak English. Enjoy it." He touched her cheek lightly with his fingers.

"Thank you, Giovanni. How thoughtful." Lucy kissed his cheek again. How comfortable she felt with him…too comfortable.

Then he caught her gaze with his own and she couldn't move.

A warm light filled his eyes and for a moment she felt that he might want to kiss her. Or, maybe, she wanted to kiss him. That must be it. He said himself that he only saw her as a sister. How could it be possible that a man as sophisticated and handsome as this one would want to kiss a tom-boy?

But then his soft hand stroked up her arm. He pulled her closer and she let him. She could feel his warm breath and see the depth in his eyes. It was too much, too close. No one had ever looked at her this way and she began to tremble.

Giovanni took a deep breath. He closed his eyes, lingered a kiss on her cheek and then turned to head down the stairs.

"Wait." Lucy drew a shaky breath. "You told your family that God gave me the gift of healing. Is that what you really think?"

Giovanni stopped and looked back at her with the oddest expression. He shrugged as though nothing was out of the ordinary. "When have you ever known me to say anything other than what I think?"

"But…"

"*Buonanotte, Lucia*." He retreated down the stairs.

She put her hand over the place he had kissed. Her hands still trembled. Then she remembered the gift in her hand. She stroked the small book and opened the cover. On the left page, Giovanni Castello had scrawled his name as a child.

She must control her emotions. Nothing between them had changed. She'd have to write to him when she got back to the States. Lucy put the book on the nightstand next to her bed. "I'll read you later, but first the tub."

Lucy slipped out of her skirt and blouse and hung them in the closet. On a hook behind the closet door, she found a fluffy full-length bathrobe intended for visitors.

"These people think of everything." Lucy put on the robe and threw her nightgown over her arm.

She opened her bedroom door and headed for the bathroom. A deep, claw-foot tub sat under a small window on a floor of shiny black and white tile. She giggled and turned on the hot water to fill the tub. A jar of bath salts caught her eye. *Lavender*. She sprinkled some in the tub and turned the water off.

Lucy took the bandage off her knee; bruised and swollen, but healing nicely. She stuck one toe in the water and then eased her way into the tub, careful to settle down so her knee would not get wet. Utter contentment escaped on a sigh. She washed her hair and pinned it to the top of her head. Lucy leaned back, closed her eyes and propped her knee against the side of the tub.

A spring breeze touched the room through the opened window. Soft talking and laughter filtered up from the patio below. The strums from a mandolin floated by.

Thank you, Father, so much for this. You have given me a rest even when I didn't think to ask for one. She prayed for her family and for the

Castello's and her mind went to the people of Messina. *Somehow, I feel as though you want me to stay.*

Lavender steam filled her senses and the music from the mandolin carried her away.

A shaft of brilliant sunlight inched its way across the room. It reflected in the mirror and shone through the large crystal that hung against the windowpane. On the opposite wall, a dozen tiny rainbows danced. It took a moment for Lucy to remember where she was. At first, she imagined herself to be in the middle of an incredible dream far from the nightmare of Messina. Then she remembered that the bed in Messina had never felt this good. In fact, she could not remember a bed ever feeling so wonderful.

She slowly opened her eyes and sighed happily at the sunny paradise. She stretched and moved her hands beneath the covers, across the downy soft robe that she wore.

That's odd. Why would I wear a bathrobe to bed? She looked about the room for clues and tried to remember the night before. Why was her nightgown folded over the arm of a chair? "What on earth?"

CHAPTER SEVENTEEN

"You were sleeping in the bathtub."

Three dark-haired little girls met Lucy's startled eyes. Elisabetta, the oldest of Giovanni's nieces, leaned her elbows on the bed with her chin in her hands. Was she the one who'd spoken?

"Your hair is red," Elisabetta said. Yes, the voice belonged to her.

"Her hair is brown too," Teresa, next in line and in height, ran her hand along the smooth satin comforter. She spoke as if this was not a new conversation.

Maria sucked her thumb.

"You're right; my hair is red *and* brown. It is called auburn." Which didn't tell her how she got from the tub to her bed. "Did you say I was sleeping in the bathtub?"

The little girls nodded in unison.

"No, that's not possible." Lucy searched her memory. She had set the book there, on the nightstand. It rested in the same place. Then she put on the robe, filled the tub, got in, and…

"*Oh, no.*" Lucy felt the blood leave her face. She looked down at her bathrobe and with shaking hands peeked inside it.

"*Oh, no.*" The phrase poured from her soul. If she disappeared and never came back, surely they'd understand.

The little girls giggled.

"Who put me here? No, don't tell me." She thought of Giovanni and buried her face in the pillow. "I can't ever leave this room," she moaned.

The girls' laughter grew.

A soft knock came at the door. With hands still shaking, Lucy quickly wrapped the robe tighter and pulled the covers up a little higher.

"Yes?" she squeaked.

The door opened with a creak and Rosa Castello stepped inside.

"*Buongiorno, bambina*. Elisabetta, Teresa, Maria, out." She pointed to the hallway. The giggling girls ran from the room.

"You must have been exhausted. Did you sleep well?" Giovanni's gracious mother pulled back the curtains to let even more light into the room.

"Oh, *Signora* Castello. I'm so sorry. I must have fallen asleep in the tub. I'm so embarrassed."

"Don't be. Please, call me *Mamma*." Rosa sat on the bed next to Lucy, took her hands and held onto them. "Giovanni told us how hard you've been working. And that was your first hot bath in two months? I would have done the same thing. Actually," Rosa gave Lucy a motherly smile, "all of us have fallen asleep in the tub one time or another, even Giovanni."

"Who found me?" Lucy lowered the covers a bit.

"Teresa."

Lucy let out a huge sigh. "Thank goodness. And she told you?"

Rosa patted Lucy's hand. "Yes. I was going to wake you, but you were sleeping so soundly that it seemed a shame. So Adella and I drained the tub and put the robe on you. I'm surprised you didn't stir at all."

"How did I get here?" Lucy whispered.

"I was going to ask Papa, but when Giovanni heard you had fallen asleep, he wouldn't let anyone else near you." Rosa glanced at the book on the nightstand and a smile floated on her lips. "Come and get dressed. Breakfast is still on the table." She stood and looked at down Lucy. "We want you to feel welcome. No matter what happens, you're a member of our family now. You don't ever have to be embarrassed and you'll always have a bed waiting if you need it." She kissed Lucy on the forehead.

"Do you need to borrow some clothes while you are here? I understand most of your things are still in Rome."

"You're as wonderful as Giovanni told me." Lucy climbed out of bed. "Yes, I would love to borrow something. All I have is my uniform, and it's seen better days."

Rosa opened the wardrobe and dug to the back. From it, she pulled a beautiful lightweight skirt in the traditional fashion of Sicilian women. Nearly floor length and brightly striped with blue and white, it had white lace trim all along the bottom. A white cotton blouse with matching lace and blue slippers completed the outfit.

"I won't know how to act! Thank you." Lucy hugged Rosa. "I'll be down in a moment."

"Don't be long. I believe Giovanni is waiting to have breakfast with you." The door clicked shut behind her.

Lucy held the skirt to her waist. Her knee had been skillfully wrapped in gauze bandage and secured with the tiniest knot. Only one person could do such beautiful work. A blush crept over her again.

His mother was gracious about it. But I know Giovanni. He's going to take great delight in teasing me. She started to giggle. *I'm embarrassed, but it is funny.*

Lucy put on the skirt and blouse and slipped her feet into the shoes. They felt a little snug, but oh well. She pulled her hair into a soft ponytail and tied it with her blue ribbon.

Birds played in the fountain outside and the morning sunlight danced off the stone patio.

Lucy rounded the corner and hesitated. Giovanni sat alone at the breakfast table. He had the newspaper opened and a cup of strong black coffee on the table.

She took a deep breath. He looked up and smiled.

"*Buongiorno, bella addormentata*." Giovanni stood to help her with her chair.

"Please don't." Lucy slid into the chair that Giovanni pulled out. Being called little monkey was bad enough but Sleeping Beauty? She'd never live it down.

"How can I not tease you? I brought you to my home, and you fell asleep in the tub. I'm glad that you forgot to lock the door, because if you remembered, we would have had to break it to get to you." Giovanni laughed lightly.

She should just hide. Lucy put her hand over her eyes.

"Have some coffee." Giovanni poured a steaming cup. The wonderful aroma brought her hands away from her face.

"I know you; milk and sugar. Unlike Messina, we have both here." Giovanni set the china bowls in front of her.

"All right. You win. It's funny." Lucy took a bite of a pastry covered with honey glaze. Heaven could not taste any better. "Thank you for carrying me to bed and for wrapping my knee."

"You're welcome, and don't worry, your knee is all I saw. *Mamma* guarded your honor the entire time. I know you don't like the idea of me looking at you, but *Lucia*, you own the most beautiful knee I've ever seen. And I've seen quite a few."

Lucy hid a smile. "I will be eternally grateful to your mother then, who apparently knew that my honor needed to be protected." She drank from her coffee to keep from laughing.

He turned in his chair and leaned an elbow on the table. "I see *Mamma* dressed you. Is it Sunday or are you going to a *festa*?"

Lucy smoothed her skirt. "A *festa*. We're not doing surgeries today so I declare a holiday. Your mother is just wonderful, Giovanni. It's so nice of her to loan these clothes to me, but I'm afraid I don't do them justice. I just don't look Sicilian."

"Where you come up with these ideas, I'll never know. Did *Mamma* welcome you to the family this morning?"

"Yes, how did you know?"

"Then you're now Sicilian, so you look like a Sicilian. You think all Sicilians have dark hair, don't you?"

"Yes and olive skin."

"*Lucia*, there have been so many different races living on this island over the centuries that we've become a mixture of a lot of things. My brother, Vito, for example had blond hair and blue eyes."

"Still, there *is* a difference. Look at your family and then look at me. I stand out like a sore thumb."

"Yes you stand out, but more like a white rose among red ones. Maybe it's good that you don't know how beautiful you are. Still, I wish I could show you what I see. You might be surprised."

Lucy tried to turn her head but his gaze was too compelling. She grabbed her coffee and took a sip.

"I think you look splendid. Don't ever say anything negative about yourself again, all right?" He put his hand on hers and squeezed gently.

What could she say? She'd never felt pretty. She'd never cared to be pretty. Did it matter?

"*Lucia*?"

"Okay." Maybe it did.

"Good." Giovanni let go of her hand. "*Papà* has asked that I help in the olive groves this morning, so we won't be leaving until after the midday meal. Have you decided whether to stay or come with me today?"

"If you don't mind, I'd love to stay around the house so I can get to know your mother." Wait a minute. She raised an eyebrow. "Your family doesn't rest in the afternoon? I thought all Italians took a break after *pranzo*."

"Normally, yes. But, today will be an exception. It pleases me that you and *Mamma* are becoming friends. Is there anything I can pick up for you while I'm in town?"

"The only thing I can think of, is maybe more plaster. Since the rain seems to be letting up, it'll be so much easier to use." Lucy looked hard at her empty plate. She really could eat more.

"I was thinking about what *you* might need." Giovanni shook his head. "But you're right we do need plaster. If you'll excuse me, *Lucia*, I'd better join my brothers before they come to find me." He stood and then leaned in with a gleam in his eye. "I wouldn't want to have to beat them in front of you." He kissed Lucy on the top of her head, touched her cheek with his thumb, and then headed down the patio steps.

Lucy climbed the stairs to her room. What a wonderful morning. She had spent it with Rosa, Celeste and who was the other? Adela, yes, that's her name. The herb garden had to be the most beautiful place she'd seen so far. Who knew it was below the stone patio on which she'd shared breakfast with Giovanni earlier. A rock wall covered in vines of yellow jasmine supported the patio and surrounded the piece of heaven. Blossoms fell a full ten feet from the top of the wall to the ground below; a great green and yellow curtain to frame Rosa's garden. A stone walkway wove in and around rows of garlic, basil, oregano, parsley, thyme, rosemary, lavender, roses and any other plant suitable in flavoring the wonderful meals produced in the kitchen.

Lunch was wonderful too. But now Giovanni and his father had gone off to town. The family now rested and the house grew still. This would be a perfect time to read. Ahh...time to read...she closed the bedroom door and picked up Giovanni's gift. A comfy chair made her welcome and she propped her injured leg up on a hassock. She stroked the outside of the book and imagined a young Giovanni trying to read his way through it.

She turned the page, began to read, but then stopped to look out the window.

"It all happened just across this island." Lucy thought about Mt. Etna that rose not far from Giovanni's home in Messina.

Her gaze fell to the pages.

Through the fields below the great volcano, Persephone often walked as she picked violets. Hades, the king of the underworld, saw her and instantly fell in love. He sprang from a dark cave and carried her to his kingdom in Hades. Persephone ate the seed of the pomegranate and Hades took her for his wife. She could not return to her mother.

Persephone's mother, Demeter, came looking for her daughter. She even lit a fire in Mount Etna so that Persephone could find her way home, but to no avail. Persephone had vanished. Only the maiden's playmate had seen what had happened.

When Demeter found out, she became outraged and shook Olympus to its core. She refused to attend the counsel of the gods and laid a spell on the land so it would bear no fruit or wheat. Famine threatened the world.

Zeus had to intervene. He commanded that Persephone be allowed to visit her mother for half of the year. She would live with her husband for the other half.

Zeus gave Sicily to Persephone as a wedding gift and it is there that she arrives every year to end the death of winter and bring with her new life and spring.

Lucy read the final page and sighed. What a beautiful story. On the page facing the last paragraph, was a message in Giovanni's clear hand.

You are my Persephone.

Ti amo.

Giovanni

I have chosen to believe.

Lucy's throat went dry. She read the message again and now her hands trembled. Could this be possible?

From outside, across the garden, came the blood-curdling scream of a child.

At the hospital in Palermo, Giovanni threw a tarp over boxes of medications and dry plaster. He tied it to one side of the truck bed while Michael tied the other. His father loaded his new, used, microscope in the cab.

"Giovanni!"

"Papa, did you call me?"He stopped at the sound of his name and looked around.

"No." Giovanni Sr. looked over the truck door.

"Giovanni!" he heard his name again.

Horses' hooves hit the ground behind him. Giovanni turned to see Antonio riding a horse…hard.

Covered in dust and flecked with foam, Antonio and his horse slid to a stop.

"Teresa has fallen from the patio wall!"

Michael went pale.

Giovanni placed his hand on his brother's arm. "How bad is she?"

"We thought that she was dead, but *Lucia* breathed into her mouth and Teresa started crying. Her arm is badly broken. Giovanni, the bone has come through the skin."

They jumped into the Ford and slammed it into top gear.

Thank you, God, that Lucia was there to revive Teresa. She probably would have died. Giovanni's second prayer in twenty years raced through his heart. *Please. You know I can save a limb that has sustained an open fracture… I know Lucia is too good a doctor to wait, but please don't let her do anything to Teresa's arm.*

Giovanni leapt from the Ford before it fully stopped. He ran through the front door and across the great room.

He took the stairs two at time and found his mother just outside the nursery; anxiety written all over her face. She grabbed her son by the shoulders.

"*Mamma*, let me by." Giovanni tried to go around her.

"Calm down," Rosa demanded. "*Lucia* saved Teresa's life. She's done the best she could with her arm. We need to be grateful."

Giovanni closed his eyes.

Too late. The words reverberated inside him.

Lucia had taken Teresa's arm off.

Giovanni drew a deep breath and prepared himself once again for the role he always played in his family.

He squared his shoulders and pushed his emotions inside his heart. He must be strong, especially for the little girl inside the nursery, maimed for life… and now also for *Lucia*, who he knew would take the brunt of his brother's anger.

"You're right, *Mamma*, we need to be grateful." Giovanni managed to stroke her cheek. "I'll be all right."

Dread filled him.

He hesitated, gathered his courage and then entered the room.

Giovanni first saw Lucy. She sat on the bed next to Teresa, who slept soundly. Then his eyes fell on his sweet niece. She looked so peaceful, except he could see that she had been crying. Teresa's little chest rose and fell under the covers, her dark curls lay all about her face on the pillow, her good arm tucked under the sheet and her other under a cloth soaked with liniment.

A cloth soaked with liniment?

"What is this?" He could not help but sound sharp. "Why haven't you wrapped her arm?"

Lucy looked up at Giovanni like a frightened child. Her voice lacked its usual confidence.

"Giovanni, I'm so glad you're here," she whispered. "Don't worry, it's clean. I haven't wrapped it because I wasn't sure you'd like the way I did it." Lucy wrung her hands. "I did the best I could. I've never fixed this kind of fracture by myself before. I wish you could have been here. Please Giovanni, look at it, make sure I did it right."

Giovanni stopped in his tracks and turned a searing gaze at Lucy. She had done hundreds of amputations. Why did she need his approval?

Lucy rubbed her hands in alcohol and gingerly lifted the cloth that covered Teresa's injury.

Giovanni forced himself to look at his niece.

He caught his breath.

"She still has her arm," he whispered, his throat tight and dry.

"Yes." Lucy cringed. Was that fear he heard?

"It's clean, I've set the bones. There's always such a risk of infection with this kind of injury, that I wanted you to make the final decision. If you'd rather amputate, we can take her down to the kitchen right now."

Giovanni did not know what to say. Relief washed over him in such waves that he found it hard to breath.

Lucy turned pale and began to tremble. "Examine her. Please tell me if this is what you want."

Giovanni made himself focus. He cleaned his hands and ran them carefully along Teresa's swollen arm; it had been set to perfection.

"This is not yet commonly practiced even by seasoned surgeons." Goose bumps rose on his arm. "How did you know to do this? Are they teaching the setting of open fractures in Boston?"

Lucy put her hand on her chest and closed her eyes. "I'm so relieved. I know it's not commonly practiced. I wasn't sure what you'd think. We weren't allowed time in Messina to do anything but amputate. I never thought to mention to you that I knew how to set a compound fracture."

She spoke quickly. "I was so afraid of infection, I couldn't wait for you. I put a bottle of either in my medical kit the night I delivered Max. I forgot to take it out because we left Messina so quickly. I always keep a small vile of carbolic acid in my bag as well..."

Giovanni almost laughed aloud. Lucy's nervous chatter used to annoy him, now he found it endearing. She hadn't even heard his question.

He grabbed her by the shoulders and forced her to face him.

"Who taught you to set a compound fracture?" This time he raised his voice just above a whisper.

"Daddy did." Lucy looked into his eyes, intense.

She unbuttoned her left sleeve and rolled it up above her elbow. "I'm surprised you never noticed my arm as many times as you've seen me with my sleeves rolled up."

Giovanni took her arm in his hand and ran his expert fingers across it. Sure enough, he saw a slight misalignment of the bone and scarring on her skin.

"Your father did this? When?"

"I fell out of an apple tree when I was eight. He had read about Dr. Lister's work with carbolic acid and felt the risk worthwhile to save my arm. None of the doctors in town agreed with his decision, but as you see my father saved my arm."

Michael burst through the door. "Where is she?" He turned on Lucy. "If you've hurt her I'll..."

"You'll do nothing." Giovanni stepped between his brother and Lucy. "Get out."

He pushed his brother back outside the room.

"*Lucia* has saved Teresa's life and she has saved her arm. I've met only a handful of doctors who can properly do what she has done." He softened his tone. "Go downstairs with Adella until we're finished here. Your daughter will recover. Right now she just needs to sleep."

Giovanni stepped back in the room and closed the door behind him. "I'm sorry about that."

"He's frightened for his daughter. I understand." Lucy leaned over Teresa again and re-covered her arm. "Thank you, Giovanni. I'm so relieved. I was so afraid you'd be upset with me."

"Upset with you?" He closed his eyes for a moment. How he regretted his explosions at her expense.

"*Lucia*, I couldn't be more pleased with you." He ought to kiss Lucy, right here in the nursery. He moved to the door. "I'm glad I picked up the plaster. Let's wrap this arm. "

Lucy eased herself on the bed to pull Teresa into her lap, in case she should wake.

"Let me do that this time; she's your patient, Doctor," Giovanni whispered. How many had they done this with? Giovanni slid beneath Teresa and held her in his lap.

Lucy spread a towel beneath the little girl's arm and in almost no time had the arm wrapped in a beautiful white cast. "It's amazing how fast this stuff dries when there's no rain." Lucy touched her work, satisfied.

Giovanni wiped Lucy's hands in a towel. Couldn't he please take her in his arms? "Let's let Michael and Adella in. Then, maybe you'll go for a walk with me?"

Could she feel the tension? Lucy nodded once, but she did not speak.

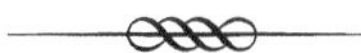

Giovanni headed down the hallway. He wanted to run like a boy and his palms sweated like a coward. He turned to see if Lucy followed him.

She had disappeared.

"*Lucia*? Where did you go?"

She stuck her head out of her bedroom. "I just want to take this apron off. I'll be down in a moment. Where shall I meet you?"

"In the herb garden." Giovanni could not think of any place better. "Meet me in the herb garden."

CHAPTER EIGHTEEN

From the balcony on the patio, she could see Giovanni's silhouette in the moonlight. He sat on a small stone wall that gave support to flowering vines, which sweetened the air around them.

The full moon cast a blue light on everything and reflected like a white marble in the fountain that bubbled in the middle of the garden.

Lucy tried in vain to steady her breath against her pounding heart. Her hand clutched the little book he had given. Somehow it gave her courage to face him or did she carry it as evidence should the evening go awry? She crossed the garden path and Giovanni stood to meet her.

He offered a gentle hand to guide her to sit on the wall next to him. Lucy handed him the book, watched his face and waited for him to speak.

Giovanni stared at his gift. A gentle breeze rustled the vines. He set the book on the wall and took a deep breath.

"Vito died when I was eight."

Lucy nodded.

"When I was ten, Giuseppe died as well. Both funerals took place in the church we visited yesterday, in Palermo. I can remember sitting in the exact same spot that we sat in. I was so young and my parents so overcome with grief that they paid little attention to me. Of course, now I understand, but then I felt so alone."

He stared off across the garden to the place where his brothers rested. The pain that was once such a mystery touched his face. He set his jaw and squared his shoulders and Lucy longed to comfort him. She touched his fingers.

He wrapped his hand around hers. "I prayed as hard as I could. Twice I lost my best friend. Twice I asked God not to let me live my life alone. I asked Him to please send just one person that I could be close to, someone with whom I could share my most intimate thoughts."

Giovanni turned his head slowly. He looked down at Lucy's hand and then up into her face. The warm light that had illuminated him last night filled his eyes.

A feeling both terrible and beautiful pierced her heart. Lucy became afraid; afraid that he might actually love her and then again, that he actually might not. She began to tremble.

He smiled.

"All my life I thought that God had turned a deaf ear to my request. Yesterday, as I watched you praying, I've seen you pray so many times. You were leaning on one knee. You looked so peaceful. The memory of the first funeral came back to me, out of the blue, vividly, as though it happened yesterday. It was then that I realized; God had answered my prayer. He took twenty-six years and answered my request better than I ever could have. He sent me you. Only God could have created a person who would complete me the way that you do.

"*Lucia*, I've asked you for your age, but you've never asked mine; I am thirty-four. That makes me eight years older than you are. You were born the year Vito died. It could be a coincidence, but I cannot convince myself that it is. The odds of someone like you meeting me here are astronomical. I tried to calculate them last night and I couldn't. Once that reality took hold of me, I was left with no other choice. I must not just believe in Him, I must follow Him."

"What amazes me is that I had completely rejected Him, and yet He still brought you to me." Giovanni gave a dry laugh and shook his head. "Am I making sense?"

Lucy squeezed his hand. "Yes." Excitement grew. "You're telling me that you believe in God, that you've become a Christian."

"Yes."

"And?" She leaned toward him. "I can see you're not finished,"

Giovanni took a deep breath; he stood to his feet and pulled Lucy up with him. He took both her hands in his, he looked into her soul again with his dark liquid eyes, so soft and kind and full of hope.

"I have a confession to make." He gave a sigh.

"Go on," Lucy whispered, her heart in her throat. "You can tell me anything."

"*Ti amo, Lucia*," Giovanni said, softly. "I've always loved you. From our first argument on the dance floor in Rome, through all of the blood, the death, through all of the arguments, I have loved you. You've been Persephone; full of light and life. I've been Hades; dark and angry. God has used you to bring me back to life; I don't want to live my life without you. My greatest hope is that, despite how I've treated you, somehow you'll love me, too."

The world seemed to spin and Lucy found it hard to breathe.

She tried to speak, but her throat went dry. Her eyes filled with tears.

Giovanni shifted his weight; hope faded from his face and he slowly hung his head. "I've said too much. I've overstepped my boundaries. I told you that I was your friend and now I've ruined even that. I'm sorry *Lucia*...I..."

Lucy did not hear anything else he said. Her heart pounded in her chest and a sob escaped her throat. She collapsed into him before he could stop her. Her arms slid around his waist as she buried her head in his chest.

"I didn't mean to make you cry." Remorse flooded his voice.

His arms closed tightly around her. He kissed the top of her head and stroked her hair. She could only cry harder.

"I will be your friend and your servant forever." He rested his cheek against her hair.

Lucy found her voice."You don't understand."

"What, *Lucia*? What don't I understand?" He pulled her up by her shoulders, wiped tears from her face and searched her eyes.

"I love you, too." How foreign those words felt on her tongue. "I've fought the feeling since the first time you let me lead in the operating room. I never dreamt that you could fall in love with me. I didn't think you saw me that way..."

The look in Giovanni's eyes made Lucy's heart stop. She had heard that joy could be fierce, but she had never seen it until now.

"Have no doubt that I love you." Giovanni placed gentle hands on the sides of her face.

Lucy lost strength to move.

"Let me *show* you how I see you." He brushed her lips with his, he kissed her softly at first and then like a man who has found his prize.

Not at all prepared for the shockwave of emotions that washed over her, Lucy started to cry again.

His soft eager lips kissed up her cheek and then sought her mouth once more.

Her knees started to buckle, so she leaned into him. Giovanni pulled her into a strong embrace and kissed her again.

He pressed his cheek to hers. "Marry me." His warm whisper caressed her neck. "Please, *Lucia*, say that you will marry me."

"Yes." Lucy barely choked out the word before he kissed her again. This joyful kiss turned into laughter and he lifted her off her feet.

Lucy laughed even while tears filled her eyes. She belonged in his arms. She never wanted to leave.

He set her down, but he did not let her go.

"You've been in love with me since Rome?" Lucy could barely speak.

"The moment you called me a pig, I knew." Giovanni stroked her face; he traced her eyes, her nose, her lips. "I was completely frustrated, thinking that I would never see you again unless I went stayed in Rome to work with the university. Then the earthquake happened. The need was so great that I knew there would be little chance of going back. I thought, once again God had let me down." He pressed his face against hers again. Lucy memorized the feel of his cheek on hers, the smell of his skin.

"But He didn't let you down?" She wanted to hear him say it.

"No, He didn't." Giovanni pulled back to look into Lucy's eyes. "I can hardly believe that you love me. After all I've said and done, I will make it up to you for the rest of your life."

"After all you have said and done?" Lucy laughed.

She placed a timid finger along his cheek. Her heart danced when he leaned into her caress, then grabbed her fingers and kissed them. "Giovanni, you've honored me. You've treated me like an equal, with respect and honesty and genuine friendship. You even let me lead in the operating room. No one's ever allowed me that privilege, not even Daddy. On top of that, you keep insisting that I'm beautiful. How could I not love you?"

"Even though I called you a monkey?" He tightened his arms around her.

"Even though you called me a monkey." She tilted her head to look up at him with a smile. "You are such a rascal."

"I hope you can put up with me." He leaned in close again and his breath washed over her.

"I hope so, too." Lucy bravely moved up on her toes and closed the gap between them to press her lips to his. He responded right away with his hand cradled to the back of her head.

Did he remember her words from a few weeks back?

He rained light kisses on her face, her eyelids, her nose, her cheeks."I'm honored, Dr. James." He rested his face to hers, his smile reverent.

She would never be the same.

Giovanni broke into laughter. "So this is why you didn't want me to tell your father that you fell from the orange tree!" He rubbed Lucy's arm.

She gave him a playful smile. "Are you going to yell at me?"

"I might." He laughed again, then fire filled his eyes. He pulled her close again, closer than before. A shudder run through his body just before he brought his lips down on hers. This kiss was different, raw and powerful, it stole Lucy's breath. It rent her heart and locked it with his and she knew when he said he loved her it would be forever.

Weak and light-headed, Lucy used him for support. But she kissed him in return.

A chuckle rose from deep in his chest.

He leaned his cheek to hers once more, breathing hard. His strong hands stayed around her until she regained her balance.

"I love you," Giovanni whispered in her ear.

Lucy's heart thrilled.

"I love you, too." Lucy rested her head on his shoulder and closed her eyes.

From above their heads Antonio shouted, "Hey, everybody, Giovanni's finally getting married."

"What?" Papa asked.

Lucy and Giovanni looked up in time to see the Castello family assemble at the balcony to watch.

Lucy buried her face against Giovanni's neck, but he lifted her chin, his smile radiant.

He looked up at his family. "Should I kiss her?" he asked with a voice so loud, all of Palermo must have heard him.

"Yes, kiss her!" The Castellos cheered.

Giovanni looked back at Lucy, heat rose in her cheeks.

"You'd better get used to this." He grinned and waggled his eyebrows. "We're a *very* open family." He kissed her one last time, then lifted her off her feet and spun her around while his family cheered again.

He kept her in his arms and carried her all the way back up the steps of the patio before he put her down.

The Castello family surrounded them with cheers.

"*Evviva! Giovanni* e *Lucia*. God bless the bride and groom."

Lucy struggled to find sleep. Her bed, so comfortable; her room so beautiful; and her heart so happy—she kept looking around from her cozy nest. She thanked God over and over and re-lived the events of the evening in her mind.

In her heart, Lucy could see Giovanni's face when he laughed; she could hear him ask her to marry him again and again. She let out a soft giggle when she remembered the feel of his arms around her and the way he would not let go of her hand once he had set her on her feet at the top of the patio steps.

"She's said yes." Giovanni told his mother when his family gathered all around them. Apparently, Rosa had been aware of his intentions.

She gave Lucy a warm smile. "*Benvenuta a famiglia, Lucia.*" Rosa kissed Lucy first on one cheek, then on the other.

Lucy sighed with contentment and closed her eyes once again, in an attempt to sleep.

A dream began and in her dream, she could hear someone weeping from a great distance. She opened her eyes. The house, completely still, felt cavernous.

What was that about? She snuggled back into her pillow and closed her eyes.

She heard it again. The sound, very faint, tugged at her. Someone was crying, weeping as though their heart would break. She opened her eyes and sat up. She could hear the muffled sounds come from the very walls of the house.

Her heart started to break. *Who is that Lord?*

Lucy swung out of bed. She slipped her feet into the downy slippers that Rosa had provided. She pulled the matching thick blue velvet robe over her head and buttoned the front.

Her reflection in the standing mirror distracted her. *At home this would be something to wear to a party not a robe to cover a nightgown.*

The muffled sound of crying reached her ears again and pulled Lucy to reality. She opened her door and crept out into the hallway. Giovanni's bedroom door had been left open, so she slipped to the edge and peeked inside. His bed had not been touched.

She turned and went down the stairs, then rounded the corner and saw a single light shining in the great room. Rosa sat on the overstuffed sofa in front of the fireplace, not yet dressed for bed. Papa Castello stood beside her, beneath the crest, his hand on the mantle, his head bowed.

Lucy reached the landing and Rosa came to meet her. Arm in arm they walked to the sofa.

"*Mamma*, who's crying?" Lucy did not feel like sitting, so she stood. "Where's Giovanni?"

Rosa placed her hand on Lucy's cheek. "Giovanni is in the chapel."

"Should I go to him? Is he praying?"

Papa woke from his vigil and turned to face Lucy. Square shoulders and kind eyes commanded respect and admiration. "The house of Castello has followed The Christ since the days of the Emperor Diocletian. Since that time we have in unbroken succession served God with our whole hearts, by life and by death."

"The inscription on the crest." Lucy came to stand under the crest next to the elder Giovanni. This family was really that old? "Your family has been serving God since the days of the Coliseum?"

"Yes." Papa raised an eyebrow. "Did Giovanni explain to you the meaning of our coat of arms?"

"Not completely." Lucy shrugged. "I saw it in the house in Messina. I thought it might have something to do with God because Giovanni didn't want to talk about it."

"He'd forsaken The Lord years ago." Papa watched Lucy with interest, his expression kind. "We've been praying for our prodigal son for a very long time. What you don't know is that when he turned 18, Giovanni vowed, as have generations of Castello men, to give his heart to God and to serve Him. But his vow wasn't genuine. He only did it to please us. When he returned from London, he said that he could pretend no longer. He said that he didn't believe and he returned the ring of his knighthood."

"His knighthood?" Lucy stepped back, her eyes went wide. "Giovanni is a knight?"

"He was." The elder Giovanni no longer looked like a farmer. Lucy looked in wonder at the gold filigreed sword shining against the onyx background. "He will be again. He's reclaiming his vows right now. This is between the Almighty and Giovanni. It's something that he must do alone."

A door clicked shut at the far end of the house. Papa and Rosa turned to watch the archway closest to the fireplace. A minute later Giovanni came through it.

His disheveled hair gave him an air of nobility. Would he be drained of energy? No. He had light in his eyes that had not been there before. He had always stood erect, but now his shoulders seemed even straighter and though his face gave the evidence of tears, on him rested peace and strength. How many generations of Castello's had given their lives to God?

Giovanni went to his parents first.

His father opened a plain wooden box on the mantle. From it, he pulled a very old ring, set with onyx. The stone itself had been engraved. It bore a golden sword with a cross-shaped hilt. Papa placed the ring on Giovanni's right forefinger. The men held each other at arm's length for a moment. Papa kissed his son and then they embraced.

"It is good to have you back, Giovanni." His father gave his son a strong pat on the back. "This is indeed a day for celebration."

Giovanni went to his mother next. She kissed him on the forehead and then he took her into his arms and Rosa let out a quiet sob.

"*Ti voglio tanto bene, Mamma*," Giovanni whispered. "I'm sorry that I hurt you."

"*Ti voglio bene, Bambino*." She stroked his face. "You're forgiven. Let's not bring it up again."

When at last Giovanni released his mother, he turned to Lucy. "I'm glad that you're here." His deep, rich voice touched her soul and with his smile, Lucy knew he was a new man.

He stroked her cheek with his fingertips. "I want you always by my side." He turned back to his parents and asked a silent question.

"By all means." His father tucked a joyful Rosa under his arm. "We know of her commitment to our Savior, and it is plain how much she loves you." Papa handed the box to Giovanni.

Giovanni opened the box and pulled from it another very old ring. This one, made for a woman, had been set with an emerald and engraved on the sides with an olive branch.

"These rings go together. They were crafted in the sixteenth century," Giovanni said. "They last belonged to my great-grandparents. The symbols on them match the symbols on the crest. We all wear rings that are similar."

Giovanni's parents held out their hands. Their rings were almost identical except that Rosa's stone was sapphire.

Giovanni turned Lucy to the coat of arms once more. "The basement of this house was, in its first use, a prison for Christians who were to be taken to the Coliseum in Rome."

What? Lucy gasped.

Giovanni rubbed her hand. "Later, it was used to hide Christians from persecution. The words below the sword, as I told you say; 'In His service by life or death.' What is etched under the lamb is a scripture reference. Matthew 10:28. Which says, *'Do not fear those who kill the body but cannot kill the soul. But rather, fear Him who is able to destroy both the soul and body in Hell.'* Those words were scratched into the foundation stone of Casa Bella by someone who was martyred, as an encouragement to Christians facing death."

Giovanni searched Lucy's face and went on.

"The sword is both a sword and a cross. We are a family of accomplished swordsmen."

"You are?" Once again, she saw Giovanni in a new light.

"Yes."

Oh. "This is how you so easily disarmed Officer Jackson." Lucy looked up at the swords that hung on either side of the crest.

"Yes. These swords all belong to my brothers my uncle and my father. That one." He pointed to the far right. "Is mine."

"But you're a doctor."

"Yes, I am." Giovanni looked down at her with a curious smile. "Does this knowledge of me, of my family, cause you to see me so differently?"

Lucy examined her heart and appealed to God. She looked back at Giovanni, afraid to say what was in her heart, but knowing she could not depart from the truth at this important moment.

"This knowledge causes me to see you more clearly." She searched his face and tried not to be afraid to lose him so soon.

"Giovanni, I am not nobility. I am just an American. I believe you when you say that you love me, but shouldn't you be marrying someone who is noble, too? Will I make you happy? Will I be what you need in all of this?" She motioned to the grandeur around them.

Giovanni grew soft. He put his arm around her shoulder and kissed her temple. "You are exactly what I need." He drew her attention back to the crest.

"As I said, the sword is also a cross for, without doubt, we are Christians. The crown represents God the Father, our king. The lamb of course is God the Son. The flames above are the Holy Spirit. The olive branches on either side say that we are men of peace. The Castello family has taken a solemn oath to do justice, to love mercy and to walk in humility before God."

"That's from *Micah*, isn't it?" No wonder he'd hidden this from her.

"Very good." Papa smiled his approval. "Yes, Micah 6:8. We serve the poor and protect the innocent."

"Look, *Lucia*," Giovanni opened the box to let her peek inside. "Here is your wedding band."

Lucy saw a simple band engraved with an olive branch that wrapped all the way around it.

Giovanni closed the box and handed it to his mother. He took Lucy's left hand in his and got down on one knee in front of her. He held on to her hand and looked into her eyes with strength and sincerity.

"But I've already agreed to marry you with all of my heart." This was a little awkward. "Do you need to ask me once more?"

"This is a tradition of the House of Castello." Rosa stepped to Lucy's side. "Listen and you'll understand." She directed Lucy back to her son.

"As Christ gave His life for His bride, the church," Giovanni said. "So will I lay my life down for you *Lucia*, my bride. I declare this before God and all of heaven."

Rosa whispered into Lucy's ear.

Lucy turned to her speechless.

Rosa smiled and nodded to Lucy.

"And I will honor and serve you my husband all the days of my life," Lucy repeated. She meant every word.

"And will you willingly follow the footsteps of Christ with me even if it means certain death?"

"Yes." Lucy choked the word out before Rosa could give her the answer.

"I will," Rosa whispered. She smiled at her future daughter-in-law.

"I will," Lucy's heart trembled inside her. *This is better than a fairy tale.*

"Then I claim you as my sister and as my wife." Giovanni slipped the ring on her left ring finger and kissed it.

Giovanni rose to his feet and planted a gentle kiss on her lips.

"I didn't think anything could make tonight more beautiful." Lucy's eyes filled with tears.

"I will now take my place beside my brothers and my father." His eyes shone, too.

He pulled Lucy into the most wonderful heartfelt hug, his face buried in her hair.

Lucy hugged him tight, rejoicing in her heart while Giovanni prayed.

"Thank you, God, for bringing *Lucia* to me," he whispered. "Thank you, God, for taking me back, thank you for not giving up on me."

The locomotive slowed to a stop. Lucy gave her hand to Giovanni and he helped her from the train. How amazingly easy it was to forget the starkness of this place after the beauty of Giovanni's home. She followed him toward the baggage car, to look for the medications that had come with them. Lucy's hand went once again to the place where her ring, on a chain for safety, rested beneath her blouse. Giovanni had done the same with his; after all, Messina had not yet become a place to wear jewelry.

Had someone called her name? She stopped and searched through the crowd. Sure enough, her father stood next to Father Dominic.

"Lucille. Over here." Henry James waved his arm.

"Daddy!" She waved back. "Giovanni, Daddy's here."

"Go to him. But please let me be the one to bring up our engagement. We've known each other for such a short time it will come as a shock. I want to tell him the right way."

"You've been trying to protect me since the day we met. How could I not see it?"

"Because I behaved so badly. I'll always protect you *Lucia*. Go on." Giovanni gave a nod. "I'll get the bags."

Lucy ran to her father and threw herself into his arms. "Daddy, I wasn't expecting you for two days. What a wonderful surprise."

"Lucy, darling." Henry James kissed his little girl. "I could wait no longer to see you. Father Dominic's been telling me what wonderful work you've been doing. I'm so proud of you."

Lucy greeted the priest with a kiss on the cheek.

"You look rested." Father Dominic's statement almost sounded like a question.

"It's amazing what just two days can do to change a person's outlook on life." Lucy avoided his gaze.

Giovanni approached them with a steward, who pushed a stack of crates on a cart. He greeted Father Dominic with a warm hug.

Giovanni extended a hand to Henry James. "Dr. James, I hope you didn't wait too long for our return."

"I arrived here early this morning, so I haven't had to wait long at all." Dr. James shook Giovanni's hand. "I understand that you two have become friends and from what Father Dominic tells, me quite a good team."

"Yes." Giovanni gave the steward a tip. "Your daughter has made a believer of me in more ways than one. You've a right to be very proud of her. I've rarely met anyone with her skills. I'm looking forward to knowing the man who helped her develop them."

With everything in the mule cart, they headed through Messina. The sun shone, but the odor of damp smoke still clung to the streets.

Lucy examined a man asleep in his cot and watched her father with a wary eye. The minute she had seen her father at the train station, she remembered that he had a strong distaste for anyone with dark skin.

Lucy's encounter with Officer Jackson, made her wonder if he might have a distaste for Italians too.

What puzzled her most was that her father always followed God faithfully and she had never given his prejudice a second thought until she came here. How could he reconcile following the God of Love and not loving anyone because of color? How could she be so blind as not to see it?

Right now, her father acted normal. He chatted cordially with Giovanni all the way to the hospital station. He even joined them in their work once they had settled in and now cheerfully applied himself, like he had always been a part of their team.

Lucy let her gaze wander to where her father injected a child with smallpox vaccine. *He seems happy.*

Her gaze traveled across the room to where Giovanni inspected the remaining vials of vaccine, writing the date of arrival on each bottle.

The events of last night still felt like a dream but the weight of the emerald ring around her neck assured her of reality. What would happen when Daddy found out?

In the pit of her stomach, she had a feeling that things might just explode.

CHAPTER NINTEEN

To the right of Dr. James, stood the daily line of *profughi*, who came with their injuries or illness; a runny nose, a broken finger or worse. Lucy's father saw to their needs one by one.

"Just imagine." Maybe she could test the waters a bit. "There will be a real hospital for these people to heal in before long."

Giovanni looked up from the box of vaccines. "Not just one, but two, and I hear that a clinic will be opening up on this end of town." He gave Lucy a mischievous glance. "We'll actually be tearing this place down next week."

Her father looked up from the woman he vaccinated, to acknowledge what Giovanni had said. Clueless, he kept right on working.

Lucy shot a warning smile to Giovanni. "Everyone who's come to Messina has worked so hard. We're actually starting to see a difference."

"*Dottore* Castello, *Santa Lucia*." Giovanni's favorite assistant pushed his way in from the back of the line.

"Pietro, it's good to see you. Your cast doesn't come off until next week. Is everything all right?" She made sure to give him her full attention.

"My *Mamma*, she is very sick. Please, will you come to her?" Pietro took Lucy by the hand and pulled.

"Have you eaten today? Why don't you go and ask cook for some bread and cheese. Dr. Castello and I will be ready in a few minutes."

"No. I don't want something to eat." Pietro walked past Lucy and went to Giovanni. "I have to take care of *Mamma*."

"*Perche tu l'uomo della casa*." Giovanni placed the lid on the crate.

"*Si*." Pietro stepped closer and Giovanni put a hand on the boy's head.

Lucy's heart melted. "He's so young to be so grown up."

"What did he say?" Henry James paused from his work.

"He is the man of the house so he must take care of everyone before he takes care of himself." Giovanni looked down at his friend. "*Andiamo a casa tuo*. First go gather some food for your family from the kitchen. Meet us at the mule cart. Dr. James, are you coming?"

"Daddy?"

"Go ahead, daughter." Dr. James looked up from the refugee in front of him. "I can manage this."

"Thank you Daddy for bringing fresh clothes." Lucy and her father stood in line at the mess tent.

"I thought you'd want to get out of that beautiful nurses uniform." Her father gave her a rub on the back. "Word has reached Rome about the work that you and Dr. Castello have been doing here; you deserve to dress like a doctor. Some of your former patients live near the university, you know."

"I'm sure our patients are all over Italy by now. I had no idea when I volunteered how extreme things would be. Is this what the Civil War was like?"

"It was chaos too, but in a different way. A lot of the surgeries were done outside. I was just a boy at the time, but it's something you never forget.

"Dr. Castello says that when he first arrived they worked outside."

"Speaking of Dr. Castello, I haven't seen him in a while. Where is he?"

"He and Father Dominic had a meeting at the American village. I could have gone too, but I'd rather eat dinner with you."

"Welcome home. Nothing seems right when you're not here." Cook's bushy brows scrunched together whenever he smiled, especially when he handed her food.

"*Grazie*, it's good to be back." Lucy took her food and Cook patted her cheek with his finger tips.

"They've sure taken to you." Henry James raised an eyebrow.

"I've taken to them too." Lucy handed a plate to her father.

"Canned meat, potatoes and tea? Where on earth did this meal come from?" Henry James scratched his head.

"From America of course." Lucy picked up her fork and spoon. "They sent what would travel well. Unfortunately, the refugees in Messina are so set in their ways, that they won't eat meat from a can. Nor will they touch the potatoes, and as for the tea, Sicilians drink coffee. Many of them had never even seen tea before. They thought it was tobacco and tried to smoke it. So it was decided that food from America would be given to the soldiers who will eat anything and of course to us. At any rate, I am glad to have good tea."

"I'm curious about your time here. I was very surprised that you decided to stay when the *Venezia* left. " Henry James helped his daughter with her chair; they sat at the door table. "Tell me everything."

Lucy searched her memory; where should she begin? "Daddy, so much has happened, I feel like I've been here for years."

Lucy told her father about the long hours, the unending line of patients in the cold damp tent, working without anesthesia and losing all those children. Then she told him of the people they saved. When she finished she tried to read her father's face. *He seems much quieter than I remember him..*

"I'm very proud of you." Henry James smiled at his daughter. "I'm sure that your mother would be too. I knew you would come away from here a different person. I was glad to see that arrogant doctor honoring your skills. You seem to be getting along. Tell me truthfully, how is he treating you?"

"Actually- *I've got to choose the right words.* -we've become great friends. God has been so good to me in that respect. We fought terribly in the beginning, but we always seemed to be put in circumstances that forced us to get along. Finally, we gave up our differences and when we did we became a wonderful team. At first, I was put out when Dr. Davidson told me I would be assisting him, but I never knew that working closely with a partner would make everything go so much better.

"Daddy, those doctors in Rome were right, Dr. Castello is extremely gifted. I've never met a surgeon with his skills, except for you." She patted her father's hand. "I feel like I'm better for having worked with him."

Henry James studied her face. "Then why won't he come to Rome and work in a real hospital?"

"Because Giovanni- *rats* -has such a compassion for the poor; they're often so neglected and go untreated. He's chosen Messina as his mission field." *Maybe he didn't notice.*

"When did you start calling him Giovanni?"

Uh oh. "We've been partners for over two months. In the first three weeks, we worked eighteen hour shifts seven days a week. Now we work twelve. How would I not call him by his first name? Tell me how things are going in Rome."*Yikes, yikes, yikes.*

"Well, that's part of the reason that I'm here, my darling." Henry James took Lucy's hand. "The work that we've been doing in Rome has been a great success and we'll be finishing early. I've been asked to stay for another year."

"That's wonderful. I'd love to stay." *I believe in miracles.*

Her father shook his head, took a bite of ham and then dabbed his mouth. "I've chosen instead to return to America the last week of June. Lucy we'll be heading home in three months, just in time for the 4th of July. I was hoping to convince you to come back to Rome with me until we leave. We could do some sightseeing; maybe take a train up to Florence."

No, no we can't leave. I can't leave. I've got to stall him. She felt a cold chill on the back of her neck. "There's still so much work to be done here. I've promised these people that I would stay until September."

"But this station isn't going to be here that long. Giovanni, I mean Dr. Castello himself said that it would be taken down next week. Have you thought that through?"

"Actually," Lucy said slowly, "I have. Dr. Castello is turning his home into a clinic and surgery. It sits just outside the city limits. The house is still standing and with little repair it will be very functional."

"Is that the clinic that Dr. Castello mentioned earlier today?" Her father turned discerning eyes upon her.

"Yes." *Oh man. Here we go.*

"And exactly where are you going to live?"

"I-in the American Village."

She saw her furrows in her father's brow, and then he gave a warm smile. *Huh.*

"Watching you work with Dr. Castello actually made me a bit jealous. Come back to Rome and work with me a bit too."

"Daddy, I love to work with you." Lucy put her napkin on her empty plate. "You've been my greatest inspiration. Somehow though, I feel called to Messina."

Henry James straightened up in his chair. His eyes grew serious.

Jehoshaphat, he knows.

"Do you feel called to Messina? Or called to Dr. Castello?"

Cat's out of the bag. Kill me now and get it over with. She took a deep breath. "Both."

Her father's low steely voice made her shiver. "Lucille, you've only known him for two months."

"Yes, but we've been together for almost twenty-four hours a day." Her stomach tightened.

"You don't know anything about him." He tossed his napkin on the table.

"Daddy, you're wrong. I know him well."

"How well?"

Lucy swallowed hard. *At least Giovanni will be merciful.* "He's asked me to marry him and I've said yes."

Dr James stared at his napkin and a dark cloud drifted across his face.

"Daddy, say something. Giovanni is a wonderful man. Please get to know him before you draw any conclusions."

"This is my fault." He rubbed his eyes with his fingers and then looked up. "Lucille, I've raised you to think independently and right now I really regret it. Most of the time you make responsible decisions, but you're very impulsive. If you decide to marry this man, you will be separated from your family. I cannot, give you my blessing."

"Why not?" Lucy felt the color leave her face. She leaned forward. "How can you object to him when you don't even know him?'

"I have many objections without having to know him." Henry James shoved his plate away and leaned an arm on the table. "The first is that he doesn't live in Boston. In fact, he isn't even American; he lives half a world away. Let alone that he's not even Anglo Saxon, he's Latin. He's Italian and Sicilian at that. Who knows what heathen blood runs in his veins.

"Our family is unadulterated and you want to mix with another race? Add to that the fact that he is not even a Christian. How can you even consider marrying someone who doesn't believe in Jesus?"

"But he does." Lucy remembered his shining eyes and his new commitment just the night before. *I have to defend him.* "He's just recently given his heart to the Lord. And this prejudice against other races is not biblical. Father, all my life I've heard this double standard come out of your mouth, but I never thought about it until now. *You* are the one who taught me that God created all of us in His image and yet you don't believe it in your heart. We have Italian friends in Rome, what would they say if they knew how you thought? They're all right for friends, it's fine to work in their country, but that's as far as it goes."

"Enough!" Lucy's father's brow tightened with severe firmness. "I'm relieved that at least he now acknowledges God, but Lucille. I know without hearing it from anyone that if he goes to church it will be a Catholic one. I do *not* want you to marry a Catholic."

Lord, please give me wisdom. "Daddy, in my lifetime I have been devoted to God, to medicine and to my family. I have rarely willfully disobeyed you. I love you with all of my heart, but you're wrong. To think the way you're speaking goes against everything I've learned from you about God." Lucy pushed herself away from the table. "I will *not* be returning to America with you, and I *will* marry Giovanni."

Lucy turned away from her father. Her eyes went to the flap in the tent. This would be a great time for Giovanni to emerge from the other side. No such luck.

"I understand your compassion for the poor people of Messina." Henry James touched his daughter's arm, his voice kind. "You've always had a love for the poor; I know, I've encouraged it. I think you've transposed that love to Dr. Castello, because he's been working here with you. Please, for my sake, don't do anything hastily. Wait, give it time. I think when this is all over you'll find that you don't really love him, you love the work you're doing while you're with him. Please, promise me that you'll not marry him until fall, and I'll not insist that you come back to Rome with me. If by September, you still think that you love him then I will give my blessing."

Lucy grew rigid, her skin felt cold and her hands began to shake. *He just said we were leaving in June now he's talking about September. He's trying to manipulate me. He's never done that before.* "We've not even discussed a date yet, but I feel as though I can wait until fall. I'll talk it over with Giovanni." *I need some space.* She stood to her feet and kissed him on the cheek. "Good night, daddy."

Lucy walked into the surgery, now so familiar it felt close to her heart. Everything was peaceful and in order. She sank onto her stool to sort things out. Her mind went back to the first few days and how foreign everything felt; how unfriendly Giovanni had been. Now that she knew him and his protective nature she could see right through his mask. *How am I going to get Daddy to change his mind about him?*

The clop, clop of hooves and a loud snort from Jonah brought Lucy out of her trance.

"Let's go find her." Giovanni said. "I hope dinner with her father went well."

"I'm sure everything's just fine." Father Dominic answered.

On her side of the tent wall, Lucy sat quiet as a mouse. It was such fun to eavesdrop. She counted to ten and right on cue, the flap moved aside and Giovanni walked into the room.

"There you are. What are you doing down there?" He pulled her to her feet and kissed her cheek.

"Giovanni, *please.*" She pushed him away playfully and wiped her face.

"I told you to get used to this. The priest is family too you know." He pulled her back to his side.

"Don't I get a chance?" Father Dominic beamed.

"You've told him?"

"He's telling everyone." The priest gave a fatherly smile. "Since the day I met you I wanted this. Congratulations, dear heart."

How could she *not* hug this man? Lucy slipped under his arm. He kissed the top of her head and hugged Lucy like a bear.

"Let go, I can't breathe." She squeaked.

Father Dominic released her with a rub on the top of her head.

Lucy, still laughing, staggered to the table and leaned.

Giovanni moved to her side, crossed his arms and leaned his shoulder to hers. "What a great meeting."

"Really?" Lucy looked up at him. "What's the news?"

"Some of the portable houses, at the American village, have already been finished. We saw them this evening. *Lucia*, they're beautiful. When everything's done, there'll be three hospitals plus our clinic and a few others. And...are you ready?"

"Yes." Lucy looked up into his shining eyes.

"They're bringing *electricity*."

"*Electricity*? Are you sure?"

Giovanni nodded.

Lucy clasped her hands. "How much easier things will be. When?"

"Soon. They're taking measurements for the wires this week. This tent will be disassembled, as they need materials for the new houses. We're going to go ahead and set up my villa." Giovanni, paused and smiled. "I mean, *our* villa.

"I'm so excited I can hardly contain myself." Lucy glanced at their ragged surroundings. This would be just a memory. "I have to keep my stool."

" *Lucia*, it gets better." Giovanni glanced at her stool and put his arm around her. "*Padre* and I have been discussing the dilemma of where we should live."

"What about the American Village?"

"That might be a problem. They're building a thousand new houses. Other nations are building them too. That will give Messina a lot of new homes, unfortunately, there are still nearly fifty-thousand people living here."

Father Dominic leaned against the opposite table. "The villages are a good beginning, but everyone knows that they're just a start. Your villa is intact enough for us to live in. Why take a residence that a peasant could use?"

"So *Padre* and I were just discussing the possibility of living there ourselves." Giovanni turned toward her. "We'll take the downstairs bedrooms and bath. You, Sister Francesca and the others can live upstairs. The house is still big enough that if we have a severe case of who knows what, we'll be able to take them in too. What do you think *Lucia*? Even my mother wouldn't object to us living together under those circumstances."

"I can see nothing wrong with it either. Besides, we've become such a team, it'll be nice not to have to separate. When do we begin the move?"

"As soon as your father leaves."

Oh yea, Daddy. She had almost forgotten how awful dinner had been.

Giovanni tilted his head, his gaze swept her face. "How did supper go?"

"He's threatening to disown me."

"I'll just excuse myself." Father Dominic inched his way toward the door.

"No. Stay, *Padre*. You're as much a part of this as Giovanni." Lucy relayed the events of the evening. This was so annoying, so embarrassing; she turned away.

"Don't worry." Father Dominic's steady gentle voice soothed her troubled heart. He pushed his glasses up his nose. "I've seen God work out situations far worse than this one. Still, more than almost anything, I long for peace among Christians." He stood and stroked her cheek. "If you'll excuse me, I think I'll go spend some time in prayer."

Father Dominic left and Giovanni put Lucy back under his arm.

"I think that your father is afraid of losing his only daughter. He's right; you would be living half a world away. You probably remind him of your mother too." Giovanni pulled Lucy to his chest. "I want you to take tonight to think about your decision."

"But..." Lucy's voice cracked.

"Shh, let me finish." He placed a gentle finger on her lips. "I promise to understand completely if you decide not to stay with me. I'll always love you – enough to let you go if I have to. I don't want to stand between you and your father."

From her resting place, Lucy could hear the strong steady beat of Giovanni's heart. He pressed his cheek against her hair and she felt safe. She tightened her hold. "I already know what my answer will be."

He grazed her cheek with his soft lips and Lucy could take no more. Love was so beautiful. Even if it meant never seeing her family again she would stay with this man.

"Tell me in the morning," he whispered in her ear.

CHAPTER TWENTY

Henry James threw the blanket off his legs and sat up. The argument that occurred between himself and his daughter this evening disturbed him very much. He always hoped Lucy would marry someday, but he never imagined that she would choose someone so foreign, or want to live in a place so far away.

Careful not to wake anyone, he climbed out of bed and wandered with his candle through the dark hospital, in the direction of the mess tent.

From outside the flap, he saw the glow of a lantern. Curious, he stepped inside and found Giovanni across the room sitting at the table made from a door. A pile of books decorated the table and the young man seemed engrossed in the one he balanced on his knees, his feet propped up on the chair next to him. In front of him, lay a plate filled with several odd looking cookies and a glass of milk.

Giovanni must have heard footsteps, because he peered over his book and smiled.

"Ah, Doctor James, come and sit with me."

Henry James walked across the room and pulled out a chair.

"Would you care for *biscotti*? My mother made them, they're wonderful."

"No, thank you, I won't be able to get back to sleep if I do." Henry James sat. He measured Giovanni under his critical eye; olive skin, dark hair, gray eyes. What combination of blood would produce dark gray eyes in an olive skinned man?

He felt Giovanni's gaze, but he did not say a word. His candle flickered. He had to know. "What are you reading?"

Giovanni tilted the book on his knees, so Lucy's father could see "Holy Bible" embossed across the front.

"That's Lucy's Bible. I gave it to her." The urge to snatch his gift away almost won.

"Yes." Giovanni moved his feet to the ground, but kept the book in his lap. "I have a lot of catching up to do."

"Lucy tells me that you've recently become a Christian. The last I knew of you, you weren't a believer at all." Henry James crossed his arms and leaned back in his chair.

"Yes," Giovanni said again. "I've dedicated my life to God and His service. Although I must admit, I still have many questions. Your daughter has helped me to see things quite differently than I once did."

"Lucy is a remarkable young woman." An inch is all Henry would give.

"That she is." Giovanni nodded.

"I understand that your interest in my daughter is more than just professional," Henry James leaned forward.

"Yes." Giovanni closed the Bible and put it on the table. He leaned forward and focused his dark gray eyes. "Lucy told me of your conversation earlier this evening. I'd hoped to come to you myself, with our decision to marry, so I could properly ask you for her hand."

"If she told you of our conversation, then she must have told you my answer." At least the man had the decency to use Lucy's English name.

"She did." Giovanni did not bat an eye. "I understand your concerns Dr. James. I'd be surprised if you'd answered in a positive manner too quickly. I want you to know that I love Lucy enough to set her free if she wishes. I told her so this evening. If she does marry me, she'll lack for nothing."

Unexpected. Maybe a different angle would prove Henry's misgivings. "What about her medical career? Would you make her stop practicing in order to be your wife?"

"Absolutely not." Giovanni tilted his head with a slight smile. "She's too gifted. Lucy would be free to choose whatever she would want to do."

Henry James lifted his glasses and rubbed the bridge of his nose. Dr. Castello certainly was a lot more gracious than he had imagined.

"There are only two things, then that I must object to. Knowing Lucy, she's told them to you already. The first is that you're not just Italian, you're Sicilian. The second is that you're Catholic. Fix those two things and you would have my blessing."

"Though, I could change the church I attend, I believe such an action would be pointless." Giovanni sat up a little straighter. "As long as I'm serving the one true God, what does it matter which church I go to? As to being Sicilian and Italian, I could not love my heritage any more. There's nothing I can do to satisfy you on these matters. Lucy can see beyond the problems of race, and religious differences. I'm surprised that the father who has taught her so much cannot.

"In any event, Lucy has shown me the value of prayer, and you can be assured that I'll be praying for resolution. I would truly like for us to become friends. Please, as a favor to your daughter, seek the Lord on her behalf as well."

Had an arrow pierced his heart? Should he give in to the tug at his consciounce? Henry James stiffened. "I *will* be praying; praying that

Lucille comes to her senses. I firmly believe in racial separation. To think that my daughter has chosen someone like you is a bitter pill."

He looked away from Giovanni's penetrating stare. A mouse scuttled across the tent from under a table.

"Sometimes it takes a bitter pill to make a person well." Giovanni stood and collected his books. "If you will excuse me. Our days start early around here and I probably should get some sleep." He placed the last cookie in front of Lucy's father. "Really, you should try it."

Giovanni sat on the edge of his cot for a moment. From the other side of the curtain, he could hear Lucy breathe. What a shame to know that her father felt the way he did. The world was so full of prejudice. In his own beloved country, the separation between northern and southern Italians was a prime example.

His mind went to the history books he read over the years. How many wars had been fought between Protestants and Catholics? He could not count them all.

Giovanni knelt to pray. *Somehow you've got to help me resolve this. I don't know how you've kept my family in your service all this time, but here I am, one more Castello, asking for your guidance. I will wait for your answer.*

The curtain moved and Lucy sighed. She seemed so very upset that evening. Maybe he should check on her. In silence, he stood, went to the foot of his bed and pulled the curtain away from the wall an inch to watch her sleep.

Angela mia. Her red curls ran riot around her head. She lay curled up in a ball, shivering; her blanket had fallen to the ground.

How could I not have noticed the night breeze coming down from the mountains? Giovanni reached behind and pulled the blanket off his bed along with his burgundy wool cardigan. He slipped back through the curtain, and covered her first with his sweater and then with the blanket. Then he grabbed her blanket to take back with him.

Someone cleared their throat.

Giovanni froze. Please don't let it be Henry James. *This would be hard to explain*. He looked around the room and found Sister Francesca in her cot, with one eye open.

He smiled at the nun and put a forefinger to his lips.

Sister Francesca sat up a little. "Is everything all right?" She spoke without a sound.

Giovanni blew a kiss to the old woman and motioned for her to lie back down.

Sister Francesca did as he asked with a smile.

The sun rose just a bit earlier this morning and that suited Giovanni just fine. Spring had arrived in full force which meant the rain would finally go and things would dry so much easier. He had been up since four; a habit he had learned from his uncle a long time ago. Now that Giovanni's life had been changed he saw the logic. This was time to be with God; man to man…so to speak.

He gave one last look at all the patients he had tended to; everything and everyone had been taken care of. That left only one more thing to do; the icing on the cake to his way of thinking; breakfast with his favorite girl.

From outside the tent the ring of hammer and saw reached his ears. Foreigners were teaching his beloved *Siciliani* to work with wood. *That should bring us a good share of injuries today*. He chuckled.

He remembered Lucy's Bible and ducked back inside the dormitory to grab the book from the foot of his bed. He found a note on his pillow.

I will cling to you forever.
Ti Amo,
Persephone

Giovanni stuck the paper in his pocket. Lucy must have realized that he watched her last night. He walked into the mess tent and spotted her at the door table. She looked like the sunrise with her shiny dark red braid and hazel eyes. Then he noticed that she wore his sweater and he felt like singing.

Giovanni grabbed a roll and put it on his plate. What? No more coffee? Cook was nowhere to be seen. With great reluctance, he chose a steaming cup of tea. He sat next to Lucy and took a sip.

"Tea." Giovanni made a face. "This tastes like dish water. How can you drink it?"

"Like this." Lucy sipped her tea. "Umm. Did you get my note?"

"Yes Persephone. Spring will live forever in my home. I'm glad you're going to stay. How did you know which pillow was mine?"

"The same way you knew where I was. I've listened to you snore for over two months now."

"I do not snore."

"All right then you breathe loudly." Lucy eyes sparkled. "I like my new sweater. It's so soft. Is it cashmere?"

"Yes, it's cashmere. It's a nice color for you, but the sleeves are too long."

"No they're not, see?" Lucy shoved the sleeves up to her elbows. "You brought a cashmere sweater *here?*"

"Yes. It's old. I wore it in college. Besides, you don't seem to mind." He put his napkin in his lap and reached for his roll.

"It was very sweet of you to cover me last night, but now Sister Francesca wants me to trade beds with her. I guess she knows you as well as your mother. You won't mind having her just on the other side of the curtain will you?"

"*San Giuseppe!*" Giovanni dropped his roll onto his plate. "She knows about us?"

"Giovanni, you've been telling *everyone*. She was bound to find out." Lucy nodded.

He ran his hand through his hair. "She'll not give us any privacy until after the wedding. I'll have a talk with her." Lucy's laugh was his favorite sound. Then last night's conversation with Henry James came to mind.

"I spoke with your father last night."

"I know, he's already told me." Lucy squeezed her tea bag on the side of her cup with a spoon. "He seems a little better about you and me, but he's still objecting. Daddy has decided to leave by train this afternoon. I think he feels uncomfortable around us. Giovanni, he's never acted this way toward me."

"Somehow we'll help him to see that he is not really losing you." Giovanni dipped a piece of his bread in olive oil. "One day I might actually get to know him."

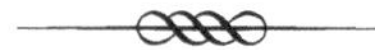

Henry James stared out the window at the beautiful coast of Italy. He did not see a thing. Instead he kept re-living the events of his visit.

Part of him wanted to be glad to see his daughter so in love. She had always been such a tomboy; he had given up the notion that Lucy could ever be normal. It would take someone foreign to find her attractive especially with the way she often behaved.

Giovanni loved Lucy a great deal, Henry James could be sure of it. Giovanni Castello also had the means to provide for his daughter even better than she was provided for now. The fact that he came from a prestigious family would give him bragging rights back home.

On the other hand, he simply could not put aside the fact that Giovanni was Italian. There would be a lot of people back home he could never tell the truth to. And the fact that Giovanni was Catholic made him cringe.

The more Henry James thought, the more his stomach churned. He had intended to spend this year with his daughter. Why on earth did he let Lucy volunteer to work in the hospital station? To that point, they were having a marvelous time.

Now he lived in a foreign country; alone. Would he travel home by himself too? In his mind, he imagined Lucy in a wedding gown marrying that Sicilian. Sickening.

In the satchel at his feet the leather spine of his Bible peeked up at him. *All who call on the name of the Lord will be saved*...Shouldn't he give in? Shouldn't he choose what God wanted? What about what Henry James wanted? No. His daughter should....correction, Lucille *would* return home with him. He pushed the satchel back under his seat until the Bible was out of view. Then, he pulled out a pen and stationary and wrote a letter.

My dearest Lucille,

It is now plain to me that you do not love me. I hope I am wrong. I will leave the choice up to you. Leave him now and all will be forgiven. Stay with this man and I will consider you dead.

Your Father,
Henry James

Jonah made the turn toward home without prompting from his driver. The crunch of gravel together with the clop of his steady walk seemed to announce the fading of another day. A front wheel ran over a piece of pavement cracked from the earthquake and the cart bounced.

"He's going to be shocked when we no longer head in this direction." Lucy grabbed the side of the cart and braced her feet against the dashboard.

Giovanni let the reins hang loose across his lap. "Yes, but he'll have his own stall."

"Do you think the coach house will be ready soon? He's been such a good mule." Lucy imagined Jonah clean and happily munching hay.

"It will." Giovanni turned his head slightly.

"Do you think we've told enough people?" The cart rocked again and Lucy bounced.

"Scoot closer to the middle. I promised your father I'd keep you safe." Giovanni pulled her by the waist to his side. "What were we talking about? Oh, yes, do I think we've told enough people about the move?

Yes. I don't think anyone will have trouble finding us. There's someone living in that house."

"That's odd." Lucy readjusted her seat. "As many times as we've driven by here, we've never seen them."

"I didn't think anyone would *want* to live there. It looks like it could fall any minute." Giovanni turned the mule to the left and drove him to the front door of the crooked house. "This was a nice villa once, I knew the people who lived here. I have an awful feeling about it now." He gave a sober glance in Lucy's direction. "I've had my fill of fallen houses."

Giovanni knocked on the door and a few minutes later a peasant with a gruff, unshaven face opened it.

Lucy held her breath. He was not much taller than she, but his body was large and hard, probably from a lifetime of physical labor. His shifty eyes and bushy brows made her want to duck behind Giovanni. *This guy is scary looking*. She backed up a step.

The man took one look at Giovanni and his stern face stretched into a huge smile.

"Giovanni!"

"Gasparone, I'm glad to know you made it. How is your family?"

Lucy watched not moving.

Gasparone and Giovanni hugged and kissed both cheeks.

She shook her head. *That would get a man punched at home*.

"This is Gasparone Di Foustino. He's a master fisherman and the only one I will buy from." Giovanni put a hand on Gasparone's shoulder and the other on Lucy's "This is *Lucia* my fiancé."

"Fidanzata?" Gasparone smiled even wider; his yellow teeth lacked one on the side. He grabbed Lucy before she could stop him. He squeezed her tight and gave her a big kiss on the cheek. "*Giovanni! Che bella!*"

I'll never get used to this. Lucy tried to regain her composure once Gasparone let her go. The odor of fish rose from her clothes.

Gasparone opened the door wider. "Come in."

They followed him into the well-lit villa. Whoever built the house made sure windows decorated every wall. It was clean and neat, but the floor moved in a funny way when she walked so Lucy stepped lightly.

"This is my mother *Prudenza Di Faustino* and my daughter Elena." Gasparone wrapped an arm around Lucy and guided her into the parlor that still had several pieces of furniture scattered about. His mother and daughter gave short curtsies.

"*Piacere*." Lucy curtsied in return.

"And this is my Maddalena. She died three years ago." Gasparone stroked a faded photograph in a handmade frame.

"She was as sweet as she was beautiful." Giovanni pulled Elena under his arm. "And you're going to look just like her." He pinched her nose. "Lucia, why don't you take care of *Signora De Faustino* and Elena? That way I can have a talk with Gasparone."

"Sure." Lucy took Elena and sat on the davenport. She dug through her medical bag for the vial of smallpox vaccine.

"*Amico*, this house is not safe." Giovanni's muffled voice floated from around the corner.

I hope he takes Giovanni seriously. Lucy vaccinated Elena and her grandmother. She heard footsteps and both men appeared from the kitchen.

"Lucia we need to be going," Giovanni said pleasantly. He gave her a hand up.

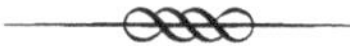

"Will he listen to you?" Lucy leaned back on the wagon seat and propped her feet up on her bag. Jonah walked at a steady pace, the hospital tent in the distance, lit by the final rays sent from the bright red sun which sunk behind the mountains.

"He says he will." Giovanni's mouth tightened. "I hope he doesn't put it off."

A bird flew buy with a worm in its beak, on the way to its nest in a tree. It landed and tiny birds with mouths wide open greeted their mother. "Look Giovanni."

He pulled the cart to a stop. A familiar warmth lit his eyes. "Life. How beautiful. Maybe that will be us one day. Would that be all right with you?"

Lucy felt heat rise in her cheeks. "Yes. I love children."

Giovanni chuckled and pulled her under his arm. "I didn't mean to embarrass you. I think you'll make a wonderful mother."

"You do?" Lucy turned back. He could be so disarming and the thought of being a mother excited her.

"Yes." He moved the mule on.

Lucy snuggled into him and he tightened his hold. "I hope Daddy comes around by then"

"We'll name a grandson for him and then he wouldn't be able to resist."

"*Henry* Castello? That sounds odd don't you think?"

"*Enrico*." Giovanni smiled into her ear. "I can't wait to meet him."

"*Enrico*, hmm, I like it. Will he be number one or number two?"

"I'm thinking, number three."

Lucy pulled away. "Number *three?*"

"*Si.*" Giovanni gave a sly nod. "The first will be Vito, the second Giuseppe and number three Enrico."

"Isn't it tradition in your family to always have a Giovanni? What happened to him?"

"He can be number four."

"Number four. All boys and no girls? That's typical."

"Of course not. We can have daughters too. I love girls." He waggled his eyebrows. "Do you want to know their names?"

"Why do I encourage you?" Lucy rolled her eyes. "We're not even married yet and you're naming children."

"I have become an optimist."

"Now I've heard it all."

Giovanni pulled Lucy back under his arm. "I like it better this way. Tomorrow we start the move, you know."

"I like it better this way too." She caught him smiling at her. "Believe it or not, I'm going to miss the days that we lived in a tent."

One by one someone lit lanterns, inside the walls of their ragged home.

"So will I," he said softly. "We'll tell our grandchildren all about it."

"I suppose you know their names too."

The sky glowed deep pink and blue, with the last rays of the sunset that poured over the harbor of Messina. Stars filled the sky and the musty smell that comes with the beginning of summer, hung gently in the air, even though May had not yet come to a conclusion. The day had been just like so many of the others, busy and fulfilling, with a deep sense of satisfaction; the kind that only comes from serving God without reservation.

Giovanni walked out the back door of his villa and paused for a moment, to marvel at the colors of the sunset. How his life had changed. He would have noticed, the beauty of a sunset before, but he would not have allowed himself to enjoy it.

Such a deep sense of peace had come over him since he had given his heart to Jesus. *Who would have known how much strength comes from peace*?

He walked forward and rested his hands on the stone railing. His gaze fell to his ring, which he now wore whenever he could. His mind traveled back to those lonely days in London, where he learned to nurse his rage until it nearly consumed him. What a waste of time.

It was in London that he first met a well-known group of scientists; all a part of a growing movement, which firmly held that men of science did not believe in God. Dr. Montgomery and Dr. De Stanza, who worked with Lucy's father, belonged to that group.

Giovanni had good reason to leave London and return home. Cold and elitist, "The Humanist Society of London" enlisted the kind of men who found science more important than the betterment of man. They backed their selfish, money driven decisions with the declaration that there was no God. Morals only applied when convenient.

Giovanni had been angry enough with the Almighty to go along with the group. He had even convinced himself that he could be one of them, until he realized they looked down their noses at the underprivileged people he loved to devote his time to. These men actually believed that people had been born poor, because they came from a lesser form of the human breed. The more educated a man, the wealthier a man, the more "evolved" a man's condition.

When Giovanni challenged their way of thinking, they dismissed him, saying that he kept his morals stuck in an outdated era. So, Giovanni struck out on his own. He sought to help where he felt God had failed.

Soon an impressive reputation followed. When it came to the practical application of medicine, Giovanni's surgical skills far surpassed those around him. King Edward found his skills so superior, that he took notice and he gave Giovanni work alongside of Sir Joseph Lister.

Suddenly, his humanist friends found him valuable. He made them look good. However, Giovanni had grown weary of their selfishness; they might be men of science, but he could never be one of them, even though they still tried to include him in their group.

He clinched his fists. What they would do to try to discredit him once they found out about his faith in God?

He who is quick-tempered acts foolishly. The Word of God whispered in his heart. It had been months since he had been *really* angry. Not that the cure was complete; some underlying issues still needed to be dealt with. Father Dominic said that he would probably always have a temper to control, but the Master Surgeon had begun the surgery and Giovanni expected a full recovery.

He took a deep breath and relaxed, with the sensation of air filling his lungs. He scanned the orange grove for Lucy. They had put in a lot of extra hours lately and the effects had begun to wear on her.

They had hoped to be able to operate the clinic on a set schedule, but the hospitals had not yet been finished, so they could see no way to do that.

By eight in the morning, the great room swam with people. At least traumatic injuries had come to a minimum. But, Messina still housed a lot of refugees, and sooner or later, every one of them needed medical attention. The house on the hill had become a very popular place.

The living conditions of the people they helped had become Giovanni's biggest concern. True to the tough nature of Sicilians, many, given the choice to move, still refused. They preferred to live in hand made shacks in front of their former homes, even though the city would soon be plowed under. With so many people living under such conditions, Messina would teeter on the brink of an epidemic, until everything became normal again.

The orange grove grew darker in the evening mist. Lucy must be down there somewhere; probably under a tree with her Bible in her lap. His heart swelled. She had done a brilliant appendectomy that afternoon. He remembered her words a few months back and chuckled. She did have a tough time in the kitchen, but she could perform an operation with the skill of few he had seen.

Life would be perfect right now, if not for the letters from Henry James. Lucy received another one that day. Giovanni really should find her; she must be hurting, she had to be, although she rarely allowed him to see her disappointment.

He descended the steps and walked out among the trees. A smile rose to the surface when he passed the one she had fallen from.

"*Lucia*? Where are you?"

The rustle of trees in the night air gave answer.

She must be further in the grove than he first thought. He spotted the massive banyan tree that grew in the corner with branches the width of a man's waist and roots that snaked to the ground from above. Every year, the tree grew in size; this one had been here a very long time.

She'd better not be in that tree. He made his way across the property. Pictures of his childhood flashed through his memory. How often he and his brothers played among these trees. One day, maybe, his own children would play here as well. He grew excited at the thought and then chuckled when he remembered how his normally outgoing Lucy, so practical and nonchalant in the doctor's office, would grow shy when the discussion turned in that direction. "*Lucia*?"

"I'm here." Her voice floated down from above. "Giovanni, I'm stuck."

He stopped, looked up and held back a laugh. About halfway up the huge tree, he could just see her silhouette in the fading light. "*Santa Maria*. How did you get all the way up there?"

"I used the ladder, but it fell and now I can't get down. Please don't fuss at me. I know I deserve it for being up here at all…but the sunset was so beautiful…" her voice trailed off with a slight tremor; had she been crying?

"Stay there." He waved at her. "I'm coming up."

Apparently, she had not found the wooden steps that his Papa had nailed into the tree years ago. Giovanni walked around the bottom and tested them; they were still firmly in place.

"You've climbed this tree before." Lucy bent over a branch to watch him.

Giovanni managed the steps and the branches without any problem. He paused on the thickest branch and offered his hand.

"Come and sit with me. This was my favorite place when I was a boy."

Lucy shimmied down the trunk and the two of them settled on a part of the tree that was very much like a natural chair. They could lean back against the trunk and rest their arms on another branch that crossed in front of them.

Giovanni tucked Lucy under his arm. "I'm simply going to have safety nets strung under all of these trees to catch you, should you fall." He gave her an affectionate squeeze.

Lucy gave a weak smile leaned into him and played with the button on his waistcoat.

"Talk to me *Lucia*, what's bothering you?"

Lucy pulled her father's letter out of her pocket and handed it to him.

"It's too dark for me to read this." Giovanni tried not to laugh again. "What does it say?"

"Daddy says that he's made friends with the port authority in Rome. He says that I simply must return to Boston with him or he will have me deported. Can he do that?"

"I don't think so." Giovanni searched his memory. What were those visa laws again? "*Zio Vincenzo* is an attorney, I'll ask him. In any event, I had *Padre* send our application for a marriage license three weeks ago. Once the license is approved, in the eyes of the government, we'll be married. You will virtually be seen as my property."

"Your *property*?" Lucy sat up and frowned. "Is that how you see me?"

Ah, the fire returns. That's more like it. He handed the letter back. "Of course not, but *Lucia* you must understand where it is you'll be living. There are some very old laws here, some which have been in place for centuries.

"In a lot of ways it's good, there are a thousand years of understanding among Italians; you will be my wife and there will be no questions. In a lot of ways it's not; here a wife is simply expected to obey her husband whether she wants to or not. That you work with me, that I choose to give you freedom, will be a source of a lot of gossip I can assure you. It might even become a scandal. Are you sure you're ready for that?"

Her arm slid around his waist and Lucy snuggled into his shoulder. "Is that a yes?" He smoothed her hair away from her face.

"Scandals seem to follow me. As long as we're together."

"Speaking of together. I have a surprise for you."

"You do?"

"How would you like to spend a couple of days in Palermo?"

"But I went last week. It's your turn to change Teresa's cast."

"No. I mean that we'll go together and spend two whole days. You've been working very hard lately bambina, I think a few days off would do us both some good."

"But how? We can't close the clinic." Lucy waved at the villa.

"Doctor Hertz, from the Dutch village, needed some time so I traded with him."

Lucy walked into the great room at Casa Bella; the great room aglow with light that reflected in the wall of windows. This place felt like a warm hug.

"*We're home*." Giovanni let the front door close with a thump.

"Mmm, I smell dinner." Lucy breathed in the scent of garlic and tomatoes. "You were right. I didn't realize how much I needed this. You're always taking care of me."

"I always will." He gave her hand a gentle squeeze.

"Where is everyone?" Lucy turned about. An afghan had been tossed on the arm of a chair, children's books lay scattered in front of the fireplace, but the room contained no people.

Giovanni raised a knowing eyebrow and pointed upstairs. "Listen, you'll hear them. It usually takes a minute."

The sound of small feet running floated down the stairs.

"Here they come." Giovanni glowed with anticipation.

"They sound like a herd of elephants." Lucy kept her eyes on the stairs. Before they knew it, the room filled with family members.

"Giovanni! *Lucia*!" The children surrounded them, and covered them both with hugs and kisses.

"Both of you are here at once?" Rosa emerged from the kitchen, her white apron, spotted with tomato sauce, still tied around her waist. She grabbed Lucy, kissed her, and then turned to Giovanni.

"*Mamma*, it's good to see you." He kissed her.

"Finally, the two of you are back." Rosa patted both of her son's cheeks at once. Giovanni scrunched his face and the children laughed. "I've not had both of you here together, since the night you became engaged. It's good to have our family complete again. Hurry and wash, dinner's ready. We'll wait for you." Rosa gave Giovanni a swat on his behind.

"*Hey*." His eyes went wide. "I'm too old for that."

The children laughed.

"Not as long as I'm your mother, you're not."

"I'm doing what she says." Lucy grabbed Teresa by the hand and they ran to the steps. "Let's get out of here."

Rosa clapped her hands. "Children, help *Lucia* and Giovanni to their rooms. Hurry, the pasta's in the water, we don't want it to become mushy."

"Giovanni, will you say the blessing?" Rosa gave an encouraging nod.

Lucy leaned an elbow on the armrest of her chair to watch him. His stinky brothers grinned. This place felt like home.

Giovanni bowed his head and his eyes went wide.

"No joking! Just pray." Rosa saw everything.

Giovanni bowed his head and closed his eyes. So contrite. Once finished, he lifted his head, put his napkin in his lap and scanned the room. "You've given the servants the night off again."

"Yes." Rosa gave him a stern look. "Why shouldn't they go home in the evening?"

"A cook is paid to cook, *Mamma*." Giovanni elbowed Lucy.

"I'm not even sure we have servants." Michael Sr. waved his fork at Antonio. "It's been at least a week since I've seen the butler. What's his name? I don't remember."

Lucy stifled a laugh. This was about to get good.

Rosa pointed a finger at her sons, one at a time. "When I pay *you* for your opinions' then you can have your say. I see three grown men who need to help with me with dishes later."

The children giggled. Celeste and Adella exchanged approving smiles.

"Aw, *Mamma*." Antonio groaned. "Have a little mercy."

"Why are you begging *Mamma*?" Michael Sr. picked up a basket of bread and passed it. "Giovanni started it. We should let him do the dishes."

"No. Because his sidekick, there would help him. He's always had it way too easy."

"You mean, *Lucia*?" Michael Sr. gave her a playful glare from across the table. A platter of sausages and peppers came her way. "She's still here? She must be trying for sainthood. Why else would she hang around the likes of him?" He nodded in Giovanni's direction.

"That *must* be why everyone in Messina calls her *Santa Lucia."* Antonio took a bite of sausage.

"*Santa Lucia*, you've been engaged for almost two months now, are you still willing to marry this man?" Michael grinned at Giovanni, who turned to listen to her answer with interest.

"Yes." Lucy tried to keep her tone indifferent, but a smile played on her lips. "You do realize, you ask me that every time I visit. Why?"

"I wouldn't marry him," Michael Sr. shrugged. "I know what he's like. I'm surprised he's been able to keep you this long."

Giovanni laughed. "Don't worry *Lucia*." He leaned toward her. "I wouldn't marry Michael either. He isn't as pretty as you."

The children giggled a bit louder.

"Does he order you about?" Antonio looked down his nose. "It's all right, you can tell us. We know he can be like a general."

"Giovanni, your brothers are smarty pants just like you." Lucy dabbed her mouth then turned in her seat to face Antonio.

"You didn't answer the question." Michael Sr. set his glass back on the table.

"No, he does not." Lucy looked at Michael directly, then she turned to Adella. "Does Michael order you about?"

"He wouldn't dare." Adella leveled her eyes at her husband.

Everyone laughed.

"Giovanni?" Sometimes Antonio had the swagger of a pirate. "I want to know what it's like to work with your *fidanzata*. Does she discuss lace and fashions while you do surgeries?" He changed his voice to sound like a girl. "Geeovannii, don't you like the way my dress matches the pearl handle on my saw?"

The children giggled. Rosa narrowed her eyes. Papa took her hand and bit his lip.

"Or does she get upset, when you pay more attention to your patients than you do her?" Michael Sr. put his napkin over his head like a kerchief and changed his voice too. "Stop looking at that bunion. Look at me."

"Have a scalpel, *Caro mio*." Antonio handed Michael Sr. his butter knife and batted his eyes like a girl.

Rosa put her fork down. "Boys, that's terrible! Are you trying to cause them to argue?"

"It's all right *Mamma*, they're just having fun." Giovanni turned to his brothers. "I think it's smart to work with my *fidanzata*. That way I can have the pleasure of looking at her all day long."

Oh, brother. Lucy took a bite of her sausage but her cheeks warmed.

"I couldn't ask for a better partner." Under the table, he gave her hand a squeeze. "She's as steady as any man and just as professional." Giovanni raised an eyebrow at her. "Just the other day, *Lucia* did an amazing appendectomy."

She covered her eyes with her hand. With what they ate for dinner, surely her partner had a plan to one up his brothers.

"This man came to us with a fever and vomiting and complaining of sharp pains right about here." Giovanni rubbed his stomach, at the area of his appendix.

Rosa narrowed her eyes at her son, but she kept quiet.

"We knew right away what was wrong. *Lucia* started the surgery without me because I was stitching someone's head. By the time I joined her, she had his stomach opened up like a picnic basket. You could see everything beautifully. That man's appendix was *so* swollen I could hardly believe it. It was big and round." Giovanni searched around the table. "It looked just like this." He skewered a large sausage on his fork and held it up like a prize.

"Ohhh! Ewwwe!" Everyone at the table moaned.

"Stop, please." Antonio covered his ears.

"That's nothing." Giovanni continued with a straight face. "It smelled just like Papa's socks after a day in the olive groves." He sniffed the sausage while his brothers gagged. He put it on his plate, cut it in half and then took a bite. "Umm, delicious. Here *Lucia*, I couldn't possibly eat all of this." Giovanni gave her half of it.

Everyone at the table moaned. Michael Sr. put down the sausage that he had been eating and glared at his brother who smiled sweetly.

Lucy laughed so hard, she found it hard to breathe.

"*Giovanni*." Rosa's mouth tightened. Did she find it funny too? "Must I wash your mouth out with soap?"

"I apologize *Mamma*." His face oozed innocence. "They wanted to know what it was like to work with *Lucia*."

"I have a question." Michael Jr. sat beside Lucy, his face still red from laughter.

"Yes Michael?" Giovanni turned to his nephew. "What's your question?"

What fun to watch him with the children in his family.

"I've read that there are so many buffalo in the American west, the herds stretch across half the continent. Is it true?"

He wants to be a cowboy in the worst way. Lucy re-arranged her napkin. "If there were that many where would we live? You've been reading paperbacks again."

"What's a buffalo?" Filipo sat up on his knees.

"You've seen the drawing, in our geography book." Michael Jr. nudged his cousin.

Excitement rose. Lucy had been out west not long ago. "They're twice as big as a bull and they have a head like one too only its set a bit lower and very shaggy. It takes a skilled hunter with a brave horse to bring down a buffalo."

"Have you ever seen one?" Ricardo wiggled in his seat.

"Oh yes." Out of the corner of her eye, Lucy saw Michael whisper something to Antonio. "You remember the uncle that I told you about, the one who owns a cattle ranch and lives in California. My brothers and I spent the summer with him three years ago. I saw buffalo and learned to ride in a western saddle. I even learned how to throw a rope."

Giovanni peered at her sideways. "Throw a rope? What exactly does that mean?"

Lucy looked around the table. Her eyes stopped at Giovanni's brothers. *Me and my big mouth. Now I've done it.* She held her breath for a moment and then gave up.

"When a cowboy catches a cow, he does it with a rope, on his horse." Lucy tried to only look at Michael Jr. "He'll make a loop in one end and twirl the loop over his head. At just the right time, he'll throw the loop over the head of a cow and his horse will help to stop it. If you give me a rope and start to run away, it is very likely that I'd be able to catch you."

The children all started to laugh.

"That is impossible." Michael Sr. leaned forward.

"I don't know." Giovanni turned to Lucy with a chuckle. "I've seen her wrestle. My inclination would be to believe her."

Rosa's eyebrows went up. "Your uncle taught you to do this?"

Lucy nodded, heat radiated from her cheeks.

Rosa turned to Giovanni. "She wrestles?"

"Only bad guys."

"You can rope a cow?" Michael Jr. sat on the edge of his seat.

"Yes. But, Uncle Roy is so much better than me. He can catch a cow at a full gallop with the reins in his teeth."

"I don't believe it." Michael Sr. scowled. "I'm going to get a rope."

"Oh, no. I'm absolutely not going to rope any people. Someone could get hurt."

"Please *Lucia*." The children bounced up and down.

"You won't hurt me. How much rope do you need?" Michael gave a look of challenge to Lucy, but he addressed Giovanni. "A wild woman from the American west, brother. Well done."

Giovanni raised an eyebrow at Lucy. "Take him up on it. If he breaks a leg I'll set it."

Fine. "I'll need about thirty feet."

"Let's go watch." The children scraped their chairs on the tile.

"What about dessert?" Rosa's question sounded more like an attempt to make everyone sit down again..

"Who wants dessert?" Antonio helped his wife with her chair. "I want to watch *Lucia* make a fool of my brother."

Giovanni followed Lucy out to the patio. *She certainly is not typical*. He watched her handle the rope his brother brought to her. She made a large noose with a slipknot.

"We actually could use a metal ring or an eyelet." Lucy began to roll the rope into a coil. "That way the noose would slip easily, but for tonight we'll get away with this."

She stopped and let her hands fall in front of her, the rope still in her grip. "Daddy would be livid if he knew I was doing this. You're sure this doesn't bother you?"

"If you have a talent, I believe that you should use it." He laughed. "He's bull-headed, everyone knows it. Go ahead, catch him like a bull."

"Don't run." Lucy let half of the coil fall to the ground in a neat pile. She looked up at Michael Sr. "I don't want you to fall."

"No...you have to catch me. Remember?" Michael Sr. kept his hands out to the side, ready to move.

"All right, you've asked for it." Lucy followed her "cow" with a steady gaze. The rope in a large circle above her head.

"She's doing it, just like in my books." Michael Jr. jumped behind her.

His father made a dodge to the left and then to the right, but Lucy anticipated his movement. The rope landed in a neat drop, around his shoulders.

Antonio and Giovanni burst into laughter and the children cheered.

Lucy pulled Michael in and then tightened noose around his shoulders. "You're a very slow cow." She wrinkled her nose at him and then set him free.

"*You* will make an excellent Castello." Michael gave her a hug and kissed her cheek. "You should have Giovanni teach you to fence."

"With her temper? She doesn't need to handle a sword." Giovanni quite liked the idea.

"Hey." Lucy grinned at him.

"Why not?" Antonio gave him a nudge. "She's got an excellent eye, she's light on her feet. You know *Lucia*, Giovanni is so good they wanted to make him a master instructor at the Royal Academy, just under our Uncle Vincenzo."

"I thought he was an attorney." Lucy wrapped the rope into a coil and handed it to Michael.

"He does a lot of things." Michael tucked a laughing Ricardo under his other arm like a football. "If Giovanni won't teach you, we will. And the next time you come we'll fence for you."

"If anyone teaches her, it will be me." Giovanni pointed at his own chest. "And the next time we come, I'll take you both.

His brothers laughed. Antonio grabbed Giovanni's shoulders and mussed his hair. So Giovanni had no option other than to lock Antonio's head under his arm.

Michael Jr. jumped on Giovanni's back. Lucy laughed and covered her mouth.

Rosa walked by with a silver tray full of cookies. She leveled her eyes at her sons. "Stop your wrestling and come have some dessert."

"*Si, Mamma.*" Giovanni winked at Lucy and let Michael Jr. slide to the ground. He went to her side but not before he gave Michael Jr. a playful push on the head. They pointed at each other in mock anger.

"My life was so dull until you came along." He took her hand in his.

"How could it be dull with all of these beautiful people around you?" Lucy flushed from laughter.

"You were missing from it." He gave her a pull toward the wicker furniture, where his mother waited. "Come, *Signorina* Cowgirl, let's have some coffee with *Mamma*."

"I apologize for interrupting dinner *Mamma*." Lucy let go of Giovanni's hand just before she sat. They found a place to rest on a small sofa.

"We were almost finished anyway. Besides, we've come to look forward to your interesting conversations. Would you care for *biscotti*?" Rosa held out a silver tray full of cookies.

"*Si, grazie*." Lucy picked one full of almonds and dipped it in her coffee.

"Ah, my guitar. That's heavy for you with one arm. *Grazie*, Teresa." Giovanni winked at his niece and eased the guitar out of her hand. The little girl climbed into Lucy's lap and Giovanni began to play. The deep tones filled the night sky and floated on the warm breeze.

"That's the song you played on the piano the first time I visited here." Lucy hugged the child in her lap, careful of her cast.

"I can't believe you've been with me this long and I haven't sung it to you." He stopped playing. The moonlight on her hair and the sweetness in her face made his heart jump. "It's a love song about a man who is looking at Naples from a boat. The area he is looking at is called *Santa Lucia*. He sings about how beautiful the city looks from the water. I always imagined that he was just returning from a long journey. That he had a family waiting for him and loving arms to greet him."

He looked into her eyes and hoped she could see the depth of his love.

Lucy turned pink and squeezed Teresa gently. She had such strength of spirit.

What an honor, to be given someone so pure. With all his heart, he longed to take her into his arms and love her until all doubts vanished . But, for now, he must wait. In less than a month, *Lucia* would be his at last. Tonight, he would make love to her heart, through music. The words to this sweet old melody would just have to do.

"Sul mare luccica
L'astro d'argento
Placida 'e l'onda
Prospero 'l vento;
Venite all'agile
Barchetta Mia;
Santa Lucia! Santa Lucia!"
(T. Cottrau – Longo 1835)

The next morning came, exquisite and beautiful, the kind of morning that made Sicily famous; the air cool and the sky as blue as a baby's eyes. A golden mist hung on the ground, as a token of the warm afternoon to come.

On the patio, Lucy had the hardest time choosing between soft crusty bread smeared with mascarpone cheese or indulging in one of Rosa's breakfast biscotti.

"Hey Annie Oakley." After the night before, Michael applied his new nickname every chance he got. "Where's Buffalo Bill?"

"I'm not sure." Lucy chose to ignore the jab. "He wasn't in his room when I left mine."

"Giovanni came down early this morning." Rosa placed a pitcher of goat's milk on the table. "He wanted to visit Vito and Giuseppe, I believe he's still there."

Even in the sun, Lucy felt cold. She put her *biscotti* down. "When he talks about his brothers he becomes so sad. I need to find him."

"You should go to him." Rosa took Lucy by the hand, led her to the steps of the patio. "Before you go, I want to thank you for giving my son back to me. The deaths of his brothers hit him very hard. It was then he began his journey away from God. When he moved to London, he hardened completely. He became so angry, so serious. God is changing him, I can see it. He hasn't played at the dinner table for years." Rosa's eyes glistened. "And he sang to you last night. You don't realize what a miracle it is to hear him sing again."

"God is changing him," Lucy said softly. "He's the one to thank not me."

"Yes." Rosa gave Lucy's hand a gentle squeeze. "But you've been his instrument."

He's a wonderful man, *Mamma*. He deserves a good wife. I hope I can give him what he needs."

"I think you'll do just fine." Rosa hugged Lucy.

Lucy walked across the herb garden, passed the fountain and then down the stone path toward the family cemetery. The ruins of a church built long ago, now covered in flowering vine, gave solemn witness.

Giovanni stood at the foot of the graves. His normally straight shoulders sagged and the old gray cloud, so familiar from the days of the hospital station, loomed in his eyes.

He took a deep breath and made a slow turn to face her. Lucy remembered how he used to hide his pain behind sarcasm, but now he hid nothing at all.

"*Buongiorno, principessa*." His voice sounded flat. "God must have heard my heart because I was just wishing you were here."

Lucy came to his side and he took her hand in his. She said nothing. When he felt this way; he only needed to hold her hand so she let him.

Giovanni turned back to study the graves.

She watched his face again and felt for certain that she knew what went on in his heart. "You're still angry at God aren't you?"

Giovanni grew darker than he had for a long time and gripped her hand. "I am."

His eyes turned black just before he closed them. Giovanni breathed in deeply and the released the air slowly. He relaxed his jaw.

"*Lucia*, I'm tired of living angry." Giovanni took another deep breath."I'm weary of this battle."

Lucy prayed in her heart for guidance.

"You're praying for me." Tears softened his voice. "You're always praying for me." Giovanni pulled Lucy into a gentle hug from the side. "You're always here when I need you."

Giovanni squared his shoulders. "I'll seek God until I find a solution. If I'm to lead our family properly, I must do so without the anger."

Lucy hugged him back. Water splashed in the fountain and a bee buzzed by. Her stomach growled.

"Was that you?" Giovanni held her by the shoulders, his eyes full of light again...

"Yep." Lucy giggled.

"How do you stay so slender?" He took her hand and led her down the stone path toward the house. "Come on, let's get some breakfast. We'll take care of Teresa's arm and tonight: you and I are going to the opera."

Lucy stood in front of the dressing mirror in a beaded gown of emerald green; could this reflection really be her own image? How was it possible that this exquisite garment hung, unworn, in the back of someone's closet? Adela had helped her dress and Celeste had done her hair, both seemed to be just as excited to help as Lucy was to go.

"I can't thank you enough." Lucy hugged the women one by one.

"One more thing." Celeste pulled out a small atomizer. "This is perfume from my home in France. It doesn't take much, but tonight you cannot be without it."

Lucy felt like a princess. Her prince waited patiently for her at the bottom of the stair. Meticulously dressed in his black tuxedo, Giovanni had combed his hair back stylishly; on his finger he wore his onyx ring. Every bit as handsome as she remembered him on the night they first met, Lucy's heart fluttered and her stomach tightened. He turned his black eyes on her and she almost ran back to her room.

Watch me trip. Lucy put her gloved hand on the mahogany banister for balance. Like a magnet her eyes were drawn back to Giovanni.

"*Sei molto bella*." A slow smile spread across his face and he watched every step she took on her way down the stairs.

"You make me feel beautiful." Lucy's hands trembled, but not out of fear.

"I've always told you that you are."

Lucy touched the crook of his arm and Giovanni put his hand on hers. "You're trembling, bambina. You're not nervous are you? I want you to have a good time tonight."

"I'm excited." Lucy smiled into his handsome face. "This is my first date."

CHAPTER TWENTY- ONE

The grand marquis at the world famous *Teatro Massimo* read; '*La Bohème*', by *Giacomo Puccini*.

The sad and beautiful tale of lovers separated by death, captivated Lucy from the haunting first notes until the final curtain.

Giovanni became quite still during the performance. At the end when the heroine, Mimi, died he took Lucy's hand in his and held onto it until the lights went up again.

Lucy hung tightly on Giovanni's arm, not wanting to wake from such a perfect dream. He led her through lively streets, then down to the marina and the waterfront. They strolled arm in arm along the water's edge beneath the glow of street lamps, between gilded palaces and extravagant hotels on one side and the midnight sea on the other. Couples greeted as they passed; gentlemen with a tip of their hats and ladies with a smile.

He paused and looked up at the Hotel Victoria. The faint strains of music floated from inside. "This is what Messina was like you know. Its waterfront was much like what you see here, with people on the promenade and lights everywhere."

"Do you think they'll rebuild it?" Lucy found that she missed the devastated city.

"It will never be the same." Giovanni pulled her closer. "There's just no way to put back a building that's three hundred years old. But they will rebuild and one day things will feel normal again."

"Are you hungry?" Giovanni led her down some steps and paused in front of a line of sailboats. "I shouldn't even ask you. You're always hungry. How about some dinner?"

"That sounds wonderful." Lucy looked back the way they came. "Where?"

Giovanni slipped off his jacket and loosened his tie. "Come." He walked her out on the stone pier. There, tied to a hook, floated a small boat with a pair of oars inside it.

"In that?" Lucy tried not to giggle.

"No." Giovanni turned in the direction of the water. "Over there."

Behind him, moored to the farthest point on the pier, a beautiful pleasure yacht glistened in the moonlight. "You've not really seen Palermo until you've seen it from the water."

"Is this yours?" Goose-bumps tickled her arms.

"Yes, it's yours too." He gave Lucy a pull toward the boat, his face lit with pleasure. "My brothers like to use it, so I keep it here. My parents are not much for the water but my brothers and I, we love it. It means a lot to me that you're excited."

Giovanni jumped on first and then he lifted Lucy to the deck. "Welcome aboard *La Santa Rosa*. Let me show you around."

"Okay." Lucy grinned.

"The deck is easy enough to see. She's a full forty feet long. My brothers and I have spent a lot of time making this boat exactly what we wanted. We built the bench there, in the stern. It has lots of storage for life vests and other things. This bench," He lifted the lid on a box in the middle of the boat, "is for fishing tackle. Let me show you down below." He went to the door of the cabin and opened it.

"You really love this boat, you're glowing." Lucy couldn't help but laugh at him.

"Yes. I read *Treasure Island* when I was a boy and I've dreamt of being a pirate ever since. Come on, you'll love this."

Lucy followed him down a few wooden steps into a very pleasant cabin with a bunk for sleeping; big enough for two, a well equipped galley and a dining table built into the hull.

"The head is right through there." Giovanni pointed at a small door toward the rear of the cabin. His eyes glowed with delight. "It even has a small shower. That was my idea. I built it."

"We'll have to take a trip sometime." Lucy tried not to look at the bed. "We could sail all the way around Sicily."

"Or up the coast to Venice." Giovanni opened the door and Lucy went back up the steps. "Do you want to go out?"

"Really? Yes, but it's dark." Lucy watched Giovanni untie the ropes.

"We won't go far." He pulled up the anchor, took the wheel and kicked his shoes off. The boat began to glide through the harbor. "You should take your shoes off too or you'll find it hard to stand." He peeled his socks off one at a time and tossed them to the side.

"I'm not having any problems." Lucy shrugged.

"Suit yourself." He turned the wheel to the left a bit. The boat dipped and Lucy grabbed the mast in front of her. "Last year Antonio and I put in an automobile engine and a propeller for nights like this, when there's little wind. Do you sail much in Boston?"

"Believe it or not, I've lived all my life near the Atlantic, but I've never sailed at all." Lucy peered up the mast; it seemed tall enough to hook the crescent moon glowing overhead.

"Come and take the wheel." Giovanni motioned for Lucy to stand in front of him. "The first time you steer a boat is something you never forget."

Lucy tried to let go but she nearly fell over.

"I've never seen you look so graceful." He smirked. "Take your shoes off."

"Okay, fine." Lucy kicked her shoes to the side and her feet slid out from under her. "These silk stockings make it even worse." She re-gripped the mast.

"Then take the stockings off."

"You've got to be kidding."

Giovanni tilted his head and looked at her feet. "I won't watch you."

"You better not." Lucy waited.

He raised an eyebrow and then slowly turned around.

Lucy hurried to roll up her stockings

"Are you finished yet? "Can I turn around? I want to see your knee again." He turned his head a bit.

"No. Don't you dare." She stuffed them in her shoes and pulled her dress back into place. "That's better." Her confidence returned with her balance.

Giovanni turned around and beckoned her to stand in front of him.

Good; a reason to be close. "Now what do I do?"

"Put your hands here and…here." Giovanni placed Lucy's hands on the wheel. His breath tickled her neck. Did he find it hard to keep his hands where they belonged?

Maybe I should step away. But you know, with all the opportunities he's had in the last two months, Giovanni's never pressed his advantage. What a wonderful guy. She leaned against him.

Giovanni cleared his throat and pushed away gently. "Now you decide where we'll go. Pick a place somewhere out there." He motioned beyond the harbor, to the black Tyrrhenian Sea. "When you want to stop, pull this lever all the way down. I should be back by then."

"Where are you going? Giovanni, I might run us aground."

He laughed and shook his head. "I'm going to get dinner. If you see land directly in front of you, stop the boat." Chuckling quietly, he ducked inside the cabin.

Lucy could hear Giovanni open and close cabinet doors in the galley. She gripped the wheel until her fingers started to ache. Ahead on the water floated a lone pelican. *Please don't let me hit him. Please don't let me hit him.*

The pelican drifted on by in the wake of the boat. He looked at her and she looked at him.

"Don't act so smug, you've done this before." Lucy glared at the bird.

"Who are you talking to?" Giovanni emerged from the cabin below with a huge picnic basket.

"That bird over there."

"The pelican? How funny." He walked the basket to the stern of the boat and put it on the bench. Then, he came to relieve Lucy.

"Apparently, we have not sunk. Well *Lucia*, what do you think?"

"I'm having the time of my life. I can see why this is so popular." Wisps of hair floated around her face, she smiled and wrinkled her nose. "What a sense of freedom. How do you ever decide when to turn back?"

"That's the hardest part." He dropped the anchor, turned the engine off and planted a light kiss on her nose. "Let's eat."

Rosa had sent a marvelous dinner. The basket contained a large thermos of Italian egg drop soup, Giovanni called *stracciatelle*. It also contained a warm salad of sorts; *caponata*, that went on yummy, crusty bread, and one more unopened container.

"What's in here?" Lucy pulled the tin out of the basket and popped it open. It looked like tiny pieces of fried… "Are these fried clams?"

"Try it before I tell you." Giovanni skewered a piece with his fork and held it for Lucy to try.

"Whatever it is it's good." Lucy liked the crunch. "It kind of tastes like fried clams."

"Good." Giovanni ate some himself. "This is squid. It's called *calamari*. I've known some Americans to be squeamish."

"You should know me better than that." Lucy took another bite from Giovanni's fork. "Weren't they serving us donkey for a few days at the hospital station? The cook said it was beef, but that was *not* beef in our soup."

Giovanni laughed. "I'm not sure what it was, I'm just glad no one got sick on it."

With the dishes empty, Giovanni stood, stacked everything and set it to the side. He opened the bench that he had sat on and pulled out a soft wool blanket.

"Come sit with me." He unfurled the blue tartan covering. "You're shivering."

"They only want one thing." Aunt Lucinda's warning came to her clear as day. Lucy eyed the blanket with suspicion. *He's a good man, but he is a man.*

Giovanni's face grew soft.

"I know what you're thinking. I know what this looks like, but nothing could be further from the truth. *Lucia*, I wanted to be alone with you because we're never alone. We always have someone around us, Father Dominic, the nuns, our patients, my family...It is completely selfish, but I want to spend time with you, alone, just you and me. Please come and get warm. I won't do anything to make you uncomfortable."

How could she have misjudged him? "I'm sorry." She slid next to him and settled under Giovanni's arm, on the inside between him and the boat. She let him cover them both with the blanket. They leaned against the corner with their feet propped up on the bench.

"Your feet are cold too." He touched her toes with his and she giggled. "Scoot up." Giovanni pulled Lucy closer and covered her feet. "Better?" he smiled into her eyes.

She nodded and leaned her head on his shoulder. She watched the lights from the city, rocked by the gentle sway of the boat as it tugged on its anchor.

Palermo twinkled in the night. The city lights rose from the water to the sky, along the shadowy slopes of *Monte Pellegrino*. The mountain framed the background of Palermo, a noble sentry that forever guarded the island of Persephone. The lights, the mountain and the city, melted together and shimmered in the waves like images in impressionist's dream.

"I can't believe how beautiful this is." How had her lonely life come to be so wonderful? Lucy sighed in utter contentment. "I can't believe how late Italians stay out at night."

"That's because we nap in the afternoons." Giovanni rested his well-shaved cheek next to hers.

"What tower is that?" Lucy let him wrap his arms around her and his hands take hold of hers. How safe she felt.

"That's the church that we visited yesterday. Over to the right you can just see the Palace and see the lights from the market? They are there." He nodded to the right.

Giovanni rested his soft cheek on hers once more and the faint scent of soap and after-shave, washed over her, warm and inviting. She felt his chest rise and fall and his thumb caress the back of her hand, her ring and the finger that wore it.

Giovanni brought one of Lucy's hands to his lips and kissed it. He began to sing in quiet tones, the first phrase of "*Che Gelida Manina*" from *La Bohème*.

*"How cold your little hand is, Let me warm it for you."*He sang in English.

"*La Bohème* is such a beautiful story." Lucy sighed. "How odd that Mimi's real name was *Lucia*. Did you realize that before we went tonight?"

"Yes." Giovanni tilted his head to look into her eyes. "You have my word *Lucia*, that unlike Mimi, you will always be taken care of."

He wrapped his arm around her again and pulled her just a little closer. He leaned his face to hers. Would he kiss her? He did not.

"You're not even going to try to take advantage of me are you? You love me enough to *not* touch me?" She turned in his arms to look into his face. She wanted him to see her heart. "We're alone on this boat in the middle of the water. I love you so much that I would find it very difficult to deny you anything. I love you so much more because you're treating me like a lady." She placed her palm on his cheek and he pressed it to his face with his hand.

"I promised you, and I promised God." Giovanni looked into her soul. "What kind of man would I be if I broke my promises? Besides, waiting will only make our wedding night that much sweeter."

"You make it sound so simple."

"Don't be deceived *Lucia*, I find it very hard to resist you. I'll not kiss you out here, because if I do I will not be able to stop..." His voice trailed off.

At the word "kiss" an odd expression crossed his face. The air felt very warm, but Lucy began to shiver. Giovanni drew closer and Lucy found that not only had she lost the strength to move, she did not want to move. Passion filled his eyes and she thought for a moment that he *would* kiss her.

Lord please give me strength. I want a lot more than a kiss. I'm afraid I'll not refuse. She moved her hand back into his, he gripped it and took a deep breath. And then she remembered what Rosa had told her right before she came down the stairs.

"*Gesù, Maria!*" Lucy said loudly. She squeezed his hand.

"Ha, ha, ha, ha!" Giovanni threw his head back in peals of laughter. He put his hands on her cheeks and kissed her square on the forehead. "Who told you to say that?"

"Your mother." Lucy was laughing too. She tried to catch her breath. "She said if things got too warm that I should shout it. She said it would make you stop."

"Ha, ha, ha!" Giovanni laughed again. "I wasn't going to do anything, were you?"

"Well, no." Lucy played with her thumbnail. She remembered the look in his eye and poked a finger to his chest. "Are you telling me that you were in complete control? That you weren't thinking…" her voice trailed off and she buried her face in her hands. "Oh, I'm so frustrated. I'm a doctor. I've seen it all. I know *all* about this. Why is it so hard to have this discussion?"

"Because at this moment you're a young woman in love, not a physician." Giovanni gently lifted her chin. "You always know what I'm thinking. I've learned not to hide from you. So yes, I was thinking; about our honeymoon and how perfect I want it to be for you. Lucia, I want you more than I've wanted anything in my life. I'm so grateful God has given you to me; that I'll never use you badly. So, no matter what I want or think, I *will* choose the right thing." His eyes began to glow again. "You *do* take my breath away."

He breathed once more, and he relaxed his grip. He stroked Lucy's cheek with his fingertips and kissed the top of her head. "I think it's time for us to go home. *Gesù Maria. Ha, ha, ha, ha.*" Giovanni rose from their cocoon. He wrapped the blanket around Lucy and pulled up the anchor.

It was one o'clock in the morning when hand in hand, Giovanni and Lucy climbed the stairs at Casa Bella. They walked the upstairs hallway, all the way to Lucy's bedroom door. With each slow tick of the hall clock, Giovanni's control slipped a bit more.

The flame that kindled in his eyes, while on boat, still smoldered. He knew she could see it, because he could no longer hide it. At least here at Casa Bella, he could not take things too far.

"Now, I will kiss you. Here, where I will be forced to let you go." Giovanni pulled her close and wrapped Lucy in the kind of embrace he had only allow himself to give her once before.

He kissed her with all of the love in his strong heart. He thrilled at the softness of her lips and the sweetness of her breath. She felt so fragile, in his arms, like a flower, easily broken. Yet she did not resist. She allowed him to crush her, so he did. She invited him to kiss her again and he could not stop.

He rejoiced at the beauty of the gift in his arms. If only God would make time pass quickly. If only, somehow, God would help him make her wedding night a joy.

Lucy trembled beneath his touch and he released her. Was his kiss too much? Maybe too strong? "Are you all right?" He searched her eyes.

"I'm fine," Lucy whispered. She touched his soul with the light in her eyes.

"You trust me, even in this matter," he whispered back and joy filled him.

"With my whole heart, I trust you." Lucy smiled the impish smile he loved so much. "I'm just new to this. And don't worry, I won't shout. It would wake everyone."

A soft laugh escaped him. Giovanni kissed her temple and drew her close again.

"My wife. God could not have given me a more perfect wife. There are still times when I can hardly believe you're real."

"I'm real, all right." Lucy spoke against his shoulder. "In three weeks I'll follow you anywhere."

He could never deserve such a precious thing.

"In three weeks, I'll give you a gift that belongs to no other." Lucy put her hand over his heart. Her gentle touch made him weak.

"A gift I will treasure my entire life." Giovanni whispered back, his soft voice rough and masculine. "My heart is yours *Lucia*."

He lingered a kiss on her cheek and whispered in her ear. "You can trust me *cara mia;* even in this will I take care of you."

"I know you will." Lucy offered her sweet lips once more.

How could he refuse? He kissed her one last time, softly, tenderly, she leaned into him and he held her tight. With much effort, he stopped and forced himself to pull away.

"God will bless our decision to stay pure," Giovanni said, as much to himself as to Lucy. Hopefully time, indeed, would move fast. "I read about it just this morning."

Lucy still held his hand, he did not want to let go. He stroked her velvet cheek with his fingertips. It took every ounce of his strength not to pull her close again.

Down the hall, a door opened with a slow creek. Giovanni smiled, glad for the interruption.

Teresa stumbled towards them in her footie pajamas. She rubbed the sleep from her eyes and wrapped her good arm around Lucy's legs.

"My arm itches."

"I know." Lucy stroked her head. "Why don't you go climb into my bed, you can sleep with me. I'll be there in a minute."

Giovanni stooped to Teresa's level and straightened the sling that held her cast. "*Buonanotte, cara.*" He kissed his niece on the cheek. Giovanni stood and pulled Lucy toward him. For a moment, he let himself drown in her eyes. She certainly must have felt what he did. "*Buonanotte, cara.*" Giovanni kissed Lucy on the cheek.

Lucy followed Giovanni out of the train and into the humidity. After several hours sweating in a hot train, the humid air actually felt good. She scanned the dusty station to find Father Dominic.

The priest stood by the mule cart. He smiled and waved when she spotted him, then pulled a handkerchief from the folds of his robes to mop the perspiration off his bald head.

"He has an odd look on his face." Lucy readjusted her shoulder bag.

"He does." Giovanni squinted in the sunlight. "I've seen that look before. Something's not right, I wonder what it is."

Father Dominic greeted the couple in his usual manner. He hugged Giovanni and kissed Lucy on the cheek. He tightened his lips.

"*Padre*?" Giovanni touched his shoulder.

"Not here." Father Dominic lifted Lucy's bag into the cart. "Let's get in the wagon, so we can talk."

Lucy's stomach tightened; she looked to Giovanni. He shrugged and put the rest of their bags next to hers.

The ground under her toes began to vibrate.

"Did you feel that?" She grabbed Giovanni's arm.

"No." He made a slow turn. "But you always feel a tremor before the rest of us. Maybe that will be it."

He gave her his hand; did the ground just vibrate again? Lucy waited, eyes wide. Jonah gave an uneasy snort.

The vibration became stronger and then stronger still. Lucy struggled to stand. Debris fell, the cloud of dust that rose around them blocked out the sun and Lucy coughed violently.

Giovanni wrapped his arm around her. "Breathe through this." He placed a handkerchief in her hand and moved it to cover her nose and mouth. He grabbed a hold of the cart and kept Lucy on her feet. Then it stopped as quickly as it had begun.

Lucy still struggled to breathe. "It's been months since we've felt something that strong."

"Are you all right?" Giovanni moved her hand and the hankie back over her face.

"Yes." Lucy gave a gentle push on his hand. "I think I can breathe now. Are you okay?"

"I'm fine." He looked over to the other side of the cart. "Padre?"

"I'm here." The priest had been hugging Jonah's neck. He wiped his glasses on his robe.

Giovanni held out his hand and Lucy stuffed the hankie in her pocket with a sheepish smile and climbed into the wagon. "I put one in my pocket this morning and now it's gone."

"I was trying to help you into the cart." Giovanni shook his head and swung up beside her. "I'm not worried about the handkerchief, I bought ten new ones for us to share just yesterday, remember?"

He gave Father Dominic a hand up. "We'd better get going *Padre*."

Giovanni slapped the mule with the reins and they took off.

They nearly flew to the middle of the city, where a number of doctors had already lined up wounded. They jumped from the wagon and raced to the people stretched out on the ground.

"Dr. Castello, Dr. James." The voice belonged to Dr. Donelson, the English physician who had an office at the American village. "Help me get these children into this wagon."

Lucy turned to see the poor man with several crying children at his feet and a baby in his arms. Her heart broke at the sight. She picked up a screaming two-year-old.

"Come on *bambina*, let's put you in the wagon."

Giovanni grabbed another child and placed it next to the one in the cart. He yelled above the noise. "Let's take these people to our clinic. It's the closest and there's plenty of room,"

Doctor Donelson nodded and loaded the last child.

"*Padre*!" Giovanni shouted across the bedlam; he met the priest's gaze. "We're going to the villa. Send people as you find them."

They got to the house and Lucy ran ahead, while Giovanni secured the mule. She handed a child to Sister Francesca. The dependable nuns had everything set for them.

Lucy skidded to a halt. Sister Francesca had the oddest look on her face. "Sister what's wrong?"

Henry James stepped out of the shadows.

CHAPTER TWENTY-TWO

"You're coming home with me *now*." He towered over her.

" I have work to do." *Seriously?* Lucy wheeled around and headed for the dining room, but her father grabbed her wrist and yanked her into the hallway.

"I'll have no arguments. You're my daughter; you *will* do as you're told."

"What's the matter with you?" Lucy tried to pull free from her father's vice-like grip. "Ouch! Daddy, please, these people are hurting. I have to help them."

The front door closed with a thump.

"This is exactly the kind of thing we've been preparing for." Giovanni led the English physician into the great room, emptied of its furniture except for the chairs, scattered about for waiting and cots placed up against the walls for emergencies.

"Once these cots are full, it will be very easy to throw mats down and line people up on the tile." Giovanni pointed to the stack of mats rolled up in the corner.

They walked into the dining room where two metal tables stood. The big dining table, up against the wall, held supplies and instruments, all in neat order.

"A third table is in the kitchen." Giovanni held one of the kitchen doors open. "We've been using it for general exams."

"I'd heard this clinic was put together nicely." Dr. Donelson clapped him on the back. "Well done Dr. Castello. The new hospitals can't be finished soon enough. I've never seen a place so prone to earthquakes."

"It's a good distance from your surgery. But you know you're welcome to use this place whenever the need arises." The house was too quiet. Giovanni looked around. "*Lucia*?"

"I'll not have you associating with these greasy Italians any longer." Henry James dragged Lucy with him toward the rear of the house.

"*Giovanni!*" Lucy planted her feet and wrestled to break free, but her father grabbed her other hand and pulled her toward the back door.

With a swift motion, the door opened and Father Dominic stepped inside.

The priest wrenched Lucy free and stood between she and her father.

Giovanni came around the corner with Sister Francesca at his side. The crying child Lucy had given her, still in her arms.

"Exactly *what* is going on here?" Giovanni pushed his way in front of the priest.

"My daughter is coming home with me *today*!" Henry James took a step toward Lucy.

Both men blocked his way.

The sound of wounded carried in through the front door made heads turn.

"Dr. James was trying to... take Lucy home with him." Father Dominic leveled his gaze at Giovanni.

Wow. Lucy's eyebrows went up. *He's really angry*.

Giovanni's eyes turned black and he squared his shoulders. He ran a light finger over the red fingerprints on her arm, and then shot an icy look at her father. "We'll finish this discussion later. You can make yourself comfortable in the study or you can help. There's an extra table in the kitchen. Decide." Giovanni turned back to Lucy with a low, steady voice. "*Lucia*, Dr. Donelson is waiting the dining room, would you help him set up?"

"Thank you." Lucy spotted the child that Sister Francesca held, lifted the girl and kissed her forehead. Lucy placed the bleeding child into her father's arms.

"Here Daddy, a greasy Italian needs you." Lucy ran out of the room.

Henry James stood by himself with the injured child in his arms. He wanted to hide his face. At the same time, he wanted to throw a fit. Nothing had gone the way he had planned it. He looked at the beautiful little girl with large scratches on her face, her jet black hair, matted to her head with sweat and dirt.

Something in his heart stirred. Forcing his daughter was not God's way. But why? Why did it have to be Gods way? Maybe if he helped his conscience would stop bothering him. Yes. He would help the huddled masses and then he would take Lucy home.

Henry James helped his last patient slide off the table. He washed his hands in the shiny kitchen sink and dried them on a fluffy hand towel. This was a very nice house.

He pulled out his pocket watch, opened it and touched his wife's picture as he always did. Nine o'clock, what a day. It had been a lot like the two weeks he spent on the Venezia; hectic and grueling. The factory fire in Boston a couple of years ago had been similar and then before that, the days he served in the War Between the States. He had only been a boy then, but working in those hospitals had helped him discover his life's calling.

"Is that the last one?" Dr. Castello's voice came from where he worked, in the next room. Henry James stood still. Should he join them or not? He kept his mouth shut and listened.

"I believe it is." Dr. Donelson's accent and formal speech gave away his country of origin.

"Do you need one of us to drive you home?" Lucy sounded weary.

"No. I've had his carriage brought here. It's just outside." The priest seemed friendly enough, when he wasn't angry.

"Then I'll just let myself out. *Grazie, arrivederci*."

"*Ciao*." The back door closed. "He's the sweetest man."

"You look tired, *principessa*." It had been a real treat to see Dr. Castello in action. Lucy was right. There were few to equal him. Maybe the other reports about him were true as well.

He wiped his forehead with his handkerchief. Henry James wanted to relax and enjoy the camaraderie that hard work brings between co-workers. These people were doing a bang-up job. In any other circumstance he would have been proud to associate with them.

Any other circumstance? Henry James remembered what he had done to his daughter. He hung his head, he regretted his actions…except…

Giovanni prayed for a reasonable solution, almost the entire day. Now the day was done and it was time to face the music. In the kitchen, Henry James stood quietly by himself.

"Dr. James, if you are not too tired, I'd like to go into the study to talk. Sister Francesca will bring us some food. You must be hungry, I know your daughter is." Giovanni went to the kitchen and washed his hands. He grabbed a fresh towel from the cupboard and dried his hands. Maybe he could lighten things up a bit.

"Giovanni." Father Dominic called from the hallway. "May I have a word with you first?"

"Please excuse me." Giovanni gave a slight bow. "I won't be long." He followed Father Dominic to the study.

"Is this what you wanted to tell us?"

"Partly." Father Dominic grew sober. "Giovanni, Dr. De Stanza was here today. He said the humanist group you belonged to wants to observe how your clinic operates. Apparently they believe you're still one of them."

Giovanni shoved his hand through his black curls. "*Padre,* what I told you still stands; I've not been one of them in years. After our big falling out in London. I was so relieved to be rid of them. Then, somehow, they found out who my family is and when I gained recognition from King Edward they latched onto me.

"They can only have sent Dr. De Stanza for one reason. They must need money, or my name on some project that will bring them money. Where is he?"

"He's staying in the American Village. He says he'll be here first thing in the morning."

"There could not be worse timing." Giovanni felt a weight in the pit of his stomach. "Of all of the members of that group I trust him the least. The man has no moral conscience. He must not find out that *Lucia* is living here. No matter what we tell him, he will just believe that I'm having my way with her. He'll spread it all over Messina and then all over Rome. He will convince her father. I don't want her hurt."

"Giovanni." Father Dominic leaned against the desk and crossed his arms. "He already knows Lucy lives here. He came from Rome remember? Dr. James and Dr. De Stanza traveled together.

Giovanni sighed loudly he leaned against the desk as well. "There's more isn't there?"

"I'm sorry." Father Dominic picked up a Marconi-gram that lay on the desk along with a stack of unopened mail.

Giovanni took the paper, and read it.

"It's from my uncle. Apparently *Lucia* is within her rights to stay if she wants to, but because she and her father are foreigners, the authorities will not stop her father from forcing her to leave."

Before he could say anything else, Father Dominic handed him one more envelope. He turned it over and read the outside. Giovanni ripped it open and pulled out the contents.

He smiled and his heart grew light. "Well *Padre*, it seems that we are officially married."

"Congratulations," Father Dominic leaned a hand on the desk. "Giovanni, you know as well as I do that unless a marriage is consummated, it can easily be annulled."

They heard a knock at the door.

"May we come in?" Lucy held a tray full of fruit, cheese and bread. Sister Francesca carried a tray of drinks and Henry James followed.

"Yes, come in." Giovanni gave a weary smile, his heart heavy again.

They pulled chairs around the coffee table in front of the fireplace and put the food in the center.

"*Padre*, would you please say the blessing?" Giovanni watched Lucy and asked God for an answer. *Padre* could marry them tonight and then he could take her somewhere, but where? There really was nowhere to go in Messina at this point. Besides he did not want such a thing for his most treasured gift. He had wanted Lucy's wedding night to be full of joy, not tears. And what about this house full of injured people? He could not in good conscience leave them. *Please Lord, show me what to do.*

Henry James, forced Giovanni's attention. "that the work you're doing in this clinic is wonderful."

Henry James sat up straighter and leaned forward, his hands gripped the chair. "Nonetheless, I feel that I should get right to the point and I will be blunt."

"By all means." Giovanni leaned forward too. 'Let's put the cards on the table."

Henry James looked once at Lucy and then back at Giovanni. "It has been brought to my attention that this place is more than just a clinic. I know you people are living here; Lucy is living here, with you, Dr. Castello. I am also aware that the two of you are almost inseparable; that you have been traveling extensively together.

"Given the reputation you have in Rome, at least among your friends, you must understand that I'm appalled. That you would corrupt my daughter after promising to take care of her is reprehensible."

Giovanni felt Lucy's gaze. He had never wanted her to know just how ugly a man he had once been. He wanted to defend himself, but he could not lie, so he did not. "You're right, about some things Dr. James. But you are not correct on all counts. I've not always been the nicest person, but it is my understanding that God has forgiven me. I have always kept my word and I do not lie. For the sake of this argument, I'll repeat what I told you some months ago. I love your daughter and I've asked her to be my wife. Through some stroke of God's mercy, she has said 'yes.' However, Lucy is not just the woman I've chosen to marry, she is my working partner. We do spend a lot of time together. We have traveled together, but always very publicly. I can assure you, that I love her and I respect her. I've never tried to touch her in the wrong way."

"This is exactly what I expected you to say." Dr. James frowned. "I would like to believe you, but I don't know you well enough."

"If you can't take my word will you take your daughter's?" Giovanni turned to Lucy. "*Lucia*, am I telling the truth?"

"Daddy, Giovanni isn't lying. We've never been together in a manner that was inappropriate. You know *me* well enough; I've never lied to you, even if it meant that I would be punished for my actions."

"I thought I knew you." Dr James turned steel eyes at Lucy. "But even that seems to have changed. You will return to Boston with me, but I'll not live with a harlot. I've decided to send you to California. You can live with your aunt Lucinda. The two of you belong together."

Giovanni straightened in his chair and leveled his eyes at Henry James. Anger, grew in the pit of his stomach and he welcomed it. He opened his mouth to put Lucy's father in his place.

"There's an easy way to resolve this question!" Lucy stood up, fire in her voice. "Come on, Daddy." She walked toward the door. "Let's do one more examination tonight."

She spun around to face her father. "If I'm not a virgin, then I'll come home with you without another word. If I am, then I'd say you owe both of us an apology." Lucy stood at the door of the study with her hands on her hips.

Giovanni would have been tempted to laugh if the situation had not been so serious. She might have come from America, but Lucy surely had the temperament of an Italian; he could not have been more proud.

Henry James shifted in his chair. "I don't have to examine you to know what's been going on here. I've been working with Dr. Castello's friends. They seem to think it rather funny that my daughter, *the Christian*, has fallen for his charms.

Lucy, from across the room, looked into Giovanni's eyes for a moment; he knew what she would do.

"Fine Daddy. Giovanni will examine me. Giovanni, give me a moment, I'll be in the kitchen." Lucy turned and disappeared into the hall.

Giovanni picked up on her cue. As if nothing was out of the ordinary about Lucy's request, he took one last bite of his bread, wiped his hands and mouth with his napkin and stood. "Sister Francesca." He nodded at the nun. "I'll need you for a witness."

"I'll have nothing of the sort." Her father took the bait without blinking an eye. "You stay here." Henry James followed his daughter into the kitchen.

Giovanni turned to the nun at his side. "I can't think of anything more horrible. Please go hold her hand, since I cannot."

Sister Francesca gave him a sympathetic rub of the arm and followed Henry James.

Giovanni slid back into his chair and rested his chin on his hand. "At least this will be resolved tonight," he mumbled.

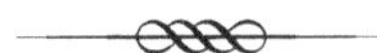

Lucy stormed out of the kitchen with her father close behind. She ran through the study.

"This is not the end of the discussion, daughter." Henry James tried to follow, but Giovanni put his hand squarely on the man's chest and pushed him backward. The back door closed with a bang.

"You've hurt her enough." Giovanni kept his voice low and firm.

Henry James turned red and his fists balled up. Then he shifted his gaze to the ground.

How disgraceful! This man deserved to be punched; except that he was *Lucia*'s father. Giovanni clinched his jaw and turned away. "Padre? Let's give Dr. James my room for the night. I'll take the spare cot in your room." He turned back to Henry James. "You go to bed, I'll see if I can convince Lucy to sleep in the same house with you."

Lucy ran down the steps and out into the shadowed orange grove. Who would ever dream of such utter humiliation? To think her own father thought so little of her. To think he would actually take the word of strangers over her own; that he had to see for himself. She should run and never look back.

Lucy ran harder until she tripped and caught herself on the banyan tree. She thought to climb it but her eyes filled with tears and she sobbed so hard she struggled to breathe. So she sank to the bottom of the tree with her back against the trunk. She pulled her knees to her chest.

I can't believe what just happened. God, please help me. I don't know if I'll ever be able to forgive him. I never want to see my father again.

"*Lucia*?" Giovanni called from across the garden. With everything in her, she wanted to answer, but shame made such an awful weight. Lucy pulled her knees closer and hid her face.

"*Lucia*? Answer me, bambina." His deep musical voice was a balm on this gaping wound. Tears spilled down her cheeks. Here was someone who always protected her. Giovanni would set things right.

"Giovanni?" She wiped her eyes with the palms of her hands. "I'm by the big tree."

"This is where I thought you would go." His gentle voice came from nearby and then he stood over her.

"I can't believe what just happened." Lucy hid her face in her arms and he sat on the ground beside her.

"He never should have embarrassed you that way. I should have stopped it." Lucy heard such anger in his voice, she turned back to him.

Giovanni's face became gentle again.

Lucy shook her head with a sniff. "At least now he knows the truth. I can't believe he thought I was lying. The most horrible part was how shocked he was when he saw for himself; it was all over his face. I'll never forget that look; it made me feel dirty even though we've done nothing wrong. Then he wouldn't apologize. And he still insists that I'm going home with him. Why would he believe such an awful thing of us?"

"Because the men he's working with believe it of me. *Lucia*, I have a reputation."

"Why?" Come to think of it, she didn't know much about his life before they met.

Giovanni shrugged and looked at their hands. Then he looked into her eyes and she wanted to pull him close. "I had forsaken God, so I did whatever pleased me. Although I was never as bad as they wanted to believe. I've never taken advantage of a woman."

"You're a virgin then?" Lucy asked, afraid of the answer.

Giovanni took a deep slow breath; he took her other hand in his and held them both together. His eyes grew wide, his voice grew soft and for the first time his hands trembled. Was he afraid? "With all of my heart I wish I could say that I am. You deserve nothing less. If this changes your opinion of me I understand."

What should she think? Aunt Lucinda's words floated through her mind. *Men are considered virile if they do, women are considered whores*. "Women are held to God's standards Why aren't men?"

"Men who follow God are," he said softly. "If I had only heeded the vows that I took at eighteen; the vows that I just renewed, I would have been as chaste as you. I have ruined everything."

This is where my faith is tested. Do I show mercy? He was a thirty-four year-old unbeliever when we met, why am I so disappointed? I should have known this side of him existed.

Lucy listened to her heart. She could feel Giovanni's stare. She could also feel his disappointment grow. Lucy hoped to hear God tell her what to do but all she heard was the chirp of crickets and the call of the nightingale.

She pulled her hand from his and turned away. Lucy put her head in her arms again, surely her heart would cave in. *Now, I am alone*.

Giovanni stroked the back of her head just once. He stood with a sigh and brushed himself off.

"*If any man is in Christ, he is a new creation*." The last sermon she had heard before she left the States, came back to her.

Old things have passed away; behold all things have become new. Lucy lifted her head from her arms; Giovanni was gone.

"Giovanni?" Lucy called loudly. Her heart pounded, fear gripped her. She stood to her feet to see in the darkness of the trees. "Giovanni where are you?" Desperation grew. *Oh, Lord God, what have I done? I've hurt him.*

She turned back toward the banyan tree and ran right into him.

"I would never leave you out here in the dark by yourself." Giovanni's voice was barely audible. "I was just at the next tree."

"I'm so sorry." Lucy sobbed and melted into his chest. His arms, slow to close around, her lacked their usual strength. "How could I ever reject you?"

"Then we're all right?" He touched the back of her head. "You forgive me?"

"Giovanni, there's nothing to forgive." Lucy stroked his face, she kissed his cheek. "You're a new creation. God has made you completely new. All the old things that you've done are simply gone. You've read Second Corinthians, I know you have. I don't want to lose you. Please." Lucy looked into his noble face. "Please, will you forgive me?"

"Yes, *amore*." He buried his face in her hair, and his arms became strong again. He held her tight. He breathed in sharply and kissed her hair and then her cheek and finally touched his warm lips to hers in a slow kiss, full of love and tenderness. His kiss grew both in strength and passion, it brought healing and forgiveness. He kissed her again, this time like he had done just two nights ago. She melted into him and her heart became one with his and his with hers.

They breathed together and Giovanni kissed her face, her temple and forehead. "I love you." His whisper caressed her.

"I love you too," came from the depths of her soul. He was forgiven and his sins forgotten. She would never bring it up again. Lucy dug in her pocket and handed him his own handkerchief. That was all it took to make him laugh.

"Will you come back inside?" He kept his arms around her.

"I will if you want. I'd much rather stay right here." She snuggled into his chest.

"I'd much rather keep you here." Giovanni tightened his hold and pressed his cheek to her head. "One day I will. For now, I think we should head in, but not before we do some planning."

He stroked her cheek, she could see his eyes shining in the darkness.

"About Daddy?"

"Yes, and about you and me."

"Go on."

"We received two pertinent pieces of mail today. The first came from my uncle. He told me that although you're welcome to stay in Italy, because you're foreigners, no one will stop your father from taking you home with him."

Lucy's heart sank. "What else did we receive?"

"Our marriage registration." Giovanni smiled and smoothed her hair. "As far as Italy is concerned you are now *Lucia* Castello."

"It came?" Lucy's heart became light again. "Then there's nothing that Daddy can do."

"Actually, *Padre* reminded me, that until our marriage is consummated, he has a right to appeal for an annulment."

"We could take care of that tonight," Lucy heard herself say. "Father Dominic could marry us and then... the words got stuck in her throat, she found it hard to look him in the eye.

"Then what?" Giovanni dipped his head to make her face him. "Where could I take you? Upstairs with the nuns? To the American Village? There used to be a very beautiful hotel just on the water downtown, but there's nothing now." He leaned his face lightly to hers. "And what of this clinic full of injured people? Would we return in the morning to care for them?"

"Yes." Either she loved this man or she didn't. No more trepidation. "I don't care where we go. I've never needed anything fancy, you know that."

"I know that, bambina." He lifted her chin and brushed his lips against hers. "Our time will come. You will be my wife. On that day, I'll show you exactly how much I love you. But we've always done things the right way and we need to continue. This marriage contract will hinder your father for a while. In order to take you he will now have to appeal for an annulment. That will give me time to find a place for all of these people to go."

"Are you saying that you want me to return to Rome with him?" Lucy's eyes filled up with tears again.

"I'm *sending* you to Rome with him." He put his finger on her lips and pulled her closer. "Let me finish. First, I will write a letter and you can personally take it to the local magistrate." Giovanni gave a wry smile. "*Zio* Vincenzo, my uncle who just wrote. For me he could stall the proceedings for at least a year. Second, Dr. De Stanza is coming to ask me for money in the morning. I know without asking that he's the one who convinced your father that we behaved immorally. I do not want you here when he arrives."

"Why not? I would love to confront him." Lucy frowned.

"Yes, I'm sure you would do a good job of it too." Giovanni chuckled and then he grew sober. "*Lucia*, there are some things a man must do for himself. Protecting his family is one of them. I'm asking that you obey me in this. Go to Rome with your father. Seek out my uncle. I will deal with things here and then I will come for you." He wrapped both his arms around her again.

"What if it doesn't go our way? What if I end up back in Boston? Or even California?" Lucy felt a cold chill and started to shiver.

He tightened his hold "You're trembling. Don't be afraid, *amore*. I want a list of all of the possible addresses that I will need to find you. I *will* find you *Lucia*. As God is my witness, I will find you, I will marry you in a church before the Lord and I will make you mine."

Then as if he needed to confirm his claim on her, Giovanni kissed her once more. He would protect her, he would come for her. Lucy would leave in the morning and she would wait for him to come.

CHAPTER TWENTY-THREE

Lucy climbed out of bed the next morning and stumbled across the bedroom. She had been waking up at four-thirty for so long she hardly noticed the darkness around her.

She lit a lamp, opened the armoire and stared at the clothes inside it. *I'll just need a few things for the journey. It's funny, I never even needed most of what I brought.*

She took out a sage green frock and closed the door. Lucy pulled on her dress; she could hear someone tinkering in the kitchen, down below.

I can't believe this will be our last morning together for a while. She wrapped her hair into a smart French twist, the way Celeste had taught her. *I just don't want to leave him.*

Lucy wrinkled her nose at her reflection in the mirror. *No matter what I do, I simply see an overgrown twelve-year-old.*

The faint aroma of coffee floated through the crack under her door. *Mmm.*

Lucy gave the door a slow push so it would not squeak, slipped through it and headed down the stairs.

At the landing, Lucy slipped into the hallway to avoid the sea of people, asleep in the great room. The house would have been dark as ink, except for the glow of a single lamp that came from the direction of the kitchen.

Lucy walked down the hall, went through the study with its homey smell of leather and books. She went through the door that led to where Father Dominic and Giovanni lived. Sure to be extra quiet, Lucy crept by Giovanni's room; inside it, her father just might be awake.

Lord, please give us some time alone before I leave.

Lucy caught another whiff. *His coffee always smells like chocolate.* She pushed through the swinging door at the rear entrance of the kitchen.

Giovanni leaned against the counter with a cup in his hand. He had a second cup set out, just for her.

"*Buongiorno, bambina.*" Giovanni kept his voice just above a whisper. He poured coffee into Lucy's cup, kissed her "good morning" and then handed it to her.

"A thought occurred to me as I was dressing." Giovanni tilted his head in her direction; he looked at her from head to toe and smiled.

"What did you think?" Lucy smiled back. Over the past months, these few precious moments in the morning had become their time to talk and pray before everyone else woke.

"With very few exceptions, we've been together almost every hour of every day since January."

Lucy nodded, just glad to be next to him.

"I used to think I was so strong and independent that I didn't need anyone. You've become such a part of me, I'm not sure I'll know how to function without you." He pulled her under his arm. "You haven't left yet and I feel your absence strongly. Don't be surprised if you are only in Rome for a few days before I steal you away."

"I'm counting on that." Lucy leaned against him. "Did you bring your Bible?"

"*Si.*" He nodded and finished the last of his coffee. "You really don't mind that I keep it? There are plenty at Casa Bella, but this one smells like you." Giovanni took her hand and pulled her to the kitchen table where Lucy's Bible lay.

"Of course not." She placed the lamp in front of them and they sat side by side. "I have another one at the Drake's house. What are we reading?"

"Psalm ninety-one." Giovanni thumbed through the pages until he found it. "It goes against reason." He stroked his hand across the page in front of him. "Most books become tedious after I've read them two or three times, but this one becomes more interesting every time I open it. This time last year, I never would have believed it."

Thank you, Lord for this miracle. "*Caro,* if you read, I'll pour more coffee."

Lucy sat silently with her heart in her throat as Giovanni read the psalm and then several passages in the book of Matthew. When he led the morning prayer, she almost broke down.

Just like every other morning, by the time he finished, the house had begun to stir. Father Dominic always came through the door first. He poured a cup of coffee and they discussed the day's agenda. Today, he would to drive Lucy and her father to the harbor. The nuns came in next. They bustled around the kitchen, with their cheerful chatter and soon breakfast was served; first to the patients, then to everyone else.

Breakfast in the sunlight, on the patio was as good as a hug. This morning, the house, the trees, the mountains, the smells, seemed much more beautiful than ever.

Lucy found Giovanni watching her with dark eyes like he used to do, when they were still at the hospital station.

"You know where the Drakes live?" Even with such beautiful sunshine, her world turned gray.

"Don't fret bambina. I know Rome as well as I know Palermo; I'll find you with no problem." He held out his hand and she slipped hers into it.

"You can remember where my uncle lives?"

"Yes, I have the letter and his address safely hidden. I'll get it to him."

"Have you seen your father this morning?" he asked gently.

"Yes. He's eating in the kitchen. I think he might be regretting what happened last night."

Giovanni said nothing, but he tilted his head and his eyes grew soft. He was right. She *could* tell what he was thinking. "I know. I have to forgive him, even if we never see eye to eye again." Lucy squeezed his hand. "You are not to worry either, I'll be all right."

Giovanni lifted Lucy's trunk onto the wagon. He remembered the day he unloaded it and how frustrated he had been that she came. Now, more than anything, he wished she could stay.

Henry James came out the front door first, followed by Lucy and his aunt. The man barely said a word all morning. He threw his carpet bag up beside Lucy's, turned to Giovanni and grimaced. "That you behaved well with my daughter has changed my opinion greatly. I only hope that you will come to see that I'm taking her home for her own good."

Giovanni gave a half smile and shook his head. He spoke with a low voice. "At least legally, Lucy is now my wife. So you will have to make an appeal, before you can take her out of the country."

He paused and then looked directly at Henry James. "You may believe your own lie, but I do not. You're not doing this for Lucy's good;

you're taking her selfishly and in doing so you will probably never have a good relationship with her again. That you would so damage someone who loves you as much as she does, is beyond my comprehension. All I can do is pray for you."

Giovanni quickly turned from Henry James. He and went to Lucy and took her hand.

"Bambina, it's time." His thumb stroked her ring finger.

"I'll be back soon." Lucy smiled up at him, but her eyes glistened.

Giovanni steadied his heart. She had such strength.

"Just don't climb any trees. I've heard Rome has a shortage of lemon drops." Giovanni touched his fingertip to her chin. She looked as delicate and fragile as she did on that dreary January day, when she first arrived. The scent of rose water in her hair brought back the memory clearly.

"No sword fights." Lucy poked a finger to his chest. How could he resist her?

With everyone around him watching, Giovanni pulled Lucy up and kissed her tenderly.

Henry James snorted and turned his head.

"I will come for you Persephone," he said, softly, so only she could hear. "If I have to travel the world to find you, I will." He held her for a moment and lost himself in her hazel eyes full of tears.

"I'll wait for you. You know I will. I think you'd like California." She pulled out of his arms and let go of his fingers last. Lucy took a step up into the wagon and refused her father's hand.

Father Dominic gave the mule a slap with the reins and the cart rolled down the driveway. Lucy turned to look at Giovanni one last time, the wagon rounded the corner and she disappeared from sight.

Giovanni clinched his fists and gritted his teeth, but the gentle touch of Sister Francesca at his arm steadied his heart.

"*Lucia* needs you to be strong." Sister Francesca steadied her dark eyes on him. "She's depending on you to set things right."

"Yes she is." For the first time in months, he steeled his heart.

The clock on the mantle struck nine.

Sister Francesca stuck her head in the study. "Dr. De Stanza is here."

"Thank you, Sister. Bring him in. "Giovanni stood and straightened his waistcoat. He walked around the front of his desk, leaned against it and crossed his arms.

"Ah Dr. Castello, it's good to see you." De Stanza stood in the doorway for a moment, before he sauntered into the room, followed by the odor of too much cologne. His appearance had always struck Giovanni as odd. Why would a short bald man think that since he could no longer grow hair on the top of his head, he should grow it on his chin? It only made him look like a very ugly elf.

"I see you've not lost your fondness for working among the peasantry and…" his lip curled, "…clergy." De Stanza offered his hand.

"No, I have not." Giovanni kept his arms crossed. "Surely, you're not here to remind me of the obvious. I know you would never come to simply observe my clinic. Tell me why you're here."

"But that's exactly why I'm here." De Stanza squinted through his monocle. His hand dropped to his side while his gaze roamed the room. "I want to watch you, really. News of the work you're doing here is all over Rome. Finally, it dawned on us that working with the underprivileged as you do, is actually very clever. People love to give, quite generously, to a cause that's worthy. We've decided to help you in your efforts by extending an invitation for you to rejoin our group…"

"So that you can put your name on the clinic and earn a little extra recognition as well." Giovanni gave a sly smile and rubbed his fingers together to indicate money.

"Yes and why not?" De Stanza seemed so weasel-like Giovanni's skin crawled. "If it's for the betterment of the humanistic cause you should be all for it."

Enough of this conversation. "In the last six months, your group has done next to nothing to help the people of this city; simply putting your name on this clinic is not the way to start. Besides, I thought I had made it quite clear that I no longer wished to be associated with you."

"But you were so amiable at the party in December." Spittle flew out of De Stanza's mouth as he spoke. "We were under the impression that we might be able to reach an understanding. After all, we're humanists, we should work together."

"I came to the party, out of obligation to Dr. Mortellaro." Giovanni moved left to avoid the shower. "As head of the University Hospital, he has a stellar reputation. We've remained friends since I graduated.

"That he chooses to allow you and Dr. Montgomery to work with him is entirely his decision, not mine. As for the matter of being a humanist, I've had a change of heart. I never fully embraced everything you stand for and in the past few months, have come to reject your way of thinking completely. I do not feel inclined to associate this clinic with you."

De Stanza narrowed his beady eyes at Giovanni. He reached across the desk and picked up Lucy's Bible. "Ah, I see the problem. She must really be quite charming to have you reading this." He gave a leer, his teeth yellow from tobacco. "You don't really believe this do you? Or are you pretending to read this in order keep her where you want her. Yes, that must be it." He snickered. "It's been such fun helping her father realize, exactly why you would want his daughter as a partner."

Giovanni grabbed the Bible from the irritating little man, placed it back on the desk and then stood towering over him.

"I call myself Christian now, that's why I'm reading the Bible." Giovanni took a step forward and De Stanza backed up. "I will never give you my name or my money. If I ever hear you say anything derogatory again about either Dr. James, the daughter or the father, I will make your life miserable. You know I have the power to do so. Now leave."

Dr. De Stanza took a few more steps back, his eyes as big as saucers. He turned to leave and Giovanni followed him.

From the next room, the bang of the front door said someone entered with an injury. The voice that followed made his heart stop.

"Really Daddy, I can manage by myself. It's just a sprain."

"Daughter, you are *so* stubborn. I don't know how I've raised you without your mother."

"I think I hear your *puttana* now." De Stanza gave a mocking snort and straightened his shirt. A cold smile crept across his face. "I must congratulate you Dr. Castello. Once again you've succeeded in an area in which we have failed."

"That's enough." Giovanni grabbed De Stanza by his collar. He dragged the annoying gnat into the great room and over the patients, who started to applaud. Then Giovanni tossed him out the front door. The people on their mats began to cheer.

"I forgot to take out the rubbish." He brushed his hands.

The patients applauded louder.

"He called *Santa Lucia, puttana.*" A peasant spat.

The peasant on the mat next to him sat up. "Every now and then that worm comes to our neighborhood. He asks questions about you and *Santa Lucia;* none of us have ever trusted him. If he comes back we'll make sure he regrets it."

"If he gives you any trouble let me know. And I know you're angry, but please don't spit in my house."

"*Mi dispiace.*" The first peasant batted his eyes.

Giovanni chuckled and turned his attention to Lucy and her father.

His heart skipped a beat.

"*Santa Maria*! What happened to you?" Giovanni stepped over three people.

Lucy hobbled between her father, on one side and a peasant with bandages wrapped around his head, on the other. Wet from head to toe, her auburn hair matted to her head and mostly undone, hung sideways, onto her left shoulder. The skirt of her dress had a tear from the knees down; the right sleeve ripped near the shoulder, was soaked with blood.

"*Santa Lucia*, she is hurt." The peasant held her hand.

Lucy smiled.

"I can see that." Giovanni waved his hand toward Lucy. "So are you, what are you doing walking about?"

"I was the only one who could stand; we couldn't bear to see her this way."

"*Grazie, amico*." Giovanni patted the man on the back. "I can take her from here. Please go lie down."

Giovanni lifted Lucy off her feet and carried her into the dining room.

Her father followed.

"You were gone so long I almost forgot what you looked like." Wet or not, it felt good to hold her. He scrunched his face. "You smell terrible."

"Yes, I know." Lucy rolled her eyes. "Giovanni, what does *puttana* mean? That's a word I haven't learned yet."

"Sister Anna." Giovanni looked over his shoulder to the nun who swept the floor. "Would you close those doors?" The nun gave a nod and shut the doors behind her.

He set Lucy down on the table nearest the window. "I don't think I want you to know what it means. It's ugly and simply not true and I do not want my wife to repeat such words."

"But, how am I supposed to learn?" Giovanni held up a finger and Lucy stopped talking.

"*Lucia*, there will be times when you'll simply have to trust me. In the meantime, I really want to know, what happened to you?" Giovanni looked for bruises on Lucy's head, he moved gentle fingers through her wet hair.

Henry James came to Giovanni's side. "There's nothing wrong with her head, I've already checked; except for maybe on the inside." He tapped his temple with a finger.

"Didn't I say the same thing to you once?" Giovanni examined Lucy's eyes.

"You know, that's really not very funny." Lucy pulled back.

"Shhh." Henry James pointed at her. He turned back to Giovanni. "And, you handled her beautifully."

Giovanni stopped his examination. Maybe Henry James was the one who hit his head.

Lucy started to speak, but her father silenced her with another point of his finger. Lucy shut her mouth with a smirk.

"Do you know what *puttana* means?' Giovanni straightened up.

Henry James scowled. "Yes."

"Then you agree with me."

"Of course."

"Would you, mind telling me what happened?"

"We were heading to the harbor." Henry James rested a hand on the table Lucy sat on. "I had no idea how many people knew her. As we traveled, every few feet, someone would come to the cart to shake her hand or give her a flower or who knows what. I was so frustrated. They made us so late that the boat left without us. Then we rounded a corner and …"

"Giovanni." Lucy grabbed his arm. "The house that Gasparone and his family live in has finally collapsed."

Giovanni's stomach grew tight; he put a hand to his head. "We told him that would happen. Why don't people listen to reason? Did anyone get hurt?"

"Yes." Lucy threw her hands to the side, like he should have known. "*I* did."

"And where's *Padre?*"

"He's still there. He said he'd catch up to us."

"Can you talk and let me look at your arm at the same time?" Giovanni really enjoyed the change of atmosphere.

Lucy scooted around, to allow him access to her shoulder.

Giovanni took out a pair of scissors.

"Just rip it." Lucy looked at the dress and then up at him. "This frock will never be the same."

Giovanni grabbed the sleeve at the shoulder; the fabric gave easily. Lucy winced. "Sorry, bambina."

"Anyway," Lucy took a couple of deep breaths. "Gasparone isn't home; he's out fishing beyond the harbor."

He swabbed her arm with disinfectant.

Lucy sucked in air. "His mother came running and said that Elena was trapped inside."

"*Mamma Mia*." Giovanni shook his head. "You were the only one who could go inside to pull her out?" He chuckled in spite of himself.

Lucy gave a sheepish smile. "Carlo was there with some others from his neighborhood, but they were all too heavy. They were going to send Pietro inside. He's so young, I couldn't let it happen."

"Take a breath, your rambling." Something about her voice made Giovanni concerned. "Slow down."

Lucy took a deep breath. "Elena was so scared, and the house was so unstable. She wouldn't come out on her own, so I crawled in after her. I found Elena huddled in a corner hugging her mother's picture. I was able to coax her into crawling out of the hole that I came in through and that's when this happened."

Lucy followed Giovanni with her eyes. "Do I really need stitches?"

"Just a couple this time." He picked up a string of catgut with some tweezers. "I promise I won't yell at you."

"This time*?*" Henry James frowned at his daughter.

"I'll tell you about that later." Giovanni sat next to Lucy on the table. "Go ahead *Lucia*, finish your story."

Lucy put her hand on his arm and squeezed. "The floor gave way. I probably only fell a few feet, but Giovanni that basement was full of water. When I landed I twisted my ankle so instead of catching myself I went under."

A wisp of cold air touched Giovanni's heart. "*Lucia*, please, tell me you didn't swallow any of that water." He saw the answer in her eyes before she spoke it.

"I did." Her bottom lip trembled.

"We induced vomiting as soon as she was pulled out, but she was down there a good twenty minutes before we could get to her." Henry James stepped with ease from father to physician. He took the hand of Lucy's injured arm. "I'll hold her steady."

Giovanni quickly stitched Lucy's arm and then pulled her boot off to check her ankle.

"You're right." He smiled up at her trying not to focus on anything else just yet. "This is just a sprain."

Giovanni stood and breathed in. "Why don't you go upstairs and put on some dry clothes. I might be able to get a good enough sample from the water in your dress to see just what you've swallowed." He helped Lucy off of the table.

"That won't be necessary," Henry James said.

Giovanni thought the man would be obstinate again. But, Henry James reached in his pocket, pulled out a small jar of water and handed it to him.

"Your surgical skills are unparalleled. But even more than that, I understand your expertise in this area is legendary. I'm choosing to trust you with my daughter."

Lucy, in a thick white nightgown and robe, sat on the chair in the corner by the window. Her arm throbbed, her ankle throbbed. At least she was bathed and dressed, thanks to Giovanni's patient aunt, who now sat next to her on the hassock. It felt good to be back in her own bedroom, especially since she'd thought not to see it again for quite a while.

Lucy played with her braid. Somehow, between the time she entered Gasparone's house and the time she had been pulled from the basement, her father's attitude made a change. Maybe there was hope after all. *Please Lord, don't let me have swallowed anything awful, don't let me get sick. Not now, not just before the wedding.*

The clunk of footsteps on the stairs reached her ears.

The door to her bedroom opened with a creak and her father stuck his head in just as he used to do when she was a child. "May we come in?"

"Yes." Lucy could not help but giggle. It seemed that whoever pretended to be her father yesterday had left and the real Henry James had come to pay a visit.

The two men entered the room and sat on the edge of her bed. Neither one of them said a word, they just kept looking at her and then at each other.

"It's bad isn't it?" Lucy let go of her braid.

A gentle breeze blew the curtains; Sister Francesca stood to re-tie them.

"Daddy, Giovanni, what have I swallowed?" Lucy scooted forward.

Giovanni looked at her father.

Henry James motioned back to Giovanni. "Go ahead, tell her."

"*Vibrio cholera;* a lot of it." Giovanni took her hand.

"Anything else?" Lucy felt blood leave her face. Sister Francesca stroked her shoulder.

"I saw nothing else that was harmful." Giovanni shook his head, his voice strained. "Just a lot of the Cholera bacteria. There's a strong probability that you're about to become very sick."

Lucy tried to remember what she had read in school. "I should have about twenty-four hours before the symptoms become hard to control, but I could start reacting anytime."

Her heart ached. How she wanted to hug them, worry etched on both of their faces. There was no way to fix what had happened and now they would be the ones to deal with the mess.

"I'm sorry." Lucy fingered the sash on her robe. "If I didn't get Elena out of the house, she would've been the one who fell through the floor. I would rather this have happened to me than that little girl, but I don't want you to have to deal with it either."

"We might not have to." Giovanni smiled, but it did not touch his eyes. "Some people show no symptoms at all. If that's the case, you'll simply be isolated until you're no longer contagious."

Lucy blinked back tears. "Giovanni, I didn't know what else to do."

Giovanni rubbed her hand in his. "I would have done the same thing myself. Have you ever seen cholera?"

"Only in the textbooks."

Giovanni closed his eyes and pinched the bridge of his nose. "In any event, your father and I both agree on our course of action."

"Lucille," Henry James voice rang with confidence. "I'm sending you to the hospital in Rome with Dr. Castello."

"You're sending me with Giovanni?" Should she clean out her ears?

"Yes. I'm going to stay here until we can find a place for all these injured people to go and then I'll join you,"

Henry James stood and gave his daughter a hand up. "Shall we ask the Lord for help?" He held his hand out to Giovanni, closed his eyes and started to pray.

Lucy and Giovanni stared at each other. Sister Francesca joined the circle. They all looked at Henry James, who poured his heart out to God and then back at each other. Giovanni raised his eyebrows in a silent question.

Lucy shrugged and closed her eyes

From somewhere outside, a cock crowed three times.

CHAPTER TWENTY-FOUR

The cab pulled up to the stone steps of the hospital. What a grueling journey. The half moon overhead peeked out from behind the clouds. The streets of Rome still busy even at ten o'clock.

Inside the hospital, Lucy felt at home right away; after all she had worked here before she came to Messina. The bright and clean hospital, smelled so familiar, that Lucy began to relax. This was the right decision.

Giovanni walked to the desk and signed in.

"Dr. Castello, Miss James, welcome to Rome. We received your wireless; we've been expecting you. Where's the patient?" Dr. Mortellaro had entered the room from the right. He extended his hand to greet them both.

Lucy stiffened right away.

"He is not one of them." Giovanni whispered in her ear.

"*Doctor* James is the one who was in the accident. We wanted to be safe and bring her here for observation."

Dr. Mortellaro grew very serious. "Yes of course, *Doctor* James. Are you sure?"

"Quite sure." Giovanni nodded.

Dr. Mortellaro took Lucy's hand, he seemed like a wonderful man. "You would be hard pressed my dear, to find anyone who knows more about this than Dr. Castello. You're in good hands."

"We've set up a room in isolation, right this way." Dr. Mortellaro walked very quickly; he motioned for them to follow. "You'll have the hospital at your disposal. This young woman's father has been such a great help to us. We'll do whatever you ask. Does he know yet?"

"Yes, as a matter of fact we'll be expecting his arrival within the next day." Giovanni allowed Lucy to step in front of him. "Would you mind directing him to us?"

"Not at all." Dr. Mortellaro opened a door and led them into a stark white room, meticulously clean and completely barren except for a clock and a lone crucifix over the door. It contained two beds, one for normal use and one, obviously for a patient with cholera. The mattress had been covered in a waterproof fabric and a top sheet lay in neat folds, at the foot.

"You'll have everything you need in here," Dr. Mortellaro said. "There's a private bath through that door. Please let us know what else we can do for you." He bowed and closed the door.

"*Lucia*?" Giovanni's voice brought her back to reality; that bed was so distracting. Would she use it?

"*Lucia*?" He touched her arm. "Why don't you take a nap? I'll unpack and Sister will find something for us to eat." He looked at the nun. "Do you mind?"

"Of course I don't mind, *Lucia* is always hungry."

The door clicked shut. Could that sweet nun catch this? Lucy scoured her memory. No. but if Giovanni…

Giovanni put his arm around her shoulder.

She pulled away. "Please don't. You know better than to kiss me."

Giovanni forced her to look at him. "I wasn't going to kiss. You're right I do know better. I was going to hold you. I *can* hold you. You know that don't you?"

Lucy nodded, but she looked at her feet.

"What else do you know?"

"You can't get this by touching me or breathing the same air." Lucy lifted her head slowly.

"I helped a lot of people with cholera in London. You have to let me take care of you. *Lucia*, I will take care of you." He pulled her back under his arm. "I'm going down the hall for a moment. When I come back, I expect you to be in bed."

Giovanni knew the halls of this hospital well. He had learned his trade at The University Hospital of Rome; later he began his career here. He had been back often, to help many people, but he never dreamt that he would return with a patient so dear to him. *Lord please guide me, don't let my emotions rule my decisions.*

Giovanni rounded the corner toward the laboratory, with a very specific formula in his hand. He wanted to make sure it would be mixed properly. Out of the door to the lab came Doctor Montgomery.

Giovanni hesitated. He did not need Lucy to become any more upset. *I need you right now*. Peace filled his heart and in that moment, Giovanni knew that God had arranged the meeting.

The door thumped shut.

I must have fallen asleep. Lucy opened her eyes. Giovanni sat close by, in a chair with her Bible in his lap and a floor lamp next to him. How long had he been there?

She tried to shake off the sleepiness. "Where'd the lamp come from?

"I borrowed it from Dr. Mortellaro." Giovanni moved his chair to her side and took hold of her hand. "You've been asleep for quite some time. Let's sit you up, so you can eat some supper."

Lucy sat up and her head pounded. No need to mention it yet.

Giovanni put the tray on the bed in front of her. "You're running a slight temperature. After you eat, I want you to drink this." He brought a large pitcher to the bed stand and filled a glass with something that looked like watered down orange juice.

"What's in it?" Lucy took a bite of chicken soup.

"It's a mixture of water, salt, sugar, baking soda and orange juice. If we keep you hydrated, the bacteria you've swallowed will eventually just run its course and you'll recover. The key will be to keep as much liquid in you as possible." Giovanni frowned. "And to keep you clean. *Lucia*, this might become very ugly before it is all over."

Lucy shivered. She'd read all about this. "I know what's coming. I also know that God is faithful. I trust Him and I trust you." She set her empty bowl on the tray, took a sip of Giovanni's concoction. Might as well be brave about it. "This tastes good."

"There's one more thing." Giovanni spoke slowly. "If this begins, it will happen suddenly. We need to move you to the other bed, just in case, and then I have a surprise for you,"

Lucy looked at the ugly bed with its waterproof sheets and then at his serious face. Would she really be that sick? She took a deep breath. "Well, at least it's next to the window."

Lucy climbed out of the first bed. Would overacting bring a smile? "Ouch, my ankle, I forgot."

Yes, finally.

Sister Francesca came to her side.

"Just wanted to see if I could make him smile." Lucy shrugged apologetically. "Actually, my ankle is much better."

Lucy slid into the other bed and chose not to see the empty buckets on the floor. Some things only made this worse. "All right, where's my surprise?"

"Just a moment." Giovanni opened the door and held it. He leaned out into the hall and then backed up a step.

Into the room walked Henry James.

"Daddy!" Lucy threw her arms open.

"Lucy, my love." Her father gave her a hug.

"When did you get here?" She pushed his spectacles up his nose like she used to when she was a child.

"Not long after you did." Henry James sat on the side of the bed. "As soon as word got out that, you were in trouble every doctor in town came to our aid. The clinic was cleared in no time."

"Thank the Lord for that. The people of Messina have always been amazing. I'm glad you got to see it for yourself."

"You're both here with me." Could this be the reason for her accident? She took the hand of each. "You're not fighting are you?"

"No." They answered almost in unison.

"Will you be able to work together?"

"Yes of course." Giovanni glanced at her father. "*Lucia*, we don't want you to concern yourself about anything except getting well."

"Dr. Castello is right." Henry James patted her hand. "You keep your spirits up and leave the rest to us. With the Lord's help you'll be set right in no time."

"I have no doubt about that." Lucy finished her drink and then set the empty glass on the nightstand. She squeezed each hand again and lay down on the pillow.

Giovanni sat nearby to keep a watchful eye on *Lucia*, asleep like an angel. The thick, frumpy nightgown she wore made her look all the more adorable. He really should send someone to the doll-makers for a stuffed bear to keep her company.

Lucy's father sat to his right. Giovanni still was not sure just what to do with the man. He had been mean enough to cause Giovanni to distrust him. Yet, now, he seemed open and honest. Maybe Henry James was simply a concerned father, just as Giovanni had first assessed him.

"She was able to keep her drink down. As long as *Lucia* can drink, then we have nothing really to worry about except keeping her clean. It remains to be seen what will happen tonight. For some reason symptoms always increase in the middle of the night," Giovanni rested his chin on his hand.

"Yes, I've worked with cholera patients too; although not with the success that apparently you've had. We could have a long night ahead of us. Why don't you get some sleep?" Henry James nodded in the direction of the other bed. "I'm rested. I can watch her."

"We've been keeping this kind of schedule for months now." Giovanni determined to act as though there had never been any difference between them. "It really doesn't bother me, but perhaps you're right. It will help to be rested if this begins in full. Don't let me sleep more than an hour."

"As you wish." Henry James adjusted his spectacles on his nose. "When you wake, I'll leave for a while. Lucy is your patient, having her father here will only hinder your work. If you really need me I'll be in the chapel."

"Thank you for being so understanding." Giovanni extended his hand in hopes of a truce. "She's about to experience a different side of me. I'm grateful that you'll allow me to do my job. You know it's much easier to help a stranger."

Henry James tightened his lips. Then he took Giovanni's hand. "When Lucy was a child, she fell from a tree. Did she tell you about it?" He went to his daughter's side.

"Yes." Giovanni remembered his promise about the orange tree; it felt like years ago.

"Setting her arm was one of the most difficult things I've ever done. But it had to be done so I did it. She cried horribly." Dr. James stroked the mended arm that lay on the outside of the covers. "You can do this, you have to. God will help you and so will I. Try to rest."

Giovanni walked to Lucy and laid a gentle hand on her soft hair. *Lord please have mercy on this woman I love so much. Please don't put her through this. Please keep me focused and alert. Give me wisdom and I will always give You the glory.*

He climbed on the other bed and forced himself to sleep.

The sky outside the window was black, the clock said two-thirty. Giovanni, in his chair again, tried to read the book of *Numbers* but his concern for Lucy kept him distracted.

Maybe conversation would be better. He glanced at Sister Francesca. She had her chin in her hand and her eyes closed in prayer? Or did she sleep? *Oh well*. Henry James had left fifteen minutes ago, so that thought was no good either. He turned back to the book in front of him.

Lucy stirred in her sleep and Giovanni watched.

Nothing.

He looked down at his book.

Lucy caught her breath and Giovanni looked up. Shiny beads of sweat gathered on her forehead and his heart went to his throat. He shoved his emotions aside and put the book down. "Sister, here we go."

With Lucy still asleep, he dragged her body to the edge of the bed. She threw up violently into the bucket on the floor. What came next would be worse.

Lucy woke. She gagged and gasped for air. Then her muscles contracted in a most painful way, she cried out and grabbed her stomach. Too weak to rise, she collapsed into the bed, only for strong hands to sit her up and remove bedclothes and nightgown in one swift motion. Cold air hit her skin and an awful odor filled her nostrils. Lucy whimpered.

"You're all right bambina." Sister Francesca wrapped a towel around her shoulders; "We're right here. Come on, let's take a bath."

"Can you take her by yourself?" Giovanni's voice came from somewhere Lucy could not see.

Her head pounded and the room spun around her. She leaned on the nun.

"Yes, she can walk. We'll be fine," The nun said, in a soothing voice. She guided Lucy to the bathroom. Sister Francesca filled the tub with a few inches of hot soapy water mixed with a disinfectant and helped Lucy in.

Lucy shivered painfully, while the nun washed every inch of her. She pulled Lucy's hair into a tight braid and then pinned it to her head.

"Let's towel you dry." Sister Francesca helped her stand and rubbed Lucy vigorously until her limbs stopped shivering. The nun pulled a fresh nightgown over Lucy's head and buttoned the front.

"There you go, *bambina*. Come on, back to bed."

"Thank you." Lucy let the steady nun lead her slowly back. Humiliation threatened to crush her. She could feel Giovanni's concerned gaze but how could she look at him?

She crawled into her clean bed and heat rose in her cheeks. He must have cleaned it. Lucy turned on her side, away from him, exhausted.

Giovanni sat next to her and poured a glass of his Cholera drink.

"This will make you feel better." He held the glass for her to take.

Lucy sat up, took the glass and drank but she kept her eyes on the glass. She finished it and put the glass back on the nightstand.

"*Lucia*, look at me." Giovanni's voice was strong enough to make Lucy turn. "You need to fight *with* me. What are your symptoms, doctor?"

Oh. Yes. Fight the disease. "Abdominal cramps, muscle contractions in my legs stomach and arms. My mouth is dry, I'm weak and I can't control my bowls."

"And what do you do for a patient with those conditions?" He asked, with the same demeanor he used when she had first met him.

"Bed rest, fluids, keep the patient clean." Lucy nodded. She'd stay focused.

"That's better. Let me help you lie down."

The room faded away and Lucy drifted off.

Lucy woke to the faint chirp of crickets. Out the window, in the garden the shadowy outline of pear trees shimmered in the summer breeze.

Giovanni sat in the chair next to her bed. The clock behind him said four forty-five. "Are you still here?" Lucy reached for his hand.

"Of course. Will you drink some more for me?" He poured a glass full.

Lucy sat up slowly and took the drink in her hands. "Where's Daddy?"

"He was just here. He'll be back soon."

"And Sister?"

"Behind me on the bed." Giovanni moved aside so she could see the nun, sound asleep. "She snores like a freight train."

"She does, doesn't she? I once thought her snoring was an earthquake until she flapped her lips. Listen, she'll do it." Lucy held up a finger. Sister Francesca exhaled. They laughed.

"You're hurting, I can see it." Giovanni took her hand once more.

"I don't feel like dancing, but by our wedding day, I imagine I'll be ready."

"Speaking of dancing, let's go to the embassy ball in December, as kind of an anniversary celebration. What do you think?" Giovanni leaned back in his chair.

"I think that's a wonderful idea." Lucy put her throbbing head on her pillow and turned to see him better.

"By December there will be two Doctor Castellos living in our home." Giovanni rubbed her hand while he spoke. "Won't that confuse the snobs in this town?"

Lucy smiled.

"My *Lucia*." Giovanni touched her cheek. "We haven't prayed yet this evening, do you mind?"

"Where did I ever find someone like you?" She squeezed his hand.

"On the dance floor at the American embassy, don't you remember?" He smiled her favorite smile. "I was extremely rude and I called you a monkey."

Lucy lay still on her pillow. The room glowed with the gray light that comes at the start of a new day, just before the rising of the sun. Shadows ebbed and so, she hoped, did the battle that had raged throughout the night.

After the first episode, she had two others, both just as painful as the first. *Lord, I can't imagine going through this alone and yet so many people do.*

Her thoughts turned to Sister Francesca and then to Giovanni. *They were so patient with me last night and so encouraging. Please will you allow them to get some rest today?*

Lucy let her eyes wander about the room; Sister Francesca must have gone somewhere. She turned a little, to see the chair next to her and found Giovanni with her Bible draped across his lap. Instead of reading however, he had his eyes closed and his head rested to his fingertips. His lips moved. He must be praying.

What a beautiful sight to wake up to. You could not have given me a better gift. Thank you. She watched Giovanni pray; his black curls over his fingers and a slight smile on his lips. He seemed so peaceful. What a marvel that this man, once such a stranger, had become her soul mate.

"You had a rough night." Gray eyes opened. He leaned back in his chair. Giovanni searched her face. What clues did he see? "How are you feeling?"

"You had a rougher night than I did." Lucy moved to the edge of her pillow. "My head is throbbing, but believe it or not, I'm hungry and I'm *really* thirsty."

Giovanni stood up. "That's good news. Sister just left to find some breakfast. Here have some coffee." He poured another glass of Lucy's drink. "Let me take your temperature first, though."

"Did you get any sleep last night?" Lucy sat up and crossed her legs under the covers. "Hey, that's mine."

Giovanni stuck her own thermometer under her tongue.

"No, I did not sleep and yes it's yours. I needed to borrow it for a patient. Do you mind?" Giovanni stood over her with his hand on her forehead. He moved his hand to her cheek.

Lucy placed her hand on top of his.

"Don't worry about me." Giovanni rubbed her cheek with his thumb. "I feel fine. As soon as Sister gets back, I'll lay down for a bit." He placed his fingers on her neck and pulled his watch out of his pocket.

The door opened and Sister Francesca came in with a tray of food.

"There you are." Giovanni stuck his stethoscope in his ears. "Our princess is awake, I think she'd like some breakfast."

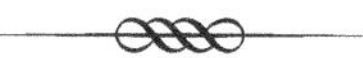

Lucy pulled out her prayer journal to write. Sister Francesca carried the empty dishes out the door.

Giovanni eased himself onto the other bed and turned on his side to face her.

"Sweet dreams." Lucy called over her notebook.

He put his head on the pillow and winked at her.

He looks so tired.

His eyes began to droop and soon he drifted off.

I've never seen him sleep before. He's adorable.

Lucy closed her journal and stretched out too. A gentle breeze moved the curtains and the room felt so cool and comfortable. She wrenched her eyes open one last time to see his sweet face and then she sank into a dreamless sleep.

Had she slept long? Lucy rubbed her eyes. "What time is it? Her father stood over her and the smell of lunch drifted from a tray near her bed. The bed next to hers had been neatly made.

"Two forty-five. Are you hungry?"

"Yes. Where's Giovanni?"

"Hello to you too." Henry James chuckled, poured a glass full of her drink and handed it to her.

"I'm sorry. Are you going to join me for lunch?"

"Yes." Her father ran his hand across her head.

Lucy sat up and took a good drink from her glass; she looked about the room. The door to the bath had been shut and she could hear Giovanni sing softly from behind it.

She grinned at her father.

"Lucille, you're not allowed." Henry James narrowed his eyes.

She'd never listened before, why start now? "What are you singing?" she asked loudly.

"It's a love song." Giovanni answered through the door. "Shall I sing it to you?"

"Only if you're clean." Lucy laughed and dodged her father's attempt to put his hand over her mouth.

"I *am* clean and I'm also completely naked," Giovanni said. "But since you've asked, here I come."

"WHAT?" Lucy pulled the covers to her chin and Henry James turned quickly.

Giovanni jiggled the doorknob.

"*No*, Giovanni, don't you dare." Lucy dove under the covers and pulled the sheet over her head.

Giovanni jiggled the doorknob again and the door creaked.

"But *Lucia*, don't you want to hear me sing?" She heard his bare feet on the floor and then he gave her sheet a tug.

She held it up tight. "Not anymore."

"But *Lucia*, you're a *doctor.*" He emphasized the word. "What I'm wearing shouldn't bother you at all, should it Dr. James?"

Her father burst into laughter. At that moment, she loosened her grip and Giovanni yanked the sheet off her face. She squealed and laughed. Giovanni stood in front of her, dressed head to toe, except for his bare feet.

"Oohh." She threw her pillow at him. "You said you had no clothes on."

Giovanni ducked and caught the pillow. "No, I said that I was naked. Under my clothes I am." He sat on the edge of her bed, and dropped Lucy's pillow on her face.

"There's no doubt you've had a good rest." Lucy giggled and moved her pillow behind to sit up.

"I do feel much better." Giovanni stroked her cheek with his thumb. "How does lunch sound Dr. James?"

"Wonderful," they replied in unison. Lucy laughed again, glad that her father had chosen to play with them.

"Thank you Daddy." Lucy patted his hand. Henry James set her tray in her lap, Lucy breathed in the scent of lentils and rice. "Oh wow, this looks terrific. This was my first meal at the hospital station. Can we pray?"

"She's feeling better." Giovanni shook his head. "I can't believe how much food your daughter eats for someone so thin. I've often wondered if I should check her for tapeworms."

"I've often wondered that myself, except that her mother was the same way." Dr. James looked out the window; his expression became extra soft.

"Thin as a rail, always upbeat, always smiling and always hungry." He pulled out his silver pocket watch, opened it and touched the faded picture stuck inside. "This is Maggie." Henry James handed the watch to Giovanni.

Giovanni smiled softly, first to her father and then to Lucy. "She was beautiful. She has the same sweetness in her smile that you do." He handed the watch back to Henry James. "Thank you for allowing me this privilege."

Emotion flashed through her father's eyes. Henry James quickly handed a tray of food to Giovanni, then took one himself.

Henry James said grace and Lucy dug in.

"I've noticed a new scar on your knee Lucille." Henry James moved his tray to a better place on his lap and then wiped his mouth. "Dr. Castello mentioned another set of stitches back in Messina, how did you get hurt?"

Giovanni pressed his lips together.

Uh, oh. Lucy swallowed hard. "It all started when I fell out of an orange tree at Giovanni's house." She cringed and ducked.

"*Lucille*!" Dr. James sat up in his chair. "Will you never learn?" He shook his head and slid back again. "No I suppose you won't."

Lucy told how she fell from the orange tee.

Giovanni jumped in, like she knew he would, to finish with the tale of the earthquake and baby Max. In his typical fashion, he made Lucy out to be a great big hero.

Daddy did not smile. "So against the wishes of the priest and the direct orders of your superior, you climbed down into an unstable basement?" Her father turned to Giovanni. "You do realize that I forbade her to enter that house yesterday morning and look at what happened. She could have been killed."

Awesome. It was so good to have her father back to normal.

Henry James leveled his eyes at her. "I'm glad that you saved the baby daughter, but you're lucky *I* wasn't there to yell at you." He pinched the bridge of his nose. "This 'tom boy' behavior is nothing new you know. Several summers ago, I sent Lucy and her brothers off to California to visit her aunt and uncle. When she returned, her hands were so callused I couldn't believe it."

Lucy stifled a laugh and watched Giovanni's reaction; his eyes were dancing.

"Do you know that Lucille spent the entire three months roping cattle, with the ranch-hands?" Henry James threw a hand in the air. "Her aunt and uncle had all kinds of social functions arranged for her to attend. She barely made one of them. *My daughter*, covered in dust and dirt and roping cows."

"Yes, I'm proud to say that *Lucia* has quite a few hidden talents. You know, I've seen Annie Oakley in action."

Henry James once again turned a sharp eye on Lucy.

"Oh, I'm feeling so much better today. Maybe I'll *get off easy*." Would they would take the hint?

"Last night actually went better than I expected it to." Giovanni took her empty tray. "The fact that you've been able to keep fluids down has helped tremendously." He poured another glass. "We'll stop picking on you now." He handed the glass to Lucy. "If by this time tomorrow you're as good as this, I'll say that you're right."

Over the last few months, Lucy had learned to read Giovanni quite well. Behind his smile and soft eyes, his demeanor said he believed her battle had just begun. Lucy's gaze fell to the dreaded buckets on the floor. She drank the entire glass with determination.

Nine o'clock. Why, when a person didn't want to watch a clock did his eyes seemed drawn to it? This quiet hospital made time drag, except… Giovanni looked at Lucy. She was worth it. With dinner done and another liter of cholera drink in her Lucy slept peacefully. Maybe tomorrow would bring hope of a quick recovery.

His gaze fell to her ring, and then to his own. He belonged at her side, and she at his.

"Oh, no," Lucy sighed in her sleep.

Giovanni sat up, at full attention and instinctively, he moved to drag her, once again, to the side of the bed.

Lucy's body reacted.

CHAPTER TWENTY-FIVE

Surely this night would be her end. Lucy's body, racked with pain, chose to expel every ounce of liquid that it contained and she could do nothing about it. Her muscles cramped with such violence, that she often came close to passing out.

She no longer cared what happened to her, she only knew that she hurt all over. Her head pounded, the room spun, cold air pierced her limbs and hands guided her up and down to the bathroom with every wave.

She had a vague awareness of Sister Francesca and Giovanni; their presence brought her comfort. Once or twice she woke up in the tub or was her life all about bathing? Once or twice she woke up in Giovanni's arms; her head against his shoulder, her body wrapped in a towel. *Shouldn't this bother me? No, he's taking care of me. I can hardly hold my head up. Maybe I'll just sleep.*

A glass was at her lips. Incredible thirst drove her; her tongue swollen and her mouth so dry. Giovanni held her up and slowly, slowly she drank every drop. How wonderful. He wiped her mouth and set her on her pillow.

Heavy eyelids shut and then an iron hand dragged her to the edge of the bed. All that sweet hydration came back up with such force; Lucy thought that her stomach would come out her mouth. She began to cry.

"You're all right." Giovanni soothed by her ear. He put his arm under her shoulders and held the glass to her lips again. "Go ahead and cry bambina, but you're all right. This reaction is normal. Just drink slowly. One sip at a time, swallow it *Lucia*, you have to swallow it."

She blinked back tears and watched his concerned face as she drank. Sister Francesca took her hand. *What would I do without the two of you? I often wondered what it would be like to be his patient. Now I know. He's patient, he's kind and he's strong; they both are. Oh please Lord let me recover.*

Henry James walked in the room. With the rising of the sun, the night's battle had come to an end. Lucy, in a restless sleep, had lost so much weight. Her eyes sunk in, her fingers and lips showed signs of dehydration and her skin had that awful, but familiar, blue pallor.

Cholera. He knew it well. He hated the disease. In a city as big as Boston it visited often enough. Mostly in the slums where sanitation was lacking, but every now and then it would surface in other neighborhoods too. This drink young Dr. Castello had invented seemed simple enough. Too simple, in fact to actually work, but apparently it did because Lucy still lived.

Sister Francesca sat in the chair next to her. "If Dr. Castello hadn't been so adamant: we probably would have lost her last night. She had quite a fight, thankfully she's still here."

"I know." Henry James put a soft hand on his daughter and then he turned his eyes upon the man who had kept her alive. Grateful admiration crept into his heart.

Giovanni, sound asleep in the other bed, did not stir a muscle.

"Shall I wake him?" Sister Francesca started to rise.

"No. Let him rest while he can. Just tell them I was here." Henry James touched Lucy one more time. He should leave before he began to cry.

"This is the third night." Giovanni was not sure why he had to say it, but he did. His muscles ached and his head hurt from lack of sleep.

"I know." Sister Francesca stood at the nightstand stirring the pitcher with its life-giving fluid. She looked as tired as he felt.

Into Giovanni's mind crept the faces of all the people he helped with this disease over the years: those who lived...and those who did not. His stomach became one big knot.

"This is one of the most violent cases I've ever seen." He closed his eyes and did what he had seen Lucy do so many times. *My God and Father, please have mercy on us. Please help her recover. Please keep me strong.*

"Shall I get Dr. James? Do you need a rest?" His aunt sat on Lucy's bedside.

"No. I'm not leaving anymore."

Lucy moaned softly and Giovanni stood ready.

"Neither am I." Sister Francesca moved an empty pail into place and the battle began again.

It must be light outside. Lucy floated in and out of a restless sleep. Sometimes she dreamt about Messina, sometimes about Boston, sometimes she believed herself wide-awake even though she still slept.

Her world began to spin. Something solid stuck in her mouth and then liquid filled her throat. She coughed and gagged then swallowed by reflex.

Lucy woke to find herself, cradled like a baby, in Giovanni's arms. He had a glass on the nightstand and a large eyedropper in his hand.

"You are awake," he said, with a smile. "Good. Can you sit up for me?"

Lucy tried to answer, but her throat felt too dry to speak. She found his eyes and nodded. Lucy moved in his lap and tried to control her limbs. Giovanni re-adjusted his hold and supported her back. Lucy sat up.

"That's better." Giovanni acted so upbeat. Something must be wrong.

Oh. He fought for her life. Lucy watched him fill the eyedropper.

"I'm going to put this in your mouth," he said. "All you have to do is swallow. Can you do that?"

She nodded.

Drop by drop, Giovanni fed her until the entire drink was gone. It felt so good on her throat.

Anxiety coursed through her. *Please don't let me throw up.*

They looked at each other and waited and finally Giovanni closed his eyes. "Thank you God, for small steps." He smiled into her eyes. "*Lucia*, I have to show you something."

He shifted his weight, moved his feet to the floor, lifted Lucy in his arms and stood.

"Where are we going?" Lucy whispered.

"Just to the window. *Lucia*, can you see?"

Lucy looked out into the garden. "What is that? Are those flowers? Why are those people standing there?"

Tears filled Giovanni's eyes. "They're people that you've helped. Word has gotten around Rome that *Santa Lucia* is sick. They've been coming in a steady stream since yesterday. They've been praying non-stop. Can you see all of the flowers they've brought? And that's not all."

Giovanni turned her around to see the other side of her room; in the corner stood a table, piled high with letters.

"These are all for you. They're from Messina." Giovanni's voice choked with emotion. "*Padre* sent a wireless. People are outside of the gate of the clinic praying for you just like the people are doing here. You helped them, and now they want to help you." Giovanni put his cheek to her forehead "*Lucia*, you have to recover, with so many people praying, how can you not?"

Lucy could not say what she felt in her heart and tears of joy filled her eyes.

"Oh, no, bambina," Giovanni said softly. "You mustn't cry, you need those tears."

"Yes." She managed to whisper.

Giovanni sat back on her bed and moved to place her in it.

"Let's try some more." She nodded toward the empty glass on the stand.

"That's what I like to hear." Giovanni patted her hand. "Let's rest just a moment and then we will."

Henry James pulled out his pocket watch and touched his wife's picture. He took a deep breath and walked into his daughter's room.

Giovanni sat on Lucy's bed. He held her unconscious body in his arms and fed her the cholera drink with the eye dropper.

"If I put it on the back of her tongue, in just the right place, she'll swallow it on her own." Giovanni squirted more down her throat, his face set like flint.

Henry James sat on the bed too. "It will be easier if you just hold her and let me work the eye dropper."

Giovanni handed it to Henry James and scooted over, all the while, balancing Lucy in his lap.

The two of them worked, until every ounce of the drink was gone.

Henry James could see pain etched across Giovanni's face, even though the physician maintained a professional demeanor. Henry used to hide his feelings too, right after he had lost his wife.

"I want to thank you for taking such good care of Lucille." Henry James wiped Lucy's mouth and they laid her head back on the pillow.

"Don't thank me until she recovers." Giovanni would only look at Lucy.

He touched Giovanni's shoulder. "I know, what you're thinking, but we're not giving up."

"No," Giovanni said. "We are not."

Lucy slowly opened her eyes. The light from the lamp made her squint. She knew by the labored beat of her heart that things had not improved.

She could hear the soft prayers of Sister Francesca, from the other side of the room. Next to her, in a chair, his head in his hand, the love of her life bowed in prayer. Her heart broke for him, but she could not cry because she had no tears.

Lord Jesus, please, you know that I will come home gladly whenever you call, but please let me stay for his sake. If I must go, please get him safely home to heaven to live with us. Don't let Giovanni grow bitter or lose his faith in you.

With all the strength she had, Lucy reached for Giovanni's hand.

He lifted his head; he had been crying.

"I'm so sorry you have to see me this way," she whispered.

He grasped her hand gently and leaned over her. "I don't see anything but how beautiful you are."

"You've always made me feel beautiful." Lucy held his hand to her cheek remembering the first time he stroked her face.

"I know what you're thinking," she said, once she caught her breath. "You're thinking about our night at the opera and your promise to me. You *are* taking care of me *amore*. Giovanni, I'm not Mimi."

His eyes filled with tears, but he fought them back. "You always know what's going on in my head. You know then, that I'm also thinking how much I love you. *Ti amo, cara mia.*"

Lucy held his hand tight and savored the words she loved to hear most. "Promise me."

"Anything."

"Promise me that if I don't make it, I will see you in heaven one day. Don't allow my passing to take you away from Him."

"I promise, *bambina*." He placed his hand back on her cheek.

More than anything, Lucy wanted to kiss his sweet face, so overcome with worry. "It's all right." she stroked his hand. "You can cry. I want to cry too. I don't want to leave you."

"I don't want you to leave." His heart ran down his cheeks.

Lucy struggled once more to breathe. "Giovanni?"

"Yes."

"Where's Daddy?"

"I'm right here, my love." Henry James sat next to Giovanni. He stood, leaned over his daughter and smiled.

Lucy took his hand too. "I want you to love each other."

"We do my dear."

Lucy closed her eyes for a moment exhausted, but she smiled.

"Good. I love you Daddy."

How comforting to feel the weight of their hands; both strong and caring. "Giovanni?"

"Yes, my angel."

"I'm so glad God brought me here. I don't regret one minute of it. I love you." Her eyes fluttered, Giovanni became blurry and the room felt far away.

No, I want to see him. A single tear forced its way from the corner of her eye and Lucy knew no more.

Giovanni felt his heart rip. His breath came in short gasps. He laid his head beside Lucy and wept silent tears. *God, I will do anything if you would only spare her. Please spare Lucia. Please.*

He took a hold of her hand, so shriveled that her ring swam on her finger, put it to his cheek and laid his head down again.

Henry James stumbled out of the room.

Giovanni prayed alone.

The door opened again. Giovanni kept his head next to Lucy; who cared what person had entered? He felt a warm hand on his back. He turned to find Father Dominic.

"*Padre*." Giovanni stood and hugged his dearest friend as tight as he could. The priest had held him countless times over the years. He would always be grateful to this teacher/friend sent by God.

Giovanni let Father Dominic go, pulled the second chair closer to Lucy and the two sat.

"Your parents are here with Michael and Adella, so is your uncle Vincenzo," Father Dominic whispered. "They're in the chapel praying. The children all sent drawings. Teresa in particular is very concerned."

"Really? They're all here?" What a wonderful family. He could always count on them.

Father Dominic took his hand. He looked so old tonight. "Giovanni, God might decide to take *Lucia*, you know that don't you?"

"Yes." Giovanni's heart trembled. His eyes filled with tears again.

"Are you prepared for that?"

"I don't know." Giovanni stroked her limp arm. "How can I let her go? I waited so long to find her. I should have sent her home when she first arrived or later, with her father. I would rather live knowing that she was alive somewhere else, than to have her suffer this way."

"But that's not what *Lucia* wants." Father Dominic squeezed Giovanni's hand. "She came to us prepared to lay her life down, for you or me or anyone else that God sent her way. I know, given the chance, *Lucia* would do again exactly as she has done to this point, even if she knew this would be the outcome. That's just who she is. My question is, what are you going to do from this point on?"

Giovanni's mind went back over everything that had happened since December. It had been so horrible and yet, because of *Lucia,* it had been wonderful too. The sweet moments on the boat would always live in his heart. He looked down at Lucy's ring, he touched it and then he touched his own. She would be so disappointed if he lost faith. And the thought of never seeing her again, well, that was unacceptable. Giovanni turned to his oldest friend. "*Padre*, I give up. I'll not contend with Him any longer. I know He's God and that He's good. If *Lucia* dies, I'll never be the same, but I know that I must serve Him.

"She's always saying how God can bring something good out of the worst of circumstances. I believe the book of Romans says that too. I keep trying to figure out how. Maybe, I'll better serve the people in Messina having also lost everything to the earthquake." A wave of emotion fought to overcome him.

Giovanni regained his composure and focused on Lucy. Her breathing had become so shallow.

Giovanni forgot to breathe as well. He felt for a pulse. "Her father should be here."

"I'll get him." Father Dominic stood and prayed for Lucy. "We'll get through this together, I promise." He hugged Giovanni one more time and left.

Giovanni lay his head down next to Lucy and took her fragile hand in his. "*Lucia, ti amo*." His voice cracked and his heart shattered. "Go and be with God if you have to. I will love you with every breath, and I *will* see you in heaven."

The chapel, filled to capacity, made Henry James uncomfortable. He wanted to hide his face from these people; all these Italians, all Sicilians, all Catholics, who all prayed for his daughter; most of them, complete strangers.

Giovanni's mother knelt to his right. She held his hand, with her head bowed. He had never seen such devotion. Even from his home church, even when his beloved Maggie had died. Yet, here in a foreign country, with a group he had shunned, he had found true believers. They embraced him with genuine affection, they grieved with him and they prayed, not just the short prayers that he had been used to hearing. These people had been praying for several hours now and they had yet to stop.

They acted more like Christ than anyone he had ever met.

For whoever calls on the name of the Lord will be saved. The words from *Romans* whispered in his heart.

Please forgive me. Henry James bowed his head. *I've learned my lesson. I can plainly see that these people belong to you. If it's your will for my daughter to serve you in this country then who am I to stand in the way? Please spare Lucy. I'll give consent for her to marry. I was wrong to disobey you.*

He rose at Father Dominic's urging and walked the hallways of the hospital alone, until he came to Lucy's room. He put his hand on the doorknob and hesitated. He did not want to experience the drama he knew lay inside. Henry James took a deep breath, he steadied himself and opened the door.

There, unconscious on the bed, was his beautiful Lucille. Even in this awful state she looked so much like her mother he felt the urge to call her Maggie. Next to her, in a chair, with his head on the bed and her hand in his was the young man she had begged him to accept.

Why had he been so stubborn? Did this young couple deserve the joy that he and Maggie had shared even if it was brief? Of course they did.

Would he have married Maggie all over again if he knew she would leave him early? Without doubt.

Henry James knew Giovanni to be as in love with his daughter, as he had been in love with his wife.

Like a ray of light, Henry James saw things in such a different way, that he felt as though he saw through the eyes of God.

Giovanni had become *him*, Lucy had become *Maggie*. The story was happening all over again.

He remembered how abandoned he felt by everyone except his God. He had been by his wife's side all by himself that evening. He held her hand, with his head on the bed, just like the young doctor in front of him.

When Maggie finally breathed her last, he had almost no time to grieve at all. He had to be strong for his three children instead. But at least he *had* children as evidence of the love he had shared with her. Giovanni did not even have that.

Overwhelming love and compassion filled his heart for Giovanni Castello. He had fought a good fight. Both physical and emotional exhaustion lay heavy, on the young man. Sometimes a person could do nothing more than to trust in the hands of The Almighty.

Henry James pulled out the chair next to Giovanni, determined to help him stand firm, even if Lucy should die. It would be the best gift he could give to his daughter. He sat in the chair and rubbed Giovanni's back.

Giovanni straightened up and wiped his face. "Would you like to sit here? I've been next to her all evening."

Henry James felt worse; even in his grief, Giovanni could be so gracious. "No, I love her, but you're *in* love with her. Stay where you are."

"How did you let go of her mother? Maggie wasn't it?" Giovanni searched Henry's eyes.

"You might have to let her die, but you don't have to lose her. Maggie has been with me, in my heart, all these years. She's waiting for me. *Lucia* will wait for you too." Henry James had never spoken his daughter's name in Italian before. Would the young man notice?

Giovanni gave a grateful smile. "You never fell in love with anyone else did you?"

"No. There was never any one else like Margaret."

Giovanni gave a slow nod, he turned back to Lucy.

The clock on the wall struck two.

"This is almost over, I can feel it." Giovanni said softly.

"I can feel it too, but we will fight to the end."

"Yes, we will." Giovanni turned to him and Henry saw a will of steel in his exhausted face.

CHAPTER TWENTY-SIX

The deafening silence of the hospital made even the slightest sound seem harsh, offensive and loud.

The night dragged on minute by minute; the tick, tick, of the clock, echoed off the walls along with the sound of Lucy's ragged breath. With each labored effort, Giovanni felt a moment of relief, only to listen anxiously for the next.

He kept a steadfast vigil; he watched her chest rise and fall in a slow rhythmic motion. Giovanni leaned further back in his chair, the room started to feel comfortable and warm and his eyes became very heavy.

Now he fought to stay awake too. Giovanni stood and paced the room; sometimes he prayed for strength, sometimes he asked God to take him instead.

At last, Henry James urged him to sit still, so he did. Giovanni rested his chin in his hand and felt the heaviness of sleep descend over him again. He felt angry, he felt helpless; he could not stop it.

She has been resting for quite some time now. A voice whispered through a murky dream. *How long has it been since she last had any fluids? Has she lost what you last gave her?*

Giovanni sat bolt upright in his chair.

"Dr. Castello." Henry James touched Giovanni's hand. "How long has it been since Lucy last had any fluids?"

Giovanni turned quickly, his heart started to pound. He stood and looked at Lucy's face, her breathing was shallow, but nonetheless, she still breathed.

Giovanni pulled out his pocket watch. "It's been almost fifty minutes." He did not want to get excited. He lifted her sheet to see if she had expelled what he had given her. He felt her nightgown and the bed around her, then turned to Henry James, his hands trembled.

"She's dry." Giovanni pulled the covers over Lucy again. "Let's not get our hopes up, but maybe she'll take more."

Henry James walked to the dresser, poured another glass full of liquid and picked up the eyedropper.

Giovanni lifted Lucy into his arms. He stroked his angel's face.

Henry James waited patiently with the glass and eyedropper in his hands.

Giovanni gave a slight smile and moved Lucy so that he could support her head a little better.

Henry James's eyes filled with tears just before he closed them to pray, Giovanni supposed, just as Lucy had done so many times. Just like his daughter, when Henry James opened his eyes again, Giovanni saw strength.

"Now I know where she learned to do that."

"Do what?"

"*Lucia* always prays for strength in a difficult situation. I can't count the times she's done what you just did, especially when we were living in the hospital tent. I had a hard time believing that someone who is so soft and feminine could be so tough at the same time."

"Maggie was just like Lucy." Henry James squirted a few drops into Lucy's mouth. "She loved God with every fiber of her being. She's the one who taught me to pray and now it's second nature. God has never failed me in all of the years that I've served him."

"You feel that way even though she died?" Finally a connection with Lucy's father.

"Yes."

Henry James looked out the dark window and then at Giovanni; tears filled his eyes.

No words would suffice.

"Let's change the subject." Henry James moved on the bed.

"Yes, let's," Giovanni breathed.

"This drink you've come up with is common sense. I wonder that no one's thought of it before now. Where were you when you first used it?" He squirted more drops down Lucy's throat.

"London." Giovanni steadied his voice. "The thought occurred to me that if the body is mostly made up of water, salt and sugar, and this bacterium causes the body to expel just that, then our focus should be on replacing the elements lost. I noticed that if a person was strong enough to last, the bacteria would eventually die and they would live. So my goal became keeping patients hydrated long enough to outlive the bacteria."

"How beautifully simple." Henry James swirled the eyedropper in the glass. "Unfortunately, I know many people, physicians included, who still believe this can be transmitted by touching, or breathing the same air, so they wouldn't be inclined to do what we're doing."

"Old beliefs die hard." Giovanni moved a stray hair from Lucy's face.

Henry James shook his head. "You should have heard what was circulated when I set Lucy's arm. People thought I had given her a death sentence."

"Yet her arm healed beautifully." Giovanni touched her scar. "And still, many doctors refuse to learn, opting for amputation instead.

"You know, she saved my niece's arm, just recently. I'm so grateful she was there when I wasn't. There are very few physicians that I would trust with my family, *Lucia* is one of them."

"That doesn't surprise me." Henry James leaned in and gave her more drink. "God always brings good out of a bad situation."

"How do you mean?" Odd that he would say that.

Henry James glanced at Lucy's scar. "Lucy's fractured arm, as painful as it was for her at the time, became one of the catalysts that drove her to medical school. So in a way, because she broke her arm, she was able to save your niece's arm."

Giovanni nodded.

"I didn't realize you'd lost a brother to cholera,"

"How did you know that?" Giovanni sat up straighter.

"Your mother told me. Now that I know, it makes sense that you became such an expert. I know that the loss of your brother was what drove you into medicine and finally to develop this drink. How many lives have you saved with this?" Henry James continued to feed his daughter.

"A lot, I never counted them all." How often he wished he could have saved Vito. "So you're saying that God used the tragedy of my brother to save lives?"

"That is exactly what I'm saying. Was Vito the kind of person to sacrifice himself for the lives of others?"

"He was helping victims of cholera when he got it himself; probably from drinking the same water that they did. But yes, to answer your question, he did sacrifice his life and he did it with no regret."

"I get the feeling that he would be very pleased to know his death brought the healing of so many. Am I right?"

"Yes, I know he would have it no other way." A cold place in Giovanni's heart grew warm.

Dr. James paused, Giovanni gave his full attention. "That's the essence of Romans 8: 28 exactly. "*All things work together for good to those who love God, and are called according to His purpose for them.*"

"And what good has this brought?" His heart strangely light.

Henry James cleared his throat. "It's brought us together. Let's get Lucy through this one way or another and then maybe we could work together on a few things. For starters, I can see the need to find a better way of feeding a person who cannot eat on their own, some way to get fluids and nutrition either into their stomach or even into their veins directly. What are your thoughts?"

Giovanni got excited. "I've been thinking about just that for quite some time. If we could figure it out, then a patient could receive exactly the amount of fluids lost and not dehydrate at all. Cholera would no longer be life threatening."

The dark of the night, faded to gray; a nightingale sang somewhere close by. Giovanni sat still in his chair. His body had stopped protesting a long time ago and simply became numb. To his right, Henry James looked twice his age, with his tie undone and his spectacles hanging on the end of his nose. They had worked and talked all night.

"I don't know what else to do." Giovanni rubbed the stubble on his face. "Either she will live or she won't." *Please Lord, let her be all right.*

"I'm embarrassed when I think of my behavior toward the two of you."

Giovanni made a slow turn. He had *not* expected this conversation to come from Henry James, but the man continued anyway.

"I apologize, Giovanni and I'm asking for your forgiveness. You're a good man and I know it. If Lucy recovers from this, I'll give my blessing for you to marry. If she doesn't, then I hope that you'll continue to see me and her brothers as family, for that is how I will see you."

With a concerted effort, Giovanni stood from his chair and extended his hand.

Henry James stood as well and pulled Giovanni into a fatherly hug.

How God has changed me in a year. Giovanni hugged him back. "Of course I forgive you."

Both men sank back into their chairs.

Ping. Lucy's ring fell off her hand and hit the floor. She gave a deep gasp, she gave one more and then she stopped breathing.

CHAPTER TWENTY-SEVEN

Lucy stood on the stone patio at Casa Bella. The sky, bluer than she had ever seen in her life, dazzled her eyes. The sun, a brilliant yellow, drove away any shadows, and yet Lucy found that she could stare into it without blinking. Out beyond the patio she could see the herb garden, over run with the most beautiful white flowers.

Behind the herb garden, she saw yet another garden, in the middle of a grove of willowy almond trees, heavy with fruit.

She ran down the stone steps, across the first garden and followed the path to the second. She stopped just before she got there.

This isn't supposed to be here. This is supposed to be a graveyard. Then she saw that the garden had become the most beautiful graveyard she had ever seen. It only contained three headstones, and yet the garden seemed to go on forever. A path wove its way around the graves and then to a three tiered fountain in the middle.

She turned to the fountain and saw three people standing by it; a young man, a boy and a woman. Lucy approached them slowly, but not out of fear for fear had no place in her heart.

"Mother," she cried. Joy filled her heart. She stepped forward and took her mother's hands. Then, unable to resist any longer she hugged

Maggie James. "I've missed you so much." Lucy loved the warmth of her mother's arms around her.

She turned to the young man, who had the most amazing blue eyes and to the boy. They both watched her, their faces peaceful and gentle.

"I know you." Lucy took the young man's hand. "You're Giovanni's brothers. You're Vito and you're Giuseppe. What are you doing here?"

"We want to ask you that." Vito gave the bow of a gentleman. He kissed the ring on her hand held her gaze with his own and smiled. "You should be with our brother. What are you doing here?" His voice sounded so much like Giovanni's.

"I don't know." Why she hadn't looked for Giovanni sooner? Lucy searched her memory, then looked into Vito's deep blue eyes. She put a hand to her head. "No, wait a moment, I do remember. I've been sick and Giovanni's been trying so hard to make me well."

Then, with all of her heart, she wanted to see him. "Where is he?" Lucy turned to her mother, but she found herself alone.

"*Lucia*!" Giovanni's call came from across the herb garden.

"Giovanni? Where are you?" She turned. Lucy now stood in the orange groves behind Giovanni's house in Messina.

"*Lucia*!" He called again, his voice filled with pain.

Her heart hurt. "He's upstairs. He needs me. He thinks I've died."

She ran in the back door and then up the stairs. Lucy rounded the corner to the upstairs hall and found that she had walked right into the hospital in Rome. She stood just outside of her room.

She could hear heated voices. Lucy opened the door and saw clearly that her body had stopped breathing. Giovanni moved to give her mouth-to-mouth resuscitation and her father fought to pull him back.

"*No. You might get it too!*" Henry James grabbed him.

"*Let go of me. I know the risks. I would die to save her!*" Giovanni pulled free and lifted Lucy into is arms. With tears streaming down his face, Lucy watched Giovanni try, desperately, to breathe life into her limp body.

"It's all right." Her father pulled at Giovanni again. "She's gone. Let her go."

"*No*!" Giovanni pushed Henry James to his chair. "Just one more time."

Lucy ran to Giovanni. She wanted to touch him, but she could not. "Lord *please* let me stay. Please, I want to stay."

Lucy felt air fill her lungs with a rush; nothing ever hurt so bad or felt so good. Her body felt too heavy to move, but she knew she had made it. Giovanni leaned over her. He had his hand beneath her head and his mouth next to hers. Lucy breathed again, to force painful, wonderful air to fill her lungs. A tear fell on her face and then she opened her eyes.

Lucy let her gaze travel slowly about the room. Sunlight poured in through the window and a balmy breeze moved the curtains. *This room is too quiet.*

She looked to her side. Could her heart melt at such a sight? Giovanni slept in his chair with his head on her bed and two days growth of beard on his face. He cradled her hand and snored softly.

Her father slept as well. He leaned back in his chair; his head tilted all the way and his mouth open. Nothing could be more beautiful.

She gathered her strength and stroked Giovanni's tangled hair.

He stirred.

"*Buongiorno, amore*." Her raspy voice sounded strange. "Giovanni, I'm still here."

Giovanni raised his head quickly; he looked around as if he wasn't sure who had spoken. He turned his eyes upon her and Lucy smiled.

"*Lucia!*" Giovanni lifted her into his arms and kissed her cheek. "You're back." He held her close for the longest time.

Joy filled her heart. His rough cheek felt like heaven and she breathed in his warm, familiar scent.

He took a sharp breath.

"Have I made you cry?" Lucy stroked the back of his head.

"Yes." He laughed and released her so she could see his eyes full of tears and full of love.

He looked over his shoulder to Lucy's father. "Dr. James, she's awake."

"What? Where?" Henry James sat up with a snort. He looked for the spectacles that had fallen to his chest. "Is she coherent?"

Giovanni smiled. "Do you know where you are?" He seemed to touch her soul with his.

"I'm in your arms, *amore*." Lucy smiled back.

He placed her on her pillow and took her hands.

"What a dream I had. Did I die this morning?" She could not take her eyes off him.

"You died yesterday afternoon *Lucia*." Giovanni stroked her cheek. "I thought I had lost you."

"God let me come back. I know He did. He used Vito."

"How did you know?" Giovanni searched her eyes. "You must have heard your father and me talking about him." He moved a stray hair away from her eyes and tears filled his again. "All things work together for good."

"What did you say?" Lucy stroked his face and he kissed her hand.

Then, Giovanni bowed his head and prayed. "Thank you God, for using my brother to save my wife. He would have wanted it. Now I understand."

"This is a small wedding?" Henry James looked about the crowd that filled the stone patio at Casa Bella. "I've never seen so many people at a reception; and the food! They must have been cooking for weeks."

Lucy hugged her father's arm and laughed. Such wonderful mayhem. "I've never seen these people do anything small. I'm not sure that they know how."

Her brothers danced with Giovanni's nieces. Uncle Roy stood at the far side of the patio with Michael Junior. He had brought a beautiful western saddle, inlayed with silver, as a wedding present and now explained its functions to her new nephew. She would most likely end up giving the saddle to Michael.

"Look." Lucy nudged her father. "Aunt Lucinda is dancing with Giovanni's uncle Vincenzo. Don't they make a nice couple?"

"I never knew what she said to you, Lucille." Her father shook his head.

"I never knew why she said it. How'd you find out?"

"Giovanni told me. I'm afraid I didn't pay enough attention to what happened in my own home."

"It's okay Daddy." Lucy kissed his cheek and smiled at her aunt. "Being so sick cured me of that. I've a good idea how awful I looked and even then, Giovanni thought I was beautiful. It's his opinion that matters most anyway."

"Finally, you see the truth." Giovanni came to his wife's side as though he knew she had been thinking about him. He grabbed her about the waist and placed a tender kiss on her cheek.

"*Stasera, cara mia*." He smiled his promise in her ear, so no one else heard.

"*Gesù Maria,*" Lucy whispered back.

Giovanni threw his head back and laughed. He pulled her close again and whispered. "You really want me to stay away tonight?"

Lucy giggled and then she grew warm.

"That's what I thought." Giovanni kissed her lightly and her heart fluttered.

"Save it for the honeymoon!" Antonio shouted from next to the banquet table.

He and Michael waved at them and toasted with *cannoli*.

"You can kiss her all you want as far as I'm concerned. She's *your* wife." Henry James laughed.

The patio certainly was warm.

"Don't be embarrassed." Giovanni pulled her close to his side and awkwardness faded to joy.

He's always made me feel so safe. Thank you God.

Lucy's mind went back to their first encounter in Rome. Even then he tried to protect her. *I should have known who he was from the start.*

"What are you thinking?" Giovanni slid his hand slid down her arm and hugged her waist. "You seem far away."

"I was remembering our first dance."

Giovanni's hand tightened. "I'll never forget that day. I danced with the most beautiful girl in Italy." He kissed her temple. "It seems my uncle might have the same thoughts. It's been a long time since I've seen him look at someone like that. Maybe I should tell him to call her a monkey."

"Maybe I should tell her to call him a pig." Lucy swatted him. "How long has he been alone?"

"About ten years." Giovanni had at a twinkle in his eye. What did he know that she didn't? "The men in America must be blind as bats. I cannot see how your aunt is not married. She's very handsome."

"If you'll excuse me." Henry James bowed to the couple with a mischievous grin. "I'm going to speak to your uncle." Off he headed across the patio.

"A little help. Exactly what *Zio Vincenzo* needs." Giovanni chuckled. He turned toward Lucy with a tilt of his head. Today his eyes were black. No question what he had in mind.

"May I have this dance Dr. Castello?" he asked with his beautiful rolling accent.

"You may." Lucy curtsied and smiled and gave him her hand.

Index of Italian Phrases

Aiuto–Help

Andiamo–let's go

Andiamo a casa–lets go home or to the house

Andiamo a casa tua – let's go to your house

Amico/a–friend m/f

Arriverderci–Good bye

Bambino/a/i–Little boy, little girl, children

Basta–Stop, enough

Benvenuto/a–Welcome m/f

Benvenuto a casa, figliolo – Welcome home, son.

Benvenuta bambina–Welcome little girl or child(fm).

Bella–Beautiful. (che bella – how beautiful0

Bella addormentata–Sleeping beauty

Bellissimo/a–Beautiful m/f

Biscotti–delicious hard cookie for dunking.

Bravo/a–Well done m/f

Buongiorno–good morning

Buonanotte–good night

Buonanotte, a tutti–Good night everyone

Buonasera–good evening

Nuovo Castello–New Castle

Cannolo/i–crunchy pastery filled with sweet creamy cheese. mmmm

Caponata–cooked vegetable salad, so good!

Casa – House

Che Gelida Manina–Beautiful song in the opera La Bohème.

Come va?–How's it going?

Ciao–Hi / bye

Dottore/ Dottoressa- Doctor m/f

Dio mio, l'donna testarda My Lord, the woman is stubborn

Evviva!–hurray!

Festa – party, holiday or celebration.

Figlia/o–Daughter/son

Figli–children

Fidanzata–fiancé

Gesù–Jesus

Grazie – Thank you

Grazie a Dio.-Thank God.

Grazie a Dio, sei a casa.- Thank God you are home.

Impossibile–Impossible

La Boheme, by *Giacomo Puccini–very famous opera. (look it up)*

Mangia–to eat

Maria–Mary

Mi dispiace, signore- I'm sorry, sir.

Momma mia–Mother of mine.

Momento–moment

Monte Pellegrino–large mountain which stands sentinel over Palermo

Nonna/o–grandmother/grandfather

Pranzo–lunch

Perche'–because / why

Perche' tu l'uomo della casa–because you are the man of the house.

Per favore- Please

Permesso–Excuse me, (to get by someone)

Prego–You're Welcome

Pronto–Now, quickly

Principessa–princess

Pioggia dal terremoto–Earthquake rain

Peloritani–mountains around Messina

Piccola scimmia–little monkey (female)

Porco–Pig (A very bad thing to call someone in Italian)

Profughi-refugees

Puttana–whore/prostitute

Riggatoni–Large tube shaped pasta

San Giuseppe–Saint Joseph

Santa Lucia–Saint Lucy (a beloved saint of Naples)

Sei molto bella–You're very beautiful

Signora/e–Mrs/Mr

Signorina–Miss

Silenzio–Silence

Sono Luigi–I am Luigi

Sogni d'oro–Sweet dreams (literally dreams of gold)

sotto le macerie. -under the stone

stracciatelle–Italian egg drop soup.

Sua moglie e' morta."- Your wife is dead.

Stasera cara mia–tonight my darling

Teatro Massimo–Theater Maximus, famous operhouse in Palermo

Ti amo–I love you. (to your spouse)

Ti voglio bene – I love you. (to friends and family)

Uno…due…tre–one, two, three

Un attimo signore–in a minute sir

Via San Francesco–Saint Francis Street

Voglio morire–I want to die

Santa Lucia Santa	**Lucia** *(literal translation)*
Sul mare luccia, L'astro d'argento	*Upon a glittering sea, a star of silver*
Placida e'l'onda, Prospero e' il vento	*Calm the wave, prosperous the wind.*
Sul mare luccia, L'astro d'argento	*Upon a glittering sea, a star of silver,*
Placida e'l'onda, Prospero e' il vento	*Calm the wave, prosperous the wind.*
Venite all'agile, Barchetta mia	*Come with agility, my small boat,*
Santa Lucia! Santa Lucia!	*Saint Lucy! Saint Lucy!*
Venite all'agile, Barchetta mia	*Come with agility, my small boat,*
Santa Lucia! Santa Lucia!	*Saint Lucy, Saint Lucy!*

(T. Cottrau – Longo 1835)

Millie Grazie, A Thousand Thanks

Mamma Rosa and Papa' Pietro for being brave enough to move to America. Mom for giving me a love of reading and writing, Dad for your strength. My brothers; Phil you've always been my champion, Rich for your pep talks, Pete for the map and for your wisdom, Bill, for your inspiration. Mary, best sister in the world. Jeff Harshbarger; You're my best friend. Thanks always believing in me.

Thanks to; Maude Howe for being so brave. Rebeca S. for lessons. Valarie for telling me I could write. To Sharron for listening so well. Gaye for all the haircuts and long discussions. Jessica, Ashley, Carol Ann, love you.

Camille for long talks and lunch.

Adrianne for loving it.

To my Publix family for all the encouragement

Thanks to Katia for helping me with all the Italian phrases.

If I messed something up, please be patient, I'm still learning.

Special Thanks to Jessica D. You taught me so much.

Thank you, thank you.

To Leigh, I'll always be your Sophia. Susan, your artwork is amazing. Love you .

Steven for trying so hard. Ruth for telling me my story was really good.

Gambol, Twila, Ashley, Poopie, Max, Judah, Rocky, Abby and Jack-Jack for all the comfort, snuffles and patience

And finally to my Lord Jesus Christ; what do I have that hasn't come from your hand?

CPSIA information can be obtained
at www.ICGtesting.com
Printed in the USA
LVHW091128271018
595045LV00011B/601/P

9 781498 453073